Tales of Emoria:
Past Echoes

Tales of Emoria:
Past Echoes

Mindancer

Silver Dragon Books
a Division of
RENAISSANCE ALLIANCE PUBLISHING, INC.
Austin, Texas

ISBN 0-9674196-7-0

First Printing 2000

9 8 7 6 5 4 3 2 1

Cover art and design by Mindancer

Published by:

Renaissance Alliance Publishing, Inc.
PMB 167, 3421 W. William Cannon Dr. # 131
Austin, Texas 78745

Find us on the World Wide Web at
http://www.rapbooks.com

Printed in the United States of America

Dedication

To my parents who always wanted me to write fiction. To Bary 'The Muse' Johnson who has a gift for giving inspiration during an everyday conversation. And, to all the readers who have made these little Tales a joy to write.

Map copied from
the ancient scrolls of The Tales of Emoria

Northern Territories

Southern Territories

N
E
S
W

Translator's Note—Pronunciation guidelines for Jame and Tigh's names:

Jame is one syllable with a long 'a'. Tigh is pronounced Tig. The spelling of her name follows the Ingoran rules of grammar where the 'h' indicates the eldest daughter of the House of Tigis.

Chapter
1

All she could hope for was the peace she believed was at the end of the journey called life. She gladly reached out for the fleeting light that promised a vision, a face that had long since faded from her dreams. All she had left to hold was the belief that her shattered soul would soon be pulled together once again in the Renasyan Meadows where her ancestors awaited her.

The vision was not enough to release her from the fear and hatred that battered her body. The shouts and taunts from the frightening throng took too long to fade from her senses. Her confusion about why the villagers viewed her with distrust and, in the end, with violence, was a puzzle her curious mind would not have the opportunity to pursue. Enough was enough, and she closed her eyes—choosing what she wanted to be her last vision on earth.

****

The road showed traces of an earlier rain shower that had drenched the pair of walkers and a tall pale horse. The dry heat soaked up the moisture before the plants had a chance to benefit from it. The pair, who had experienced weather that could make the most seasoned traveler consider giving up a journey, was barely aware that the moisture soaking their clothes was from rain rather than sweat.

Tigh," Jame ventured. "It's been a while since we've been to Ynit."

Her companion studied the road as they walked along with easy strides that marked them as travelers. "I guess it has," she finally agreed, amusement flashing across her mild expression. "We haven't promised to be back there for any reason, have we?" The soft cadences of Tigh's voice were edged with a teasing that came easily with her interactions with Jame. "Or maybe there's another reason you want to go there." Tigh was suddenly standing in front of Jame with hands on her hips and an amused twinkle in her clear blue eyes.

Jame studied her companion as the taller woman let her well-hidden impish side show. The soft black leather that encased her body, the functional armor and the sword hilt peeking over her shoulder, said as much about Tigh as she cared for most people to know. Her tall muscular frame and quick mind made her a warrior that people instinctively backed away from. The mane of black hair, kept off her face by a leather band buried under shaggy bangs, and the compelling blue eyes that gleamed over a sculpted face only enhanced her reputation.

Jame took all this in every time she looked at her companion, always trying to reconcile the fighter with the playful woman standing before her. Jame, although proficient in ways of self-defense, was not a warrior. But having a warrior as a willing companion was a gift for any peace arbiter and Jame thanked the mother waters of Laur that she had Tigh.

Her appearance contrasted with Tigh's in significant ways. Because of the rough life on the road, she wore leather leggings and tunic. But they were of softer browns than the severe black of her friend. Her shorter, slender form was muscular and fit from constant walking and carrying much of what she needed on her back. With gentle green eyes, and long, red-blonde hair with bangs as shaggy as her companion's, Jame's features were not as striking as Tigh's but were more attractive because they did not intimidate. They matched her profession by welcoming interaction.

Knowing that she'd been caught, the arbiter tried to think of a cute response but knew she couldn't deceive Tigh. Sighing, she did the only thing that would get her out of the box she'd put herself in. Flinging her body forward, Jame tackled the solid warrior who had the good grace to topple flat on her back in the middle of the road.

"You...speechless?" Tigh was having a problem laughing with the extra weight on top of her.

A grinning Jame crawled off the warrior. "I was just seeing how many words I could get out of you at one time."

"You doing some kind of research?" Tigh, the first on her feet, reached out a hand to Jame.

After taking the hand and being effortlessly pulled to her feet, Jame shrugged at the question.

"That's what I usually say," Tigh chuckled as she gathered Gessen's reins into her hands. The horse, accustomed to the antics of her companions, had taken the opportunity to forage for a snack by the roadside.

"You're in a good mood," Jame commented as they continued down the road. Tigh flashed her a brilliant grin and Jame grinned back. This was the Tigh only a few had the good fortune to know.

As they crested a small hill, Tigh's head suddenly stiffened and her features slipped into a grim expression. The warrior stopped and concentrated on sensations nipping at the edges of her keen hearing. Jame held as still as possible, always fascinated by how her playful companion could instantly turn into an alert deadly warrior.

"There's a village. Sounds like trouble." The warrior swung onto Gessen and held a hand out to her companion. Grasping Tigh's arm, Jame was quickly behind the warrior and holding on tight as Tigh pushed Gessen to a dirt-flying gallop.

****

She no longer felt the pain. Rather than fear, she felt relief that this ordeal was almost over. The irony that one such as she would come to a violent end formed a sad smile on her battered face.

A new sensation penetrated her hazy mind. A noise—sharp and clear. Hoofbeats, galloping hard, creating a solid echo as the noise of the crowd slipped away, giving way to its insistent tattoo. Her strength of curiosity belied the fact that she was ready to give up on the world and she cracked open the eye that was not swollen shut. A pale horse could barely be seen in the cloud of yellow dust billowing in its wake. Much to her relief, her tormentors' attention was already on the unwanted intrusion.

As soon as the armor-clad warrior pulled up on Gessen, she was on the ground, leaving her companion to settle the animal. Just to make sure she didn't get any argument about her purpose, Tigh reached over her shoulder and slipped out her black-bladed sword with a no-nonsense scrape against the leather sheath. The villagers, recognizing the black leathers, had the good sense to back away to the safety of the rambling porch outside the village inn.

Jame, slipping off Gessen, scanned the huddled crowd for the likely leader. A thin man wearing an imposing medallion and an angry scowl rushed her way. Before he had a chance to open his mouth Jame was shouting at him. "Is this the way you show justice in this town? Where is the arbiter?"

"We can't wait around for an arbiter to show up for every little thing," the headman scowled. "We're a remote village."

"Arbiters aren't always far away." Jame shook her head. "Sometimes they can be within calling distance." She pulled her arbiter's medallion, hanging on a chain around her neck, out from beneath her tunic. "What did that person do to deserve this kind of punishment?"

"Since she came into town, all kinds of strange things have happened..." the headman began, surprised that this feisty young woman was an arbiter.

Jame impatiently shook her head. "Did she hurt anyone or destroy property?"

"Well, Hemme's son tripped and fell outside the inn and..."

"Did anyone see her cause injury or destroy property?" Jame pressed impatiently.

"Not actually seen..."

"If you don't mind, we'll take her off your hands." Jame turned her attention to her companion who was bent low over the bloody heap in the middle of the square.

"You keep strange company for an arbiter," the headman ventured.

"You're too quick to judge." Jame leveled her clear green eyes at him. "Something I'd work on, if I were you."

The man snorted, incredulous that this young woman could be so blind. "She's a wild one. Stories of her have reached even us."

"She *was* a wild one," Jame corrected, glancing anxiously at Tigh, who was still checking the body. She prayed they weren't too late. "She's been cleansed."

"I hear that doesn't always work as well as they let on." The headman scowled as he rubbed his chin.

"It depends on who they were before they were recruited for the Elite Guard." Jame straightened and challenged him to make some kind of comment to that.

He backed off, knowing that he had already overstepped his boundaries with this arbiter. "You're a brave one," was his only comment before turning and striding back to the other villagers anxiously huddled around the inn.

Shaking her head, Jame trotted to her companion. How could she explain that she was safer with Tigh than with anyone? Stopping a few paces away, she tried to gauge the condition of the unfortunate woman. There was so much blood on her face and clothing that it was hard to determine the extent of injury or much else about her, for that matter.

Tigh turned to her, then glanced around, noting that the villagers were watching them with a mixture of fear and hostility. She put two fingers to her lips and let out a shrill whistle, rewarded a few heartbeats later by a dust cloud kicked up by Gessen. Tigh and Jame carefully wrapped the woman in a blanket that Tigh retrieved from a saddlebag.

"Shock?" Jame asked.

Tigh's haunted eyes held hers for several heartbeats before nodding. The warrior once caused this kind of pain and worse and she had to live with the memory. Jame reached over the battered woman and put a comforting hand on Tigh's shoulder. Tigh swallowed and allowed their bond to calm her. "I'm going to have to hold her on Gessen."

Jame nodded as Tigh signaled the horse to kneel on her front two legs. The warrior carefully lifted the woman and, using an enviable combination of strength and balance, she straddled the saddle. When Gessen was back on her feet, Jame picked up a pack that obviously belonged to the woman and hung it on the saddle.

"Which way?" she asked as she took the reins.

"That way." Tigh nodded to a distant low line of bluffs.

****

Tigh's instincts were correct about the ridge. It was pocked with shallow caves and shelter bluffs. They easily found a cave large enough for them and Gessen, yet hidden from the main trail. Armed with their herb kit and several strips of cloth they kept for emergencies, Tigh made a thorough check of the woman's wounds. She patiently cleaned and dressed them, a skill she learned while her warrior tendencies were cleansed from her. It was believed that the rehabilitation of the Guards was enhanced by learning to ease pain instead of inflicting it.

Jame fetched water from the small creek that meandered along the base of the bluff, and gathered wood for the fire. After the flames were hot enough to give off some needed warmth and a small pot of stew was set to simmer, she crept next to the warrior for a closer look at the woman they had saved. Although it was matted with blood and dirt, Jame could tell that her hair was a pale blonde, unusual for that part of the world. The arbiter also noted the absence of the faded look of most villagers who worked hard just to survive. High born, she mused to herself as she inspected what was left of the woman's clothing. It had the fine weave and delicate cut found only in the larger cities to the west. Tigh, after finishing the stitch to a small gash on the woman's arm, picked up a bracelet and handed it to Jame.

After flashing Tigh a questioning look, Jame studied the intricate interlocking of metals and semi-precious stones. "Artocian?" she ventured. Tigh nodded as she carefully rolled the woman onto her stomach and cut away the remaining material, revealing a cross pattern of welts that could only have been made by a whip.

"By the Children of Bal," Jame gasped. "The headman said that no one had actually seen her do anything wrong. It's the usual excuse—blaming the different-looking stranger for any mishap that occurred while she was in town."

"And different-acting," Tigh added as she thoroughly cleaned the welts.

"You think she is what she appears to be?" Jame crooked her head at her companion.

For an answer, Tigh pushed cascading hair from the woman's shoulder blade. A small clear image of a feathered quill and ink jar was etched in the skin. Jame bent closer for a better look. "I don't think I've ever seen this mark before."

"She's with the University at Artocia," Tigh explained, rummaging through her saddlebag for a clean tunic. With Jame's help she removed the rest of the tatters from the woman's spare frame and slipped the tunic on her.

"What would she be doing here?" Jame frowned as she checked on the progress of the stew. Tigh stepped outside the cave to wash in the cold stream, taking the time to think over an answer. She had never heard of an Artocian scholar venturing into such a remote place. It was clear she wasn't visiting family.

Upon reentering the cave, the warrior glanced around to make sure everything was secure. It was instinct to never let down her guard. Jame ladled some of the stew into two wooden bowls and pulled a second metal spoon from the saddlebag. Tigh sat next to her on a smooth stone—evidence that they weren't the first people to use the cave.

"I'll save out some of the stew," Jame said quietly as she handed a bowl to Tigh. The warrior nodded, glancing at their patient.

"I think we have a bit of a mystery here." Tigh scooped a spoonful into her mouth and chewed thoughtfully as she contemplated the injured woman. "She's not completely unworldly, for a scholar." Jame gave her a quizzical look. "She's conscious but keeps her eyes closed, determining whether we are friend or foe." Jame blinked at her, surprised, then turned to the woman, then glared at the warrior.

"You can be so infuriating sometimes," Jame muttered as she put her bowl down and went to the woman's side. "It's all right," she assured her. "We rescued you away from those villagers."

Slowly the woman's good eye opened and flicked around, taking in the cave, the woman next to her, and finally the dark-clad figure sitting by the fire. She swallowed with difficulty. Before a word was uttered, Tigh was handing a water bag to Jame. The woman's eye widened at the closeness of the warrior. It was clear she knew of one of her saviors.

Jame tipped the water bag to the stranger's dry lips, and to her surprise, she drank deeply. "I'm Jame, Peace Arbiter-at-large for the Southern Districts. This is Tigh, Peace Warrior."

The woman looked as though she could have said several things about that particular title for Tigh, but she, a scholar, knew better than to judge a manuscript by what others said about it. "Seeran. Historian, University of Artocia," she rasped. "But you've already determined that."

"I've been to Artocia," Tigh explained.

"I think I would have remembered if Tigh the Terrible had been in the city," the woman responded hoarsely.

The warrior looked down at her hands, an action Jame knew her companion unconsciously performed when she was reminded of her former title. "I wasn't Tigh the Terrible then," she said softly. Jame looked at her questioningly, surprised that Tigh avoided her eyes. The arbiter quickly let it go. She knew that Tigh would tell her when she was ready to.

"Are you hungry?" Jame turned her attention to Seeran, who was studying the passive warrior. She had heard that Tigh the Terrible had been cleansed, and that she had dedicated her life to good. This person did not behave like the warrior whose exploits exploded from the scrolls of the chroniclers. A demon who could freeze a soul with a single glance and who was a master of intimidation. This person was impossibly passive, letting her companion control the situation. "Hungry?" Jame patiently prompted. She was more than accustomed to the effect her friend had on people.

Seeran focused on her. "A little." Before she had a chance to say more, Tigh was near the fire, rummaging through a saddlebag for their spare bowl and spoon.

"She's very efficient." Jame bit back a grin at Seeran's puzzlement over Tigh's behavior.

"I would like to hear your story sometime," the scholar stated thoughtfully, taking in more details as she studied her rescuers. As a historian, it was her skill to paint scenes and etch words in her mind. She now saw the joining ring on Jame's finger and the identical one on the warrior's hand as she handed the bowl to Jame. She had heard that Tigh the Terrible traveled with an arbiter but not that they were joined. There was definitely an intriguing story here, a gentle arbiter and the most vicious warrior since Ranblan the Destroyer.

Jame grinned at Seeran's raised eyebrow after the first mouthful of the delicately flavored stew. "Tigh's an Ingoran." The other eyebrow shot up as the good eye rested on the black leather-clad warrior settled on the stone near the fire, carefully sharpening and oiling her sword. People from the city-state of Ingor did not believe in eating the flesh of animals.

"How surprising," was all Seeran could mutter as her inquisitive mind pushed through the blur of discomfort from her wounds and exhaustion. Perhaps what began as a horrible day would turn out all right after all. She watched as the warrior carefully laid out a fur on the opposite side of the fire and placed her sword to one side of it. She paused, then pulled a large hide from the saddlebag and put it over the fur before obsessively checking the area outside the cave once again and scanning the interior. When the warrior was certain that everything was as it should be, she stretched out on the fur and dragged the hide on top of her.

"Night, Tigh." Jame's voice betrayed the great affection she had for the reticent warrior. She glanced across the fire while Seeran worked on another spoonful of stew. The historian watched the interaction with interest. So the arbiter had really succeeded in taming the wild warrior.

"'Night, Jame," the warrior whispered, revealing a gentleness that was reserved only for her companion.

Jame smiled as she turned her attention back to scooping another spoonful of stew into Seeran's mouth. "She spent most of last night in search of a capricious child who had run off in anger and had gotten lost in the woods when darkness fell. We were visiting the village on the other side of the valley. Our supplies were low so we stayed in an inn. I'm usually able to arbitrate for a room and meals, and traveling supplies. Last night I went to bed rather early and missed out on the all night hunt."

"The people let her help, by herself, that is?" Seeran hesitated, wording it as kindly as possible.

"She is not what she used to be," Jame explained gently as she helped Seeran drink some water. "Is there anything else you need before I turn in?"

"You've done so much already. For a stranger, that is." Seeran was suddenly shy at all their attention to her.

"We are only too happy to help." Jame smiled, settling the leather hide around Seeran's battered body. "If you need anything just give a little shout. Tigh will be awake and at your side before she even realizes that she moved. Bowstring reaction. It's something that takes getting used to."

"I can imagine," the scholar murmured.

She drowsily watched as Jame stepped outside to clean the cooking utensils and made sure the fire was properly banked. When the camp was in order, the arbiter crawled under the hide next to Tigh.

Waiting to drift off, Seeran gazed at the huddled pair across the fire. It had been an astonishing day for her. *One for the chroniclers*, she smiled to herself, *one I lived to chronicle myself—A tale of being rescued by the most notorious warrior from the Grappian Wars.* It was rarely mentioned that she was strikingly beautiful, only that those now clear blue eyes had glinted with feral joy at commanding an army and rushing into bloody battle. She was said to have been merciless, gleefully inflicting pain without remorse. This was the woman sleeping just beyond the fire. A shiver ran down Seeran's spine as she tried to store that thought away. This gentle, passive woman was not Tigh the Terrible. Not anymore. The small smile returned. It was, indeed, a story for the chroniclers...a story that was hers to tell.

****

When Seeran's eyes opened again, the sun was stretching long, dancing fingers into the cave. The aroma of sweet herbs steeping in steaming water and the crackling of the flames were the only things that penetrated her senses until she became more attuned to her surroundings. Just on the edge of her hearing was the muffled bubbling of water and the whisper of voices outside the cave.

A fair-haired head popped around the mouth of the cave. Seeing that Seeran was awake, Jame grinned and disappeared. A few heartbeats later, she entered the cave holding a leather bundle overflowing with roots and greens.

"The morning meal will be ready in no time," Jame announced as she untied the bundle and laid it out on the flat rock and sorted through the greens. Some were destined for the pot and others to be cut up and eaten raw. Seeran watched with interest, having only heard of the Ingoran diet but never witnessing its preparation.

"Are you also Ingoran?" the historian finally asked as her curiosity took over.

Jame gave out a wry chuckle as she glanced up from her work. "No...um, actually I'm Emoran." Seeran couldn't have been more shocked than if Jame had slapped her. The Emorans were a legendary tribe of fierce warrior-women. Not the type of people to produce a peace arbiter. "I know, I know," Jame laughed at Seeran's expression. "I'm the black sheep. It happens."

"There are many old stories about the Emorans, but nothing from modern times." Seeran frowned as she tried to remember everything she had read about the tribe.

"We've settled down quite a bit since the Wars of Farror that helped us establish our territory." Jame's eyes twinkled good-naturedly.

"Settled down? As in peaceful co-existing?" Seeran inquired.

"Uh...not quite. But enough that it's pretty peaceful most of the time." Jame shrugged. "We're a tribe of warriors. It's in the blood."

"That's more in keeping with what I've read about the Emorans." Seeran nodded, then focused on the tall, imposing shadow blocking the entrance to the cave.

Tigh swept keen blue eyes around the cave before settling them on Jame. The warrior held up a handful of small round tubers. Jame's face lit up and Tigh couldn't keep back an affectionate grin.

"Have I ever told you how wonderful you are?" Jame beamed as Tigh knelt next to her and deposited the tubers near the pile of greens.

"Plenty where that came from," Tigh said softly as Jame leaned over and casually brushed her lips on the warrior's cheek. That got a delighted grin from the warrior.

"Now check on our patient while I prepare this feast." Jame waved her small knife in Seeran's direction. Tigh was at Seeran's side before the historian had time to blink.

The warrior raised an eyebrow at Seeran's startled expression, which quickly relaxed into an embarrassed grin. With silent but gentle efficiency, the warrior carefully checked her wounds, replacing the bandages and ointment as needed. Seeran watched her curiously, observing the complete focus Tigh had on her task. As the warrior put away her herbs, Seeran tried to sit. Strong hands reached out and helped her scoot back against the wall. Several furs were placed behind her, cushioning her tender back.

"Thank you," Seeran said as she wiggled into a comfortable position.

Tigh blinked at her. Kindness and kind words directed at her still came as a surprise. "You'll be fine." She nodded, busily straightening her kit. "Nothing's broken. No internal bleeding."

"That's good to know," Seeran responded, noting that the warrior was more comfortable with the art of healing than with the art of communication. "I guess I got lucky you two came along."

Tigh raised an eyebrow. Seeran almost laughed. *Who needs words with a face that expressive?*

"Not so lucky for being there in the first place," Jame commented quietly. She shook the heavy, flat pan full of sizzling vegetables that she had brushed with oil and sprinkled with herbs. The aroma filling the air told them that the morning meal was almost ready.

"I guess you're wondering why I was in Raighton." Seeran studied the wall on the far side of the cave.

"We don't mean to pry," Jame quickly responded. "If it's private..."

Seeran chuckled as much as her sore face muscles allowed. "No, no. Nothing like that. In fact, it's kind of embarrassing, actually." She looked at the steady, expectant eyes of her benefactors. "I was, uh, in search of stories."

Tigh and Jame blinked at her. "Stories?" Jame questioned as she divided the meal among three plates, handing one to Tigh and carrying the other two over and settling in front of Seeran.

"Yes. It's a part of our training as historians," Seeran explained, accepting one of the plates. Picking up a piece of the grilled tuber and popping it in her mouth, she was grinning before it was chewed and swallowed. "This is the most incredible food."

"Stories," Tigh prompted.

"We have to spend time witnessing history, so to speak. If we can't see it for ourselves, then we gather the story from eyewitnesses...visit the locations where events took place...that sort of thing," Seeran explained between mouthfuls.

"And this is why you were in an isolated village in the middle of the Argurian Plain?" Jame asked, still puzzled.

"You see, the hard part is finding something that hasn't been chronicled yet." Seeran looked from the warrior to the arbiter.

"Ah." Jame slowly nodded. "And you thought there must be a story here."

"Actually, I decided to go to the least popular place among the historians. There's sometimes a problem with all of us trying to get the same story."

"There are reasons why casual visits to the Argurian Plain are not desirable." Tigh rolled her eyes.

"So I discovered." Seeran cleared her throat. "But I did find a story. One that has never been chronicled."

"Really?" Jame reached out and touched Seeran's arm.

"Yes." Seeran finished chewing another mouthful. "And it happened when it was least expected." She practically beamed at the pair of expectant eyes waiting for her to go on. "You," she laughed as if stating the obvious. Tigh stared in mid-chew as Jame frowned in deciphering what the historian was saying. "The story of Tigh the Terrible and Jame the Arbiter."

Tigh and Jame looked at each other, then at Seeran. "Jame keeps a journal. So we've been chronicled," Tigh explained, returning her attention to her plate.

"A journal is only a small part of chronicling. It represents one viewpoint out of many," Seeran returned. "Don't get me wrong. Journals are wonderful because eyewitness accounts can be hard to find and are often unreliable."

"What story do you think you have here?" Jame asked. "We just travel around arbiting cases."

"You seem to do the dramatic rescue rather well." Seeran noted the blush creeping up Jame's neck. "And there are rumors. Of villages being saved from raiders, of sudden peaceful negotiations, of grateful merchants when their stolen wares were mysteriously returned..." She looked at her audience and received very noncommittal expressions. "Rumors, of course. But the only thing all these miraculous events have in common are the two of you."

"You seem to know a lot about these rumors," Tigh commented, taking Seeran's cleaned plate.

"We historians pay a lot of attention to stories floating on the wind. It's a good way of finding some amazing tales to chronicle."

"We've been at this for a few years, you can't possibly chronicle all that we've done." Jame leveled reasonable green eyes at her.

"Much of history is lost to time." Seeran smiled at her. "We can only hope to capture the essence of what passes by every day. What do you plan to do with me once I am well enough to travel?"

"The choice is yours." Jame glanced at Tigh.

"Even if I choose to travel with you? At least as far as the first major city." Seeran raised expectant eyes first to Jame, then to Tigh.

"We have no choice but to take you to the nearest city," Tigh sighed. "It's too dangerous for you out here alone."

"So if you happen to do anything worth chronicling?" Seeran almost laughed at the exasperated look on the warrior's face.

"Most of the time our lives are uneventful. Even boring." Jame shook her head. "We just travel from town to town offering our services."

"Then I'll have a chance to see what most historians never do." Seeran almost beamed. Her audience eyed her with wary apprehension. "A look at heroes when they're not doing something heroic."

Tigh rolled her eyes and rose with the dirty plates and strolled out of the cave to the stream.

"She doesn't like to be called a hero," Jame confided. "Her past haunts her too much for her to feel that she deserves it."

"I think that history will see it differently." Seeran met the green eyes across from her.

"Yes. I think you're right." Jame grinned. It might be interesting to have Seeran around for a while.

Chapter
2

Four uneventful days later, Seeran believed her
companions when they told her their life was generally
uneventful. If it weren't for the change in countryside
from stark scrub to an old growth forest, there wouldn't
be anything to write about at all, except, of course, her
enigmatic companions.

The historian's wounds were healing rapidly, a tribute to the warrior's skill. A long cloth wound around
her head dipped down to cover her swollen eye, pro-
tecting it from the sunlight. With Jame's help, she
managed to fashion the borrowed tunic and leggings
into something that fit her thin frame and height. Fortunately, her boots had not been damaged during the
incident in the village.

Jame had yet to tell the story of how she and Tigh
met and formed their unique partnership. Seeran could
only speculate that they met at Ynit where the warriors
of the Elite Guard were cleansed when the Grappian
Wars were over. The enhancements that turned them
into effective warriors made them unfit for society
when they were no longer needed to fight. Discovering
how they cleansed the warriors would be enough of a

story for Seeran, since it was a tale that had yet to be
chronicled.

Tigh had wandered off again like a cat sniffing out
a scent. Jame was outwardly relaxed as usual, but Seeran noticed that she was less talkative. Playing the
observer, the historian refrained from asking if anything was amiss.

The warrior had been gone for quite a while and
Jame had long ago stopped making an effort to converse. "Tigh seems to have found something," the arbiter offered as they paced along on the rugged forest
trail.

Their way was suddenly blocked by four figures
dropping cat-like from the trees overhanging the path.
The strangers' lithe muscular bodies, including their
faces, were clad in a patchwork of leather and armor,
exposing as much skin as not. Menacing swords were
strapped to their backs and the foremost warrior
grasped an intricately carved staff with a well-worn
leather grip.

Seeran's knees weakened from the shock of the
confrontation. She nervously glanced at Jame, noting
that the arbiter's attention was riveted on the staff.
They stood frozen for long heartbeats until Jame let out
the breath she was holding and relaxed her tense body.
She nodded to the person holding the staff.

The historian blinked in surprise when the foursome dropped to their knees and bowed their heads.
Jame rolled her eyes and stepped forward. "Stand up,"
she muttered as the strangers rose with their eyes still
on the dirt path. She reached out and touched the chin
of the warrior in front of her, causing the head to rise
and gray eyes to meet hers. "Well met, Argis."

"Well met, my princess," the tall woman responded,
holding the staff out for Jame to take. Resigned, Jame
grasped the wood, trying not to let the memories of its
feel overtake her. The women pulled down the cover-

ing from their faces, revealing the strong young features of warriors.

Princess? Seeran's mind shouted, glad she didn't gasp the word out loud. Within half a heartbeat, she realized that these women were Emorans.

"I can't imagine what would bring you so far from home," Jame muttered softly, not anxious for the reason.

Argis glanced at the three scouts behind her and they silently faded into the forest. "We will walk."

"This is Seeran, a historian." Jame turned to the intrigued scholar. Argis thoughtfully studied the woman, then nodded.

"Well met, Seeran." The warrior bowed.

"Well met, Argis," Seeran returned.

Argis glanced around, then raised a questioning brow at Jame.

"She's close by." Jame smiled. Argis nodded as they continued down the trail. "Now tell me, why are you here?"

"There's been trouble," the dark-haired warrior began. "The Lukrians have been more aggressive than usual. They've joined forces with a group of warriors from the Wars. Warriors from the Elite Guard who escaped cleansing, if the rumors can be believed." A cracking branch echoed from the trees. "I guess our friend doesn't find this to be happy news."

Jame shook her head. This news was more than disquieting for her companion. Only a former Elite Guard knew the full consequences of uncleansed Guards at large. She turned to Argis. "Will the Council talk to her?"

"Given the circumstances, the Council voted to allow her to work with us...if she chooses," Argis answered carefully.

"So, has the Council finally admitted she'd be an asset to our society?" Jame asked, trying not to sound bitter. Her people had been less than pleased with her choice of a life companion.

"They're not ready to go that far." Argis shook her head, then turned a serious eye to Jame. "But we can't survive this without her."

"I'll need conditions." Jame knew that Tigh would do anything that the arbiter asked, and she'd especially not hesitate to stop these renegade warriors, whether the Emorans wanted her to or not. But this was an opportunity for Jame to get Tigh accepted into her world—a world she was destined by blood to return to someday—and she didn't want to live the rest of her days without Tigh by her side.

"The Council anticipated as much." Argis almost allowed a glint of humor to touch her eyes. Jame may not have the leaning to be a warrior in the traditional sense, but, in many ways, she was a better fighter and strategist than the rest of them combined.

"She'll be allowed to enter Emoria?" Jame pressed.

"She'll have to give up her sword," Argis returned. "At least until you've met with the Council and settled your terms."

Jame nodded thoughtfully. "I will speak to Tigh."

"You have a duty to your people, no matter what she thinks," Argis shot back, desperately trying to control her temper and her feelings towards her princess.

"She understands and respects my duty to my people," Jame returned, letting a little of the anger she was feeling show. "But you forget, we have a duty to each other."

"Your joining has not been recognized by the Council," Argis reminded her.

"That doesn't make it any less real in our hearts." Jame stared off into the trees.

Argis, not wanting to get into an old argument, shrugged it off. "This is something that you'll have to work out with the Council."

****

The trees opened onto a clearing dominated by a small lake. It was late in the day and Jame was not surprised to find a neatly made fire surrounded by a close circle of stones. A familiar leather pouch hung from a teepee of sturdy sticks tied together with a vine. The three scouts materialized in front of Jame, Argis and Seeran and cautiously approached the camp to make a quick investigation.

"I guess we camp here tonight." Jame grinned. Tigh had a knack for finding the most pleasant places to camp.

"Why hasn't she shown herself?" Argis demanded as they settled their belongings around the fire.

Jame, rummaging through one of Gessen's saddlebags, looked up. "She will. She's probably gathering food for the evening meal. If you want me to cook, you'll be eating Ingoran. If not, that lake probably has fish in it."

The four Emorans exchanged glances. Fish sounded good but they were sick of each other's attempts at cooking on the long journey to find their princess.

"We will try Ingoran food," Argis solemnly stated.

"Very well." Jame winked at Seeran, as she pulled out her cooking pans and utensils from the saddlebags.

Seeran couldn't believe her good fortune to be caught up in an honest to Bal adventure involving a legendary people such as the Emorans. She had listened with interest as Argis talked about what was happening with the tribe since the arbiter had last visited. Much of it was like any city gossip, yet there was an intriguing hint of the exotic.

The sun was almost gone when Jame settled into the task of preparing the evening meal, separating out the herbs and greens for whatever delicacy her erstwhile partner found. Four Emorans were suddenly on their

feet and peering into the darkened edge of trees with
their hands on their belt knives. Tigh stepped into view
carrying a large bundle.

"Argis," she greeted blandly as she entered the circle of firelight, then cast her eyes over the scouts she
had played hide and seek with most of the afternoon.
"More mouths to feed than usual." She held up the
bundle, then went to Jame, squatting next to her.

Jame looked up at Tigh and captured her blue eyes
sparkling in the dancing firelight. They gazed at each
other for long heartbeats before Tigh shrugged and
placed the bundle on the ground, carefully opening it.
Jame sucked in a breath of relief and looked down at
what her partner had foraged. A squeak of delight had
the skittish Emorans on their feet again as Jame flung
her arms around Tigh's neck and gave her a happy hug.

Tigh learned early on that Jame liked to eat and
took special delight in certain foods. Much to her surprise, she also discovered that she took as much delight
in offering these foods to her companion when she had
the good luck to find them.

The Emorans, eyeing this display of affection, sank
back down onto the ground and continued cleaning
their weapons. It was obvious that their princess was
very fond of this warrior and the warrior seemed to be
just as attached. Too long a time had passed since the
Council predicted that Jame would return to them bro-
ken-hearted, ready to forget this life away from the
tribe. After being joined for five years, they still
seemed to be very much together and happy.

Jame separated several plump apples from the usual
assortment of roots and greens. "A special treat for
after our meal." She grinned as Tigh gave her an indulgent look and ruffled her bangs.

"You live such a life that apples are a treat?" Argis
leveled her gaze at Tigh, the flames casting dappled
shadows over her strong features.

Tigh rose and stepped into the firelight, emphasizing her height and solid body, her expression set as she met the Emoran's eyes. "We travel to places where apples are not common," came her response after she made sure the Emorans felt the full impact of her presence. This gift had nothing to do with the enhancements that turned her into a warrior of the Elite Guard. Her ability to command attention was from the blood of her ancestors.

Argis tried to keep an awed expression from her eyes as she slowly nodded. Although her instinct screamed at her not to prod the warrior, her loyalty to her princess overwhelmed her good sense. The proud Emoran had grown up believing that she would be the one worthy enough to be Jame's life companion. They had been close friends as children and were romantically involved even while Jame pursued her studies in Ynit.

"Tigh has a knack for finding them in the most unlikely places," Jame added, not wanting any more friction between the two warriors than there already was.

Argis gave the arbiter a long look, struggling with balancing her distrust of the warrior and her feelings for Jame. She finally continued to hone her sword with slow, long swipes of the whetstone.

****

Seeran watched with fascination the wary dance Tigh and Argis performed as they went through the ritual of checking the area and making sure it was safe for the evening. The way Argis kept glancing at Tigh and Jame as they went about their chores using an enchanting wordless communication revealed the depths of feeling the Emoran had for the arbiter. *Another story to piece together,* Seeran sighed to herself.

"I'm going to check the area," Tigh said softly to Jame as the arbiter crawled into their blankets. "Get some rest. I have the feeling tomorrow's going to be a long day."

"Master of understatement." Jame sighed and moved closer to Tigh's ear. "Don't let Argis get to you."

Tigh reached out and gently squeezed Jame's hand. "Only for you," was all she whispered as Jame brought her face around and gazed fondly into Tigh's eyes before leaning forward and giving her a gentle good night kiss.

Tigh slipped out of the circle of firelight, pausing just inside the first line of trees to focus her senses on the restless forest. The scuttle of a nocturnal rodent, the creak of branches overhead and the slow flap of the expansive wings of an owl touched her keen hearing. Not a sound out of place...except, of course, the Emoran over to her left, close enough to clearly see Tigh, and something else...further into the trees.

The warrior sighed. Life with Jame was complicated enough, but it would be a lot less complicated if her partner weren't an Emoran princess. It was bad enough that Jame chose her consort from outside the tribe, but a notorious warrior from the Wars was beyond unacceptable. After the initial rejection from the Council, Jame was so upset that she didn't even bother to petition the tribe to approve her union with Tigh. Instead, they were joined according to the Ingoran customs, Jame pledging her loyalty by adopting Ingoran traditions. Tigh was forever astonished and amazed that Jame gave up so much of her own life to be with her.

A faint rustle told Tigh that the Emoran had taken a few more steps before stopping again. The warrior simply turned her head and gazed into the dark woods. After a few long heartbeats Argis stepped out from behind a tree.

"Did they teach you to see through things?" Argis crossed her arms, determined not to show that she was surprised that Tigh had heard her.

"They taught us to listen." Tigh's head suddenly whipped around as her arm flew up, catching a streak of darkness. Bare moments later, the undergrowth, maybe fifty paces into the forest, rustled—the sound rushing away from them. "Sometimes it can save your life."

Argis stared at the arrow in Tigh's hand, realizing that it was meant for her and not the warrior. She took hesitant steps forward, stretching out her hand. Tigh gave her the arrow. "Why were they shooting at me?" She examined the shaft. It was all black except for a single yellow feather.

"You don't know who they are?" Tigh carefully picked through the forest to the place where her senses told her the assailant had been. Argis, still in shock, stumbled after her. Tigh flicked a curious eye at her. "They've been following you all day."

"What?" Argis grabbed her arm and turned her around. Tigh flinched at the contact but expecting it reined in her battle-sharpened reaction.

"You were looking for us, they were following you." Tigh lifted an eyebrow and went back to studying the recently disturbed underbrush.

"Why didn't you say anything?" Argis demanded.

"I didn't know who they were after," Tigh responded quietly as she studied some small shreds of leather on the rough bark of a tree. Tigh's catching of the arrow startled the assailants enough to get their leather caught on the bark. It was a reddish color, very fine and supple. "There are three of them. Dressed in this leather. Their only weapons are bow and arrow. Faces partially covered—like Emorans." She flicked an eye towards Argis. "Small and lean—like women." Tigh's gaze lingered a little longer on the Emoran's face, noting a shift of the jaw muscle.

"We are at war with another tribe," Argis reminded her. "That's why we're here."

"Why would they be stalking you, though?" Tigh turned to go back to the camp. "Perhaps they knew you were looking for your lost princess. Someone who could be used as a valuable hostage."

"Which is more the reason we need to get her safely home," Argis countered.

Tigh straightened to her full height and leveled a serious gaze at the Emoran. "She was safe until you brought attention to her." Not waiting for a response, she turned and stalked out of the forest. Argis stared after her for a few uncertain heartbeats before shaking her head and following.

****

Dawn found Tigh wrapped protectively around Jame underneath their furs to fight off the cold night. Before sleep finally found her, Tigh had spent much of the night pushing down her anger at the Emorans for endangering her partner's life. The warm comfort of the woman who she felt she didn't deserve to share her life with always had a placating effect on her. Nothing else mattered to her. Only Jame.

Argis, wrapped in a cloak of fur, sat on last watch in the fine mist that drifted off the lake. She tried hard to accept that Jame was never going to leave Tigh. What was harder to accept was that Tigh had much stronger feelings for Jame than any of them had imagined.

The proud warrior shook away thoughts that she now owed this enigmatic warrior her life. Suddenly, angrily, she snapped the stick she had been absently whittling and just as quickly sank into sadness. She was destined to live a life that was not her choosing. Unable to live with the companion of her choice, she was bound by Emoran honor to protect with her own life the companion of her lost love.

A pair of piercing blue eyes startled her out of her reverie. Tigh had reacted to the snapping of the stick and was propped on her elbow ready to protect Jame if need be.

Never removing her eyes from the stony blue gaze, Argis rose to her feet. After several long heartbeats, she turned and stomped off to the lake to wash the lack of sleep from her eyes.

Tigh looked down at the tangle of red-blonde hair. Gently brushing a few strands away from her companion's face, she could see that Jame was still deeply asleep. She hated to wake her, but the sooner they were on their way, the sooner they could get her to a place of relative safety.

The warrior lightly kissed Jame's cheek and was rewarded with an annoyed twitch. She next chose the ear and lingered a little longer, moving quickly out of the way to avoid Jame's suddenly rolling body—still asleep but not as deeply. Allowing a grin to tug at the corners of her mouth, Tigh leaned forward and brushed her lips against those of her partner. The response this time was a tiny moan. Almost there. Tigh pressed her lips against Jame's and after a heartbeat was rewarded with a return morning kiss.

Green eyes fluttered opened as Tigh pulled away a little. "It must be really early," Jame sleepily yawned. It was a joke between them that the earlier it was, the gentler Tigh was at waking Jame up. If it was late, the arbiter could expect any number of rude awakenings. Her companion's imagination was limitless when it came to that sort of torment.

"It is," Tigh responded softly. "There have been developments." Jame was suddenly awake and alert. "We must travel quickly."

"Developments?" Jame wasn't going to leave it at that.

"I'll explain when we're on the road," Tigh promised.

"You won't be playing cat and mouse with the
scouts again?" Jame knew Tigh too well.

"I'm not leaving your side," the warrior breathed in
her ear.

"That bad?"

"Not good," Tigh admitted. "But not anything I
can't handle," she added with a grin.

Sighing, Jame had no choice but to accept her partner's quiet confidence.

****

"We're not going to be able to drop you off at the
nearest city," Jame said as she handed Seeran a plate of
cold odds and ends that was the morning meal.

"That's all right." Seeran tried to keep down her
excitement about going with them.

"This isn't some adventure with a guaranteed happy
ending," Jame cautioned her.

"I know that," Seeran replied. "I honestly do
understand. But I can't let this opportunity pass simply
because it may be dangerous."

"Not *may* be...WILL be...dangerous." Jame knelt
in front of the historian.

"I know it's dangerous. I'll probably be in terror
most of the time and wish I were in my safe little room
back in Artocia. But if I don't go with you, I'll spend
the rest of my life regretting this chance," Seeran
returned just as seriously. Jame glanced over the historian's shoulder to Tigh, who was standing a few paces
away. The warrior gave a small nod.

"All right. You can stay as long as you can stand it.
But remember, we may not be able to get you to safety
if you change your mind." Jame held the historian's
eyes a while longer, making sure that she truly understood the situation. The arbiter's internship had been at

the military camp in Ynit, so she knew first hand what uncleansed warriors were like. But for all the horror she had witnessed, as ruthless warriors were made fit for society, she wouldn't have traded the experience for anything in the world. That was where she met her life companion. Her soulmate.

"I understand," Seeran repeated not really fathoming what she was getting into but knew she couldn't walk away from the opportunity.

****

Argis listened intently as Tigh quietly described to Jame what happened the night before and was puzzled that Jame was more concerned about Tigh's safety than her own. Almost tripping on the undergrowth-covered path through the forest, Argis had to use all her warrior self-control not to interrupt and shake some sense into her princess.

"If I'd known we were being stalked..." Jame began, as Tigh rolled her eyes. The arbiter always got unreasonable when it came to Tigh endangering herself.

"I didn't know who they were stalking," Tigh responded.

"It doesn't matter, you were playing 'cat and mouse' with them," Jame countered.

"I was keeping track of their movements," Tigh clarified, not wanting to get into this kind of discussion.

"You were playing with them." Jame leveled heated emerald green eyes at the warrior. "Tell me you weren't."

Tigh's mouth went dry as she blinked at her partner. Facing a hostile army was easier than facing Jame sometimes. "I was...uh...sharpening my tracking skills. I don't get much chance anymore." She raised a sheepish eyebrow for good measure.

Jame struggled to keep a grin from her face. She secretly loved that childlike expression. It was endearing beyond words. "I'm sorry. It's only natural to worry."

"You know I'm always careful," Tigh whispered, glancing back at the Emoran warrior trailing close behind. Seeran was swaying on a carefully stepping Gessen ahead of them. Green eyes met blue in an understanding of the words unsaid. Despite the dangers and rigors of their life, they were determined to live long enough to retire from the road—even if it was as Queen of Emoria and her Consort.

Jame sighed as they trudged past the massive roots of an ancient growth of trees. Seeran twisted to capture the view around her, gaping at the silent rough-barked wonders. Even the forest sounds seemed to change as the domineering nature of the trees saturated the air. The historian, looking back at her companions, was about to comment on it, when Tigh's hand flew up. Everyone stopped. Gessen, trained for this kind of stillness, flicked her ears to pick up anything out of the ordinary.

Tigh looked around before her eyes settled on the massive root system of an uprooted tree. It was easily large enough to shelter all of them, with one close by to protect Gessen, if necessary. The warrior led the small party to the sheltered roots.

"What's going on?" Argis, having neither seen nor heard anything out of the ordinary, vented some of the anger towards Tigh that clung to her as easily as her well-worn leathers.

"Your scouts." Tigh flashed an impatient eye at her.

"What about my scouts?" Argis crossed her arms.

"They are no longer with us," came the dry response.

Argis was quick with her knife, but Tigh was quicker. They stood in a will of strength with Tigh holding Argis' wrist with one hand and keeping the knife up and away. Tigh's sword was in her other hand pointed at the Emoran's chest. A wide-eyed Seeran was shocked to see Jame roll her eyes at this tableau.

"Warriors," the arbiter muttered. "Argis, drop the knife. It's not Tigh's fault that the scouts are missing."

"I don't like her attitude," the Emoran growled through the pain shooting down her arm from the iron grasp on her wrist.

"You just don't like her." Jame shook her head. "Drop the knife. We've got to find the scouts."

Argis raked a cold eye over the warrior in front of her, then dropped the weapon. Tigh immediately let go of the wrist and sheathed her sword: Taking a step back, Argis rubbed the feeling back into her arm. Jame picked up the knife and handed it to the still angry Emoran.

"This can't go on. Not when we must be working together to get safely to Emoria." Jame glared at her old friend. "I know I can't make you like Tigh but at least accept her as an ally. You do owe her your life." Argis struggled to bring her rage under control. "Please. Do it for me?" Jame's appeal echoed as a child's voice in Argis' ears. It was the one plea that Argis could never deny.

Tigh suddenly found something interesting to study on the ground as the unfamiliar sensation of jealousy rippled through her. She knew that Jame wouldn't have pulled that tactic if this weren't such a desperate circumstance. The fact that she wasn't the first warrior to cave in under it bothered her more than she wanted to admit. But a charming and persuasive personality was Jame's gift and she had to use it at full power sometimes just as Tigh had to occasionally use her sword in a fight.

Argis took a deep breath and stared directly into Jame's unwavering eyes. "Only for you," the warrior

finally breathed and turned in time to catch Tigh wincing at her words.

Jame read the conflict of emotions as Tigh put on a
passive mask. She knew she had hurt the warrior in the
place where Tigh was the most vulnerable. Reaching
out a hand, she placed strong fingers under the bowed
chin. Tigh raised her head and soaked up the aching
apology in Jame's eyes. The warrior slowly nodded
and straightened, pulling her thoughts to their current
situation.

Still unsettled by the thought that she had hurt
Tigh, Jame grasped the warrior's hand. Knowing
Jame's tendency to hold guilty feelings, Tigh pulled her
into a gentle hug. "Time to see what kind of trouble
your scouts have gotten themselves into."

Chapter
3

Tigh let out a slow breath as she peeked through the branches of the massive tree she had quickly scrambled up. The scouts' hands were tightly bound and dirty rags were wrapped around their mouths, but other than that, they appeared unharmed. A continuous rope was knotted around their necks as they were led like a string of oxen by one of the red leather-clad women. The other two Lukrians followed behind the captives.

Tigh realized that the Lukrians' instructions had been to capture hostages—any hostages—and that was the reason they were stalking the Emorans. She was shocked at the tears stinging her eyes when she realized that they weren't after Jame. It was obvious they didn't know why Argis and company were away from Emoria and never got close enough to learn Jame's identity. The arbiter, after all, was not dressed as an Emoran, even though she now carried her old staff—the only weapon she agreed to learn while growing up.

The Lukrians' skills at stalking were formidable to have captured the forest-trained Emorans so efficiently. Tigh knew of no one who could sneak up on Emorans in the woods, especially those trained to be scouts. They knew the sylvan lands as well, if not better, than the wild creatures that inhabited it. Yet these scouts were taken, unharmed.

"Stop talking," the leader turned and hissed at the prisoners before shooting a warning glare at the rear guard.

"We are far enough away," one of the others stated. "They won't know these clumsy scouts are missing until they make camp tonight."

"You don't lower your guard until I say so," the leader growled.

Tigh's eyes narrowed as she took in the accessories attached to the Lukrians' belts as they passed beneath the tree she was in. Focusing on a pair of small stained leather bags dangling from the belt of the leader, Tigh barely stopped herself from cursing out loud.

****

Jame was surprisingly uncomfortable around her closest friend from childhood. Tigh had only been gone a few heartbeats, but it felt much longer as the two Emorans realized that they had too much and really nothing to say to each other. There was no middle ground. Jame knew that if she had stayed in Emoria, she and Argis would most likely be joined.

The problem was that the warrior was at once familiar and almost a stranger to her. Jame had drifted too far away from the world in which she was raised. She had already apologized several times. The first time was the strange, wonderful, but agonizing time when she made the decision to leave her family and friends to become an arbiter. The last time was when Argis came to Ynit to confront her with the reports that their princess was cultivating a dangerous relationship with the notorious Tigh the Terrible. That meeting had been...difficult. Jame almost laughed, shaking her head.

She had hoped that Argis had forgotten about her and found someone else to share her life with. Glancing at the warrior, sitting with her knees pulled tightly to her chin, Jame knew that this mission was a miserable ordeal for her. But she also knew that whatever Argis was feeling was her own fault and Jame mustn't feel guilty about it.

Seeran, sitting with Jame within the tangle of roots against the upturned base of the tree, gave in to the long days of exercise and less than satisfying sleep under the stars and dozed off.

The arbiter crept to the warrior and nestled into a mess of small, wiry roots, trying to work them into a comfortable sitting place. Argis darted glances at her but refused to take her eyes off the surrounding forest. "You should stay back. We don't know what's out there."

"I'll keep alert." Jame caught the look Argis flashed her. "I'm not the same person who left Emoria ten years ago. I've grasped enough of the warrior within me to keep up my self-defense skills."

Argis pulled her knees closer to her chin. "I'm not the same person I was ten years ago either. But you never gave me a chance to grow with you," she mumbled, forcing herself to keep the warrior's mask in place instead of allowing it to fall and shatter.

"I know that," Jame responded, thoughtfully. "But I had already grown apart from you after my first moons in school." She sighed and decided to bite the arrowhead. Their previous confrontations had been strong, emotional reactions to what was happening at the time. Now, in hindsight, Jame realized that she had been wrong not to let Argis know how she felt when she first realized that Argis was not who she wanted to spend the rest of her life with. "I should have told you then. But I was young and wasn't sure what I was really feeling. I was struggling with the idea of leaving home for good to pursue something that I wanted to do more than anything else. I truly thought that you would realize that we weren't meant to be together and find someone else. It's not like we had made any kind of formal commitment to each other..."

"You were going to be the Queen and I was to be the great warrior at your side." Argis choked on the words.

"Those were the daydreams of children." Jame shook her head, astonished that Argis still clung to their childhood playacting. "You can still be a great warrior at my side," she added softly. Argis turned her head sharply, resting intense gray eyes on her. "You just won't be my consort." Argis looked back out into the forest. "I had already grown apart from you before I met Tigh. You have to know it in your heart. Please don't hate her for it. It's not her fault."

A silence settled over them as Argis worked through the tangle of emotions that she had lived with for so long. The squeaking of the treetops rubbing together in the breeze and the scuttling of the tiny creatures in the undergrowth occupied their senses for long heartbeats. Finally, Argis took a deep breath and addressed the trees before her. "I knew in my heart that you no longer felt the same way for me. That you had outgrown our childhood dreams." She suddenly turned sad eyes to her princess. "A part of me tried to outgrow them, too. But that was too powerful a dream to let go of. I wouldn't have been just a warrior. I would have been the Queen's warrior. Being your friend distinguished me from the others. It gave me the incentive to excel, and to live up to the title of Queen's warrior."

"But you have excelled. You're the best warrior in Emoria." Jame nodded at the Master Warrior braid wrapped around Argis' belt.

"I did it for you." Argis captured Jame's eyes with her own. "I did it because I knew you would come back someday. After you'd seen the world and were ready to settle down. I would be there."

"I told you not to wait for me if I decided to pursue being an arbiter for a while after I finished my studies," Jame whispered, letting the guilt wash over her. She mustn't feel guilty. Argis made her own choice. "The last time I visited Emor."

"Had you met Tigh by that time?" Argis softly asked.

Jame studied her hands. "I had seen her when they brought her to Ynit to be cleansed. She was as fierce as a wild animal...as they all were when they were captured and caged." Jame stared into the forest, seeing not trees but a stone courtyard drenched in the orange glow of the late evening sun. "I was on my way to a lecture when a wagon with a cage on it came through the gate. It was not an uncommon sight at the time. Many of the uncleansed warriors hadn't yet been found. The wagon was coming in my direction and I got a good look at the person inside the cage." Jame shook her head as the vivid images flashed through her mind. "It looked as if she had been chased for thousands of paces. Covered with mud and blood, she was wild and feral and frightening. Despite this, she was alert to everything around her, like an animal. She clung to the bars of the cage and captured my eyes with the most compelling, icy blue I've ever seen. They made her even less human than the mud and blood. Those eyes enveloped me with her personality until I was frozen and could not look away. As the wagon passed by, she started to laugh, intentionally breaking the spell. It was then that I saw a hint of sadness and humanity touching her eyes and echoing in that laugh. In that tiny breath of time, the woman beneath the warrior peeked through and captured my interest." Argis was staring at her, not so much for the story being told, but for the reminder that Jame had always been a storyteller, blessed with the gift to weave words together into images and emotions like no other storyteller she had ever heard. "I hadn't actually met her face to face when I visited

Emoria a few weeks later, but I unconsciously knew that I had witnessed my destiny."

"How did they capture them?" Argis' curiosity got the better of her.

"They used a special combination of herbs developed as a weapon for the Elite Guard. It can be put on the end of a dart or arrow. Its effects are almost immediate and can knock a person out for many sand marks. It was ironic that they used one of their own weapons against them," Jame explained.

"I've never heard of such a thing," Argis responded, finding the possibility intriguing.

"The formula is known only to the Elite Guard and those who trained and subsequently cleansed them."

"So how did you actually meet her?" Argis asked, feeling strangely more relaxed. The true story was much less intimidating than what she imagined had happened in Ynit.

"I met her two moons later." Jame looked into her mind at the memory of that first meeting—if it could be called a meeting. "When a person completes the training to become an Elite Guard, they exhibit personality traits that are near opposite of those they possessed before the training. That's one of the reasons why they stopped recruiting career soldiers and convicts. They actually lost their ruthlessness and willingness to kill when trained. Most Guards had a mix of good and bad traits, just as we all do, and they made up the bulk of the regiment. But the recruiters set out to find law-abiding, peaceful citizens with the necessary physical characteristics and trained them to be the Elite Guard to lead these regiments."

"By the Children of Bal," Argis whispered, appalled.

"It was a terrible crime against those people." Jame had witnessed the shattered shells of the women and a handful of men who had to face what they had done during the Wars. The most difficult part of the rehabilitation was mentally restoring them to who they had been before their recruitment.

"So are you saying that Tigh the Terrible was one of these law-abiding, peaceful citizens before she became a Guard?" The truth created even more of a turmoil within Argis. It was much simpler when things were the black and white reality of her imagination.

"Yes," came Jame's simple reply. "She comes from a merchant family in Ingor. She has a solid Ingoran education and had been training to be a merchant. She won't talk about it, but she was going to go to Artocia and study to become a scholar." Jame paused and pulled the stopper from her water bag and took a long drink. "She was ready to undergo the next part of her rehabilitation—learning to be around people—but her reputation kept anyone from stepping forward to present her case. Her training to be a Guard had changed her to such an extreme that no one was sure if the cleansing had really worked on her. A part of our internship was to argue on behalf of the Guards as they progressed through the levels of rehabilitation." She took a deep breath. "No one wanted to argue Tigh's case. No one even wanted to be in the same room with her. Some argued for leaving her in that tiny cell for-ever. What was worse, she thought that this was the proper punishment for what she had done."

Argis blinked at her. Tigh the Terrible accepting responsibility for the atrocities she had committed dur-ing the Wars? She felt lightheaded as the certainties in her world shattered. "You couldn't let that happen," she whispered, knowing Jame too well. "You've always been able to see the good in people."

"I remembered that brief glimpse of humanity and I knew I had to try." Jame nodded.

"So you argued her case."

"Not quite yet," Jame chuckled. "The moment I said I was willing to arbitrate Tigh's case several others stepped forward and volunteered. Being a princess

really gets in the way sometimes. They insisted that it
was too much of a risk for me, but if I felt that strongly
about it they would give it a try. A dozen tried, one
after another. Tigh wouldn't have anything to do with
them. Although she was cleansed, she still had that
compelling personality and she frightened the arbiters
away. I finally convinced them to let me visit her once.
If she frightened or threatened me I promised that I
wouldn't pursue it. Not wanting to hold her captive
forever, they agreed."

"She's not the only one with the persuasive personality." Argis' face creased in an ironic smile.

Jame colored a little at the gentle compliment
before clearing her voice. "I have to admit I was nervous when I went to see her that first time."

*The cell was narrow but tidy. The only furniture
was a cot, a small desk and chair, and a stand holding a
chipped ceramic basin. The walls and ceiling were
whitewashed and created an austere, but not unpleasant
atmosphere. A low barred window allowed the sun and
the noises from the courtyard below to filter in.*

*The worried assistant healer placed a wooden chair
in the corridor for Jame to sit on and still be able to
observe through a barred window in the door the tall
figure stretched out on the cot.*

*"I'll be at my desk," the assistant healer sighed,
knowing that he couldn't convince the young arbiter
that this was a hopeless cause. He pointed to the cluster of whitewashed furniture at the end of the corridor.
"Don't hesitate to call for help."*

*Jame nodded and sat in the chair, taking in the
scene before her. Tigh was dressed in the simple white
cotton tunic and leggings worn by the cleansed Guards.
So different from the last time Jame had seen her. Her
clean face revealed a striking fair-skinned young
woman. The deep tan from years as a warrior had
faded during her time in confinement. A healthy fitness*

still radiated from her, evidence of the nurturing care given to the Guards during their cleansing. Stretched out on her back with her hands behind her head and staring at the ceiling, the warrior was seemingly unaware that anyone was outside her cell door.

Shaking his head, the assistant healer slowly walked back to his station down the long corridor.

The young arbiter cleared her throat. No reaction from the warrior. Jame shifted nervously before breaking the tense silence. "I'm...uh...I'm Jame, assistant arbiter." The warrior continued to stare at the ceiling. "I'm...uh...just going to talk a bit. I have a story I really want you to hear." Jame took in a ragged breath. She usually wasn't so nervous and she didn't know how to handle it. "I just want you to understand why I'm here and why I want to argue your case."

Jame waited quietly, trying to gauge the reaction from Tigh the Terrible. The other arbiters did not even have a chance to state their case before the warrior directed her powerful personality at them and intimidated them into making a quick journey back down the corridor. Jame, having grown up around warriors, was prepared for that kind of confrontation. This lack of acknowledgment of her presence was more disconcerting than overt, threatening behavior.

Sighing, Jame resolved to relate her impression of Tigh as the caged warrior was brought into the compound. Even if Tigh didn't understand, Jame would feel better for trying.

Although Tigh never moved throughout the narrative, Jame noticed a slight relaxing of her facial muscles and more blinking. She was listening at least.

The silence lengthened until Jame was convinced that Tigh was not going to speak. "Anyway, that's why I'm here. I want to arbitrate your case. If you want me as your arbiter, I'll return tomorrow with a first draft of the argument." Jame watched the prone woman, noting the nervous swallow and the eyes looking inward rather than at the ceiling. "All you have to do is agree to the preparation of the case. You will always have the choice to pursue it or not." Another swallow rippled through the powerful throat of the warrior. "Just say yes or no."

Silence enveloped them once again, to the point that voices rising up from the courtyard could be heard. Sadly sighing, Jame rose to leave, taking one last look at the unhappy warrior.

"Yes."

It was so soft Jame barely caught it. She froze and gazed through the bars, but Tigh still refused to look at her. "Thank you," was all Jame could say before treading slowly down the corridor lost in thought.

"I presume you finally got through to her." Argis cocked her head at the arbiter, feeling more than a little pride in Jame's courage.

"She let me visit and listened to the argument as I wrote it," Jame smiled sadly, "but she didn't really let me into her thoughts until my fourth visit. She had graduated by then to grunts and nods in response to what I said to her. Little did I know that this was her normal method of communication."

Tigh sat on the edge of the cot staring at the neatly written and well-presented argument in her hands after carefully reading it. Jame sat in her little chair in the corridor nervously watching her. She shouldn't care about what her client thought of the document. It was, after all, a part of the job. But she knew that there was more going on than just doing her job. She was drawn to this enigmatic person, more than she had ever been drawn to anyone. She wanted to get to know her, not shake hands and say goodbye when the arbitration process was finished.

Tigh interrupted Jame's reverie with a sigh. The warrior carefully laid the document on the cot next to her, and then rose to stare out of the window. Jame waited. She had discovered and quickly cultivated the art of patience while working with Tigh.

"Why are you doing this?" came the weary question, seemingly addressed to the window.

Jame almost responded with what she told the warrior on the first day, but something deep inside stopped her. "Because I want to," she finally answered. Tigh slowly turned and for the first time looked directly at the young woman who thought she was worth saving.

"Why?" came the question again. Those intense blue eyes, softened by the cleansing and haunted by the memories of what she had done as a Guard, reached straight into Jame's soul.

"Because you deserve it," Jame gently responded.

Tigh slid down the wall and pulled her knees to her chin. "I don't deserve it." It was a clear statement without bitterness.

"Yes, you do," Jame returned with a great deal of warmth. "You are not Tigh the Terrible. You have the rest of your life to be the Tigh you wanted to be before you were recruited."

"That's not possible," Tigh shook her head.

"Then be the Tigh you are today."

Tigh sighed. This upstart arbiter had a gentle, reasonable manner that was as persuasive as any skill she possessed. On top of that, she had a youthful air and an innate innocence that made it hard to deliberately go against her. Suddenly blinking, Tigh realized that she didn't want to disappoint this young woman. When was the last time she cared about anyone else's feelings?

"When people look at me, they see Tigh the Terrible." The warrior captured the trusting emerald eyes of the arbiter. "When I look at myself, I see a monster not worthy of being allowed to live a normal life again."

"When I look at you, I see a woman who has the right to a life outside of these walls." Jame jumped to her feet and took hold of the bars. Tigh raised an eyebrow at the feisty move. "Do you want to make up for the wrongs you did as Tigh the Terrible or do you want to spend the rest of your life in this cell feeling sorry for yourself?"

An astonished Tigh blinked at Jame. Suddenly she was on her feet and at the door with her large, strong hands holding Jame's smaller hands against the bars. Not taking her eyes away from Tigh's, Jame didn't react or try to struggle free. They stood for long heartbeats staring at each other in what began as a war of wills but quickly transformed into something else. They were so close that they could feel the warmth coming off each other and a strange tingle flowing between their hands. Confused by these new sensations, Tigh quickly pulled her hands away from Jame's and stepped back staring at the floor in front of her. What was going on with her?

Jame took a long breath and held onto the bars to steady her lightheadedness. What a strange reaction. She had never felt anything like it before.

"We'll try it your way for a while," Tigh finally mumbled.

"That was the beginning," Jame sighed. "We spent the next several moons building up a trust, then a friendship, and then finally a love."

"It was easier to think that she forced herself on you," Argis admitted.

"So you could have a reason to hate her." Jame nodded. "She's a human being—and a vulnerable one at that—because of what she has to live with every day."

A rustling behind them told them that Seeran was awake, so they sat in silence on the restored foundation of their shattered friendship.

Their reverie was broken by a disturbance in the undergrowth just beyond the trees on the other side of the trail. Jumping to their feet at the same time, Jame and Argis froze, listening as the sound came closer. Argis slipped her sword from the sheath on her back and motioned Jame to get back against the upturned tree. For once, Jame did not argue and crept back to Seeran who was watching the forest with wide-eyed fright.

Suddenly the noise stopped. When the echoes died away, Tigh stepped from behind a tree.

Seeing that the warrior was alone, Argis angrily lowered her sword. "Where are the scouts?"

Tigh's eyes brushed past her to Jame, who stood and approached her partner. "Your scouts are unharmed." Jame briefly closed her eyes in relief. Argis shifted impatiently behind her, trying not to glare at the warrior. "It seems that our stalkers were looking for any hostages they could get. Fortunately, they didn't get close enough to find out your identity."

"How were they captured without being injured?" Argis demanded.

Tigh flicked her eyes at the Emoran before capturing Jame's again. "The same way they captured me," she said as Jame gasped. "That confirms who we're up against."

"They drugged them?" Argis stepped forward. Tigh gave Jame a questioning look.

"We've been trying to make peace," Jame explained. Tigh nodded, knowing that Jame would tell her everything when she had the chance.

"I think they drugged them just enough to capture them. They are moving quickly back to their territory."

"We can't just let them be taken..." Argis was interrupted by a sharp glare and a raised hand. Good person or not, Tigh still had a quiver full of intimidation skills that had marked her as the most elite of the Elite Guard.

"I want you three to take the quickest, straightest route to Emoria." Tigh looked directly at her partner who had opened her mouth to protest. "I'll catch up to you."

"If they caught the scouts, they can capture you," Jame reasoned.

"They have what they came for." Tigh shrugged. "They think that we won't notice the scouts are missing until this evening, and by that time they'll be too far away—even if we figured out what happened to them. They don't know that we know who they are, and they are certainly not expecting an attack." She turned her attention to Argis. "Capturing three Emorans is too ambitious for only three of them this far from their territory. I suspect they're part of a larger party. I'm going to follow them a bit. The more knowledge we have going into this conflict, the better our chances of defeating them. Don't worry. I'll rescue the scouts."

Argis knew better than to argue with the master strategist who led the Guards to victory after victory, finally commanding the decisive battle that ended the Grappian Wars and brought victory to the Southern Territories.

Tigh strode over to Gessen. The horse was standing nearby nuzzling through roots to the tender green shoots close to the ground. Jame gestured for Argis to stay back, then went to her warrior. They silently separated the supplies, adding most of the foodstuff and some of the bedding to the packs that Jame, Seeran and Argis carried. When the chore was done, Jame stood with arms folded, waiting for Tigh to stop adjusting Gessen's tack.

"I'll be careful," Tigh said, anticipating what was about to come from Jame's mouth.

"Be extra careful." Jame stood her ground. This was no ordinary foe they faced.

Tigh turned to her with a lopsided grin. Needing no other invitation, Jame wrapped her arms around the tall warrior and pressed her face against the soft, black leather between the bits of armor. Looking up, she found gentle, affectionate blue eyes gazing down at her. The warrior bent her head and tenderly kissed the arbiter. "After I rescue the scouts, I'll have to rescue you from Argis," she breathed into Jame's ear.

"My protector," Jame softly chuckled.

Both grinned as they separated. Tigh shot one last glance at Argis and Seeran before leaping onto Gessen's back. "I'll find you as soon as I can," she assured her partner as she nudged the pale horse through the lush underbrush and onto the trail.

Chapter
4

Tigh was more than a little surprised at the cockiness of the Lukrians as they led their prisoners along a well-used road as if it was an everyday sight. When the others on the road realized that this strange little procession were Lukrians, they passed quickly or hung behind, afraid to even circle widely around them. A little fear didn't stop the discreet stares from safe distances. No matter what the tribe chose to call themselves, the Lukrians looked like Emorans. The passing hot season brought disturbing rumors down from the Phytian Mountains and these legends walking the earth only fortified the whispers.

Tigh, more infamous than legendary, had taken the time to exchange her black leather tunic for one of finely cut fawn-colored leather that reflected her Ingoran heritage. Not expecting to see Tigh the Terrible dressed as an Ingoran merchant, she could pass without recognition, unless she somehow attracted the wrong kind of attention. Even the sword on her back brought little notice since it was not unusual for a merchant traveling alone to have some sort of weapon as protection.

The road was crowded even for a land as populated as the Balderon valley. Discreetly guiding Gessen past small groups of travelers, Tigh discovered that the Festival of Bal was to begin that evening in the city of Balderon. Mentally rolling her eyes, the warrior knew that the influx of people would not only make it more difficult to track the Lukrians, but it increased the possibility of her being recognized.

Keeping the Lukrians in sight, Tigh trotted the pale horse behind a pair of wagons heaped high with pumpkins and other colorful squashes for the festival—a reminder that the cold season was fast approaching.

"Good day to you," greeted a rather portly man on a stout gray horse. He had the controlled friendly air of a merchant who enjoyed talking to people but was always on alert for a potential customer. The bald spot on his head was deep red from the sun, telling Tigh he had most likely traveled across the Argurian Plain.

"Good day, good merchant." Tigh nodded.

The portly merchant studied the tall, muscular woman who was sporting a sword sheathed in a well-worn scabbard for a heartbeat. His initial impression when he spotted the warrior was all but confirmed upon closer inspection. There was only one thing such a merchant could be selling. The thought brought a genuine grin to his face. "Salonis Grender, recruitment consultant."

Recruitment consultant. Tigh kept her expression passive as she bit back her disgust and anger at the seemingly benign title. It didn't matter that the enhancements and training that she had been subjected to were outlawed as soon as the Grappian Wars were over, she would never cultivate a liking for those who pursued that particular line of work. "Paldar Tigis, arms merchant," she returned.

"I thought so, the moment I saw you," Salonis exclaimed delightedly. He then glanced around and lowered his voice. "So you've heard the rumors?"

"I'm always hearing rumors." Tigh shrugged, thankful for growing up in a mercantile household and knowing how to converse with a fellow merchant.

"I thought I'd be the first on the scene, so to speak," Salonis continued, interpreting Tigh's evasive answer as typical Ingoran caution. "I should have known an Ingoran would get a whiff of what was going on—even this far from your part of the world."

"We enjoy the fresh air," Tigh commented, blandly. "Sometimes there's more in it than the scent of flowers and flowing water." It was a patent Ingoran response that strangely put others at ease. Ritual was an important part of merchant interaction.

After glancing around once more, Salonis leaned in closer to the warrior. "What do you make of them?" He nodded towards the Lukrians.

"Emorans." Tigh shrugged.

Salonis chuckled. "That's what they want everyone to think."

"Why do you think that is?" Tigh raised an eyebrow at him.

Salonis blinked at the warrior, then respectfully grinned. "You mean, why all of a sudden is there a tribe of Emoran imitators for this little rise to arms and not for the Grappian Wars?"

"It's something to ponder," Tigh returned, wondering how small the little rise to arms really was to lead the recruitment consultants to believe that there was a job in it for them.

"Rumor has it they're already fighting amongst themselves," the merchant confided. "This group seems to confirm that with those prisoners and all."

"Warriors are warriors, no matter what they choose to call themselves."

"At least they're not so stupid as to call themselves Emoran." The merchant winced as a Lukrian bringing up the rear of the little group slapped one of the prisoners who appeared to have a need to comment on something. Tigh clenched her teeth and hoped that that was the extent of the abuse the scouts were receiving. "They call themselves Lukrians."

"Interesting." Tigh pretended to ponder this. "Lukrians are a splinter tribe of the Emorans." Catching the merchant's sudden interest, she added, "or so the legends go."

"It doesn't matter what they call themselves. They just need to be good fighters," Salonis stated, then lowered his voice. "This new faction...I hear they're based in those mountains somewhere." He nodded his head at the distant peaks rising above the valley. "They're looking for the best fighters they can find." His voice went even lower as he leaned towards Tigh. "Rumor has it the leaders are uncleansed Guards."

Tigh raised an eyebrow and her faced registered as much surprise as a well-trained Ingoran merchant ever did. "I thought they had all been caught."

"That's what they say." The merchant shrugged. "But we know how that is."

All too well, Tigh grimly mused to herself.

"But merchants in our line of work go where the business is." Salonis straightened and gave Tigh a conspiratorial wink. "Silver is silver."

"You're so right." Tigh managed a grin before settling her gaze on the Lukrians. Silver is silver, but where would a handful of uncleansed Guards find enough silver to start another war? Her gaze lifted a bit as she looked beyond the walled city in the distance to the peaks dancing in the clouds much further away.

****

Seeran's tight calf muscles and burning lungs reminded her, too late, that adventuring required a physical conditioning that wasn't part of the curriculum at the University of Artocia. The forest gave way to a rocky terrain, forcing the historian to keep her eyes on where she was placing her feet. The impatient, searing looks thrown over the shoulder of the grumpy warrior told her that she was not endearing herself to the Emoran. She expected to be abandoned after each step because she was holding them back from getting Jame safely to Emoria. Historians were supposed to be unobtrusive observers, not the recipients of hostile glares.

She decided that complaining or asking for a brief rest would only make things worse with the warrior. Pushing away the discomfort, Seeran recited long epics to herself, concentrating on remembering every word. Lost in the world of word images, she miraculously kept walking—almost keeping pace with her companions. Intent on a particularly difficult passage filled with alliterations and mythical allusion, she walked for several heartbeats before she noticed that the Emorans had stopped. Looking up from her careful scrutiny of the broken ground, Seeran was surprised to see a low hill blocking their way.

"Stay here while I have a look around," Argis muttered as she started up the rocky slope before Jame could respond. The arbiter stared tensely at the warrior's receding back for a few heartbeats before taking a deep breath. Spotting several small boulders, she pulled the pack off her back and plopped it onto a sizable rock. "May as well have a little something to eat while Argis is in a protective mood," she mumbled as she rummaged through the pack.

Seeran stood in place, the feeling of being a burden crashing down now that she wasn't concentrating on the simple act of walking. Jame, realizing that Seeran hadn't followed her, flashed her a puzzled look. "Come, sit down and have something to eat. Keep your strength up."

Seeran moved stiffly to Jame and carefully eased down on a boulder. The arbiter sat cross-legged on the boulder next to the food. "I'm sorry. It's just that if I'm holding you back..."

Now Jame was alarmed. "Wait. What are you talking about?"

"I'm holding you back," Seeran said, mournfully. "I can't walk as fast as you."

Much to Seeran's surprise, Jame grinned at her. "You think you've been holding us back? You should have seen me when Tigh and I started traveling together. I thought I was in pretty good shape after growing up in Emoria and keeping up an exercise routine when I was a student," the arbiter laughed as she motioned the historian to an assortment of berries and hunks of white cheese and grainy bread. "She's got the stamina of a horse and extremely long legs. It was a half season before we found a compromise."

"But Argis..."

"Argis has lived in Emoria her whole life. She doesn't understand a woman who hasn't spent her life running, walking and climbing," Jame broke in. "The only opinion you have to worry about is mine. If that weren't true, Argis would have been barking at you all day as if you were a first season warrior. I think you're doing admirably for one not used to walking on anything but well-maintained paths and roads."

Seeran, nibbling on a piece of cheese, worked on putting Jame's words into perspective. "She must be an excellent teacher because she certainly put the fear of Hador into me," she joked weakly.

Jame looked at Seeran with a growing respect. "You're stronger than you think. Emorans respect strength more than they respect the ability to whack someone into the next moon. Believe me, after this trek today, Argis has more respect for you than she did this morning. The harder she glares at you the more she wants to push you to develop that strength. The teacher in her sees potential and it's difficult for her not to want to develop it."

"I think you're just trying to be kind." Seeran bowed her head in shame.

Jame shook her head. "You want to learn about Emorans? The best place to start is with how we think. Talk to Argis...ask her why she glared at you all day." Almost laughing at the expression on Seeran's face, Jame added, "She may scowl and complain, but she'll be secretly pleased that you want to know these things from her. In our society the ones who are the most successful are those who speak up and ask questions. It shows courage, curiosity and persistence—the qualities that make one a leader."

"I'm no leader," Seeran joked. "I'm too content being a slave to my work."

"You showed all three traits by seeking out your stories in a place where no other scholar would venture." Jame grinned.

"That wasn't courage, that was foolhardiness." Seeran shook her head.

"There's a fine line between the two," Jame commented while she thoughtfully munched on a berry. "Talk to Argis. She has a lot of insight into this. She's spent a good deal of time instructing her warriors in the difference between foolhardiness and courage."

They looked up as Argis nimbly scampered down the hill towards them. She took the hunk of cheese and bread that Jame held out to her, eating them contentedly as she gave in to her hunger.

"See anything interesting?" Jame asked after Argis finished her food and washed it down with a long swig of water.

"There's a large valley just over these hills," Argis began as she pulled herself up onto the boulder next to Jame and Seeran. "To the east is Balderon and beyond that are the Phytians. We're making good time."

Jame flashed an amused glance at Seeran, who simply let out a breath in relief.

"The road into the city winds close to the base of the hill just beyond this one. The quickest way is to follow it to the mountains," Argis ventured, pushing down her unease at being around people who were not Emorans. "It's heavy with travelers headed for Balderon."

"Then that will make it easier for us to be on the road without drawing attention," Jame reasoned. "I have a set of Tigh's clothes that should fit you well enough. If it's a festival or celebration of some sort, we can camp outside the city with the people who can't find accommodations."

"I'll only agree to it because I won't rest until we have you safely home." Argis captured Jame's eyes with her own. "I'm considering your...offer...to be your warrior and nothing more when you are Queen." With that, she jumped down from the boulder and looked up at her surprised companions. "I will try to do justice to Tigh's clothing."

****

The airy balls of multicolored light hissed as they shot upward. They remained suspended longer than gravity dictated and threw off sparks in all directions before winking out into darkness. Before the eye had time to adjust, a fiery dragonfly flashed and melted in a cascade of tumbling sparks...

"Seeran?"

The historian blinked, then spun around to face her companions, embarrassed that she had simply stopped to stare at the street corner fireworks display. "Sorry," she mumbled, surprised to see amusement rather than impatience in both the Emorans' eyes.

The laughing crowds shifted and pressed around them as they continued their search for a door with a crossed sword and bow etched on it. The decision to camp outside was quickly abandoned when Argis saw the campfires spiraling away from the city walls as far as they could see. Giving in to her unease around strangers, she thought it would be wiser to find an

Emoran safe house. Over the centuries, the safe houses were created to allow the secretive Emorans to travel without mixing too much with outsiders. Gradually, other women, such as merchants and warriors who habitually traveled, discovered the Emoran establishments and frequented them more often than not.

"They're usually just off the central plaza," Jame offered, noting the rising flush on the warrior's face from a mixture of frustration and claustrophobia from the crowd. Argis could return seasons later and find a specific, nondescript tree in a forest, but streets and buildings jumbled together in her mind. The noisy, festive throng only aggravated her sharp edged nerves. The urge to take her sword and use it to persuade the crowds not to get too close to her was so strong that she had to concentrate on not giving in to the impulse.

"How can we find it in all this chaos?" Argis growled.

Seeran, born and raised in the city of Glaus, stood on her tiptoes and peered in all directions over the heads of the surging people. "This way," she calmly announced before expertly winding through the crowd. Argis and Jame blinked at each other, then shrugged before pushing after the historian.

They managed to go several blocks with Seeran steadily leading the way. The Emorans were less successful in the art of plowing around inattentive people. Both struggled to keep the historian in sight and not cause injury to anyone. Argis nearly crashed into a tipsy group of loudly dressed women when she was briefly distracted with the colorful language Jame had acquired in her travels.

As with most central plazas, the one in Balderon was a formidable expanse of smooth cobblestone, relatively quiet and empty in spite of the festivities in the surrounding streets. At the center of the plaza was an imposing granite statue resting in an octagon-shaped shallow pool.

The trio stared across the dark water at the brilliant military leader who had liberated the city from the Kuntics, the legendary barbarians of the east. The larger-than-life warrior with wavy hair cascading from beneath a half helmet stared out at them, victorious eyes sparkling in the light from torches placed to highlight the face. In full armor atop a magnificent warhorse, the statue looked as if it could come to life at the sound of a battle cry and splash through the water to lead a charge to another victory.

"She was the greatest of them all," Argis whispered reverently.

Seeran, brow wrinkled in puzzlement, read the dedication plate on the lip of the pool. "That's Hekolatis. An Emoran."

"Yes." Jame nodded, mesmerized by the noble stone figure. She'd been nourished since birth on the tales of this legendary military hero who had led the Emorans in the age when they were the greatest armed force in the known world. "She led the army that liberated this whole region from the Kuntics. I'm glad the Balderons didn't let her memory die."

"This is interesting," Seeran mused as she continued to read the lengthy dedication. "It says that Hekolatis promised the people of Balderon that if they were ever threatened by an army of conquerors, an Emoran warrior would come and ensure victory for the Balderons."

Jame and Argis exchanged puzzled glances as they stepped next to the historian to read the inscription.

"It must be something that the Balderons made up." Jame shook her head. "Probably to give the people hope after rebuilding the city."

"Ah, but it could be true." A voice behind them caused the trio to spin around. Argis had her hand over her belt knife. Before them was a benign looking portly man of middle age dressed in the flamboyant robes of a merchant from the eastern territories. "Of course, since Emorans only exist in legends, any woman warrior could do the job just as well."

Argis raised an eyebrow at this and relaxed a fraction, lowering her hand from her knife.

"Made up or not, it's a nice sentiment," Jame stepped in smoothly.

"Very nice," the merchant agreed. "I'm Salonis, by the way, recruitment consultant," he added, glancing at Argis.

"Here for the festival?" Jame amiably asked.

The merchant glanced around, then lowered his voice. "Actually I heard there might be some business for me here. I'm only telling you this because your tall friend there might be able to find gainful employment, if you know what I mean."

Argis swaggered forward until she was looking down at the man. "Gainfully employed sounds good. Tell me more, little man."

Salonis took a step back, cleared his throat and nervously rubbed the sunburn on the top of his head. "It's obvious you're a warrior, probably fought in the Grappian Wars. I know, better than anyone, how difficult it's been for you warriors to adjust to peacetime." He paused to gauge the Emoran's expression but she stood, arms folded, waiting patiently for him to continue. "I just happen to know that we may be on the verge of another war."

"Who would dare go against the Southern Territories after what happened in the last war?" Argis demanded, pulling herself up a little taller.

"Ah, that's the question, isn't it?" Salonis leaned forward. "I hear that there are a few disgruntled, uncleansed Guards forming an army up in those mountains, even as we speak." He dramatically pointed to where he thought the mountains were. Jame struggled to keep a straight face.

"If you mean those mountains," Jame pointed in the opposite direction, "it would be difficult to hide something as large as an army up there. People live and work in all the habitable places."

"If rumors are to be believed, they live in a warren of caves deep in the belly of one of those great mountains," Salonis responded.

"And if this is true, which side are you the recruitment consultant for?" Argis shifted her weight with an air of casual edginess.

Salonis pulled a blue silk rag from his sleeve and patted his forehead with it. The merchant had spent his career around warriors and never had he felt the kind of menace that flowed off this woman. She was magnificent. "I never offer my services to aggressors who are mentally unstable."

"Harder to get your fee from them, huh?" Argis flashed him a sarcastic grin.

Salonis chuckled nervously. "I like a warrior with a sense of humor. If you're interested, I'll be at The Tiger and Bear. An experienced warrior such as yourself will be needed when that army in the mountains starts to move."

"I'll think about it." Argis nodded.

"Good evening to all of you." The merchant knew when to step away, allowing the potential recruit the time to consider his offer. Young, experienced warriors were drawn to war like puppies to trouble and rarely resisted the temptation.

"Have a good night, merchant," Jame returned as Salonis disappeared into the crowd that was spilling onto the plaza from the surrounding streets.

"Things are more serious than we thought," Argis muttered grimly as she jumped up on the lip of the pool and scanned the buildings facing the plaza. "There," she breathed in relief before dropping back down to the cobbles. "Come on."

A few heartbeats later, they stood before an ancient wooden door covered with faded sea green paint and an etching of a crossed sword and bow. Argis pulled the heavy brass knocker and let it drop against the thick wood. A little panel slid open and eyes looked them over before the panel clicked shut. The muffled sounds of several bolts being pulled was followed by the door easing open and a low voice telling them to enter.

They followed a tall woman with gray streaked auburn hair and a lean body softened by age and indoor work. The narrow darkened corridor they were in opened onto a cavernous common room.

Pausing at the threshold, their guide turned to them, taking in their packs and travel-stained clothes. "We're a little tight for rooms right now...the festival and all. The best we can do is one room for all of you."

"That would be more than fine," Jame returned. "I'm Jame, Peace Arbiter-at-large for the Southern Districts. This is Seeran, a historian from the University in Artocia, and Argis, Master Warrior and weapons instructor from Emoria."

"Well met," the woman greeted. "I'm Wence, proprietor of The Sword and Bow. We offer food, drink and a safe place to stay for as much of a donation as you can afford or in exchange for a service or goods."

"Thank you." Jame smiled as the trio descended several steps into the spacious room, banked on three sides by fireplaces tall enough for Argis to walk into. The benches at the tables and lining the walls in the corners were padded with Emoran-woven coverings. Tapestries depicting Emoran victories hung on the walls next to heroic displays of swords, bows and spears. Women occupied nearly every table. Some already had too much of the celebrated Emoran ale, others were trading soft words over steaming cups of spiced tea. On the benches along the walls, women who had been strangers just sand marks before were chatting like warrior bunkmates.

The smell of stew and fresh-baked bread hit their senses at once, reminding them that they had been on

meager rations all day. "There's a table over there."
Argis nodded.

"Looks good," Jame responded, turning to Seeran.
The historian was blinking at the sight before her. She
hadn't given a thought of what an Emoran safe house
was like when Argis mentioned it. The idea of sleeping
anywhere that wasn't outside and on the ground was
met with relief. Never did she imagine that a place like
this existed in the city she grew up in, or in Artocia
itself, hidden in plain sight, so to speak. "Seeran?"

The historian snapped out of her musings and gave
the arbiter a sheepish look before following her to the
table where Argis was seated and already talking to one
of the servers.

"Do you have any Ingoran dishes?" Jame asked as
she sat down with relief to be off her feet.

"Our cook always has a pot of Ingoran stew on the
fire. You'd be surprised how many Ingoran merchants
pass through," the girl chatted amiably. "We even had
one earlier today."

"I'll have a bowl of the Ingoran stew then." Jame
smiled at her.

By the time they had eaten the generous food offerings, the trio had relaxed enough to sit back and let the
friendly atmosphere of the common room occupy their
senses for a while. By the time Wence informed them
that their room was available, they were more than
ready to call it a day.

Wence led them up a back flight of stairs to a more
intimate version of the common room downstairs. A
few women were gathered, quietly talking or playing
cards. Each wall, except the one with the fireplace, had
two doors. Small brass renderings of animals distinguished the rooms from each other and Wence led them
to the door boasting an artfully cast wolf.

The room, even with three narrow beds, was larger
than either Jame or Tigh were accustomed to. A welcoming fire flickered in a small fireplace and an even

more welcoming tub of steaming water sat in one corner.

"A bath. Thank you, thank you!" Jame exclaimed.

"It's an Emoran tradition, as you well know," Wence stated with a wink.

"I've spent too much time away from Emoria. I've learned not to expect those things that are traditional to us," Jame returned graciously.

"Enjoy then. Put that statue outside the door if you have need of anything." She pointed to a stone rendering of a wolf resting on the floor next to the door. With that, the proprietor slipped out the door, leaving the trio eyeing the tub.

"You should go first, my princess," Argis said.

"That's not fair to Seeran. I'm not her princess," Jame disagreed. "We'll just go in alphabetical order." The expression on the warrior's face was almost comical as she tried to think of a way to turn Jame's logic around. It just wasn't proper for her to go before a princess for anything, much less a bath. "The water's getting cold, Argis."

The warrior, too tired and filthy to argue, pulled off her gear.

"I think I'll jot down a few notes while I'm waiting," Seeran said as she placed her pack on a small table in the corner opposite the tub.

"Good. I'm going to get us a pitcher of tea," Jame announced. Argis stiffened and almost protested before remembering that they were as safe as in Emoria itself.

Jame slipped out the door. The card game had become the most engaging pastime in the common room and everyone, except a woman reading near the window, was gathered around the four players, watching with intent expressions. Shaking her head, the arbiter trotted down the stairs, following her nose to the kitchen. Most Balderon kitchens usually opened onto the alley and this one was no exception. The back of the building was of older, more eccentric construction and Jame took a few too many corridors before her nose told her she was on the right track again.

"Really wasn't planning on all this exercise," she muttered as she rounded a sharp corner and was suddenly struggling against hands that grabbed her from behind.

Chapter
5

"Have you forgotten what you were taught about blind corners?" a low voice hissed in Jame's ears.

"This is a safe house," Jame growled back. "Now let go." Upon being released, Jame turned around and glared at an unrepentant Argis. "Why aren't you taking a bath?"

"I took one." Argis straightened. "You were gone too long. I decided to make sure my princess was all right."

"I've been gone only a few heartbeats and I'm fine. I just got a little turned around." Jame turned and continued down the corridor with Argis trailing behind her. A door that was closed when Jame passed by was suddenly open as a figure popped out and put a large hand over the warrior's mouth while the other hand grabbed an arm and pulled it behind the warrior's back. Jame spun around at the commotion.

"I seem to remember a lesson about doors, too." Jame crossed her arms and studied the scene in front of her.

"You're giving away my clothing. Should I be worried?" the assailant asked the arbiter as a distinctive eyebrow shot up.

Argis was now struggling and spewing muffled curses. Tigh graciously released her.

"You ungrateful offspring of a Yitsian snow monster." Argis backed away then pounced on Tigh, sending them through the opened door and thudding to the floor. "Where are my scouts...?" Suddenly aware that they were not alone, the Emoran looked up at three sets of astonished eyes staring down at her.

"They're looking after their prisoners," Tigh calmly replied.

Argis gave her head a shake, then climbed to her feet. Jame helped Tigh up before taking in the latest handiwork of her resourceful partner. "Good job," she murmured as she wound an arm around Tigh's waist. The warrior grinned as she laid an arm across Jame's shoulder and pulled her close.

The scouts were not only free, but bathed, and from the looks of the remnants of a meal on a side table, well fed. Aside from an assortment of scrapes and bruises, they looked in good shape. The Lukrians, on the other hand, didn't look like they were having a good day at all. Seated against the far wall, their feet and hands were tied together in front, and the same dirty rags they used on the Emorans gagged their mouths.

"Are you all right?" Argis studied the scouts who were grinning and seemed to be in good spirits.

"We're fine," Poylin chuckled as the other two covered their mouths to stop the laughing from spreading to them. Argis eyed them, then turned and gave Tigh a narrow look. Tigh's expression was one of innocence.

Argis sighed. "We'll have to figure out a way to get them out of here."

"How did you get them in here in the first place?" Jame frowned, looking up at her partner.

"They were the ones who brought the scouts in," Tigh explained. "They gave them a small dose of the potion to make them appear drunk and just before they approached the door, they removed their bindings and made the excuse to the proprietor that the scouts had engaged in some early celebrations to Bal."

"Clever." Jame grimaced. "You mean they just walked into the city with bound and gagged prisoners?"

"They traveled the great road as if it were the most natural sight in the world." Tigh gave her partner a squeeze before releasing her and going to the jumble of packs on one of the beds. She pulled a scrap of parchment from a belt pouch and handed it to Jame.

The arbiter scanned the contents of the note before giving it to Argis. "So the little merchant was right," Jame mused.

"You met Salonis?"

"He spotted Argis as a potential recruit." Jame nodded at the scowling Emoran. "How did you meet him?"

"He mistook me for an Ingoran arms merchant." Tigh shrugged.

"I'm wearing your civilian clothes, why didn't he mistake me for a merchant?" Argis scowled.

"Once an Ingoran, always an Ingoran. It's the attitude, not the clothes." Tigh grinned before glancing at her partner. "I know the one who signed that order. She was a Guard, but not one of the more...zealous ones. Just a good fighter, and solid in her loyalty to the Guard."

"In other words, not the one we should be worrying about," Jame said, slowly trying to envision the Guard who could be behind a military uprising.

"No," Tigh sighed, staring into the dying flame in the fireplace. After absently placing another piece of wood on the fire, she turned to find the others quietly studying her. "The warrior we have to worry about is someone as bad as I was, or worse."

"No one was as bad as you." Argis shook her head.

"That's not entirely true." The room had shrunk to an intolerable size in Tigh's mind as if the walls themselves were pushing against her chest and her brain, making her lightheaded. Jame, following an instinct that she barely understood and never questioned, was quickly at the warrior's side and wrapping her arms around her. That alone lifted the rock-like weight off Tigh's psyche, clearing her mind and allowing her to draw a proper breath. She put a hand on Jame's shoulder and gave it an affectionate, reassuring squeeze. "There were two: an acolyte of the Shrouded One and an archivist at the Marydee Institute. They became such monsters that they were immediately locked away."

"I don't remember them at Ynit." Jame frowned. "Whatever became of them?"

"I don't know." Tigh returned. "No one ever spoke of them from the moment they were confined."

"We're safe for now, at least," Jame sighed. "I suggest we get a good night's sleep in real beds for a change. We can work out our strategy tomorrow."

"Got room for one more?" Tigh gave her partner an endearing puppy look.

Jame laughed and pulled away from the warrior, watching the expression turn into a cute pout. "Always, for you." The arbiter grinned as she held out a hand to her warrior.

****

If Wence was surprised that the Ingoran merchant who had arrived the previous day was walking alongside the Emoran with an appetite for Ingoran food, she didn't show it as the small group took over a table in the back of the common room. In the last season, the proprietor had seen too many things that hadn't quite fit together. Just yesterday she gave a room to three

Lukrians 'helping' some Emorans. She believed that they were helping them about as much as she believed that men would make great warriors one day. Chuckling at the absurd thought, she beckoned one of the young serving girls over to her.

"Two Ingoran plates go to the table next to the back fireplace." Attention to these kinds of details kept her patrons happy. There was once a time when she didn't have to worry about anything beyond the occasional spats. Nowadays, factions emerged with every new rumor that another war was about to upset their all too short peace. Her natural loyalty was with the Emorans—being a descendant of that proud tribe herself—but refusing hospitality to the Lukrians and the veterans from the Grappian Wars would cause too many problems for her.

Jame grinned when the plates with perfectly prepared potatoes and greens were placed in front of herself and Tigh. Argis just shook her head at what she considered little more than side dishes to the real substance of a meal—anything cut from an animal. Her own plate was loaded with thick chops and eggs. Seeran, looking between her similar plate and the Ingoran fare, decided to ask for Ingoran the next time she had the chance.

"You have a plan, I presume." Argis flicked her eyes at Tigh before washing a mouthful down with tea.

"Yes." Tigh nodded, breaking off a piece of the coarse-grained bread and dipping it into a green sauce. Argis stopped chewing and watched the peace warrior, not letting her go without further embellishment.

"You might as well tell us what you have in mind," Jame sighed. The two warriors were like mismatched bolts and screws—they grated even when trying to work together.

"I'm supposed to be an arms merchant." Tigh shrugged. "It wouldn't be out of the ordinary if I sold a load of weapons to that army up in the mountains. We hire a wagon, purchase a few weapons for show and keep our Lukrian friends under some hides until we are clear of the city."

"Nice, simple plan. I see only one problem." Argis put down the chop she was gnawing on. "We barely have enough silver as a donation for the meals and lodgings for ten people—if we include our Lukrian friends. What do you propose to use for the wagon and weapons?"

Tigh opened her belt pouch and pulled out a small, bulging leather bag, then handed it to Jame. Giving her partner a curious look, Jame opened the bag and peered inside. A pile of silver sparkled back at her. "Where did you get this?"

"I decided to check to see what kinds of arms were passing through this territory. A lot can be determined by what people are interested in buying and trading. So I visited a number of arms shops. While I was in one of them, a noble with too much money and too little brains was insistent that the sword the merchant had sold to her had not been forged where she said it was. Being an arms merchant, I was brought in to settle the dispute which was in favor of the shopkeeper." Nodding at the bag, Tigh added, "That's the usual commission for an appraisal of such a fine sword."

"That must have been some sword," Argis whistled.

"It was Emoran," Tigh quietly dropped as she lifted her mug to her lips.

"What?" Argis and Jame responded in unison.

"Quite a few Emoran weapons are in the shops around here." Tigh shrugged. "But this one was a ceremonial sword."

"Those swords are sacred family relics. No Emoran would give one away, much less sell it." Argis reacted as if she had been slapped.

"There seems to be a market for them."

"No one should even know they exist," Argis muttered.

"Just another piece in the puzzle," Jame mused, sensing that Tigh had figured out more than she was telling Argis.

Wence grimaced as she glanced at the lodger coming down the stairs. Rarely did she have the overwhelming impulse to turn a woman away from the safe house as she had with this one. There was coldness, a tangible menace, about this woman that prickled at the back of her neck. But there wasn't anything overtly threatening about her to make Wence refuse the hospitality of the house. In fact, unlike most of her patrons, this woman didn't even carry a sword or bow.

Tigh, sitting in her customary place against the back wall, felt every particle of air in the room turn to ice. Looking up, she was suddenly staring into a pair of granite-hard nut-brown eyes. Shocked, she stumbled to her feet, trying to keep fear from closing around her desert-dry throat.

The others looked up, startled by Tigh's actions. The warrior's attention was riveted on the tall, somberly dressed woman with flaxen hair walking towards them. Her face was hardened into an arrogant smirk as she rested indolent eyes on the former Guard. The women at the other tables cringed away from her as evil radiated in her wake.

"Well, well. If it isn't Tigh the Terrible," the woman's low voice purred when she stood before the back table. "It's been a long time, old friend."

Tigh, still trying to pull air into her lungs, gasped, "Meah. I don't understand."

An airy laugh escaped Meah's throat. "Oh, you mean this?" She held her arms out and looked down at herself like a girl showing off a new set of leathers. "Did you think that they could really keep us cleansed?"

Sparkles of light danced in front of Tigh's eyes as she realized that she was facing her worst nightmare.

"You were cleansed. The cleansing doesn't just rub off."

"That's true." The woman nodded thoughtfully. "But it only masks the true warrior. It doesn't wash her away. A small dose of this," she held up a stone vial hanging on a chain around her neck, "makes a very effective soap."

Tigh's eyes focused intently on the vial. "You are uncleansing Guards that have been cleansed?" Her voice was strained from the tension in her body.

"We're only setting things back to the way they should be." Meah's eyes flashed. "They rounded us up like animals and forced the cleansing on us."

"They were just fixing the damage they had made in the first place," Tigh growled through clenched teeth.

"They did not damage us, they allowed us to find our true selves," Meah returned calmly. "I could have dosed you anytime. Your food, your drink, even the water you bathed in. It only needs to touch your skin, you see. The really interesting thing about it is that it's harmless to anyone else. I didn't dose you because it's more fun for you to know that a sip of water, or a casual brush against a chair or table can bring back Tigh the Terrible in an instant."

Suddenly the tension flowed out of Tigh as she straightened to her full height. Something about the former Guard wasn't adding up in her mind. "You were never this cruel, Meah."

"Ah, now that's the really good part." Meah's face creased with a wicked grin. "We've discovered how to delve deeper into our true selves."

"True selves." Tigh shook her head. "You're either being deceived or are deceiving yourselves." Looking directly at the cold former Guard, Tigh continued with a low menace edging her voice, "Now that I know what's going on, the next time we meet, we'll dance to the old tunes."

Meah straightened and stared coolly at Tigh. "We will be leading the dance together. It is a destiny that you won't be able to fight against." Glancing for the first time at Tigh's tablemates, she mock-bowed and turned to leave the establishment. She flipped a coin to Wence, who stared at it for a heartbeat before pitching it into the fire.

****

For the first time in her life, Argis felt fear. Not the kind of fear that got the adrenaline gushing and focused the mind and body in battle. This was a heart stopping, voice-caught-in-the-throat, frozen-in-place kind of fear. She sat on the bed with her head in her hands, desperately trying to pull herself together. Never in her life had she felt such evil. Like a living presence inhabiting the body of that woman.

Seeran, frightened beyond imagination, didn't care if her writing was shaky and blotched as she scraped her quill against the parchment in her small journal. Impressions had to be quickly written down. She knew that she was responsible for setting down these amazing events as accurately as possible. If Tigh the Peace Warrior became Tigh the Terrible, the truth had to be recorded in order to save her again.

Jame sat on a bed watching Tigh calmly count out the silver on the wide stone windowsill, check through their supplies, jot down a few words on a scrap of parchment...acting like nothing out of the ordinary had just happened. The arbiter should have been as frightened as her companions, but all she could muster was confusion. Tigh had been terrified of Meah. For both the arbiter and warrior, this woman was a walking nightmare that penetrated only their deepest, darkest sleep. The warrior had been trembling during the confrontation with Meah. Then just as abruptly the fear was gone. Jame felt the change in her companion and had been momentarily panicked that the food the warrior had just eaten contained the stuff in that vial.

"How could they have let such monsters fight for us?" Argis muttered to the floor.

"She was a librarian from the Maymi Peninsula," Tigh answered steadily as she carefully repacked one of the saddlebags.

Argis lifted her head from her hands and stared at Tigh. "You mean you were just threatened by a lunatic librarian?"

"No," Tigh sighed. "I was just threatened by a former member of the Elite Guard who seemed to resent the fact that society wanted her to go back to being a librarian."

"Exactly what did she mean by 'delving deeper into their true selves'?" Jame asked, not sure if she wanted to know the answer.

"I think they are enhancing the methods that turned us into Guards." Although Tigh's voice was level, Jame caught a flash of the haunted expression that had been common in her eyes during their early days together in Ynit. "You thought Tigh the Terrible was bad..." The warrior left the sentence unfinished as she walked to the window and stared out at a lurking shadow from her past.

The other three exchanged uncertain glances. Jame opened her mouth to respond when a gentle knock sounded on the door. Tigh didn't turn from the window, but Argis held her sword ready. Jame knew that if something threatening were on the other side of the door, Tigh would be the one answering it. The warrior's uncanny hearing, a residual effect of her Guard enhancements, told her who was in the corridor.

Wence slipped in as Jame opened the door. The proprietor swept a glance at Argis, who sheathed her sword, then rested her eyes a few moments on Tigh's back. "Pardon the intrusion. I just want to apologize for allowing that...person into this establishment. My initial instinct was to not let her in."

"You don't need to apologize," Jame responded. "You had no way of knowing who she was or what she represented."

"I felt the evil from her." Wence shook her head. "The times have been getting too strange for me not to be paying more attention to my instinct. That is why I need to tell you about the Lukrians." She noted that the two Emorans exchanged glances. "Three Lukrians came here with three Emorans. They said that the Emorans had started celebrating the festival a little early. I could not turn them away, but I fear that they are up to no good."

The proprietor expected several reactions to this but good-natured chuckling wasn't one of them.

"Forgive us, Wence." Jame grinned amiably. "Our friend over there made sure that the Lukrians received what was coming to them for helping our Emoran scouts. They'll be visiting Emoria as our special guests."

"How are you planning to get them out of the city?" Wence's concern seemed a little stronger than the need for the usual stealth. "The Lukrians have been a common sight in these parts of late. Rumor has it they come into the city for many more supplies than what is needed by their tribe."

"I've never known the Lukrians to play fetch it for anyone." Argis narrowed her eyes.

"We're not talking about just anyone," Tigh's soft voice addressed the window.

"There have been whispers." Wence eyed Tigh's back.

"We've heard them," Jame said. "That's why we're here."

"Fighting fire with fire?" Wence nodded, agreeing with the logic. "What about what that evil woman said? Your fire could become a part of their flame."

Seeran, frantically scratching away in her journal, realized that this conversation sounded like something a fiction writer would pen. Didn't Emorans ever speak without using metaphors? She didn't know why she was worrying about it. No one was going to believe this tale anyway.

"That's not going to happen." Tigh turned from the window. "I have no doubt that whatever is in that vial can do what she says it can but everything she said about contact with it isn't true."

"How do you know this?" Argis demanded, thinking that Tigh was attempting to spare Jame the worry.

"They taught us many things in the Guard. One is how to recognize when someone is lying," Tigh returned, capturing Argis' eyes. "Only a part of what she was saying was true. I would guess that the more troubling things were lies."

"Such as being dosed by brushing against furniture," Jame mused, relaxing a bit.

"Yes," Tigh agreed. "What I don't understand is, she knew that I knew she was lying."

"So the truth could be worse than the lie." Jame felt a coldness travel up her spine.

"Or she's just playing with my mind. It's something that the Elite Guards took delight in," Tigh sighed, then turned her attention to Wence. "We're planning to hire a wagon to smuggle the Lukrians out of the city."

"Then let me offer my apology in the form of a wagon," Wence responded. "My niece can help you drive it. It's time for her to see the home country."

"This may not be the best time for your niece to visit Emoria," Jame warned. "We're on the verge of war with the Lukrians. There is also the rumored trouble in the mountains to worry about."

"My niece is sixteen. She's spent her life living and working in this establishment, longing to get out and see the world." Wence's gaze grew distant as she remembered her own lost dreams. "She's been talking about setting out on her own and I can't keep her from doing that. Even with all the danger surrounding you and Emoria right now, she would be safer with you than out on her own."

After exchanging a long look with Tigh, Jame put a comforting hand on Wence's arm. "We would be honored to have your niece accompany us."

Argis just sighed at the thought of being pestered the whole trip by a warrior-worshipping adolescent.

****

Emoran warriors were trained to endure the greatest discomforts, but the sight of a tall, healthy, young girl hanging on every word that Seeran muttered was more torture than Argis could stand.

The moment the little band set off early the following morning, Gelder, Wence's niece, never moved from Seeran's side on the wagon seat. The girl couldn't stop asking questions about the University at Artocia and about the interesting life of a historian. A bemused Seeran patiently answered the questions, delighted to be able to discuss her profession without her listener's eyes glazing over.

When they had cleared the city gates and the endless camps of festival celebrants, the scouts prepared to melt into the countryside.

"Try not to get caught this time." Tigh raised an eyebrow at them, and was gifted with three identical hostile glares before the lean young women slipped away from the road and were quickly lost in a field of boulders and scrubby plants.

Argis almost smiled at the remark, Jame noted as she strode alongside Tigh behind the wagon. Gessen trailed her owners and entertained ideas of visiting the gray and white mare pulling the wagon, but Tigh had too good of a hold on her reins.

Tenting the wagon bed with fur hides allowed the Lukrians to be tied to the wagon in a fairly comfortable sitting position. Argis was not happy with this arrangement, but Jame reminded her that she was traveling with a peace arbiter and the Lukrians were in her care until they were brought to justice.

"Oh, please, please! Describe the bards' competition." Gelder's excited voice cut through the soft grinding of the wagon wheels on the hard, packed road. Argis' scowl was matched by a muffled chorus of groans from the bed of the wagon. Tigh grinned wickedly and Jame shook her head.

"We might have to take some time off their confinement for enduring this." Tigh's breath tickled Jame's ear. "They might even bring charges against Seeran for cruel torture." Jame playfully punched the grinning warrior in the arm.

"Argis is ready to beat up a roomful of historians," Jame whispered back.

"She's not used to unarmed competition," Tigh chuckled.

Jame studied the wisps of dust that shot out from beneath each turn of the wagon wheels. "Lucky for you because they're going to make you give up your sword before entering Emoria."

"I figured as much." Tigh gazed at a mountain peak dancing above wispy layers of clouds.

"Only until I have a little chat with the Council." Jame laid a hand on the warrior's arm and waited until blue eyes met hers. "If they don't agree to everything I ask, we'll help with this problem—because it's a threat that goes far beyond Emoria—but we'll never set foot in Emoria again." This was said with a quiet, intense conviction.

Tigh stopped walking and Jame waited patiently for her response, closely watching inexpressible emotions flash across her partner's face. The warrior finally closed her eyes for a few heartbeats of tranquility, and upon re-opening them said, "We will talk further about this."

"I just wanted to make sure you understood how I felt." Jame's eyes searched Tigh's. She knew that Tigh never truly believed that Jame would give up her heritage to be with her. "We will talk further—until you do understand."

As always, Tigh had to keep herself from drowning in those emerald eyes. She didn't have the strength to deny Jame anything. Would she have the strength to do what was right for both of them, if it ever came to that?

The wagon stopped, and three sets of eyes were looking back at them. "I guess we're more interesting than the bards' competition," Tigh joked weakly.

"That's not saying much." Jame relaxed a bit. Tigh draped a casual arm over the arbiter's shoulders as they caught up to the wagon.

"Taking a break?" Tigh raised an eyebrow at Argis. The Emoran shook her head and continued to lead the procession.

By mid-afternoon the relatively straight road started to follow the contours around the outer bank of foothills that fronted the Phytian Mountains. The cooler air, despite the position of the sun, told them that they had been steadily climbing. The arid land, painted with dry shades of scruffy browns relieved by rocky grays and whites, cast a somber mood over the little band. Even Gelder stopped talking.

Around the next curve, the scouts lounged on a large boulder to the side of the road. Upon seeing Argis, Poylin slid off the rock and strode to her.

"There's a makeshift settlement in the next valley," the slender scout reported.

"An army? Raiders?" Argis stiffened, her mind already determining how to get them safely around the valley.

"Farmers mostly, I think," Poylin responded. "Families. It looks like they've just moved into the area."

"Why would anyone settle in a place like this?" Jame asked as she and Tigh approached them.

"The question is, what could be bad enough to force them to abandon their homes?" Tigh suddenly felt a chill that had little to do with the cool wind that whipped through the hills.

"They may be able to tell us more than rumors," Jame mused. "The more we know, the better chance we'll have to defeat whoever it is in those mountains."

"The more I learn, the more I feel we have no chance to beat whatever we're up against." Argis stomped the cold, hardened road, frustrated that what they thought was a straightforward skirmish between tribes involved the outside world. Emorans didn't participate in the Grappian Wars because they refused to get mixed up in the concerns of the world around them. Now they seemed to be in the middle of what might become a huge conflict.

"If rogue Guards are behind this," Tigh straightened and pinned Argis with a cold blue stare, "there is one small factor to keep in mind. The secret behind the Elite Guards' victories had less to do with fighting skills than with out-thinking the opponent. They were masters of mental manipulation."

"So you think they're starting these rumors?" Jame pulled her partner's attention away from Argis.

"Yes. The strongest weapon is fear." Tigh took a deep breath.

Argis kept her tense demeanor for a bit longer before she relaxed and straightened. "I will concede to your greater knowledge." She turned and continued down the road, not observing a puzzled Tigh and a smiling Jame.

Chapter
6

Exhaustion and grief draped the dismal jumble of rocks and animal hides that barely passed as shelters. The five score inhabitants looked as if their souls had been ripped away along with any kind of hope. They were so encrusted with grime, the only way to tell man, woman or child was by size and bearing. Although they settled next to an intermittent creek, the well they had dug found only a pocket of water caught in the cracks of the unstable rock foundation.

Peering into the stone encircled well, Tigh simply shook her head. Unless these people found other pockets of water, they would be moving on sooner than they wanted to.

"You never actually saw anything?" Jame questioned a tall man with thick shoulders and arm muscles, giving away his profession as a blacksmith. It was obvious that these people loved their village and the decision to abandon it was like turning a back on one's own kin.

"Only the fear and distrust growing in the eyes of our people." Matlo's expressive way with language was common to mountain folk. It developed from the tradition of weaving original and imaginative tales far into the frozen winter nights.

Staring into the faces of four grime-covered children sitting numbly on a rock, Jame's soft heart wept at the axiom that the innocent always suffered the most in times of conflict. "This cold feeling. It comes up from the ground?"

"In certain places it was so strong that a step away from them was noticeably warmer. The evil was worse than the cold." Matlo shivered as his senses relived the suffocating malevolence from places that had held treasured memories. It felt as if Bal was punishing them for being too happy and satisfied with their lives. "It was bad enough that it clung to these cold spots, but it began to affect how we looked at each other. Friends and families whose hearts were always open were suddenly closed with mistrust and unfounded anger. The only explanation was these sudden cold spots. As they spread and grew stronger so did our anger and mistrust. When we were away from our valley, all those feelings simply vanished."

Tigh's attention was suddenly on the blacksmith. "You took water and food with you?"

"Yes. All that we could carry." Matlo nodded, glancing at a few of the men slicing bits of whatever they could scrounge and hunt in that desolate place and sliding them into three huge iron pots simmering over dancing fires. "Wish we had some of that now," he added with a sigh.

"So it was just the cold spots that were causing your feelings of ill-will." Tigh frowned as she looked within herself, allowing the uneasy thought that something beyond rogue Guards was behind this mystery.

"It seems that way, yes." The blacksmith turned at a shout from a small huddle of people further up the streambed. "I hope they found more water," he muttered as his attention focused away from the strangers to the more important issue of survival.

"What do you think?" Jame asked as she and Tigh sauntered back to their camp on the edge of the settlement.

"I think that there is a missing piece of this puzzle." Something teased the outer tendrils of Tigh's mind. She forced her thoughts to a high-class tavern in the city of Operal, which had just been taken at the point of her well-placed strategy and sword. They were long into their celebration of victory when one of the newer Guards spoke of improvements to their training—new ways of making them even more powerful and invincible. Even as Tigh walked in that wind-swept, barren valley, she could hear Patch Llachlan's ale-roughened voice echo through the tavern, demanding to know why they hadn't received these enhancements. The new recruit explained that there was a problem that hindered the Guards' legendary skills at stealth. Maybe the cold evil that flowed from Meah was more than just another trick the Guards used to spread fear before they conquered. It could be an unwanted aftereffect of the enhancements.

"Do you think these people are safe here?" Jame's concern brought a gentle smile to Tigh's lips.

"They are as safe as any when this kind of evil is out and about," Tigh sighed as they entered their neat little camp. A small fire ringed with rocks crackled in the cooling air. Catching the warmth was a cross-legged Seeran showing an attentive Gelder how she devised her notes for her journal. The Emorans were sprawled out on the scrubby ground talking softly.

"Find out anything?" Argis was stretched out with her hands behind her head and her ankles crossed. Talking things out with the scouts had relaxed her fears a bit. She hated mind games. She knew what to do when confronted by twenty sword-wielding warriors, but the idea that a foe could attack her mind worked on fears she never knew she had.

"A little." Jame waggled her hand.

"I think the rumor that something is going on in the caverns below the mountains is correct," Tigh mused. Before Jame had a chance to question her, Tigh's keen hearing picked up a soft impact on rock. Spinning around, she saw a Lukrian standing on a boulder some forty paces away just in time to realize the sting in her shoulder came from a dart. "What the...?" She stared, stunned, at the thin reed protruding from her leathers.

Argis and the scouts were on their feet ready to go after the Lukrian when a wild laughter wafted to them from the opposite direction. The group turned as one. Meah stood close enough to be clearly heard but far enough away to bolt if need be.

Tigh, feeling warmth, both familiar and awful, fill her veins, angrily pulled the dart from her shoulder and threw it to the ground. Meah just grinned as she watched the warrior struggle with the knowledge that Tigh the Peace Warrior was no more.

"Tigh!" Jame was ready to grab her partner's arm when Argis leapt forward and landed them painfully on the stone-littered ground. The Emoran held her struggling princess, enduring as much injury and discomfort as necessary to keep her away from the former Guard.

"You are dead, Meah." An inhuman growl came from deep within Tigh's psyche as the remnants of her cleansing lay in tatters within her confused mind. The initial clarity of why she was angry with Meah quickly faded with the realization of what was happening to her. How could she be angry with the person who freed the power within her soul?

Taunting laughter met her words and Tigh's expression hardened into granite resolve. This laughter alone was enough for her anger—for Tigh the Terrible's anger. Meah was a dead woman. She couldn't help the malicious grin upon hearing the satisfying hiss as she unsheathed her sword. Taking a determined step forward, an anguished sob from behind compelled her to spin around.

Gasps caught in the throats of her companions. The descriptions in the stories of the cold-glinted ice for eyes and the granite-chiseled features were a whitewash of the truth that stood before them. Void of humanity, the glacial eyes swept across them with a sneer of contempt. The potion jolting through her blinded her to everything but the sweet surge of power.

"Tigh." Jame's tear-strained voice stung her ears. Impatiently she glared in the direction of the whimper and found pleading, heart-breaking emerald eyes. Without thinking, she was pulled into those eyes and her features softened briefly. Suddenly a horrific anger enveloped her face. Turning back to Meah, she was possessed with an irrational need to torture the laughing woman before striking the deathblow. Without thought as to where this impulse came from, she was running, as an anguished cry behind her rent the ears of all who heard it.

****

It was the deepest part of the second night of chase when Tigh finally caught up with Meah. Or, more truthfully, Meah allowed herself to be approached. The rogue Guard stood in the middle of a high meadow, shaking her head at the warrior stumbling towards her. The moonlight painted a chalky tint across the still grasses and sent ghostly flashes off Tigh's armor and sword.

Tigh's mind spun, as it had for a full day, sending her body reeling to the ground. Growling in frustration at her unruly balance, she sat clutching her head with both hands, willing the landscape to stop spinning. Someone was after her. No. She was after someone. That was it. She was angry at this person for some reason. Why was she angry?

Using her sword as a crutch, she got back onto her feet. She was Tigh the Terrible. This person she was chasing was obviously of no consequence or else she would remember what had made her so angry. She straightened and took several steps before she saw the pale figure casually standing across the meadow.

"You'd best be on your way," the warrior rasped, startled by the sound of her own voice. "I'm not in a very good mood." Those words from Tigh the Terrible usually sent the bravest warrior running.

Meah's harsh laugh fell sour against Tigh's ears, and that elusive anger was renewed with startling vigor. Lifting her sword, she rushed towards the moonlit woman, but her only battle was with the world as it tumbled against her and she landed on her back, finally giving in to exhaustion.

A cold shadow draped over her. Opening her eyes, a face she had once known intimately was leaning in close. "It's really too bad we voted not to invite you back into our fellowship." Meah's voice was thoughtful as she studied the confused eyes blinking back at her. "You've always been the best looking of the lot." She placed long fingers on Tigh's chin, then jerked her head from side to side. The warrior instinctively rolled onto her elbow as the resulting dizziness gave way to nausea.

Meah sat back in the grass waiting for the dry heaves to ease. "You know, you used to be a lot more fun in the middle of the night," she commented as a sweat-soaked Tigh thumped onto her back. Her labored breathing caught in her dry throat.

"What...voted," Tigh gasped.

"It's a simple thing." Meah casually ran a long blade of grass down the side of Tigh's face. "If you joined us, you'd insist on being in charge. Unfortunately, you've not been setting the right example lately. You've been playing at peace warrior like you believe it. If we enhanced you, you'd be more of a monster than we could ever handle."

"Peace warrior..." Tigh scowled at the idea before realizing that was exactly what she had been. How had that happened? A fair-haired young woman with sparkling green eyes was suddenly staring down at her. Startled, she blinked. The young woman was gone, replaced by Meah, who was chewing on the blade of grass, large brown eyes thoughtfully studying her.

"They always said that love would ruin a Guard." Meah shook her head, then stood. "If I see her, I'll be sure to tell her how you died." She stood for a few heartbeats longer, watching the strength flow out of the once-powerful warrior. "Good bye, old friend."

She only looked back once before following the trail into the mountains.

****

The leather thong that hung conspicuously from Argis' belt whipped around the hilt of her knife in the capricious winds that plagued Atler Pass. The Emoran had tied the thong onto her belt after Tigh ran off three days earlier. She was prepared to hog-tie her princess if she tried to bolt or cause injury to herself. Argis' primary duty, now more than ever, was to get Jame safely to Emoria.

Stopping at a rough patch of stone and partly frozen mud, she choked up on Gessen's reins and guided the horse and her precious passenger around the treacherous area.

"Careful here," the warrior called back to Poylin who was leading the gray and white mare and wagon through the pass. Seeran and Gelder clung tensely to the wagon seat as it rocked and pitched over the rough ground.

Jame swayed with the motion of the horse, her mind inhabiting another world. Unable to cope with the void that had been wrenched open in her soul, she focused on the only hope she could muster. Tigh was still Tigh.

She had been cleansed once. She could be cleansed again. All they had to do was find her and capture her. The arbiter clenched her eyes shut as the impossibility of the idea cascaded over her. It wasn't impossible. She would find a way. She had to. Over and over she repeated these thoughts to keep away the despair. Tigh needed her now more than ever.

Holding the reins close to Gessen's muzzle, Argis gazed at the mumbling arbiter lost in her own world. The warrior wanted to say something, do something. It took this terrible joke of Bal for her to face the truth that the Jame she once knew had fled with the warrior. And the Jame that Argis always wanted her to be was gone as well.

To pass the time, Seeran taught Gelder some of the memorization techniques used by historians. The girl's earnest practice gave the others something to focus on. Each Emoran mourned the loss of the Tigh they had gotten to know rather than fearing the return of Tigh the Terrible. Jame's Tigh was a unique and remarkable woman and they missed her presence.

The sun was low in the sky by the time the pass opened onto a high valley bordered on one side by a stand of trees. An overgrown track arched away from the road towards the woods. Pausing at the branch, Argis took a deep breath, allowing some relief to wash over her. Home was just a day's walk from that spot.

Easing the wagon along the ragged track, they reached the small, diamond-clear lake just within the edge of the trees, and a camp used by generations of Emorans.

The scouts built a fire and fetched water for the pot. Seeran, with Gelder's willing assistance, had taken over the cooking and prepared, as best she could, Ingoran-like dishes for Jame. The arbiter tried to eat a few mouthfuls at each meal but she had no appetite. Argis knew better than to make her eat any more than she could. Jame had to work through her grief in her own way.

Her thoughts far away from fishing, Argis cast a net into the icy clear waters of the lake and watched it slowly sink beneath the surface. A crunch of a boot on the fine-shelled shore dragged her black musings back to the task at hand.

"Jyac isn't going to be pleased." Poylin crouched next to Argis and looked up at her. "About any of this."

Pulling in the net, Argis nodded. Two small fish wiggled in the thin ropes. Argis absently shook them onto a leather scrap. "This whole thing. It's much bigger than we thought. She won't be pleased, but she'll understand."

"But we don't have what we set out to get." The slender scout ran a hand through unruly, sand-colored hair. "Not only do we *not* have the woman who could help us win, she's been turned to the other side."

Argis flung the net into the waters. "We still have Jame. She's lived and worked around the Elite Guard, argued their cases for them, and witnessed the cleansing process."

"Helping us would be fighting Tigh." Poylin shook her head. "I don't think she can do that."

"She'll do it...for Emoria," Argis countered.

Poylin scratched her head and took a breath before speaking. "Maybe, if she hadn't gotten a glimpse of Tigh the Terrible."

Net forgotten in mid-pull, Argis spun on the scout, who rose out of her crouched position. "Why would that make a difference?"

"From our point of view, we see an injured, tamed animal returning to the wild," Poylin reasoned. "She sees an animal that she's tamed and can be tamed again."

Argis hauled in the forgotten net and liberated several more fish. "Jyac will get through to her," she finally said without much conviction.

The lapping of the water against the shore grew louder as the animal sounds around them died away. Turning quickly to the camp, all eyes were riveted on the darkened trees. A figure stepped into the clearing, clad in ripped black leather, face streaked with dirt and sweat, hair wildly scattered.

Without thought, Argis dropped the net, pulled her sword and flew towards the figure. But the sword was knocked out of her hand and she landed hard on the ground from the determined blows of a royal staff.

"Jame...no," Argis cried in frustration as she scrambled to her feet, but Jame was already within a few paces of the dark figure who had dropped to her knees, eyes focused on the woman in front of her.

Jame stopped running and stood as still as possible letting reality catch up with her. Studying the kneeling and passive woman in front of her, intently capturing blue eyes with her own, she had to push down her feelings and judge what was before her.

The grass crunched behind her from several pairs of running boots. "Stay back," she hissed.

"I beg you, Jame." Argis' voice cracked with frustration.

"If this were Tigh the Terrible," Jame stated calmly, looking straight into the heart-breaking eyes staring back at her, "we'd all be dead by now." The impact of the words dropped an unearthly hush over them.

Jame stepped forward until she was staring down at her partner. She saw pain, agony, exhaustion, pleading, fear, trust...love. She saw Tigh in those eyes. Lifting her head in thanks to whatever deity heard her prayers, she pulled Tigh's head tight against her.

* * * * * * * * * * * * * * *

By stripping off her dirty and torn clothing and plunging into the chilled waters of the lake, Tigh was able to turn her world right side up. Stepping from the icy water, she let Jame rub her damp skin with their drying rag and help her into her spare set of black leathers. As Jame worked on the lace of the tunic, Tigh caught her attention by lifting her chin with a finger. The warrior studied the sallow cheeks and bloodshot eyes, realizing that they would suffer the same way—no matter the ordeal, together or apart.

"I'm sorry." Tigh choked on the words as she was socked with a wave of grief. She had nearly lost this precious gift.

"I was going to save you," Jame whispered, her voice raw but determined. "Whatever it took, I would have done it."

Tigh tried to swallow but her throat was too dry. Anyone else would have done everything in her power to destroy Tigh. She pictured Jame defiantly standing up for the warrior and convincing the most unlikely allies to join her in a mad quest to redeem Tigh the Terrible again. Ducking her head, the warrior gently kissed her partner, letting action say those things that words could never touch. It was a subject that they needed to discuss, but at that moment the arbiter's devotion to her warrior was a balm for Tigh's battered psyche.

The smell of food simmering on the fire reminded Tigh that she hadn't consumed anything of substance for three days. "Hungry?" She raised an eyebrow at Jame. Overwhelming affection radiated from the immediate grin of the arbiter.

Jame quickly filled a plate for herself and Tigh as the others helped themselves to the fish that Seeran had prepared. Tigh plowed through her food, and felt much better once her stomach was full. She was a little surprised that the recovery seemed to be swift once the potion wore off.

Looking up at her expectant audience gathered around the fire with their plates of fish and flat bread, she realized that they had too many questions and concerns to put off until morning. Jame leaned against her, contentedly finishing her meal. Argis intently watched her, not entirely believing that Tigh the Terrible wasn't lurking beneath the placid eyes.

"How did you find us?" Jame took Tigh's empty plate and put it on the ground.

"I chased her all the way to the meadow over there." Tigh nodded in the direction of the distant road.

"You mean we went right by you?" Jame blinked at her, appalled at the idea.

"You would have seen me if I hadn't moved into the trees," Tigh chuckled. "Meah said she left me to die and she wanted you to find me."

"Why didn't you die?" Argis arched an eyebrow at the warrior. Tigh gave her a long look, seeing a bit of compassion beneath the wariness.

"I don't know." The warrior shook her head. "The answer probably lies within that dart."

Argis reached into her belt pouch and removed a soft cloth scrap. Tucked in the folds was the dart. "I thought the healers might be able to detect what's on it," the warrior mumbled as she re-wrapped the thin reed and returned it to her pouch.

"Thank you for saving it," Tigh said softly. The Emoran shot her a look, then slowly nodded.

"So what exactly happened?" Jame asked. The lack of food and sleep during three of the most miserable days of her life quickly slipped away. Pressing a cheek against Tigh's shoulder, she soaked up the warrior's healing warmth.

"I chased after Meah for I don't know how long," Tigh began, trying to fit together the nightmarish images that flickered through her mind. "At least a day, I think. It was night when she finally stopped. Whatever is on that dart did turn me into Tigh the Terrible. It also made me dizzy and intoxicated. I kept forgetting what I was angry about, but she always reminded me with that laugh."

"You were angry about being changed?" Jame frowned a little.

Tigh glanced down at her partner, then looked at her restless hands. "I was angry because she dared laugh at me," she softly admitted. Green eyes captured hers and searched for the truth she didn't want to see. "The change was complete. It was as if I'd never been cleansed."

"But you're all right now." Jame tightened her grasp on Tigh's arm.

"I knew Meah was holding back on something in the tavern. I think the effects of this potion are short-lived."

"They haven't found a way to change back permanently?" Argis scratched her head.

Tigh sighed and absently wrapped an arm around Jame. "You've got to understand that this is all about mind games. Meah said she was leaving me to die but it could have been just a part of the game. Maybe she didn't give me the full potency, letting us think that it isn't permanent. Maybe I was really meant to die and my body was able to fight off the poison."

"Why play all these games?" Argis growled. "Why not come out of hiding and fight like true warriors?"

"Because the Elite Guards weren't true warriors," Tigh responded softly. "We were scholars and archivists and librarians and lawyers and merchants... It's true that we were trained to be warriors once we were recruited, but what made the Elite Guard all-powerful was what we brought to it from our lives before. Our ability to use our minds."

"How can we be sure that the potion has worn off? Or that it won't cause flashbacks?" Argis returned to her immediate concern for their safety.

"We can't be sure, but I don't think that would suit their purposes." Tigh studied her hands. "They don't want Tigh the Terrible. What I've done for the last few years would make me too powerful for them."

A wolf's howls reached their ears. Argis narrowed her eyes, then she sounded a blue jay cry. A few heart-beats later, a pair of Emorans with mask-covered faces stepped into the clearing. The masks were quickly pulled away, revealing relieved and smiling faces.

"Tas, Olet, what are you doing out here?" Argis stood sternly, crossing her arms. The young warriors approached the fire.

"We've been on the lookout for several days now," Tas, a bright-eyed warrior with shaggy blonde hair, explained. She was not as tall as the other warriors, but she made up for it with a cunning quickness. "My princess." She turned to Jame as she and Olet unsheathed their swords and touched the blades to their foreheads before sheathing them again.

"Give me a proper welcome, you two," Jame laughed as the young warriors happily embraced their old friend. "This is Tigh." The Emorans looked at the warrior standing quietly behind Jame.

"Well met, Tigh," Olet and Tas each greeted her with proper formality.

"Well met, Tas. Well met, Olet," Tigh returned, noting that there wasn't any hostility roiling beneath the surface of the two warriors, just curiosity.

"Is this just your usual impatience, Tas, or are you on the lookout for a reason?" Argis gave the smaller warrior a knowing look.

"Well...uh...I mean, it's important to know when our princess is close to Emoria." Tas shifted nervously.

"Don't give her a hard time, Argis," Jame laughed. It was as if all the years and a lifetime of change hadn't even happened. How many times had Argis ragged Tas about being impatient and impulsive and how many times had Jame admonished Argis about it?

"Just like old times, eh?" Tas grinned.

Not quite, Jame thought to herself as she allowed the bittersweet reality of returning home after so many years wash over her.

Chapter
7

Jame held the soaked cloth to her face, hoping the cold water would shock away the apprehension she felt at returning to Emoria for the first time in six years. It wasn't as if she had completely cut herself off from her people. She had sent letters to her aunt as often as she could and there were always letters waiting for her at Ynit. But being logical about it didn't stop the morning meal from tumbling in her stomach.

"I'm the one who should be nervous," a teasing voice tickled her ear.

"I guess I just don't know when to stop sharing." Jame shrugged as she pulled the cloth from her face.

"It's all right for both of us to be nervous." The warrior looked out over the lightly rippling lake. "As long as we deal with it together."

"It's not going to be easy for either of us." Jame turned to her partner. "What's happened the last few days isn't going to help."

"It may have helped," Tigh countered, rubbing her chin. Jame waited for her to continue. "The worst has happened. I became Tigh the Terrible again and overcame it."

"That's only because the potion wore off." Jame shook her head.

"We don't know that for sure," Tigh mused.

"You mean you could have fought off the effects?" Jame's eyes sparkled with hope.

"Meah did give me a powerful incentive to fight against it." Tigh picked up a smooth, flat stone and studied the interesting quartz layers running through it.

"What kind of incentive?"

"She reminded me of the old warning that love would ruin an Elite Guard." Tigh cast an affectionate look at her partner. "As I lay there trying to work through my confusion, something kept pressing against my thoughts. I was Tigh the Terrible, but I couldn't completely give in to it. My feelings were tempered by something that hadn't been there before."

Jame raised a hand and placed it against Tigh's angular cheek. "Love."

"Yes." Tigh nodded. "I guess that warning had some truth to it."

"But we don't know if that's the reason you're back to normal." Jame dropped her eyes.

"That's true," Tigh agreed. "But the way Meah said it makes me think that there's something to it. She was never the same after her lover was killed."

Jame squeezed the excess water out of the cloth into the lake and watched the droplets form independent ripples overlapping each other. "There are too many questions and too many answers."

Angry shouts forced their attention to the camp. Olet, jaw set in defiance, was up against a tree with three swords pointed at her throat.

"You know, Jame," Tigh commented as she rose to her feet and held out a hand to the arbiter, "if your warriors keep trying to kill each other, we won't have an army to fight with."

Jame rolled her eyes and allowed Tigh to pull her to her feet. "Some things never change," she muttered as she strode past Argis and Tas, who had been engaged in a bit of friendly sparring. Tigh casually followed, raising an amused eyebrow at Argis and Tas.

"Take it back, or we'll take you back in a sack," Poylin growled at the unrepentant warrior.

"Take what back?" Jame asked in a steady voice. She walked around the angry scouts and put a finger on the bottom side of Poylin's blade and gently pushed it up and out of the way. Poylin was reluctant but did not resist. The other two scouts lowered their swords, but continued to glare at Olet, who straightened and grinned back.

"She called us deaf lambs because those Lukrians got lucky," Poylin accused angrily.

"Three of our best scouts getting captured by Lukrians," Olet teased. "Maybe you're not quite as good as you think you are."

"Maybe the Lukrians used a potion that was developed by the Elite Guard that immediately renders a person unconscious." Jame folded her arms.

"I've never heard of such a thing," Olet responded, but sounded less certain than before.

"It's all too real and it can be put on the tip of a dart." Jame relaxed a bit. "Now I want the three of you to fill Tas and Olet in on how this potion seems to work. All of us must be aware of the tactics the Lukrians are using against us."

The five Emorans straightened at this suggestion but prudently held their urge to protest. Tigh hid an amused smile as Argis simply stared at Jame's unorthodox method of breaking up the all too common spats between scouts and warriors.

"She's going to make a great Queen someday," Tigh said softly. Argis spun on the warrior, catching herself. She had spent too many years thinking of this person as an enemy. Tigh's sincerity about anything that had to do with Jame continually caught her off guard.

Relaxing, Argis returned to her casual stance. "Yes she is."

****

The track the Emorans used for wagons was concealed on the edge of a large mountain meadow in a thick wooded area huddled against an imposing bluff. This alone warned the odd traveler to seek another path on their eastward journey.

"We're going through there?" Seeran had stopped the wagon and stared at the dense tangle of vegetation.

The Emorans grinned as they grabbed the greenery and revealed that it was skillfully sown onto rough wooden screens. Behind these screens was a tunnel constructed of branches and vines.

"Clever," Tigh commented from on top of Gessen.

"You haven't seen anything yet," an amused voice vibrated through her back.

Seeran studied the screens as Gelder took the reins and steered the wagon through the tunnel. The historian couldn't believe that she was actually entering the legendary Emoria. She concentrated on every detail, placing them in her mind like a painting so she could recall it all later when she put pen to parchment.

"We tend this entrance like we tend our gardens," Argis, noticing Seeran's wide-eyed interest, explained with more than a little pride. "It's as important to our survival as the food we eat."

"Are we in Emoria?" Gelder stared into the heavy woods, broken only by the well-kept track.

She was answered with a dozen Emorans that were suddenly visible among the trees, their gray and green leather and armor blending them into the landscape. Three formidable warriors stepped onto the track, blocking the passage of the wagon.

Jame's arms, wrapped around Tigh's waist, tightened and the warrior could hear her angry, shortened breath.

"It's all right," Tigh said softly.

"No it's not," Jame responded through gritted teeth.

Sighing, Tigh threw her leg over Gessen's neck and landing easily, turned to help Jame down. The arbiter glared at her, not even trying to hide her anger. "This is not the time and place." Tigh's level reasoning calmed her a little. She'd go through the charade for now, but her aunt was going to get an earful about it.

Handing Gessen's reins to a scout, Tigh guided Jame around the wagon until they stood next to Argis. The air was cut with the sibilant unsheathing of a dozen swords and the warriors paid homage to their returned princess by pressing the blades to their foreheads. A single sword hissed against a scabbard. The immediate stillness was as tightly wound as a well bucket rope. Tigh turned to Argis and offered her the black-bladed sword.

Argis grasped the sword and held it aloft by the hilt and blade. One of the three warriors in the road stepped forward and Argis delivered the weapon to her. The Emorans then faded into the woods as quietly as they had appeared.

"Why did they take your sword?" Gelder broke the thoughtful silence.

Tigh turned to the tall girl who suddenly realized that speaking up might not have been a good idea. She waggled between being fascinated by and frightened of the former Guard. "I haven't been accepted by the Emorans as a friend, much less as a life partner to their princess. An outsider has to earn the privilege to hold weapons in Emoria."

Gelder frowned a little. "It doesn't seem fair."

"Traditions come from a need to ensure survival. These kinds of precautions have allowed the Emorans to survive through long generations." Tigh turned to Jame and raised an eyebrow.

Jame took a deep breath. "I don't agree with the traditions in this particular case, but sometimes we must follow them for the greater good of the tribe."

Tigh's eyes sparkled as she gave Gelder a ghost of a wink. "The sooner we get to Emor, the sooner you can work to amend these traditions."

Jame relaxed as she gave her partner a one-armed hug. Argis shook her head, wondering how a warrior could be so placid and understanding, yet so deadly when needed. This dyadic nature of Tigh's personality was going to be more troublesome than not among the Emoran warriors, who instinctively challenged what they perceived as weakness in order to keep them all strong.

* * * * * * * * * * * * * * *

If countries are a reflection of what threatens from outside their borders, then Emoria was a study in isolationism. The route to the heart of the country was a series of concealed tunnels through narrow outcrops of stone and cleverly laid out trails that wound through rugged boulder-strewn landscapes.

Stepping from a shallow tunnel, they entered a narrow, grassy valley with a rocky creek meandering through it. Steep cliffs climbed to great heights on all sides. The wall on the narrowest end of the valley showed signs of considerable human modification. Pocked with regularly shaped openings, the larger holes were fronted by cups of protruding rock. From where they stood, two or three masked heads were just visible over the lips of these cups. Light from the late afternoon sun stretched long across the valley and spiked off the sword hilts and armor of the Emorans lining the uneven crest of the wall.

The wagon stopped as Seeran forgot to urge the patient pony forward. Both she and Gelder, as if captured in a spell, gaped at the majesty of the outer wall of the city of Emor. Only the scant whisper of rumor spoke of Emor as being a city of stone, which was often dismissed as wild exaggeration. As had happened many times on this journey, the impartial recorder of places and events was abandoned as a dreamlike haze settled over the historian.

Without a word, Argis tugged on the bridle of the horse and led the wagon down the well-maintained road, anxious for this journey to be over.

Still atop Gessen, Jame looked around Tigh's arm at the place she called home. Stricken with another bout of apprehension, she fought the urge to beg Tigh to stop. The only thing that kept her going was how it would look if she showed anything but joy at returning to her home.

Tigh was almost as spellbound as Seeran and Gelder at the sight of the tenable wall of stone. Her military mind admired the details of it, down to the positioning of the entrance tunnel tucked to one side rather than dead center. It forced the enemy to be cornered with high walls on two sides. Glancing up at the outer bluff wall next to the entrance, Tigh nodded her approval at the pockets of hiding places, most likely permanently equipped with arrows and throwing stones.

Observing the number of women on the wall, Argis stopped the wagon and returned the reins to Seeran, signaling her to wait. She caught Tigh's eye, and the warrior walked Gessen over to the Emoran.

"Please do your people honor and let them see you." Argis raised proud eyes to her princess. "Give them a tale to pass on to future generations."

Jame looked down at her old friend, puzzled and confused. "Why is this different from any other time I've visited home?"

"Your presence gives us more than hope. It gives us the confidence we need to survive this latest threat to our existence," Argis stated with a sincere conviction.

Flabbergasted, Jame would have been speechless if she hadn't been sharing a horse with Tigh. "I'm not the one they should be greeting as their savior."

"Argis is right," a gentle voice interjected.

"No, Tigh. Don't try to rationalize this," Jame protested.

"If we succeed in beating down these rogue Guards, future generations will sing songs of the youthful exploits of a legendary Queen." Tigh's soft, steady voice had its usual effect on Jame's protests.

"Just one of many ordinary Queens." Jame shook her head.

"I don't think so." Tigh twisted around to face her partner. "It's your uniqueness that will distinguish you from the other Queens."

Knowing that it was not the time and place for a discussion, the arbiter took a deep breath and placed a hand on Tigh's arm. "They'll remember both of us—if we succeed."

"Fair enough." Tigh swung her leg over Gessen's neck and landed next to a puzzled Argis. Just when the Emoran thought she had their relationship figured out, they always added a new layer to it.

Handing Jame the reins, Tigh gave her a dazzling smile. The Emoran princess, unable to resist, grinned back. It was Tigh's way of telling her to relax and enjoy the ride. Raising her eyes to the walls lined with as many Emorans as possible, she was suddenly possessed by the wild jolt of freedom she always felt when she rode her pony across that valley as a child.

"Give them something to cheer about." Tigh's proud voice tickled that child within her and she beamed at her partner. The long dormant Emoran princess burst through with all the joyous memories of magical summer days.

Jame danced the pale horse off the road into the shallow grasses as cheers filled the hollow with endlessly cascading echoes. Hundreds of swords flashed in the amber fingers of the dying sun. Resisting the impulse to gallop the restless horse to the city wall, Jame took the time to etch the images and sounds into her memory. She knew that this elation would quickly fade back to a mundane reality. All the more reason to treasure this rare bit of joy. Her feelings of apprehension gone, the Emoran princess, atop a proud warhorse, cantered forward to the endless cheers of her people.

****

Tigh couldn't remember being more proud of Jame. She knew she was ruining her tough warrior reputation, but she couldn't stop the delighted grin from taking over her features. She loved seeing Jame doing what she did best. Effortlessly, the arbiter captured her audience and held them as willing hostages to her boundless charm. Leadership and greatness didn't always come at the point of a sword.

Argis and Tas, caught in the euphoria, grinned and laughed, their swords flashing in long tendrils of sunlight. The scouts and Olet, who had settled their differences during the trek in, loped through the grasses in Jame's wake whooping and cheering her on.

Argis glanced around and stared at Tigh with a puzzled expression. The former Guard stood as if in a trance. Her eyes, intently focused on Jame, glistened with pride and unshed tears.

"What?" Tas turned and followed Argis' gaze.

She blinked and shook her head. Argis had been blind-sided by this unexpected reaction from Tigh. "I just can't figure her out."

"I have." Tas grinned as Argis narrowed her eyes at her. "Jame is her whole world."

"It's not as simple as that." Argis scowled. "A warrior just doesn't give up what it takes to be a warrior. And I know she still has what it takes."

"She follows Jame, not the other way around," Tas reasoned. "I don't know of too many warriors who would do that. We're too stubborn and proud. The question is, does this make her stronger or weaker in a fight?"

"I guess we're going to find out," Argis mumbled as she signaled Seeran to start the wagon moving. She was uncomfortably reminded of a conversation she had with Jame many years before. Jame had asked if she'd be willing to give up her life in Emoria to be with her as she pursued her arbiter career. Argis couldn't even respond to what she thought was an unreasonable question. Now she realized that her stubborn selfishness and pride helped drive away the one thing she had most wanted in her life.

The historian and the girl were staring open-mouthed at the spectacle on the wall of Emor. As the shadows thickened, torches blazed to life like overgrown fireflies, crisscrossing the wall and highlighting the constantly moving people. The wall looked like it had taken on a coat of living fire and shadows as all the concealed crevices and pockets of stone overflowed with masked, cheering Emorans. Still enraptured by the sight, Seeran absently shook the reins and the wagon slowly rumbled after the returning princess.

Tigh blinked as the wagon in front of her crunched in movement. Wiping away the tears with her sleeve, she turned to the warriors watching her.

"Don't let the other warriors catch you crying," Argis growled as she and Tas fell in beside Tigh.

"I don't cry in battle." Tigh leveled an impassive gaze at Argis.

"Emoran warriors don't cry. Ever." Argis straightened.

"Then fortunately for me I'm not Emoran." Tigh raised an eyebrow.

"That'll change if Jame has her way." Argis looked ahead at the capering horse and rider as the cheers gave way to a rhythmic chant of Jame's name.

"Then you'll have at least one Emoran warrior who cries." Tigh's attention was on Jame's reactions to the chanting of her name. The arbiter danced Gessen around several times as if not quite believing her ears. Only returning heroes received that kind of honor.

Argis' mouth fell open, unbelieving, at the response of her people to Jame's return. "How does she do that?"

"She's Jame." Tigh grinned. "She can't help it."

Tas glanced curiously at the former Guard. "The Jame we knew used to draw people to her with her quiet, reasonable nature and her ability to tell stories."

"Jame's an arbiter, she's used to taking charge." Tigh shrugged. "And it comes naturally to her because people are drawn to her. It's a gift."

"I thought the taking charge part was your job." Argis flicked a curious glance at Tigh.

"My job is to make sure the defendants—and sometimes their friends—behave themselves. Peace warriors keep the peace, nothing more." Tigh knew that neither warrior believed her. No one ever did.

"If you say so." Noticing that the wagon was getting ahead of them, Argis increased her pace. Surprisingly, Tas flashed Tigh an understanding glance as she and the former Guard strode to catch up with Argis.

****

Jyac didn't know what to think of this young woman trotting towards the wall. The Emoran Queen had been prepared to see the idealistic young girl who

lived and breathed bringing peace and justice to the
world. What she saw before her was an Emoran princess. Even the foreign, well-worn clothing couldn't
conceal the confidence and maturity in her bearing.

"What do you think?" Sark, Jyac's Right Hand,
asked as she stood with her arms crossed, gazing over
the valley. She had to raise her voice to be heard over
the roaring, rhythmic cheers around them.

The golden-haired Queen studied the rider and
horse and shook her head. "I think that life outside has
changed my niece." She turned to her friend. "But not
necessarily in the ways we thought."

"Is that good or bad?" Sark raised a fair eyebrow,
her light blue eyes twinkling in the direct light of the
dying sun.

Jyac stretched her shorter, stockier frame a little
taller to watch her niece canter close to the wall. The
studious girl she remembered was not visible in the
laughing young woman prancing her horse down the
length of the wall, setting off an echoing wave of
cheers.

Yet, even in the midst of this show, the unassuming
and self-deprecating Jame bubbled forth unexpectedly.
The shock and surprise on her face when the Emorans
spontaneously started chanting her name was genuine.
Dancing Gessen in circles as if to say, "Who, me?" simply endeared her to her people even more.

Emerald eyes captured the Queen's as horse and
rider paused in the cleared chalk-white ground below.
The delighted grin was replaced by a mature thought-
fulness as the princess saluted her Queen with the royal
staff. Jyac reached over her shoulder and pulled her
sword from its scabbard, returning the salute, setting
off another roar of noise. The seriousness that Jyac
remembered momentarily flitted across Jame's face
before her attention returned to the chanting crowd.

"I think it's a good thing," Jyac mused, feeling
more hopeful than she had in weeks.

Chapter
8

Jame drew Gessen up to the gaping, shallow tunnel into the city, suddenly wanting to find Tigh. She twisted around and could barely make out the shadowed form of the lumbering wagon, too far away for her to wait. The traditional six-guard royal escort materialized from the surrounding grasses as a horse wrangler trotted out of the tunnel and grabbed Gessen's bridle.

Realizing that nothing less than full ceremony was expected from her, Jame swung off the tall war-horse, the crunch of her hard-soled boots a contrast to the whisper of the Emorans soft-soled ones. "Thanks, Gessen," she said softly as she ran her fingers through the horse's coarse mane. Gessen snorted and would have nodded that majestic head if the stocky handler hadn't had such a good grip on her bridle.

"My princess." The lead guard saluted as the others snapped into formation. Shaking her head, Jame stepped between the three guard rows. Before they disappeared into the torch-lit tunnel, the arbiter glanced back for a glimpse of her warrior. By that time, the darkness hid even the wagon. Straightening, she pushed away the last remnants of apprehension as she entered her home after too long an absence.

The brightness of the city of Emor at night was not so much from the number of torches lit in celebration of the return of a princess as it was from generations of study in the art of reflective light. The white rock, indigenous to the Phytian Mountains, was polished to near transparency around the torch sconces and in odd spots that reflected the sparking flames. The result was immediately blinding to unaccustomed eyes and dazzling once the effect could be viewed.

Emor was indeed a city of stone, carved in a horse-shoe of bluffs rising high off the valley floor. The natural pocking of the soft stone served as the enabler for chambers and outcroppings that were connected by trails a little less treacherous than those frequented by mountain goats. Color tumbled from every possible crevice and ledge as fresco murals of legendary Emorans and their feats popped out of the shadows like giants.

Jame, blinking away the sting of tears as her eyes adjusted to the brightness, tried to mentally grasp the spectacle before her. Every place that could support a person, and some that really couldn't, was occupied by shouting women. The pounding echoes in such an enclosed space forced her ears to pop. She finally focused on the woman standing apart from a loose half-circle of elders in the center of the main square.

Her aunt still possessed the hard, muscular body of a warrior, even though a few lines were etched around her eyes and the golden hair was streaked with gray. At that distance, Jame could gauge whether there was the telltale tightening of displeasure about her aunt's jaw. It had been the only way Jame ever knew that she was 'in for it' as a child. Much to her relief, she saw nothing but delight and acceptance as Jyac stepped forward.

The royal guard backed away, allowing their Queen and princess some privacy.

"Well met, Jame," Jyac's low voice purred as she took in her niece's vibrant complexion and fitness. Life on the outside had indeed changed Jame, and by appearances, for the good.

"Well met, my Queen." Jame touched her staff to her forehead, then lowered it and grinned at her aunt.

Jyac grabbed her niece in a joyous hug as the shouts cut through the night once again.

"I'm sorry I stayed away so long." Jame's voice faltered from a wave of guilt.

Jyac pulled away and held her shorter niece by the shoulders. "You did what you had to do. I see that now."

The sound of wagon wheels reached them. Turning around, Jame stifled a grin at Seeran and Gelder's stunned expressions as they goggled at the city and the spectacle of thousands of Emorans.

"We have Lukrian prisoners," Jame explained.

Her aunt was truly surprised by this. "Really. How'd that happen?"

Jame's eyes came to rest on the one sight she'd been aching for since entering the city. Her aunt saw what had distracted her niece and smiled.

Tigh emerged from the tunnel with Argis and Tas on either side of her, blinking away the temporary blindness from the city lights. She felt better when her companions had the same reaction to the sudden assault on their sight. Fortunately, the Emorans' attention was on her partner and she received only curious looks from those closest to her. Glancing around, she mentally shook her head. Jame had tried to explain Emor on several occasions, but nothing could prepare her for this brilliant city of stone.

"I know we have some things to talk about," the Queen said softly in Jame's ear. "But that can wait until tomorrow—after I've met your friend and spent some time with her."

Jame's head spun around to witness her aunt's sincere but passive expression. "That's all that I ask for. Don't judge her before you know her."

Jyac watched as Argis and Tas strode easily next to the tall, black leather-clad warrior. She was surprised to see that Argis did not betray the anger and distrust that had clung to her like her favorite leathers after the former Guard entered Jame's life.

Jame, never one for ceremony, ran to Tigh. Argis and Tas nodded to both as they continued on to greet their Queen.

"It took you long enough to get here." Jame was relaxed and smiling, much to Tigh's relief. She didn't want to admit it, but whatever was in the potion that Meah gave her still hung heavy on her muscles and mind, causing an unnatural exhaustion. The last thing she wanted to do that night was to defend her place at Jame's side.

"You were the one who took Gessen," Tigh answered with puppy dog innocence. Jame grinned as she grabbed Tigh's arm and pulled the tall warrior into the circle of elders, who had formed a more definite arc around the Queen. "Closing ranks?" Tigh inquired softly.

"Just for show." Jame's eyes sparkled. "Makes them feel important."

"If you say so," Tigh muttered as she met the eyes of the woman she had to impress above all the others.

Before the arbiter could utter the traditional introduction, Jyac stepped forward and spoke. "Well met, Tigh of Ingor."

Tigh blinked, surprised, before finding her voice. "Well met, Jyac, Queen of Emoria." Glancing at her partner, she was startled to see tears brimming Jame's eyes.

"Thank you," Jame whispered. Jyac had greeted Tigh as a member of the family, sending a pointed message to the Council and the rest of Emoria. Tigh still had to prove herself worthy enough to be Jame's consort, but recognition made both their lives much easier while in Emoria.

"I see the changes in you. They are not what we expected," Jyac responded thoughtfully. "Perhaps we have been hasty in our judgment of your life and companion." Her eyes lingered on the passive warrior standing in deference to her partner. "I hope these changes don't include your appetite." The hint of amusement that lit Tigh's eyes caught the Queen by surprise. The dark warrior was not at all as they had imagined.

"Uh, no. I'm starving, in fact." Jame sheepishly looked down at the polished cobbled ground.

"That's good because the cooks have been working for days on those Ingoran dishes." Jyac almost laughed at the expression on both Tigh's and Jame's faces. "Come. We have much to catch up on."

The cheering started up once again as the group walked across the cobbled square to the palace caverns. It would be long towards morning before the last echoes of the celebrations faded away.

****

The attempt at Ingoran food wasn't bad, but Tigh could never figure out why cooks thought they had to make up for the lack of meat with too many herbs and spices. She mentally took inventory of their mint supply in case the spicier concoctions bothered her later. Jame could handle just about any kind of food, but Tigh's stomach was used to the mild Ingoran cuisine.

The warrior re-crossed her long legs as she half-listened to Jame explain how they acquired three Lukrian prisoners. She had spent most of the evening fending off an uncharacteristic exhaustion by studying the intimate eating chamber. The palace cavern was near the top of the bluff, allowing odd glimpses of the outside through thin sheets of quartz filling in natural and a few unnatural chinks in the rock. The smooth-walled room had a circle of leather and cloth cushions with a low-lying wooden bar arcing in front of them. The entrance was cleared of both cushions and bar, allowing food to be delivered from the middle of the room to each woman. A small fireplace behind Jyac and Jame produced enough warmth for the cool cavern.

Sark sat to one side of Tigh, and Ronalyn, Jyac's consort, sat opposite the warrior. Tigh allowed a small grin at how intently they were listening to Jame's story. The realization that everyone was silently watching her brought the warrior out of her hazy musings.

Jame, knowing that Tigh was probably listening with half an ear, smiled. "I don't think you'll be giving away any big secrets by telling them how you knew when Argis passed by the door, since they know she would have noticed if it had been opened even a crack."

Tigh mentally thanked Jame and cast a glance at her expectant audience. "That's an easy one. I knew that Jame would go barging ahead, so I just listened for a frustrated noise and hurried footfalls."

"Barging ahead, huh?" Jame squinted at her with mock indignation only to be met by Tigh's patented look of innocence.

The other three laughed, admittedly charmed by what they saw flowing between Tigh and Jame all evening, an easy companionship based on a very strong devotion to one another. Not at all what they had expected.

"I see some things never change." Jyac grinned as her niece's attention spun back to her. The Queen caught the affectionate, almost tender expression in Tigh's eyes as she focused on her partner.

"Fortunately, our princess seems to be in the right hands for keeping her out of trouble," Ronalyn, a gentle dark-haired woman with soft brown eyes, mused.

"I don't get into trouble," Jame protested, hearing a muffled snort from her companion. "We get into some interesting situations sometimes." Tigh was grinning, but wisely kept her words to herself.

"Enough adventures for many long evenings of entertainment, I suspect." Jyac had heard the rumors over the years. She imagined that they did not come close to touching the truth.

Tigh stifled a yawn and flashed an apologetic look to Jyac.

"Tigh has had a hard few days, but that's a tale left for the light of day I think," Jame smoothly explained, trying not to be concerned by the lethargy that had been pulling at Tigh all day.

"Eiget." Jyac raised her voice and a muscular guard stepped into the doorway. "Please, escort our guest to her chamber."

Tigh looked at Jame, making sure it was really all right for her to turn in. Jame leaned forward and kissed her on the cheek. "Go rest. You're safe here." Tigh smiled, then rose gracefully from the cushions.

"Thank you for the fine meal, Queen Jyac."

"Thank you for bringing Jame back to us," Jyac returned.

"Jame makes her own choices about where she wants to go. I only follow." The warrior locked eyes for a long moment with the surprised Queen before carefully stepping around cushions and Sark on the way to the door.

Eiget betrayed some nervousness as she strode slightly ahead of the black-clad warrior. Tigh could only imagine the stories about Tigh the Terrible that were whispered after torches were extinguished in the barracks. Unfortunately, most of them were true. She tried to pay attention to the maze of short corridors of stone, but a hazy aura remained draped over her brain.

A large, thick-muscled warrior entered the corridor, facing them with arms crossed. Eiget prudently stepped behind Tigh. The former Guard stopped and stood relaxed. Waiting.

The large warrior made a show of looking Tigh up and down, scowling at the passive eyes and casual stance. A hand with a braid of leather dangling through the fingers shot out at Tigh to within a breath of her face. Without taking her eyes from those of the large warrior, Tigh raised a hand and took the braid. "You look like you have about as much backbone as a new-born lamb," the warrior sneered. "It will be a pleasure making you whimper on the sparring fields tomorrow." She flicked one last look of disdain at the former Guard and disappeared into the chamber she had come from.

After Tigh tucked the braid into her belt, Eiget continued through a series of short shafts jagging between small chambers. As they turned to cut through one of the chambers, a sitting room from the looks of it, a warrior with streaming blonde hair and an impressive scar across the cheek blocked the opposite opening.

Tigh sighed as she stepped up to the woman. This time she was met with only a hostile scowl. Pelting the braid at Tigh, the warrior turned and stomped through the opening. Having caught the braid, Tigh carefully tucked it into her belt next to the other one and flashed Eiget a quizzical look.

Eiget shrugged. "She's young."

By the time Tigh stepped into the airy chamber that had been Jame's childhood refuge, she had sixteen leather braids dangling from her belt. Exhaustion over-taking curiosity, she piled the braids onto a side table. Jame would explain it to her tomorrow. After tugging off her tunic and boots, she collapsed onto the bed and within a few heartbeats was asleep.

****

Jame stood, hands on hips, bathed in the warm amber that filtered into the chamber through small crevices from light reflected off the torches that lined the outer corridor. Her splayed partner, still in her light shirt and leather leggings, was so deeply asleep that she didn't even twitch when Jame walked in.

Shaking her head, Jame picked the boots and tunic up off the polished stone floor. Scanning the carved out shelves that dominated one of the walls for an empty space to put Tigh's clothes, she realized that everything seemed to be exactly as she had left them the last time she had visited. All her childhood trinkets and scrolls sat neatly where she herself had put them. She had forgotten them but they hadn't forgotten her. An ache for that lost innocence crept over her as she realized she had never allowed a proper farewell to her life in Emoria.

Folding the tunic, she placed it on top of a pile of leathers that she probably last wore when she was twelve. The heap of braids on a nearby small table captured her attention. Frowning a little, she sorted through the bits of leather, recognizing, even after so many years, some of the designs woven into them with thick, colored thread. Counting them, she frowned even more, glancing back at her warrior. Somehow she thought that this wouldn't happen. Maybe she had been kidding herself that Tigh would be treated differently from any other warrior.

Jame rummaged through their saddlebag and pulled out light linen shirts that they slept in on the odd occasion when they stayed in an inn or were houseguests. Slipping out of her travel clothes, she eased the soft woven shirt over her head, sighing at the warm comfort of it. Sauntering over to the bed, she studied the sprawled spectacle of long arms and legs.

The only time that Jame had seen Tigh overcome with exhaustion was when she had caught a terrible cold and they were laid up for a week in a dismal inn on the edge of nowhere. Pushing fearful thoughts from her mind, the arbiter gently unlaced the warrior's leggings and tugged at the snug leather.

"There's a beautiful woman undressing me. Should I be awake for this?" Jame raised affectionate eyes in the direction of the groggy voice. Sleepy blue eyes blinked back at her. Jame pulled the leggings off, then crawled up the bed until she was hovering over her warrior.

"How are you feeling?" Jame asked softly, noting the lethargy and unfocused eyes.

"Tired," Tigh breathed out.

Jame ran a finger down Tigh's cheek, finding her skin cool. No fever, at least. "Do you think it's that potion?"

"Probably." Tigh had closed her eyes in response to Jame's soothing touch. When she opened them again, Jame was relieved to see a little more alertness there. "It's still working its way out of my body."

"I hope so." Jame bent down and brushed her lips against her partner's. She realized that this was the first time that they'd been alone since rescuing Seeran. "Come on. Sit up, so I can get you out of that disgusting, dirty shirt."

"You certainly know how to sweet-talk a girl." Tigh waggled her brows as Jame pulled her up. She knew that Tigh's mild joking was a defense against feelings of uncertainty about the cause of the thick drowsiness. The warrior could barely lift her arms as Jame tried to free the shirt from her body.

"Let's get this on you." Jame carefully pulled the clean shirt over Tigh's head and then one arm at a time. Unable to resist, Jame gathered the warrior into her arms, reacquainting her senses to the intoxication she always felt when she held Tigh. It had been a long time and her soul hungered for this closeness like her body craves food.

"What are those braids for?" Tigh mumbled against Jame's hair. The Renasyan Meadows had nothing on the paradise she entered when she held Jame close.

Jame heaved a sigh. "They're challenges."

"I gathered that." Tigh's breath tickled Jame's ear. "A serious challenge or a 'warriors will be warriors' kind of a challenge?" Feeling Jame shake with laughter, Tigh felt a little better about the situation. She hated to be responsible for the deaths of sixteen warriors.

"It's a kind of initiation. The typical backhanded compliment," Jame explained. "They insult you to your face so you'll fight them. Then they'll only show you respect and accept you as one of their own if you beat the leathers off them."

Tigh nodded against the top of Jame's head. "It'll be a nice workout. I haven't had one in a while."

Jame raised her head and looked at her partner with affection. "Oh, you'll have fun all right. I just hope it'll help change the Council's mind about you."

"Uh, that reminds me." Tigh absently rubbed her partner's back. "They took away my sword. That might make the challenges a little one-sided."

Jame slowly raised her head from Tigh's shoulder. Her eyes had that special twinkle in them, the one that told Tigh an interesting idea had just popped into her partner's head. "That's right, isn't it?" the arbiter mused.

"Why don't you take care of all the details and just tell me when and where I have to fight." Tigh brushed her lips against Jame's cheek.

"That means that I'll have to face the Council first thing in the morning," Jame sighed.

"Just remember. You're not a young girl anymore," Tigh said softly, capturing her partner's eyes. "You are an experienced arbiter. You have successfully argued the most difficult of cases and have judged countless others."

"I know. My brain tells me that this is what I do all the time, but this is different. I'm going to be arguing my own heart and my own happiness." Jame nuzzled against Tigh's muscular shoulder.

"All the more reason why you'll win." Tigh rested her chin on the top of Jame's head. "No one can resist your impassioned arguments."

"I can always use tears." Jame smiled into the shoulder.

"It works on me every time." Tigh shrugged, looking down and noticing that Jame was close to falling asleep. "Come on. Let's get under the blankets and get some sleep. Everything will be clearer in the morning."

＊＊＊＊＊＊＊＊＊＊＊＊＊＊＊

Dozens of soft footfalls reached the edge of a dreamless sleep. Blue eyes popped open. Sunlight filtered in through the quartz-covered crevices in the ceiling and...twelve spearheads were aimed at various parts of Tigh's body at very close range. Tigh, remaining frozen, stared at her masked, steadfast captors.

"Um, Jame..." She flexed the arm where Jame's head was resting. The warrior flicked a look at her partner, who was curled up on her side in contented sleep. "Jame!"

Green eyes fluttered opened, casting a curious look at her bedmate. The expression turned to puzzlement when Jame sensed that they weren't alone. Raising her head, she blinked at the dozen figures surrounding the bed. With spears. Pointed at her warrior.

"What are you doing?" she demanded sleepily as she rolled over and sat up.

"Defending the honor of our princess," the woman closest to Tigh's head announced with great dignity.

"Gindor. We're joined." Exasperated, Jame held her head between her hands. Why did she think that things would be different for them?

"Only an Emoran joining is recognized within these walls." Gindor straightened to her full height, which was only a fraction taller than Jame, and brought her spear to within a hand's span of Tigh's throat. The warrior rather anxiously glanced at Jame.

"If that were true, why wasn't Tigh given another chamber last night?" Jame leveled a steady gaze at the woman.

"The Queen has always been too soft when dealing with you." Gindor returned Jame's gaze. "She let you study and pursue a life away from home because she could never deny you anything."

"That's not true," Jame shook her head. "I fought to be allowed to follow my dream. And it's not my fault that we weren't joined in an Emoran ceremony." She glared at the circle of women, noting that more than a few avoided her eyes.

"We make our decisions for the greater good of our people," Gindor responded. "We never expected you would go against our wishes that you not be joined to this person."

"So you feel you can burst in here and arrest her for an archaic law that defends the honor of royal offspring?" Jame demanded. "Someone who I've shared my life with for nearly six years and have been joined to for five?"

The twelve straightened, never wavering in the positioning of their spears. "Yes."

Tigh turned her head to Jame. "Tell me again why it was a good idea to come here."

Jame ran a frustrated hand through her hair. "At least let us get dressed before you go through with this foolish charade."

"That's not the custom..."

"Custom?" Tigh shot a look at Jame.

"It's customary to parade the couple through the streets as they were found—usually naked," Jame explained. "In this case, I don't think anyone will be surprised to discover that we're sleeping in the same bed," she added pointedly, glaring at the surrounding women.

"Let her up," Gindor ordered as the others stepped away from the bed, keeping their spears at the ready.

Tigh rolled her eyes, then looked questioningly at her partner. Jame gave her hand a reassuring squeeze.

Tossing back the blankets, Tigh eased her long, tanned legs out over the edge of the bed. Slowly, keeping an even eye on the spears, she stood, giving her shoulders a shake to settle the shirt that clung rather than draped, barely reaching her upper thigh.

Twelve sets of eyes took in the tall, muscular warrior as Tigh absently shook the hair out of ice blue eyes, now focused and alert. Jame hid a grin as she watched the women react to her partner's formidable beauty and presence.

"Get dressed," Gindor barked. What had seemed like the right and proper action to take when they had discussed it deep into the night was less clear in the light of day.

Jame climbed out of bed and padded over to their saddlebags, her eyes daring the women to say anything about it. She pulled out Tigh's softer set of leathers and handed them to her partner. As Tigh dressed, Jame rummaged the shelves for the set of Emoran leathers she had worn the last time she had visited Emoria. As much as she wanted to slip into her familiar travel clothes, she knew the only way to get Tigh accepted by the Council was to play by their rules as much as possible.

Four of the women stepped into the corridor. Gindor signaled Jame and Tigh to follow them.

"They're not really going to parade us through the streets, are they?" Tigh fell into step beside her partner.

"I wouldn't worry too much if they do." Jame leaned close to Tigh's ear. "Everyone celebrated far into the night. I'd be surprised if the morning bell-ringer is even awake."

When the narrow, inner corridor emptied into the main gallery, four of the elders, who were trailing behind, moved forward, two on either side of Jame and Tigh. As Jame predicted, the palace was unusually empty for that time of day. Tigh glanced around and was taken by the openness of the gallery and the large chambers that flowed into it. The section of the palace they strode through lined the outer bluff wall. Cleverly crafted panels of quartz, twice the height and width of a woman, lined the wall, forcing rainbows of light to dance across the polished stone floor.

Stepping into the heavily shadowed valley had the opposite effect when usually exiting a cave. Instead of squinting away the effects of sudden sunlight, the group had to adjust their eyes to the dim early morning light, even though the sun was much higher in the sky. Full daylight reached the sheltered valley only a few sand marks a day.

Before they had a chance to progress across the square, a line of masked women stood, arms folded, in the middle of the cobbled square. Gindor, studying the newcomers with puzzlement, stepped to the front of the little procession.

"What's that about?" Tigh thought she recognized Argis and Tas and possibly the scouts.

"Well..." Jame studied the women standing defiantly before them. "It's either a good thing or a bad thing." Tigh shot her an exasperated look.

"What do you want?" Gindor demanded.

Argis stepped from her place in the middle of the line, reaching over her shoulder and slipping her sword from its sheath. "You are here to defend the honor of our royal princess. We are here to defend the honor of her life companion."

Never in Jame's life had she experienced a silence so profound or so satisfying as when the echoes of those words faded into the stone. For some reason, her thoughts flickered back to another square that they had visited not so long ago. The prediction of a great Emoran warrior saving Balderon from being conquered again flashed clear in her mind as she watched Argis stand tall and defiant in front of the Council.

"Very well," Gindor finally acquiesced, her voice reflecting an uncharacteristic lack of force.

The line of young Emorans stepped aside to allow the Council to pass, then fell into place behind them.

"Is this a good thing?" Tigh gently nudged the stunned arbiter.

"It's the most amazing thing I've ever witnessed," Jame marveled, and for the first time that morning let a radiant sparkle light her eyes.

Chapter
9

Argis stood in the back of the Council chamber wondering, now that reality was slapping her in the face, what possessed her to do this. Studying the lively tapestries hanging from the ceiling of the overturned bowl-shaped cavern, she realized that she didn't have the oratory skills or even a compelling reason to defy tradition. All she understood was the absurdity of the idea of treating Jame like a cloistered princess and Tigh as nothing more than an ardent suitor. Her brief journey outside of Emoria brought home how narrow a world the Council draped around them.

Resting her eyes on the arbiter standing quietly next to Tigh in the defendants' box, Argis had no doubt that Jame could convince anyone of just about anything. But the Council wasn't just anyone. They clung to the old ways like a newborn to a mother, never accepting any reason as good enough to be weaned away.

She knew she didn't have Jame's skill to stand up to the Council, but she remembered the words that Jame had spoken when they were younger, when Argis had to defend Tas, who had gotten into trouble over a harmless prank. Argis lamented that nothing she said would make any difference in saving Tas from punishment. Jame's response was—wise beyond her years—that sometimes just showing up made a difference. Astonishingly enough it had. The loyalty Argis showed for her friend, combined with the Council's respect for Argis as a future warrior, helped reduce Tas' punishment to a warning.

Glancing at Tas standing next to her and at Olet and the scouts, she realized that just their presence made a statement more eloquent than any well-composed speech. Besides, Jame flashed that radiant smile at her. That alone made the risks of defying the Council well worth it.

The Council lowered aged bones onto the cushioned chairs around a half moon table. The defendants' box, little more than a rectangle of small stones no higher than the ankle, was centered in front of the straight edge of the table. Lying on the table was a black-bladed sword. Jame and Tigh gazed at the sword and exchanged slow glances.

The Council members pulled down their masks, revealing various shades of gray to white hair and strong faces lined with age. Gindor, seated at the center of the table, had white hair, but her face was almost smooth with large blue-gray eyes studying the pair in front of her.

"It seems you've picked up some unexpected defenders." Gindor gazed at the tall warrior. "I'm surprised that Argis thinks you have a right to pretend to be a joined couple."

"They're not pretending," Argis interjected before remembering to whom she was speaking. Just as quickly, she re-gathered her resolve to defend Tigh. Pulling off her mask, she strode around the table and stood next to Jame. The arbiter greeted her with a reassuring smile. Tigh's expression reflected curiosity but her eyes told Argis that the former Guard did not question her motive.

The sight of an Emoran princess flanked by two tall warriors had an unexpected and unsettling effect on the Council. The feeling was akin to deja vu, except that it was something they had experienced only in their mind's eye while reading the ancient, secret texts of the Emor Mysteries.

"Maybe we should just let it be..." Riglan, a thin, wrinkled woman with a long braid of gray hair, stammered.

"Coincidence," Gindor cut in. "We're letting our imaginations get the best of us."

The trio standing before them exchanged puzzled glances.

"But what if it's real?" Poag's face creased in concern. As Gindor's Right Hand, the former weapons master had to make sure that all concerns were discussed.

A low, hollow sound penetrated the stone. The shocked silence lasted only a couple of heartbeats before Argis had her mask back on and rushed to the door with her small defiant band behind her.

"By the Children of Bal, it's happening," one of the Council members gasped.

Tigh grabbed Jame's arm. "What's going on?"

"It's the alarm—most likely an attack of some kind," Jame stammered out.

Turning to the Council, Tigh stepped out of the box and deliberately strode to the table, eyes penetrating Gindor's soul as the older woman could only stare back at her. The former Guard picked up her sword, then cast a glare around the half circle of women, daring them to utter even a word about it. She was met with eyes wide with uncertainty and skin that matched the chalky walls around them.

Jame put a hand on Tigh's back, getting her attention. "Be careful." The arbiter reached up and pulled her tall warrior's head down.

"Always," Tigh breathed. "You stay here." She held Jame's eyes long enough to make sure that the arbiter wasn't going to fight her on this.

Jame nodded and brushed her lips against Tigh's. After pulling her partner into a brief hug, Tigh ran past the stunned Council out into the square.

****

A wall of mist hit Tigh's face as she emerged from the Council chamber. In the high valleys of the mountains, the weather was as changeable as an Emoran's mind, so the saying went. Squinting through the swirling fog, Tigh was impressed by the activity where only a short time before was a silent emptiness. Standing in front of a small fountain in the center of the square, Argis was a study in determination as she deftly organized the warriors, still half asleep and pulling on their leathers and weapons.

Through the pockets of mists hovering against the bluff walls, Tigh could see the browns, grays and greens of Emoran leather streaming up the narrow trails like huge mottled snakes. That meant the threat came from the forested lands stretching away from the tops of the bluffs.

"Tigh!" Argis paused long enough in barking instructions to a knot of archers to wave the former Guard over to her. By the time the tall warrior made it to the fountain, Argis had finished her task and was staring at the cobbles, momentarily lost in thought.

"What's going on?" Tigh's voice reached the grim-faced warrior and Argis blinked up at her.

"An army of Lukrians has made camp in the first meadow beyond that line of trees." The Emoran nodded upward. "They just appeared there this morning.

Patrols and guard outposts extend to the edge of our territory, yet the first word we heard of the Lukrians was from an inner patrol—just now."

"What do you mean 'camp'?"

"Tents, fires, hundreds of warriors." Argis waved her arms. Impossible was an understatement for the Lukrians to have casually entered Emoria and take over an open meadow without being seen.

"What about the outposts?" Tigh worked to keep her thoughts calm, knowing that there was a plausible answer to what appeared to be the work of magic.

"We've sent runners out to them." Catching a series of reflected flashes from the top of the bluff, Argis took a last look around the square. Satisfied that everyone was doing what was supposed to be done, she turned to Tigh. "Need your scabbard?"

Tigh loosened her belt a bit and slid the sword through it. "That'll do."

"Let's go see what we're up against."

＊＊＊＊＊＊＊＊＊＊＊＊＊

A wrinkled but surprisingly strong hand shot out of the opening in the wall and latched onto the arm of a startled scout. "What's going on?" a voice rasped as the scout found herself the prisoner of the formidable head of the Council.

"An army of Lukrians is camped just beyond the trees," the scout sputtered.

"What?" Gindor ignored the scout struggling against the bony hand tightening around her arm and scanned the chaotic activity of the city. "We send them an illuminated invitation or something?" Finally noticing the squirming girl, she let go, shaking her head as the scout stumbled away rubbing her arm.

Stomping back into the chamber, she glared at the elders hovering around Jame, giving her a proper greeting by the looks of it. Gindor shook her head. What

was their world coming to? Their best warrior, whose
hatred for Tigh was as tangible as the rock around
them, defies the Council to defend the honor of the
former Guard. Her Queen turns a blind eye on tradition
and allows a serious breach in the law. Lukrians march
through Emoria and set up camp like it was a festival
day. Now her own Council didn't have enough dignity
to remember that Jame's presence in Emoria was proba-
tionary at best.

"What's happening?" a concerned voice broke
through her internal ranting.

Gindor glared at Jame. "Lukrians. An army of
them has broken through our outer defenses and are
camped in the meadow beyond the trees." The woman
folded her arms and continued to stare at Jame.

"By the Children of Bal, how could that happen?"
Jame felt lightheaded by the realization that the menace
they had come to stop was upon them too close and too
soon.

"We've never had a problem with our defenses
before." Gindor stepped deliberately around the table.
The other women, seeing Gindor's determined menace,
backed away from their princess.

"Before what?" Jame narrowed her eyes a bit, not
believing what she thought she was hearing.

"Before today." Gindor stood in front of Jame.

"I can't believe you're even suggesting such a
thing," Jame cried angrily.

"She was out of your sight for three days—up here
in the mountains," Gindor continued. "By all the
accounts, she had been transformed back into a Guard."

"She doesn't have anything to do with that army."
Jame's anger pressed her voice into a low, even whisper.

"Do you know that for sure?" Gindor hardened her
features. It was difficult facing her princess down like
this, but someone had to remember who Tigh really
was.

"Yes," Jame flashed back. "And I don't need my eyes to see the truth."

"I admire your loyalty to your companion. I really do." Gindor relaxed the menace and pulled on her matriarchal mask. "But she is like a wild animal that's been tamed. You can only tame so much. The wildness is still at the core."

"You are so wrong." Jame stepped forward. "She is a gentle, kind soul who was turned into a wild animal to become an Elite Guard." Noting the flicker of surprise in the older woman's eyes, Jame added, "Don't decide the case until you have all the facts—the most important lesson of my training."

Gindor, so certain of whom she thought Tigh was, couldn't respond right away. The black and white of the Elite Guard was suddenly shattered into too many shades of gray. Lifting blue-gray eyes, she met the steady gaze of her princess, startled to find a strength that she knew wouldn't be there if Tigh had a dominant hold on her. Argis' change of mind now made sense. "We have much to talk about," she finally admitted.

"Yes we do." Jame grimly agreed.

A murmuring from the other women drew their attention to one of the small scroll shelves hollowed out of the wall. "What now?" Gindor frowned.

****

Clouds tended to snag on the mountain peaks and settle over the high meadows, enveloping much of Emoria in evanescent blankets of moisture. Light drizzle accentuated the unease of the silent watchers concealed in the thickly clumped trees edging the expansive meadow.

From a lookout's nook at the top of a thick, leafy tree, Argis and Tigh studied the indolently sprawled encampment. The former Guard focused her senses on penetrating the diffused air and sounds dislocated by the turbid banks of fog. With the exception of a sparse patrol on the outermost perimeter of the camp, the Lukrians showed no concern about being deep within enemy territory.

"How did they get this far?" Argis stretched her neck to get a better view of the large tent in the center of the camp.

Tigh, splayed out on her stomach on a nearby branch, carefully deciphered as much as she could in the blotches of grays and whites. Her enhanced senses widened to encompass the meadow, the trees, and the swirl of snow where the ground rose to form a nearby rocky peak. She drew into her consciousness the reaction of the plants and animals to the visitors in the meadow in comparison to the silent watchers in the trees.

Blinking, Tigh whipped her head around to face Argis. The Emoran's throat went inexplicably dry as she gazed at the strange expression on the former Guard's face.

"What?" Argis barked in frustration.

Tigh took several gulps of air to sort out what she thought she sensed. "They're not real," she rasped.

Argis stared at her until the words sank in. "What do you mean, they're not real?"

"I don't sense them there," Tigh sighed, knowing that explaining what she felt would be difficult.

"Sense them? Don't we see them and hear them and smell their food cooking? What is there not to sense?" Argis was beyond frustration now.

"What else do you hear?" Tigh asked.

"What else?" Argis frowned a little, but was willing to go along with Tigh.

"What do you hear around us, in the forest?"

Argis took a bit of time to listen. "I hear whispering. I hear someone moving around over there. Several warriors are walking over there..."

"Do you hear any birds or squirrels?" Tigh pressed.

"Of course not. We're disturbing them," Argis started, then realized that she did hear birds and the movements of scurrying animals. Out in the meadow— all over the meadow. Squinting into the drizzle, she noticed for the first time that the colony of wiry mountain dogs was creating disturbances in the fog pockets. The small rodents showed no interest in the camp not twenty paces from their frolic grounds.

Argis turned to Tigh, her expression inscrutable. "This war isn't going to be any fun if nothing about it is real." The Emoran's serious concern almost caused Tigh to laugh.

"I never said the fighting wouldn't be real." The dark-haired warrior quirked an eyebrow.

"How do we fight something that isn't real?" Argis shifted in the small lookout notch, staring at the bustling camp. "It sure looks real."

"First, we figure out what kind of reaction is expected of us." Tigh rubbed her chin on the smooth bark of the limb she was sprawled on.

"Under normal circumstances we would attack."

"So what would be accomplished if we ran into the meadow attacking something that isn't there?" Tigh pondered the scenario. The Elite Guards' informal motto was 'nothing is as it seems'. Unfortunately, the luck it took to out-think the Elite Guards was just as vaporous.

"We would look pretty foolish," Argis returned wryly.

"What would that accomplish?" Tigh mused, as if to herself. "There isn't anyone to be foolish in front of and a story of that kind doesn't have to be true if it is told for the purpose of making you look foolish."

Argis absently rolled a twig between her fingers. She knew they couldn't sit all day waiting for something that wasn't there to go away. "What exactly are you saying?"

"I say we do what they expect us to do. It's the only way of finding out what they're up to." Tigh shrugged.

Argis stared at the casually sprawled warrior, getting a tangible glimpse of what Tigh must have been like as a victorious military leader. Reckless and cautious like a mountain cat, with the ability to keep a tight balance between the two. "So we just pretend that everything is as it appears and rush the camp?"

Tigh pushed against the bark and gracefully sat up, straddling the wide branch. "We play it by their own rules." She surveyed the ground around the trees. "We attack their illusion with an illusion of our own."

Argis twisted the twig until it was sinew, knowing she'd be foolish not to follow Tigh's greater experience. "I thought you said the fighting would be real," she groused, but her expression was friendly.

"Something tells me it will be," Tigh mused while thoughtfully studying the meadow.

* * * * * * * * * * * * * *

To say that the orders that Argis passed to Tas and Master Archer Mularke were the strangest they had ever given would be an understatement. The warrior and the archer stared at her, reaching deep into their experiences for some logical reason for this absurd battle plan.

"We run into the field, yelling, then lob stones around the tents, but be careful not to hit the tents." Tas scratched her head. "And then we stay a hundred paces away."

"Then we wait and shoot at anyone who emerges from the tents and continually shower the tents with arrows." Mularke frowned. "Why don't we just shoot at the tents now?"

"Because, if Tigh's suspicions are correct, the tents are empty right now," Argis responded, knowing that she sounded ridiculous. "Look. If we end up looking foolish, I will rake the sparring fields and change the targets for two fortnights."

Tas and the tall, blonde archer exchanged wry glances. "We trust your confidence in Tigh's instincts." The Master Archer nodded.

In the time it took the warriors to gather small stones into their belt pouches and for the archers to take their places in the trees, the fog had compressed into a thin layer knee-high off the ground. The drizzling rain diffused into an uncomfortable cleaving mist as tension sparked through the trees from two hundred Emorans waiting for the signal.

"We're ready," Argis reported to Tigh.

Tigh raised her eyes as if searching the gray sky for whatever demented deity oversaw her destiny. *For Jame*, her silent prayer intoned. *My life and everything I do, I dedicate to Jame. Give me a chance to place this victory at her feet.* "Command your force, Argis." Tigh pulled her sword from her belt and pressed the flat of the blade against her forehead in a respectful salute.

Startled, the Emoran straightened as her sword hissed from its sheath and she returned the salute. Lifting the blade, she waited until nine score sets of eyes were riveted on the length of steel before slashing the air downward.

The trees edging the meadow awoke to the sound of battle yodels and the crunch of rushing boots against the brittle undergrowth. Threescore masked warriors crashed into the meadow, swinging long slingshots. As soon as a stone hurtled through the air the next one was quickly tucked into the leather pocket and sent flying. Expecting an army of angry Lukrians to face them and charge, only their warrior training prevented them from stopping and staring when the stones passed through the oblivious enemy and clattered to the ground. More than a few marveled at Tigh's quick mind for seeing through this trick.

Argis bounced excitedly when the first lob of stones fell to the ground without obstruction. "Look at that. It *is* an illusion. And the ground is mostly stone just as you thought. How did you figure that out?"

"They had to pick a place where they'd be able to hear us attacking. Sound carries through stone better than dirt." Spotting several figures clad from head to toe in red leather rush out of tent openings, she breathed a prayer of thanks to whoever watched over her destiny. "There." Tigh's voice caught in her throat at the prospect of facing a tangible enemy.

"Archers," Argis barked. A grin enlivened the Emoran's face as she watched six score arrows arc gracefully into the sky and dive through the stretched leather of the tents. Dozens of red-clad warriors stumbled out of the tents with swords drawn, expecting to engage the Emorans at close range. By the time they realized that they were the rabbit rather than the hawk, their escape route was cut off by the constant menace of arrows.

A hundred paces away, Tas threw the slingshot to the ground and pulled out her sword. Whipping her body into a dance of ecstasy, she whooped and bounced into flips while brandishing her blade in dazzling patterns. A cacophony of yodels rose in response to this display, followed by the flashing of threescore blades. Rushing forward, the Emorans let the lust for Lukrian blood flood their veins, madly laughing as the satisfying clatter of steel against steel sang the song they lived to hear.

Argis had run several paces before noticing that Tigh was not with her. Skidding to a stop on the water slick grass, she cast a puzzled look back at the dark-haired warrior. "What's wrong?"

Tigh blinked at her. A thousand responses spun through her head. Each time she went into battle she fought her own demons along with the enemy. Blood lust was the only thing that could not be cleansed from a former Guard. She gave her head a shake, intently studying the stone strewn ground. She was fighting for Jame now. For Jame's destiny. Their destiny. Slowly raising her head, she met the Emoran's inscrutable expression. A devilish grin spread to her clear blue eyes. "Let's go teach these Lukrians the proper way to dance."

Tas swung her sword for the deathblow and was surprised when she met air where her opponent had been. Spinning around, she saw that her companions were also fighting air as the red-clad warriors disengaged and formed a concerted charge across the frolic grounds of the mountain dogs towards the former Guard.

Tigh had only heartbeats to realize that two dozen warriors were chasing after her. The manner in which the lead warrior wielded her sword told Tigh to keep away from those blades. Slinging the first blade away, she caught another while bouncing away from a near slice to her legs. It was now obvious that a scratch was all that was needed to bring her down.

Cursing, she flipped over their heads, landing behind them. No armor, not even bracers on her arms, she almost laughed at the irony as she deflected the blows from three blades. An elbow blow snapped the head of the closest woman. A quick shove with her knee sent the stunned Lukrian reeling into her two companions. Over their sprawled bodies, Tigh sliced her sword against four more blades crunching down on her. Flipping back, she got the inner two Lukrians in the chin with her knees and a quick flexing out of her feet sent the outer two flying.

Landing on her back, Tigh winced as rocks chewed into her skin. Five Lukrians were in the air over her as swift reflexes rolled her away from their free fall. Scrambling to her feet, she kicked up a stone and whacked it with her foot at the head of the warrior on top of the sprawled heap as her fist exploded in the face of the first of four rushing hard at her. A quick low crouch sent the next warrior, unable to stop in time, stumbling over her. Rolling onto her back, Tigh got her leg thrust upward in time for a belly blow to the next warrior and a nice kick, sending the winded woman against the fourth warrior.

Emorans swarmed around her, gathering up the dazed and wounded Lukrians. Staring at the damage done in just the time it took for the Emorans to catch up to Tigh, Argis was beyond stunned. Never had she witnessed such control and inventiveness or such incredible speed. It was as if a small powerful whirlwind had uprooted the enemy. Frowning, the Emoran noticed that none of those left in the wake of Tigh's power had been killed. Another mystery to the complex woman she had grown to respect.

Tigh hitched up onto her elbows to watch the activity around her. Argis strode over, looking down at the casually sprawled warrior. Not even winded. It was a truly disgusting sight.

"Make sure you clean their blades before taking them back to the city." Tigh nodded at the growing pile of weapons.

"Poisoned?" For some reason Argis hadn't even thought of that.

"It obviously has no effect on you." Tigh glanced at Tas, who was tending to a warrior.

"That's why they went after you," Argis frowned. "They knew you would be here."

Tigh flicked a glance at the Emoran. "It is not my place to question Emoran defenses or security, but I think it might be wise to consider a possible breach."

"Why does everything have to be so complicated?" Argis dropped cross-legged onto the ground, head in hands. Tigh grinned at the frustrated warrior. A well-fought battle always put her in a good mood.

Chapter 10

Poag cradled a delicate crystal object in her hands as she broke from the cluster of women around her and walked to Gindor and Jame.

"Someone leaving us presents again?" Gindor peered at the object. "Looks like a shaggy goat."

"What do you mean, 'presents'?" Jame cocked her head to get a better look at the glass.

"These crystals have been appearing in the oddest places for, I would say, several moons now," Gindor responded. "We seem to have a shy artist in our midst."

"Interesting," Jame mused.

"We may as well go to the palace. Wait for word there," the Council matriarch sighed.

"If that means the morning meal, I'm with you." Jame thought about her partner rushing off to fight without having anything to eat. She hoped that the warrior had remembered to munch an apple, at least.

The city was on alert with double guards at all posts on the wall and at the top of the bluffs. A noisy backup squad of warriors and archers were gathered in a corner of the square in front of the barracks. Curious citizens mingled in clusters swapping bits of gossip. Never had the enemy been this close to the city in such a force, and a nervous energy snapped against the air.

A woman dressed in loose-fitting Emoran leathers broke free from a knot of women chatting near the tavern. Jame had to look twice before recognizing Seeran.

"Have you heard?" The historian couldn't keep the excitement from her voice as she skidded up to Jame. "I have to say, there hasn't been a dull moment since I met you two." Seeran fell in next to Jame. "Where's Tigh?"

"She's gone to help," Jame answered, smiling at the historian's enthusiasm. "Have you eaten?"

"Actually I just woke up. Who can even think about eating with all this excitement going on?" Seeran turned completely around as she gawked at the double line of pale, lavender-draped acolytes to the High Follower of Laur, patron deity of the Emorans. Each acolyte swung gleaming metal chains holding miniature renderings of waterfalls crafted from multicolored pieces of quartz.

"I was going to invite you to join me for some food, but if you find sitting around out here waiting for word more interesting..." Jame began.

Seeran pulled her eyes from the acolytes. "I guess I should eat something."

Jame's grin faded as Jyac stepped into the square, followed by Sark and Ronalyn. Nodding her approval, the Queen scanned the activity before seeing the Council coming her way. Gindor straightened as she met the Queen's eyes, daring her to say anything in front of her people. The elder was surprised when Jyac crossed her arms, taking an immovable stance most people dreaded to see, much less be the recipient of it.

"I am not pleased," Jyac said in a low angry voice when the band of elders stopped in front of her. "Come in, Jame, I think you have suffered the company of these women long enough this morning."

Gindor leveled a frozen glare at her Queen, almost shaking in her want to respond to this public challenge. "We have much to discuss," she finally growled deliberately savoring each word.

"I look forward to it." Jyac's voice was cold and smooth as the stone behind her. Seeran almost wished she hadn't let her stomach guide her decision to join Jame. The mist in the air seemed to freeze from the cold anger that flowed off the Queen.

"We found another crystal," Poag, desperate to break the tension, piped up.

After a few long heartbeats, Jyac moved her eyes away from Gindor to the object Poag cradled in her hands. The Queen put out her hand. "I'll add it to our collection." Absently, she held the crystal up to study in the weak, misty light, allowing the tension to roll away from her. "Thank you, Poag."

"My Queen!" Poylin's voice came from a path above them. A few heartbeats later, the scout rounded a painted and smooth boulder that hid the entrance to the pathway.

"What's the word?" Jyac stepped towards the scout, followed by an anxious Jame.

"Argis sent me to tell you that they are preparing to engage the enemy and have every confidence that they will return in victory." Poylin proudly straightened, careful not to add that the warriors were loading their belt pouches with stones when she left them. A curious pre-battle strategy to say the least.

"To guarantee victory, take this back to her." Jyac handed the crystal to a smiling Jame and dug into her belt pouch for a leather braid laced with deep purple thread. "I challenge her to bring back victory."

Poylin took the braid, raising proud eyes to her Queen. "We cannot fail now," she shouted before turning and dashing to the overhead path.

"At least something's going right today," Jyac began as she turned to her niece. "What...?"

Standing with the crystal in her hands, Jame's robust tan was diluted with white and her eyes were unfocused. Jyac lunged forward as Jame swayed and collapsed into her arms.

****

"It's as confusing as Bal's maze down here," Argis muttered as she held her torch into another dark opening off one of the several small chambers they had explored. Following the snaking frozen waves of sand on the cavern floor, they found evidence of the heavy tents being dragged through the tunnels. "No doubt they came through this way."

Tigh crouched down and studied a discolored patch on the shadowed ground. She put a finger on the spot and lifted it to her nose, giving it a sniff. "How are you going to stop them from doing this again?"

"Why'd they do it in the first place?" Argis frowned. "They could have come up through these caves and attacked us in the middle of the night and we wouldn't have known what hit us."

"The answer lies in whoever created the illusion." Tigh brushed the sand from her hands and stood up.

"More games?" Argis scowled.

"At least you got to fight a little." Tigh arched an eyebrow at her. "I suggest you block all the passages. It'll be a lot more difficult for them to clean out obstructions in these dark tunnels than to break through whatever you put over the outside openings."

"I'll get the architect down here so we can do a proper job of it." Argis nodded. "What's that?"

The shadows hugging the uneven walls transformed into red-clad figures. The small band of Emorans had swords in hand in an instant as Lukrians stood menacingly before them. Tas whipped her blade at the closest enemy, almost losing her balance when she didn't make solid contact.

"They're not real," Tigh yelled from the other side of the cavern.

Tas squeaked and dropped her sword, pressing her hand under her arm. "Daughter of a shaggy goat. Don't touch them," the compact warrior warned as she grimaced from the stinging pain in her hand.

"Everyone out of here," Argis ordered as the group backed to the middle of the cavern where the rope ladder to the surface dangled. Being only illusions, the counterfeit Lukrians made no move towards them, but their menacing stance was enough to make the Emorans uneasy.

When Argis grabbed the ladder to steady it for Tigh's ascent, a soft laughter wafted out from one of the tunnels. The ladder was replaced by a sword as Argis made ready to fight.

Tigh whipped around to face the tunnel the sound flowed from. An icy fear gripped her soul as a grim memory slapped her in the face. Taking a deep breath, she turned to a tense, alert Argis. "I know who we're up against," she stated evenly.

"Is that a good thing or a bad thing?" Argis had witnessed the fear flash across Tigh's face. Anything that frightened Tigh had to be terrifying.

"Both," Tigh sighed as she jumped onto the ladder. Argis quickly sheathed her sword and followed the former Guard.

Visible as a mist-covered orb the color of a hard cooked egg yolk, the sun was almost straight overhead when Tigh emerged from one of the holes hidden in the scattering of low rocks. The laugh continued to mock her memory as she absently offered a hand to Argis, pulling the Emoran from the earth. Never did she suspect this person as their enemy, even when the evidence practically screamed her name to her. That would have been pointing a finger at someone who had died at her own hand.

Most of the Emorans who had battled that day had already returned to the city. The whooping and yodeling of celebration reached Argis' ears as they trekked through the forest. The usual elation she felt after a battle was tempered by the knowledge that they hadn't yet engaged their true enemy. Noting the somber warriors around her, she realized that the encounter in the cave had the same effect on them.

"Let's not spoil a good victory." Argis glanced around to catch her warriors' attention. "There are mysteries and questions to be sure, but right now, they're as intangible as Laur's magic waterfall. We fought well and caught the enemy at their own game."

The warriors grinned, remembering the shocked reactions of the Lukrians when they found out that their plan had been uncovered. Boastful words flitted among the women, comparing tales that would grow bolder and wilder by evening's end.

As they descended into the city, Argis could see Jyac and Sark waiting in front of the palace doors. The warrior let the relief that she was able to bring home this victory soak away the uncertainties of the day. Argis strode proudly to the Queen, followed by a slightly frowning Tigh who was glancing around trying to spot Jame.

"I have met your challenge, my Queen." Argis held out the purple-laced braid, which Jyac accepted.

"Well done, Argis." Jyac's eyes sparkled with pride at her best warrior. "As you can see, we couldn't stop the celebration from starting."

"I've never known anyone who could stop a warrior from celebrating." Argis grinned, looking around. "Where's Jame?"

Jyac and Sark exchanged enigmatic glances and were startled when an upset Tigh was hovering over them. "Where is she?" came a low growl mixed with anger and concern.

"She's with the healer..." Jyac began.

"Healer? What happened?" Tigh responded in panic. "Where's the healer?" The warrior's body was ready to bolt in any direction she was told.

"She's going to be all right," Jyac quickly assured her. "I'll take you to her." She watched with fascination as Tigh labored to calm down. The warrior's almost frantic concern surprised the Queen.

"What happened to her?" Tigh repeated as she and Argis flanked Jyac while they strode across the square.

"She met with a little accident..."

"Accident?" Tigh struggled to push her concern down.

"It was that new girl, Gelder," Jyac explained. "Kas was taking her to the upper stables. She saw her friend, Seeran, down here and leaned over one of the ledges where we put our offerings to Laur—although she had been warned repeatedly to watch where she leaned. A tribute—fortunately one carved from wood— fell and hit Jame on the head. She passed out, but the healer thinks it was more from the shock of being hit in the head rather than from the injury itself." The Queen glanced at the silent grim-faced warrior next to her, relieved to see the features softening a bit.

"Did she get into this kind of trouble when she was young?" Tigh quirked an eyebrow at the Queen.

"She did have the tendency to be in the wrong place at the wrong time," Jyac mused.

"Some things never change," Tigh mumbled, trying to calm her pounding heart.

****

With her head propped up on several thick pillows, Jame watched the healers tend to the minor wounds of the warriors returning from the upper meadow. A cacophony of excited voices competed as tales were slung back and forth of Lukrians made of mist, magic caves, and an unbelievable battle between Tigh and

twenty…no, wait…fifty…at least a hundred Lukrians.
The former Guard, without armor and wielding only a
sword, downed them all in a matter of heartbeats and
without receiving even the tiniest of scratches.

If Jame could shake her pounding head, she would
have done so at the description of her partner's idea of
fun. She also felt a twinge of concern about why the
Lukrians ganged up on Tigh like that. The only logical
answer was not a happy one. Blinking back unexpected
tears, she refused to let the emotional stress of the last
few days overwhelm her. Tigh was in a vulnerable
place among these unseen vipers trying to sap her
strength and nip at her sanity. Wiping away a tear that
crawled down her cheek, she shoved her feelings of
despair into the deepest part of her consciousness. Tigh
was her life. She would do anything to make sure her
warrior was safe from harm.

"They may not be real, but they sting like the kiss
of a whip," Tas' voice cut through the noise. The small
warrior sat on a nearby pallet, wincing as the healer
studied and prodded her hand before applying a cooling
salve.

"What's not real?" Jame tried to lift her body, but
the movement made it feel like a boulder had taken res-
idence in her head.

Cradling her hand as the salve sent cooling spikes
into what looked like a minor burn, Tas sat wearily on
the stool next to Jame's pallet. "What happened to
you?"

"My head got in the way of a falling tribute to
Laur," Jame responded with a sheepish, lopsided smile.

"Ouch," Tas sympathized. "I got this from one of
those misty Lukrians. A group of them surrounded us
while we were investigating the caves. Hidden in the
shadows, they looked so real I took a swing at one of
them. Some of the mist must have touched my hand
because it stung like crazy."

"So they're more than a magical trick," Jame mused.

"The ones up top seemed to be only illusion." Tas frowned in thought. "We fought the real Lukrians in the midst of the illusions. They simply faded when we touched them. But the ones below ground were different. A kind of menace came from them."

"Sounds like we have a mystery on our hands." Jame tried not to let her face reflect the bout of panic that had been an unwanted companion since she began her journey home.

An abrupt silence in the cavern heralded the entrance of the Queen followed by Argis and Tigh. As the warriors let out a cheer of respect for those who led them to victory, Tigh's only focus was on Jame, who was looking small and pale on a pallet in the corner. Argis watched as Tigh strode away from them, keeping down her own urge to rush to Jame's side. The traces of jealousy towards Tigh still erupted, but she practiced pushing them away with thankful thoughts that Jame held her friendship. Besides, Argis had been hit with the astonishing revelation that she liked Tigh.

Tas rose from the stool and drifted over to a knot of warriors as Tigh approached. "How's the hand?"

"It'll be fine," Tas replied, hiding a grin as Tigh's attention quickly turned to Jame.

Dropping onto the stool, the tall warrior gazed down at her partner, noting the chalky pallor and a lack of sharpness in the tired, green eyes blinking back at her. "Hey," Tigh said softly, bending forward and gently kissing Jame. "How come I'm the one who fought and you're the one who's injured?"

"I try to share when I can." Jame smiled, weakly. "It's probably a mild concussion. The healer gave me something to help keep me awake until she thinks I'm all right."

Tigh nodded, studying the pattern woven into the pallet cover. This quiet introspection told Jame that something serious was bothering her warrior. She also knew that this was not the time and place to get into a deep discussion.

"I heard you fought off only a hundred Lukrians. Getting soft in your old age?" Jame lightly teased.

Tigh snorted and flicked an amused glance at the arbiter. "Does it count that I wasn't wearing armor?" She raised an innocent eyebrow.

"Not as much as if you had been barefoot." Jame bestowed a gentle, twinkling grin that never failed to bring Tigh to her knees.

"I'll try to remember to slice my boots off next time." Tigh took Jame's hand between her own and brought it to her lips. "I suppose Laur owes you a tribute for a change."

"Oh, right." It was Jame's turn for an amused snort. "Just after she replaces the waterfalls in her temple with washing pools."

"Some people do prefer bathing to taking showers." Tigh shrugged, delighting Jame with an impish grin.

"You now owe Laur a double tribute for that sacrilege," Jame giggled.

Argis and Jyac, making the rounds among the wounded, stopped in front of Jame's pallet. "Good to see you laughing," Jyac commented as she swept a glance at the tall warrior.

"I'm feeling better." Jame grinned, giving her partner an affectionate look.

"Argis feels tomorrow is soon enough to discuss what happened today." Jyac turned to Tigh. "Is that acceptable?"

Tigh blinked at her, realizing that the Queen was looking for her input, despite her current standing with the Council. She stood and pulled the black blade from her belt. "Whatever is acceptable to you, I will agree to," she responded as she offered the sword to Argis. "I don't have permission to carry this in the city, please keep it for me."

Argis stared at the sword, knowing she should take it. "Has she not earned the right to wear it?" the warrior queried as she turned to Jyac.

Jyac looked to her intently watching niece. Jame's opinion on this subject was evident on her expressive face. The time of changing traditions was upon them no matter how hard the Council fought against it. It was written in the scrolls of the Emor Mysteries and as Queen, it fell upon her to make way for the changes. "She has earned the right." Jyac looked into the eyes of the passive warrior. "As long as you wear it for Emoria."

Tigh straightened and pressed the flat of the blade against her forehead in a salute of respect. "You have my word."

Argis relaxed and grinned at the warrior. "That's good news for the sixteen warriors anxious for you to meet their challenges. But not today. Today is for celebration."

"Why didn't you challenge me?" Tigh suddenly asked. The cavern grew silent as all ears strained to hear the answer.

Argis thoughtfully studied the tall warrior as she looked for the proper words. "You have already met my challenge and won." Her eyes flicked to Jame, then back to the warrior. "You have proven to me that you are an acceptable Consort for our future Queen."

A stunned murmur rumbled through the chamber. The shock was not so much a reaction to Argis' statement, but that it was spoken aloud after so many years of whispered speculation. Even Jyac looked startled at the proud warrior's candid words.

"Thank you, Argis," a soft voice responded.

Argis' knees weakened as grateful emerald eyes gazed at her. Unable to pull words into her arid throat, she slowly nodded.

"Come." Jyac placed a hand on Argis' shoulder. "It's time to celebrate our victory."

****

The only sounds heard within the quartz-ceilinged atrium were from the walls of water spilling over tall slabs of polished stone by means known only to Laur herself. It was the one place in the city where Tigh could get Jame away from the discordant revels of the Emorans. The festive noise aggravated Jame's throbbing head and Tigh needed to think.

An acolyte occasionally drifted through the chamber to adjust the long slats of prismatic crystals along the walls so that they continued to refract rainbows throughout the chamber as the sun drifted across the sky. The effect was like being inside a giant kaleidoscope, relaxing to the point of being almost hypnotic.

Besides smooth stone benches carved around the pools that rippled with the outflow of the waterfalls, the only other choice of seating was cloth covered pillows, delicately embroidered with countless renditions of waterfalls.

Tigh and Jame sprawled on several of these pillows close enough to a pool for Tigh to dip a cloth into the water and lay it over the bump on the top of Jame's head. The warrior cradled her partner against her and both let the warmth of their bond flow between them.

"Pretty strange goings-on," Jame sighed as Tigh doused the cloth again and gently laid it on the arbiter's head. The warrior snaked her arms around Jame's middle and pulled her closer. "That bad?"

Tigh stared at the ropes of water skittering over rough patches of rock, flinging out curious patterns of droplets. "I know who we're up against," she finally breathed against Jame's ear. Startled, Jame turned her head to face her partner and received a sharp bite of pain for her trouble. "Easy." Tigh cupped Jame's head in her large hands and eased it onto her shoulder.

"I thought we knew that." Jame looked up as she relaxed into the comforting arms of her warrior.

"I think they're following someone else's orders." The laugh in the cavern mocked her memories. Could it be another game of the rogue Guards to get to her by confronting her with her worst nightmare?

She had been newly elevated to the Elite Guards and was still learning to control the enhancements to her mind and body. The Guards needed a leader capable of dominating them and holding their respect. The only way to find this leader was through a test. Word had reached them that a Wizard from the Umvian plains had been approached by the Northern leaders to create an enhanced warrior to go against the Guards.

General Rartrice strode into her cell before dawn one morning, awakening her with a shove of a boot against the cot. Before Tigh had a chance to blink awake, Rartrice was throwing her leathers at her.

"You know where the Umvian plain is?" The gaunt war veteran watched for Tigh's nod. "You are to go there and find a Wizard called Misner and kill her."

She remembered that jolt of anticipation of making her first kill hurtling through her. She was ready to run all the way to the Umvian plains, swinging her sword in abandoned ecstasy. Her life would not be complete until that Wizard's life was stolen with her blade. The General laughed at her eagerness to fulfill this simply stated order that five other potential leaders of the Guard had already failed to carry out.

"Who is it?" Jame's soft voice brushed against her ear.

Tigh drove away her memories and looked down at her partner. "When we were in the caves below the meadow there was laughter coming from a tunnel. I've heard that laughter once before many years ago," Tigh sighed. "There was a Wizard who was trying to develop enhanced warriors for the North. I was given orders to go and kill her."

"I take it you succeeded." Jame wrapped her hands around Tigh's.

"Yes," came the whispered answer. "My first kill."

Somehow her mental conditioning allowed her to work through the mind-numbing projections Misner drove into her brain like fire arrows. A part of her subconscious was able to keep track of what was real and what was illusion, leaving her body to follow the warrior instinct that propelled her forward to the kill.

The short, round Wizard laughed at her and taunted her with the names of the five Guards she had killed. Perhaps the Wizard's success at beating those other Guards made her a little too confident, and her tendency to play with her victims distracted her from recognizing the strength in her current foe. But through burning muscles and illusions conjuring her worst nightmares, Tigh was able to keep focused on the diminutive Wizard.

Letting forth animalistic bellowing, the warrior crashed through the horrific illusions and allowed her mind to give in to being frightened and be done with it. She would either die or succeed and what she did at that point wasn't going to change her fate. Misner would never let her live. Swinging the black-bladed sword, Tigh lunged forth for the kill.

As Tigh collapsed from the psychological beating, the image of a head with startled eyes dropping several feet away from its body was etched forever in her memory.

"So you saved us from facing a foe as formidable as the Elite Guard." Jame looked up into the distant, haunted eyes of her partner.

Tigh blinked at her. "I thought I had. But she still seems to be alive."

"She was a Wizard. She could have been close to death and may have revived herself through magic," Jame reasoned.

"I decapitated her," the warrior stated softly, wondering how that eager young Guard she saw in her mind's eye could be the same person gently cradling Jame.

The arbiter sucked in a breath, distancing herself from the actions of a Guard who was long dead.

Chapter 11

Argis wove more than she walked across the midnight-darkened square. Her face was a study in determination as she flicked imaginary gnats away. The quartz-filled openings that speckled the face of the bluffs danced with the light from victory parties within. Songs slurred from the celebrants in the tavern and from the balconies of the residences higher up the bluffs. Drunken laughter bubbled up from atop the gate wall in response to words that were too low for Argis to decipher. The clash of blades echoed from the barracks, accompanied by drunken cheers and calls. Three guards were already rushing across the square to break up that little party.

"All right, Tas," an inebriated growl echoed against the bluff walls. "I know you're out here somewhere." Argis stumbled on an invisible stone and staggered around a bit. A laughing whisper whipped the warrior around too fast and she suddenly found the cobbled ground much closer to her face than she would have liked. The laughing materialized into Tas and Mularke. Trying to hold each other up but chortling too hard to care if they were successful or not, the pair managed to negotiate their way to Argis. Not bothering to help their sprawled friend get up, they collapsed onto the uneven stone next to her.

"Thought you swore off drinking so much." Mularke tried to slap Argis on the leg but missed and hit the stone ground too hard. "Laur's waterfalls, I've got to stop drinking so much." She held her aching hand under her arm.

"Now we're a pair." Tas wiggled her burned hand.

"You're a pair all right." Argis winced as she pulled her body up into a cross-legged position. "Speaking of, where are they?"

"You mean Jame and Tigh?" Tas slurred. "You sure have changed your tune about them. When you asked me to stand with you in Tigh's defense this morning, I thought it was for Jame's sake. But after the battle today, I'm convinced you actually like her."

"I treated her as the enemy and the first thing she did was save my life," Argis muttered. "I discovered that I was wrong about her."

"She's not like I expected." Mularke shook her head.

"She doesn't act like any warrior I've known, but she certainly has the skills and the courage." Tas sliced her hands wildly in the air as the others spluttered with ale-soaked laughter. "Is it true that those blades had poison on them? The same stuff that turned her crazy?"

Argis nodded. "One nick and she would have been Tigh the Terrible."

Both Tas and Mularke sucked in their breaths. "Scary." A shiver went down Mularke's spine.

"Speaking of..." Tas gazed at a tall figure with an arm wrapped around a shorter figure emerging from the Temple. "She's sober. We've been negligent in our duty."

"She's been taking care of Jame." Argis shot a serious look at Tas.

Tas held up her hands in mock defense. "Sorry. Forgot. Sacred ground. Must tread lightly." Mularke covered her mouth with her hands to keep from laughing.

Argis scowled at her friend for long heartbeats, then let the alcohol relax her. "I'll forgive you because you're drunk."

"You forgot to tell me about this strange ritual." Tigh's passive voice reached them. "What is the significance of the battle leaders sitting alone in the middle of the square...in the middle of the night?"

Jame peered at the besotted trio sprawled out on the ground. "It's an ancient time-honored tradition," she answered solemnly. "Except they should be passed out by now."

"We're having a very serious discussion." Argis straightened.

"Then that laughter must have been from someone else." Tigh raised an eyebrow, feeling Jame's shoulders shake in amusement.

"Sometimes we can be seriously funny," Tas deadpanned as her companions snorted with laughter. "How did you do that today? All that flipping and kicking. I've never seen anyone fight so much with their feet."

"It's a technique they taught us in the Guards. It comes from a land far east of here," Tigh answered evenly.

"It can't be that hard if a bunch of passive quill scrapers can learn it," Argis drawled as she leaned back on her elbows.

"I take it you're interested in learning it." Tigh tried not to sigh. The Guards were anything but passive when they began their battle training.

"It will be your duty to teach us—if you become a member of our tribe." Argis kept a steady gaze on the warrior.

"*When* she becomes a member of our tribe." Jame pulled away from her partner, ready to take on anyone

who challenged her words. Argis shook her head. She
was trying to get a rise out of Tigh and got one from
Jame instead. Not like any warrior she had ever met,
indeed.

"I stand corrected." Argis grinned.

"You're drunk so I'll forgive you." Jame relaxed,
catching an amused and very affectionate expression on
Tigh's face. "Someone   has to stand up for your honor."

Tigh opened her mouth to reply but a shout from
the Council's chamber sounded instead. A pair of
Council guards ran from the chamber entrance, frantically looking around. Upon seeing the small group,
they rushed to them, shouting disconnected words.

"Wait." Jame stepped in front of them and they
started to speak at once. "One person, please. Wolfie,
tell us what's going on."

Wolfie, a stocky woman with wild, dark hair, took a
couple of heartbeats to pull her words together. "We
were outside the Council's door all night. They called
a meeting and from what we could hear, a rather heated
dispute was going on." She glanced quickly at Tigh.
"Anyway, they were yelling at each other, then suddenly everything was as quiet as the Temple. We
waited for the noise to start again but nothing happened. Finally we eased the door open a bit for just a
look. They were gone."

"Maybe they went into one of the inner chambers," Jame reasoned.

"We searched every room." Wolfie violently shook
her head, causing the wild hair to fly. "As you know,
the only way out is through the chamber door."

Given the recent events, several scenarios flashed
through Jame's mind, none of them comforting. She
turned to Tigh, who remained passively in the back-
ground, but the little furrow between her brows told
Jame that she was thinking hard. "I think we'd better
have a talk with my aunt."

Argis scrambled to her feet, cursing. "I knew I shouldn't have had so much to drink."

"Go sleep it off, all of you. I have the feeling we're going to need you well and alert tomorrow."

Tigh held her arm out for Jame to resume her place next to her. Meeting Tigh's eyes, Jame saw the promise that they were going to get through this new ordeal together.

****

Jyac was a "see it to believe it" kind of a person and in this case she didn't want to believe what her niece was patiently explaining to her. Still in her sleep shirt and a pair of cotton house leggings, the Queen strode across the square, trailed by a yawning Ronalyn. Tigh and Jame followed after them a little slower because Jame's head still ached.

"I'm beginning to see some family resemblance," Tigh mused, ignoring the dagger looks from her partner.

"She's efficient. Like you," Jame countered, lifting her chin a little but ended up grinning at the warrior.

"This is too efficient, even for her," Ronalyn turned to them and whispered.

Jyac stopped at the entrance of the Council chamber, studying the curious scene before her. The chairs were pulled away from the table at odd angles. Papers and—more shocking—replica scrolls from the Emor Mysteries were scattered on the table. She located the scroll case leaning against a wall, gathered the scrolls and rolled them into the case.

"Um, Aunt Jyac?" Jame stepped forward when the Queen, upon finishing her task, stood staring at the table, brow furrowed in thought. The arbiter laid a gentle hand on her aunt's arm. Jyac blinked at her. "Don't you think we ought to discuss what to do about this?"

"You don't understand." Jyac shook her head, her expression confused and nearly overflowing with despair.

Jame took Jyac's arm and led her to a chair at the table, sitting down next to her. Ronalyn took the seat on the other side of the Queen, laying a comforting arm over Jyac's shoulder. Tigh roamed around the chamber.

"Now. What don't we understand?" Jame asked, gently.

"It was written that the Council would disappear one night." Jyac took a deep breath, ready to stop reacting and start thinking.

"Written in the Mysteries?" Jame probed.

"Yes." Jyac concentrated on remembering the details of the prediction. "After a battle with an enemy that was real but not real. That part made no sense...until today."

Jame frowned. "You don't really think that those writings foretell the future, do you?"

"Not until today." Jyac laid the scroll case on the table and absently played with the leather thong attached to it.

Jame glanced up at Tigh, who had stopped poking around and was watching them. "There are some logical explanations to consider before we decide that we're at the mercy of predictions written a millennium ago."

Jyac turned to her niece, wondering if she had temporarily lost her mind. "What logical explanations? Maybe one or two things can be explained, but not everything at once."

Jame looked again at her partner, who nodded encouragement to her. It was Jame's place to tell her aunt the facts as they knew them so far. The warrior knew that Jame had absorbed the long rambles of half theories and suppositions that she quietly related as they soaked up the peace in the Temple. She also knew that Jame could pull everything together into something that made sense. That was the skill of an arbiter—to create a picture from pieces gleaned from people who were either too eager or too reluctant to divulge. The arbiter had to determine which was most probably exaggeration and lie and what was the truth.

"Tigh thinks that a Wizard she, um...had dealings with many years ago is behind whatever is happening in the mountains and that the Lukrians are following her orders," Jame began as Tigh stopped her wandering around and sat down cross-legged on the fire hearth. "We know that the Wizard created the illusion in the meadow."

"What is written in the Mysteries happens, no matter who may be behind them." Jyac cut into Jame's line of reasoning before she could make her full argument. "It would be different if it was an isolated incident. But two improbable incidents in a row?"

"Tigh and Argis have come up with a theory that's worth considering," Jame ventured, shooting Tigh a look. The warrior gave her partner a short nod. "They thought it strange that, as soon as Tigh joined the battle, all the Lukrians went straight for her. Tigh guessed, rightly I might add, that the Lukrian blades were coated with the potion that, uh...affected her a few days ago."

Jyac turned to the warrior. "You fought them off without getting nicked? Impressive."

"Fortunately for her and us, her skill at evading sharp objects is very good." Jame gave her warrior an affectionate look. "The question is, how did the Lukrians know that Tigh was here in Emoria?"

"That Meah person must have told them," Jyac reasoned.

"She left Tigh for dead," Jame countered. "But, as you say, she could have been lurking around as we crossed into Emoria and saw that Tigh was alive. She then could have gone to a pocket of Lukrians hiding out near our borders and enlisted their help to try to cut

Tigh down again. She also could have used the illusions of a Wizard who was conveniently in the area. A Wizard who had personal reasons for seeing Tigh dead." Jame caught Tigh's questioning expression as the arbiter neatly presented an argument against the theory she was trying to put forth. A slight crinkling around the eyes told the warrior that Jame had thought the argument through. "But, as you say, we are not dealing with an isolated incident here. We have a pair of mysteries written on scrolls that only the Queen, the Council, and the High Follower of Laur are allowed to read."

Glancing at Jyac and Ronalyn, Tigh marveled at Jame's ability to pull in her audience. The sincere, steady timbre of her voice compelled people to listen and believe the words the arbiter spoke. Tigh thanked whoever oversaw her destiny for Jame's skill, owing her very freedom to it.

"Go on." Jyac, not liking the implications of the words, kept her thoughts back until she heard what her niece had to say.

"Let's look at what happened in this chamber for a moment," Jame continued, not noticing the delighted twinkle in Tigh's eyes. The warrior loved to see Jame at work. "The Council members are arguing, then suddenly there is silence. No sounds of surprise or struggle. Only a few heartbeats later, the guards look into the chamber and find it empty. How could twelve women be disabled and dragged away in that short of time and with no visible place to go?"

"You have a theory?" Jyac pressed.

"A theory that brings all the elements of this puzzle together." Jame nodded, noting that not only were the eyes of Jyac and Ronalyn riveted on her, but Tigh's as well. "We were convinced we saw an army of Lukrians that weren't real. Is it too much of a stretch to convince a pair of guards that they don't see the Council members who are actually still in the chamber? An illusion can work both ways," Jame reasoned. "This is what I believe happened. At least twelve assailants entered the chamber from a hidden passage. If the enemy can create openings from underground caverns out on the meadow, they can certainly find a way into Emor. Let's say that the assailants and the opening to the hidden passage are concealed by illusion. They position themselves behind the Council members and prick them with a fast-acting sedative."

"Fast-acting sedative?" Jyac inquired with an air of disbelief.

"It was used to capture the Guards after the Wars," Jame explained quietly. Jyac and Ronalyn tossed startled glances at the passive warrior by the fire. "Anyway, they subdue the Council members, then cover them with the illusion of invisibility. The guards enter the chamber as the assailants are removing the Council members, but the guards can't see them. They wait until the guards have checked the inner chambers, then take the Council away through the hidden passage."

"Even if it is as you say, it still doesn't change the fact that the predictions in the Mysteries are coming true," Jyac reasoned.

"If the enemy can enter the city unseen, they can find the Mysteries and read them," Jame reasoned.

"Why would anyone create such a masquerade?"

"What do these predictions lead to?" Jame quietly captured her aunt's eyes, seeing a flicker of fear there. "Not something good, I suspect, or your reactions to them coming true would be different."

"You're right. It's not a pleasant destiny for the Emoran people." Jyac nodded before raising respectful eyes to Jame. "What a clever niece I have. Your mother would be proud."

"Thank you." Jame briefly closed her eyes at the thought of the mother she never knew. "The Elite Guard's greatest weapon was the ability to weaken the enemy through fear and mental torture before they raised a sword in battle. There is no doubt that we are up against rogue Guards most likely led by a powerful wizard. If their goal is to cause panic, then we must not panic. If their goal is to cause fear, then we must not show fear. We fight back with mental warfare of our own. Then we do everything we can to smoke them out of their underground hiding places and stop them before they cause another full out war."

Jyac realized she was staring at her niece, letting the strong words penetrate. "According to Argis, rumors of their strength have already reached beyond the mountains. How can one small nation be expected to stop them?"

"Because the Elite Guard cannot be defeated by the strength of an army," Jame stated simply, almost laughing at Jyac's confused expression. "All it takes is the ability to out-think them. And fortunately for us, we have Tigh, the most elite of the Elite Guard. That's why they want to destroy her. They know that she can destroy them."

Tigh blinked at her partner. Interesting reasoning. Although with the new enhancements to the Guards, she wasn't sure if she could hold her own with them anymore. But she knew they had to try.

"It sounds implausible," Jyac began slowly. "But then, this whole situation is implausible. We will meet with the military leaders tomorrow and you can present your theory."

"Thank you, Aunt." A warm smile spread across Jame's face as she caught the affectionate pride sparkling in Tigh's eyes.

"A thorough search will be made of these chambers for a hidden passageway." Jyac glanced around. "Finding it will help your argument."

"We will get through this." Jame laid a reassuring hand on Jyac's arm. "We will create our own destiny."

"It is written in the Mysteries that a princess will lead a victorious campaign against a half-crazed Wizard," Jyac stated quietly as she took Jame's hand into hers. "I don't need the Mysteries to tell me that you're the only one among us who is a master of creative strategies." Jyac paused, then caught the combination of delight and pride in Tigh's eyes. "I'm putting you in command of the campaign against this Wizard."

A stunned Jame, shook her head and stammered, "No. I can't do that."

"Ask Tigh," Jyac gently urged.

Jame looked up at her partner's encouraging grin. "On one condition. I want Tigh to work out the battle plans."

"I can agree to that." Jyac nodded, feeling an odd surge of hope.

****

Jame felt the sun filtering in through the quartz windows in the roof of her cave chamber. Fluttering open her eyes, she was pleased to feel only a slight tinge of the ache from her close encounter with a tribute to Laur. Poor Gelder. The girl had been so mortified that she had injured her princess. But those kinds of accidents happened in a city like Emor.

Glancing at the body sprawled next to her, Jame grinned, thinking that this morning was much better to wake up to than the morning before. The Council. Missing. Jame stifled a chuckle at Tigh's question, before they fell asleep, about whether that was a good thing or a bad thing. The warrior could be so bad sometimes. Of course it was her way of dealing with the true seriousness of the situation. Jame reached over and ran a gentle finger over the slight tension in the warrior's brow.

Tigh's face scrunched and shook a little at the touch, but she didn't wake. Jame frowned at this sluggish reaction. Despite her miraculous display in the previous day's battle, Tigh wasn't up to her normal, sharply honed physical alertness.

Jame slowly pulled up to lean against the stone wall that backed the bed, pleased that her head had lost the aching heaviness. Squinting at the remnants of her childhood that filled the niches in the wall, Jame couldn't believe she had possessed so many things. Their importance in her life had diminished as she'd drifted away from her roots. Her first braid for mastering the staff, her first warrior leathers, her first battle braid. She had forgotten about that. She had been a part of a patrol that was ambushed by a band of raiders. For their victory in the skirmish, she received a nice scar just above the elbow and the battle braid. A heady prize for a fifteen-year-old, but, even then, she didn't feel the pride that Argis had when she'd won her first battle braid. Jame just didn't have the heart for it.

The bed shook as the tall warrior rolled over with a groan. That sounded a little too much like an admission of pain to Jame. Sleepy, blue eyes blinked opened, followed by a fleeting grimace.

"You all right?" Jame asked softly, laying a hand on the warrior's shoulder.

Tigh gingerly pulled into a cross-legged position, arching her back. "I landed on some rocks yesterday. There are probably some nice, ripe bruises back there."

"Just bruises?" Jame wasted no time lifting the back of Tigh's shirt. Sucking in a sharp breath, the arbiter winced at a pair of dark purple patches. "Ouch," she said in sympathy.

"If you're gentle about it, I'll let you put salve on them." Tigh gave Jame a sheepish look.

"My big brave warrior. What am I going to do with you?" Jame bit her lip to keep from laughing.

"Anything you want," came the inevitable response, followed by a saucily raised eyebrow.

As Jame trotted across the chamber to their packs, the soft rapid patter of several pairs of boots sounded in the corridor. She gave the door a quizzical glance, but continued rummaging through Tigh's pack for the salve. More footfalls rushing by had Tigh on her feet. Running a hand through her disheveled hair, Tigh opened the door as four women passed by. Putting a strong hand out, she grabbed the closest woman.

"What's going on?" Tigh's low voice reached the startled woman's ears before she realized who had hold of her.

"Something happened at the Temple," the young guard breathed excitedly.

"Something..." Tigh prompted.

"I don't know what it is, but the acolytes are upset." Tigh let the woman go and stepped back into the chamber, closing the door behind her and wondering what this new emergency was about.

"What's happening?" Jame walked up to her holding the jar of salve.

"Something happened at the Temple." Tigh shrugged. "The acolytes are upset."

Jame sighed. "Let me get this salve on you before we see what's going on."

"It could be important." Tigh turned to her.

"It's not more important than you." Jame held Tigh's eyes for long heartbeats. Tigh, knowing that she had to let Jame figure out the balance between her heritage and her heart on her own, did not argue.

By the time they stepped outside the palace, the square was filled with women focused on the Temple. The lavender-robed acolytes could just barely be seen huddled near the Temple walls.

"What happened?" Jame asked for anyone who heard her.

Kas, the Horse Master, turned around at the question. "We don't know. No one will tell us anything. But the acolytes are upset."

Feeling the growing impatience flow from her partner, Jame determinedly led the way around the perimeter of milling women. Argis and Tas, both a little pale but looking alert enough despite their overindulgence the night before, greeted Jame and Tigh with expressions of frustration.

"They won't let us in and no one will tell us what's going on." Argis scowled.

"So," Tigh eyed the flustered and sobbing acolytes huddled together, "all we know is that the acolytes are upset," she concluded dryly.

Jame shot her a look before focusing her attention on Argis. "Who's inside?"

"Let me think." Argis put her frustration aside for a moment. "Panilope, of course, and Jyac and, of all people, Hallie."

"Hallie?" Jame cast a puzzled look at the Temple door.

"Who's Hallie?" Tigh asked.

"Our dowser," Jame responded absently as she wrapped her mind around this mystery. "Come on, Tigh. Let's go see what this is about."

"Good luck," Argis called to their backs.

Much to their surprise, Eiget, the guard at the door, let them pass without a word. The main chamber of the Temple was a public shrine to Laur, replete with sheets of falling water and shallow pools. The sound of water was enough to bring peace to the most turbulent soul.

Tigh and Jame stood for long heartbeats in the silence. Not a drop of water could be seen or heard in the chamber. Even the stones at the bottoms of the pools were dry. Walking further into the chamber and peeking around the waterless vertical slabs of stone, their minds were too numb to think of a plausible explanation.

"This isn't an illusion," Jame muttered, holding her hand out to where there should be sheets of cascading water. Tigh stepped behind her and wrapped her arms around the stunned arbiter.

"There's always an explanation," Tigh whispered against the golden hair. "We can't let them think that there isn't. Remember your own words... 'If their goal is to cause panic, then we must not panic. If their goal is to cause fear, then we must not show fear'."

Jame turned around in Tigh's arms and looked up at her partner, her head cocked with curiosity. "I didn't know you were paying attention."

Tigh couldn't stop the burst of gentle laughter. "Don't you know by now that I can't help but listen to your voice?"

Jame's breath caught in her throat at this unexpected admission. "Really?" she finally breathed.

"Remember, it was your voice that captured me from the very beginning." Tigh grinned affectionately.

Hearing muffled voices from the next chamber, Jame sighed at her partner. "I think we'll continue this discussion later."

Tigh released Jame and let her lead the way into the rainbow chamber. Panilope, the High Follower of Laur, draped in a robe of intense purple, leaned over a smaller, older woman dangling a weighted string over one of the natural drains for the passage of circulating water. Jyac stood tensely in the middle of the chamber watching them. All three looked up as Jame and Tigh entered.

The buds of hope that Jame had seen the night before were gone as Jyac lifted her eyes to her niece. The Queen's face was set in grim shock as she moved towards them.

"This was written." Jame didn't even make it a question.

"Yes." Jyac glanced around the waterless chamber, then captured Jame's eyes. "Do you think a Wizard could do this? Suck the water from the Temple until it's dry? The prophecies are coming true. There is no doubt about it now."

Chapter
12

Frustrated, Jame turned to get Tigh's reaction to her aunt's words, only to find her partner not paying attention. The warrior, brow creased in concentration, had a hand on one of the stone slabs that supported the cascading waterfalls. Exchanging glances with Jyac, Jame placed a gentle hand on Tigh's other arm, getting her attention. "What is it?"

For an answer Tigh took Jame's hand and pressed it against the stone. The arbiter felt a strong trembling caused by some kind of rapid movement.

"It's water," Tigh said softly. "This cavern is surging with it, we just can't see it or feel it."

"What is this nonsense?" Hallie demanded as she and Panilope joined them. The dowser's face was sharp with indignation. "There isn't any water here, not even deep in the caverns below." For good measure she shook her dowsing medallion at the warrior.

"A good illusionist never does anything halfway," Tigh mused as she opened up her enhanced senses.

"You still think that the Wizard is behind all this?" Jyac threw up her hands in frustration.

Tigh ignored her and concentrated on her senses. Much to her surprise, her nose detected the faint scent of water and her ears caught the whisper of splashing and gurgling. It wasn't possible—her practical mind gently tapped the shoulder of what her senses were telling her. Shrugging off that practical mind, she quieted her thoughts, allowing the voice of the possible to overtake the screams of the impossible that filled the chamber. It took just a single act to break an illusion of this kind. The illusions in the meadow faded to nothing as soon as they were penetrated. To get to the real enemy, the warriors simply pretended the imaginary Lukrians didn't exist.

Blinking out of her reverie, Tigh turned to Panilope, who was fidgeting with a sacred silver vessel she used to give water blessings to the faithful followers of Laur. "I want to receive a water blessing," the warrior announced.

The others stared at her as if she had received one too many blows to the head.

"Water is necessary for a water blessing." Panilope's low steady voice had a dry tinge to it.

"Pretend there's water flowing down this stone." Tigh waved her hand over the upright slab. "Go through the motions of preparing a water offering."

The High Follower of Laur looked at her Queen and her princess for guidance.

Jame stepped forward and put a comforting hand on Panilope's cloth-draped arm. "Tigh has an understanding of the enemy we're up against," the arbiter reassured her. "She wouldn't ask you to do something without a purpose to it." Jame turned to her partner to double-check her sincerity. Tigh did have a wicked sense of humor that surfaced at the oddest times. A raised eyebrow told Jame that as tempting as it was for Tigh to tweak a follower of Laur, she was serious in her request.

"I guess it's better than doing nothing," Panilope acquiesced as she held the small vessel between her hands and approached the dry slab. Gazing at the polished stone, the High Follower of Laur put her mind through the silent preparation for the offering. After a few heartbeats, she turned to Tigh. "Please come and accept your offering." Tigh stood next to the High Follower. "Tigh of Ingor, Laur welcomes you to her Temple."

Panilope thrust the vessel forward. Shocked fingers, suddenly drenched in warm water, reacted and the vessel splashed into a pool of clear, swirling liquid. The roar of water startled their senses after the silence in the chamber.

The delighted grin Jame bestowed on her partner was enough of a blessing to last Tigh a lifetime. "It *was* an illusion," the arbiter cried in wonderment, catching the thoughtful look on her aunt's face. "What?"

The Queen stepped up to a pool and ran a finger lightly across the surface of the water. "A few heartbeats ago I was without hope because what was written about how the waters of Laur were restored sounded like a miracle," Jyac responded quietly, capturing everyone's attention—including Panilope who was knee deep in water, fetching her blessing vessel. "But now I see it was just a test for the outsider who is going to help save Emoria from whoever is threatening our borders."

"This was written, too." Jame nodded.

"It's confusing to read." Jyac concentrated on sorting through the memorized text. "The miracle of the flowing water is followed by a passage that is written more as a parable than a prediction. The person who performs the miracle is accused of trying to destroy Laur by pretending to be more powerful than the deity. The Emorans imprison her and fight the enemy on their own...and lose."

"It was a warning, not a prediction," Jame reasoned.

"I think so." Jyac nodded, her face relaxing.

"One more attempt to use the Mysteries to destroy Tigh is thwarted," Jame mused, thoughtfully resting a chin on her fist.

"She's thinking. Not always a good thing," Tigh said, glancing at the Queen.

The Queen, in spite of herself, emitted a delicate snort of laughter.

Jame briefly narrowed her eyes at them before returning to her thoughts. Suddenly her eyes sparked with an idea. "Maybe the parable has something to it." She turned to Tigh, an impish playfulness just touching the green eyes. "It's plain that anyone who can perform this kind of miracle in Laur's own Temple, under her very nose, figuratively speaking, is too powerful to have running around." It was Tigh's turn to narrow her eyes at her partner.

"What are you saying?" Jyac, not able to see Jame's expression, was shocked at her niece's words.

"She should be imprisoned for the safety of our people." Jame sauntered up to the warrior. "What do you think?"

"Could we make it a dry prison cell for a change? Maybe one that doesn't have a cold draft?" The warrior gazed down at the arbiter with eyes soaked with innocence.

"Hmm. That does take some of the fun out of it... Whoa." Jame was suddenly in the air, cradled in Tigh's arms and held over the pool of water. Looking down at the water, then at her smirking partner, then down at the water again, the arbiter searched for words of reason. "It would make an awful messy splash if you dropped me."

"The acolytes can clean it up." Tigh shrugged.

"Dry and warm. I think I can manage that," Jame quickly agreed. "Now let me down."

"One more thing." Tigh pulled Jame's head close enough to put her lips to the arbiter's ear. "I want a roommate."

Jame tried to keep from grinning. "You do, do you?"

"It gets lonely in those dry, warm prison cells," Tigh purred, sending shivers through her partner.

"Do you have anyone in mind?" Jame purred back.

"You'll do," Tigh whispered before turning around and gently putting Jame on the ground. The arbiter immediately slapped the unrepentant warrior on the arm.

"Get that worked out?" Jyac wiped the amused look off her face.

"Yes." Jame wrapped an arm around Tigh's waist. "We are going to pretend to hold Tigh under house arrest. It may be written, but I don't think our foes think that we would actually do it. Let's give them something else to consider while we start preparations to attack. If we think we can win if Tigh is imprisoned, we may as well look like we're ready to fight."

Tigh grinned at Jame's thoroughness. "You just want to get me into a warm, dry prison cell for a few days."

Jame grinned back as Jyac just shook her head.

* * * * * * * * * * * * * * *

"How exactly did Misner know that Tigh would figure out the illusion in the Temple?" Seeran didn't look up as she scribbled the incredible account of the last couple of days. Tigh, sitting cross-legged in front of the fire, was catching up on some much needed maintenance to her armor and weapons. Jame was draped over a favorite chair from childhood spinning a tale for Seeran that would make her the envy of her colleagues back at the University.

"Good question, Seeran." Jame reached over to the small table next to her, grabbed a challenge braid and threw it at her partner. Tigh, not thinking it worth dropping her tool and piece of armor for, let the braid bounce harmlessly off her forehead. "Good catch."

Tigh benignly picked up the braid and studied it. "Tall, red-head, not bad looking." A half dozen more braids collided with her body.

"How did Misner know that you would figure out the illusion in the Temple?" Jame repeated the question.

"It is written." Tigh shielded herself from another volley of braids. "Actually, much of our Guard training involved solving seemingly impossible puzzles. By comparison, the illusion in the Temple was an easy one." Picking up a braid, she asked, "How can I meet these challenges if I'm under house arrest?"

"Maybe we can make it a part of your reward for gaining the acolytes' undying gratitude." Jame wickedly grinned.

"You enjoyed that didn't you?" Tigh scowled, remembering being tackled by two dozen lavender-clad women the moment they discovered who restored their precious waterfalls.

"Until I had to pull them off you," Jame muttered.

"You're cute when you're jealous." Tigh grinned. "They were too...um, lavender for my taste." The expression on Jame's face was worth several pounds of silver on the Ingoran market exchange. The market price skyrocketed when Jame noticed that Seeran was scribbling away in her journal.

"You're not writing this down, are you?" Jame cried, exasperated at the historian.

An unrepentant Seeran looked up at her. "Of course. You two have a very unique, but entertaining, way of talking to each other."

Tigh and Jame exchanged bewildered glances. "We talk like anyone else." Tigh shrugged.

"Rarely does an historian have the opportunity to hear everyday conversations between heroes," Seeran continued, going after and getting twin looks of exasperation. "I know, I know. You're not heroes."

"We're just doing what needs to be done," Jame clarified.

"Because you're the best ones for the job," Seeran added.

"For this particular job, yes." Jame saw by Seeran's smile that the historian had other ideas on the subject.

"So you restore the waters of Laur and they show their gratitude by putting you under house arrest," Seeran gently probed.

"Actually, that was Jame's idea," Tigh said dryly as she returned to her task.

Seeran shot a startled look at the arbiter.

"We're trying to outsmart the enemy by pretending not to fall for one of their tricks," Jame whispered in a conspiratorial voice. "You see, in the Mysteries, the Emorans are defeated if they imprison the outsider. The logical moral of the parable is that the Emorans will win if Tigh remains free. So we confuse Misner by imprisoning Tigh."

"Argis is so frustrated at all this game playing that she spent the day sparring. I think there are more casualties from her sparring than from the battle yesterday." Seeran dipped her quill into the small, stained ceramic ink jar. "So that's the story up to now."

"That's it." Jame nodded. "And if you think Argis is frustrated, just wait until Tigh gets out on the sparring grounds to meet those challenges. I just hope the enemy makes their next move fast or we'll have a very frustrated warrior on our hands."

"I'll just have to find other ways to work off that excess energy," Tigh stated with utter innocence. Jame's attention was immediately on the warrior, who was tinkering away at her armor. Seeran blinked between them, feeling an embarrassed blush rise up her cheeks.

Jame picked up another braid and absently studied it. "Do I detect a different kind of frustration?"

Tigh feigned surprise at the possible implication of Jame's words. "I thought maybe you'd want to sort through some of your things here. Clean out some of the stuff from your childhood."

Jame's shoulders shook with amused laughter. "Right. I know how much you love puttering around and tidying up." Turning to a curious Seeran, she confided, "I have to use in all kinds of bribery to get her to do the simplest chores in our place in Ynit."

"You have a place in Ynit?" It never occurred to Seeran that there was somewhere they called home.

"A pair of rooms at the School." Jame nodded. "It's home until we settle here for good."

"Why not Ingor?"

Tigh looked up from her work and cleared her throat. "Have you ever been to Ingor?"

"Uh, no." Seeran shook her head. "But I hear it's got stunning architecture. It's supposed to be the most beautiful of cities, perched on hills over-looking the Nirlion Sea."

"It is beautiful." Tigh's mind ran through images of the sun-soaked, cheerful city. "A city built from the riches of well-to-do merchants. Not the kind of place for a poor arbiter and her warrior."

"Even though your family is there?" Seeran asked before remembering what took Tigh away from her home in the first place.

"My family has different ideas of a career for me," Tigh answered quietly. Not the response that Seeran was expecting. "They thought I could just put being a warrior behind me and go back to the family business."

"I thought...I mean," Seeran stammered.

"You thought that I would be cut off from the family and disowned?" Tigh raised an eyebrow at the historian. "Merchants are a different breed. They have dealings with all kinds of people. War is a big business and merchants can't afford to take sides or be bothered by questions of ethics or morality. I'm actually of more value to my family now because of what I know about war and because of the knowledge acquired as the companion of an arbiter."

"Interesting," Seeran responded, thoughtfully.

"Luckily for me, Tigh's spirit is more Emoran than Ingoran." Jame smiled affectionately at her partner.

"I'm the lucky one." Tigh winked at Seeran.

There was a gentle rap on the door and a young girl entered holding a tray.

"Come in," Jame beckoned, amiably.

"The Queen has sent the midday meal for you, my princess, and for the prisoner." The girl cast shy eyes in the direction of the warrior sprawled on the floor. The stories flying around the kitchen about Tigh had raised her to a divine status just short of Laur herself.

"Thank you. Just put it on the table there." Jame pushed out of her chair and wandered over to inspect the tray. "Thank the cooks for the wonderful Ingoran food."

The girl's delighted smile almost overwhelmed her delicate features. "The cooks will be happy to hear that, my princess," she managed to stammer out before skipping out of the chamber.

Turning thoughtfully to Seeran, who was gathering up her things, Jame said, "I think that bringing Tigh here will have a positive impact on Emoria."

"You just want to get them thinking more like you. So it'll be easier for them to relate to you when you become Queen." Tigh cocked an amused eye at her partner.

Jame spun around at these words, realizing the truth in them. "My clever partner. I knew there was some reason I kept you around," she laughed before giving in

to the tempting aromas from the plates of food and settled down to the serious business of eating.

****

Jame squinted into the late evening sun as she
stood, flanked by Argis and Mularke, atop the gate
wall. Despite the seriousness of the threat to Emoria,
Jame felt more relaxed than she had in a long time.
Two days of keeping her willing prisoner company had
made her think that they should take a few days off for
themselves every once in a while. A small smile
creased her eyes as she ruminated about how wonder-
fully attentive a very relaxed warrior could be.

"There." Mularke's keen eyes caught a movement
at the far end of the valley. The trio watched as a small
band of women shimmered into view.

"So they just appeared in the forest?" Jame shaded
her eyes, picking out Gindor, walking beside an apparent stranger draped in delicate, dancing cloth.

"The patrol had just passed a small clearing. Hearing noises behind them, they went back to investigate
and there stood the Council and that woman," Argis
related.

A quick patter of footfalls heralded the arrival of
Jyac and Sark to the overlook. They shaded their eyes,
staring out into the valley.

"They seem to be all right," Argis ventured.

Jyac turned to her. "That's good to hear." She
managed to pull away from the puzzle pieces scattered
about the illusive crevices of her mind. Catching
Jame's eyes on her, she knew that her niece had figured
out what was disturbing her. "Do we know who this
stranger is?"

Mularke shook her head. "The scout said she
doesn't look like she's from around here."

Studying the foreign clothing, Jame lifted an eyebrow at the understatement. "I'd say she's from the Oheria Gulf coast."

"That's thousands of furlongs from here." Jyac gave her niece a wondering look. "You've been there?"

"Five seasons ago." Jame nodded. "I am Peace Arbiter-at-large for the Southern Districts. That includes the Oheria Gulf coast."

"I hear it's an interesting place. Very exotic." Jyac was impressed by how well traveled her niece was. She had never imagined that Jame's job took her as far south as the fabled Gulf.

"Compared to here, it would be considered exotic," Jame mused. She had seen so much of the world that she learned to view each culture as unique rather than strange or different. "Their dress is more suited to the warmer weather."

"Why is someone from the Oheria Gulf coast here—with the Council?" Sark, always the practical thinker, stood with arms crossed.

"Only she has the answer," Jyac responded softly.

"There are many strangers in these mountains who are trying to do us harm," Argis reminded them. "We must be cautious with this one."

"How will we know for sure if she is friend or foe?" Mularke frowned.

"We have Tigh to determine that." Jame turned to the archer. "She still has many of the skills from when she was a Guard. One of them is knowing if someone is telling the truth."

"That's right." Argis felt a jolt of hope. "She knew when that Meah woman was lying to her."

"I just hope the Council has forgotten about treating her like an unwanted interloper," Jyac sighed. "At least they'll be happy to see her imprisoned. Even if it is a ruse."

"Imprisoned in Jame's chamber." Argis quirked an amused eye at her Queen. "We could all wish for such a punishment."

To cover her embarrassment Jame slapped Argis on the arm. Jyac smiled at the exchange, pleased that her best warrior and her niece had been able to slip into an easy friendship after so many years of estrangement. She knew that Argis would never completely get over her feelings for Jame, but the fact that she was trying was a tribute to Tigh's character.

High, excited voices wafted up to them from the valley as the Council members, rambling along like they were out for a pleasant walk, jabbered and gestured at the patiently listening patrol. "They don't look like they've been through too much of an ordeal," Jyac commented.

"You can bet they're going to be raving mad about...let's see, how lax we've become in our security, how we didn't find them and rescue them...and you can be sure they'll throw in everything else they've been complaining about since Laur was a child before we hear the end of it." For emphasis, Sark covered her ears with her hands.

"Unless this seemingly miraculous return has changed their dispositions, be ready for a steady tongue-lashing for at least a season or two." Jyac ruefully grinned.

"Sounds like some things never change," Jame commented as she leaned over the wall for a better look at the stranger strolling casually next to Gindor. Talking with her hands as much as with her voice, the folds of thin shimmering fabric caught the long rays of the dying sun. Gindor appeared to be immersed in the stranger's words. That alone signaled to Jame that there was more to this stranger than someone who had wandered too far from home. Gindor's distrust of anything not Emoran was as much a part of her as her own skin.

Jame and Jyac exchanged glances, sharing the same thoughts about the stranger. They were both relieved that Tigh could help determine if this woman was harmless or not. "I suppose we'd better be at the gate or else the Council will have one more thing to torment us with." Jyac straightened and led the way down the switch back to the City Square.

Argis, following Jame, leaned into the arbiter's ear. "Do you think that this is written in the Mysteries?" she asked softly. She had spent a part of the past two days mulling over the recent strange events with Jame and her willing prisoner.

Jame, keeping an eye on her footing, responded with a negative shake of the head. "I don't think so. We won't know for sure until I can speak privately with Jyac."

"If it's not written..." Argis paused, not wanting to jinx any hopeful thoughts.

"I know," Jame said. "It might be enough to turn our chances around. Give us an advantage for a change."

They looked up at the commotion at the gate as twelve slightly bedraggled women in surprisingly good spirits emerged into the torch-lit square. Curious heads poked out of doorways and women wandered into the street to see what was disturbing their quiet evening.

"In case you hadn't noticed, we were kidnapped," Gindor growled upon seeing Jyac. The Queen stifled a sigh and strode to the twelve extremely put out women. How the women disappeared was truly a mystery to them. They had searched every patch of rock in the Council's chambers for a hidden tunnel or even evidence of recent disturbance and found nothing. Tigh determined that the escape route was concealed with a spell rather than an illusion, since an illusion would break as soon as it was touched.

"We couldn't figure out how you were taken," Jyac began, bracing for the inevitable impatient reply.

"Right out from under your noses. While you were drunk with celebrating." Gindor waved a hand at the gathering crowd.

"Not all of us were drunk and all the guards were on duty," Jame indignantly stated.

"You, my girl, have no voice here until we say so." Gindor shook a bony finger at the arbiter.

"If we hadn't listened to her voice and the voice of her partner, there might not have been an Emor for you to return to." Argis unexpectedly strolled up to Gindor, once again challenging a member of the Council.

Gindor was about to express a heated opinion on what Argis could do with her challenge when Jyac stepped forward to the stranger who was watching the interplay with quiet curiosity. "Introduce us to your friend."

Surprisingly, Gindor stopped her confrontation with Argis and turned to the tall woman. The stranger pulled the cloth draped over her head down onto her shoulders, revealing thick, curly dark hair that reflected a reddish tint in the deepening torchlight. Her skin was sun touched, as was common to the folks from the Gulf coast. Gentle, curious eyes, the same color as her hair, blinked back at them.

"This is Goodemer, a Wizard from the Maymi Peninsula," Gindor introduced with near reverence. "She found us after we managed to escape. Fortunately for you, we still have our wits about us and can act like warriors when called upon to do so. We lost our way in the caves and when we finally found an opening to the outside, we were on the other side of Jacalore Peak. Three good days walk from here. After we had traveled a bit, we came upon Goodemer. She told us that she had been drawn here because of the news that a Wizard was up to no good in these mountains."

"How did you know that?" Jame's low voice was directed at the young woman.

"Wizards can feel other Wizards at work. It is a way to keep any misuse of our power in check," Goodemer responded with a voice that flowed like a sweet melody from the accents of her native land. "There are one or two rogue Wizards that we've tried to find over the last several seasons. One seems to have settled in these mountains and is causing terrible havoc in the natural force."

"She found a shortcut through the mountains for us," Gindor put in. It was apparent that Gindor trusted this Wizard, despite every reason to be wary of her.

"I'm Jyac, Queen of Emoria and this is my niece, Jame." Jyac felt a long night was before them and the first thing they had to do was introduce this Wizard to Tigh. Eyeing the Council, she wondered how they were going to do that when Gindor wasn't even acknowledging Jame's Emoran rights. Why couldn't things be simple for once? "This is Sark, my Right Hand, Argis, Master Warrior and Mularke, Master Archer."

Goodemer laid gentle eyes on each Emoran before returning to Jame. "I've seen you before. You are the arbiter that saved those children from being sold into slavery. I am honored to be in your presence." The Wizard performed a gracious bow to a stunned Jame. She could feel the others staring at her, a thousand questions hanging in the air.

"I was just doing my job," Jame mumbled, wishing she could feel Tigh's reassuring hand against her back. The warrior always knew when a touch was needed to help the modest arbiter regain her composure.

"It seems we have much to discuss." Jyac cleared her throat. "We welcome you as our guest, Goodemer. We also want to stop this Wizard."

A delighted grin overtook the Wizard's features as she followed her hosts to the palace.

Chapter
13

Jyac sank into her favorite chair in front of the fire in her private sitting chamber. Jame sat on the edge of a nearby chair waiting for her aunt to speak.

The return of the Council tore a hole in Jyac's faith in the Mysteries, playing havoc with her ability to focus. She couldn't turn away from her beliefs because a single incident didn't happen the way it was written. Raising her head, she found her niece intently studying her, concern lingering in her eyes. This was not the time to be incapacitated by a faltering faith. "That was not the way that the Council was to return to us," she said softly, eyes turned to the fire.

"I gathered as much." Jame nodded.

"They were to reappear one morning asleep in their own beds," Jyac sighed, making the decision to tell her niece what she had just learned from Gindor. She tried to accept that if these incidents were forced events from the Mysteries, then the whole situation was false and had nothing to do with the Mysteries at all. Leaving the one truth that Jyac knew she had to follow. A princess would defeat the Wizard. "Gindor overheard the Lukrian guards grumbling about their mysterious leaders. The Lukrians wanted to trade the Council for our prisoners. They thought that was the reason for kidnapping the Council in the first place."

"Makes sense," Jame mused, especially pleased that the Lukrians weren't completely amiable allies of the rogue Wizard.

"So they weren't very happy when they found out that the Council members were to be returned to Emor unharmed," Jyac continued.

Jame frowned as she turned puzzled eyes to her aunt. "Since the Council has read the Mysteries, they knew that they would be returned unharmed. Why did they bother to escape?"

"It seems that the Lukrians were plotting to go against their leaders and even discussed moving the Council to a hiding place until they could agree on a prisoner exchange." Jyac smiled at her clever niece. Nothing got past that sharp mind. "The Council saw an opportunity to escape and took it."

Jame's eyes brightened with optimism as her mind slid the newest pieces of the puzzle into place. "So the illusion of the Emor Mysteries has been broken. That means their present strategy has been foiled."

"Maybe buying us a little time," Jyac returned with cautious optimism.

"All we need is a crack to slip through." Jame grinned. "That was a favorite saying of a professor of mine. To learn all the family secrets, one must find where the mice get into the house. Our mouse hole is the Lukrian village."

Jyac steepled her fingers in front of her face. Jame always had a mind for strategy, making it all the more sad when she turned away from her warrior training. The same trait served her well as an arbiter, but to Jyac's mind, it was wasted on such passive activities. "There is also this Wizard from the south."

"If she is as she says, we will have the cat to go with the mice." Jame leaned back into the chair.

Jyac gave her niece a sidelong glance. "Can Tigh really tell if she's truthful or not?"

"I've never known her to be wrong," Jame responded. "It has something to do with the heightened senses of the Guards."

"So we add another animal to your menagerie." Jyac's expression turned to amusement.

"The panther and the fox." Jame thoughtfully nodded. Catching her aunt's puzzled expression, she explained, "We were given those nicknames by the people of Ampiston. We reminded them of a storyteller and warrior from their ancient stories."

"I'd like to hear that story sometime." Jyac, knowing her niece's modest nature, would have to think of creative ways of coaxing what appeared to be an adventurous life out of her. "It's time to join the others for the evening meal."

"Tigh will be pleased that she can join us." Jame's eyes twinkled in amusement. "She doesn't like being shut up for any length of time. Two moons in a narrow cell in Ynit just about drove her crazy."

Jyac thoughtfully gazed at her niece. "I would like to hear about your experiences with the Guards someday. I think that it may not have been such a bad learning experience for a princess."

Jame was stunned by this admission. With Emoran traditions crumbling all around them, she caught a glimpse of the foundation for a greater, stronger Emoria.

****

Tigh, just happy to be out of Jame's room for the first time in two days, settled into the cushions of Jyac's private dining chamber. Not that the opportunity to laze around with her partner wasn't pleasant. It had been a while since they had reaffirmed their love with such depths of intimacy. A grin tugged at Tigh's mouth as she glanced at her tablemates. Sark and Ronalyn chatted softly and Argis sipped from her mug of spiced tea, her thoughtful eyes on the enigmatic tall warrior.

"I hear you're getting let off for good behavior," the Emoran warrior drawled, lazily sitting up from her slouch and putting both elbows on the table.

Discarding her first response to that statement and thankful that Jame wasn't there to comment on just how good Tigh's behavior had been over the last couple of days, the warrior answered with an expressive lift of an eyebrow.

"The warriors are itching for you to meet their challenges," Argis continued, making a show of studying the former Guard. "But if you think you need a couple of days practice after lazing around indoors..."

"I got plenty of exercise," Tigh's low voice rumbled. Sark and Ronalyn now had both ears on the exchange between the warriors.

"I don't think fighting off Jame counts." Sark couldn't resist.

Tigh's blue eyes shifted to Jyac's Right Hand. "Whatever Jame wants, Jame gets. I know better than to put up any resistance."

"So, then, are you rested enough for the challenges?" Sark grinned.

"Completely invigorated." A catlike smile spread across Tigh's face.

"Looks like some things never change," Argis commented, keeping a steady eye on the warrior.

Tigh's attention quickly shifted to the Master Warrior. It took every bit of control she had to keep the jealous rage below the simmering point. Jame had reminded her that in a close community like Emoria one could never get away from reminders of past relationships or disputes or moments of indiscretion. Argis was testing her, reminding her that she had to share her cherished intimate memories of Jame with someone else. Someone who she surprisingly called friend.

Lifting her mug of spiced tea, Tigh met Argis' eyes. "Here's to Jame. The most remarkable person I've ever met."

Argis' startled hesitancy was just for a heartbeat before she grinned and raised her mug. "Here's to Jame." Sark and Ronalyn joined in the toast.

"So the challenge is on for tomorrow?" Argis relaxed back into the cushions.

A genuine grin crept up to Tigh's eyes. "Just name the time."

"One at a time or all at once?"

Sark sputtered her tea at Argis' casual question.

"Your choice." Tigh lifted her mug.

Sark whipped her head around to Tigh. "Warrior humor—right?" the former scout asked in a hopeful voice.

"You didn't see her fight." Argis arched a brow at the older woman.

"I heard about it." Sark sucked in a breath.

"I'll let the challengers decide." Argis turned her head to the door as Jyac and Jame walked in.

Their Queen and princess were in noticeably high spirits. Jame plopped down next to Tigh and playfully wrapped her arms around the warrior and gave her a warm hug.

"You're in a good mood," Tigh commented, reaching for the hot kettle with her free hand and pouring the aromatic liquid into the empty mug in front of Jame.

"Hmmm. Thanks." Jame disengaged from her partner and took the mug in both hands, sipping the steaming tea. The spiciness flooded her mind with tumbling memories of long evenings of food and conversation she had experienced in this chamber. Those evenings were filled with security and innocence, both lost with the passing of childhood.

"Where is our guest?" Jyac turned to Ronalyn.

"Probably still bathing." Ronalyn grinned. "She couldn't stop marveling at our warm, running water."

Tigh kept her thoughts to herself, as she did earlier when Argis told her of the stranger who accompanied the Council back to Emor claiming to be a Wizard. It wasn't her place to question the Queen's decision to allow this stranger to be treated as a guest in the palace. She just hoped she could detect if the woman meant harm to the Emorans or not.

"She's from the Maymi peninsula," Jame commented as she leaned into Tigh.

"Where Meah's from," Tigh mused. All eyes turned to them.

"I think it's just a coincidence," Jame assured them. "This Wizard knew me from when we had visited there."

"When that young man sculpted the statue of you surrounded by thankful children. If I remember correctly, it's now displayed in the Gardens of Trinagol." Tigh watched in delight as the blush blossomed on her partner's cheeks. "She made quite an impression on the Maymians." Tigh looked around Jame at Jyac.

"So it seems," Jyac chuckled.

"I was just doing my job." Jame squirmed.

"Convincing the slavers that contraption could fly was beyond inspired," Tigh continued.

"I had to think of something." Jame turned to her, exasperated.

"I think most of us would have been a little less dramatic," Tigh gently teased.

"It worked, didn't it?" Jame crossed her arms.

"It not only worked but it ensured your place in Maymian history." Tigh grinned. "It's your own fault for being hailed a hero. You gave them too good of a story to ignore."

"And what were you doing during this creative subterfuge?" Jyac directed a pointed gaze at Tigh.

Grinning, Jame rested her chin on her hand and focused her attention on her partner. "Yes. Tell us what you were doing."

Tigh fiddled with a piece of flat bread as a rare blush radiated out from her cheeks. "I was backing up Jame."

"Backing up. Is that what you call it?" Jame turned to her audience, already captive, and proceeded to recount a harrowing tale of how their attempts to foil the slavers kept failing and their only chance of freeing the children was a final act of foolhardy desperation before the slavers sailed away. Images of impenetrable swamps, flying slavers and brave children stayed with them long after Jame uttered the conclusion of the story.

"Is this what you do all the time?" Argis' incredulous voice broke the silence.

"Oh, no. Not at all." Jame protested the very idea. "Our lives are generally quiet. Almost boring. Traveling from place to place. Arbitrating local cases."

"Your personal historian seems to know a lot of stories that don't sound very quiet to me," Jyac chuckled.

"Things are always exaggerated." Jame shrugged, dipping a sliver of bread into one of the bowls of sweet mountain fruit chutney. "Personal historian?"

"I think Seeran has been doing her bit to contribute to the growing legend of their future Queen," Tigh murmured in her ear.

"For what it's worth, we've been very pleased and proud of what you've done with your life." Jyac took Jame's hand into both of hers. The speechless arbiter bestowed a beautiful smile of thanks on her aunt. "I'm going to talk with Gindor tonight. Get her to put aside her objections to Tigh, at least until we overcome our enemies."

"Good luck," Argis sighed.

"I think my luck will hinge on how our guest and Tigh react to each other." Jyac raised her eyes to meet pale blue, glistening in the torchlight. "Gindor seems to trust this Wizard and you're the only one among us who can determine if she is friend or foe."

Tigh absorbed the statement and slowly nodded. "I will do everything I can to help."

****

Nothing in her limited experience in Maymi could have prepared Goodemer for the wonder and sophistication of the palace at Emor. The clever ways of providing light had her thinking that one of her Wizard colleagues lent a hand in the illumination until she studied the light source closer. She couldn't believe the airiness of the guest chamber with polished white walls glowing orange in the reflected torchlight.

For all their fabled fierceness, the Emorans appeared to have a sophisticated culture. Goodemer didn't quite know what to make of the twelve women who called themselves Emorans, since the only exposure she had to them was in their mythology. She certainly didn't expect a comfortably furnished room, replete with a waterfall of warm water flowing into a quartz-lined pool.

The nice guard told her that the waterfall was a gift of Laur, their patron deity. The Maymians should think about adopting this deity for some relief from their hot, humid climate. Realizing that she probably spent too long in the soothing waters, she quickly dried herself with the soft linen cloth. A set of light wool leggings and tunic were laid out on the bed. Fingering the unexpected softness of the fabric, she wondered if they were woven from the wool of the shaggy goats she had seen frolicking on the steep mountain slopes. They were definitely much warmer than her filmy clothes.

After slipping into the warm wool, she added her belt pouch and a silver amulet of a wolf's head that she wore around her neck. She spent a few moments stilling her mind, knowing that her first battle in these mountains would be against the Emorans' distrust of her. Raising her eyes, she addressed her absent mentor.

"I don't know if I can do this. What if I can't convince them I'm a friend and not a foe?"

She listened to the cascading water, expecting no answer and getting none. Her mentor had faith in her ability to perform this daunting task. She just had to see through her own natural modest impression of her skill. Sighing, she walked to the door and pushed it open. Eiget, lounging against the opposite wall, straightened.

"This way." The guard led the Wizard through a baffling maze of intricately carved and painted corridors and small chambers. Goodemer, ever curious, gawked around like a child in a confectionery shop.

At the end of a narrow corridor stood a doorway covered with hanging leather strips rather than a light wooden door. Eiget stepped to the side of the opening and signaled Goodemer through. Careful not to show the nervousness rolling around inside of her, Goodemer nodded to the guard and pulled aside the leather strands, stepping warily into the cozy dining chamber. She was relieved to see a small party, four of whom she had already met.

"Enter, enter." Jyac waved the Wizard in, indicating an empty space opposite Tigh and next to Argis. "Please sit."

"Thank you," Goodemer responded politely as she dropped cross-legged onto the cushions.

"You've met Jame, Argis, and Sark," Jyac stated. "This is my consort, Ronalyn, and Jame's partner, Tigh."

Goodemer bowed her head to Ronalyn and Tigh, her eyes lingering briefly on the lounging warrior. "I've seen you before in Maymi. The story of your bravery and compassion has become a favorite among my people." She decided it was not the proper place to speak of the other time she had seen Jame and Tigh when she was a young apprentice. Her mentor had been called to Ynit to create a spell that removed all trace of the process used to enhance ordinary people into the perfect warrior. The young Goodemer spent most of that time lost in an adolescent fascination with the arbiter and the warrior.

Tigh bowed her head in acknowledgment of the compliment but could never find the proper words to respond.

"Goodemer is a Wizard," Jyac explained politely, even though everyone knew who she was. "She's here to investigate the doings of a certain Wizard in these mountains."

Argis poured spiced tea into Goodemer's cup and pushed a basket of flat bread and a bowl of chutney within the Wizard's reach. "We're curious about this investigation." The warrior's low voice accompanied the offer of food and drink.

"We seem to have a common goal of wanting to stop this Wizard before she can do great harm," Jame smoothly clarified.

Goodemer nodded as she took a sip of the warm liquid, trying to calm her nerves. This was the toughest part of her assignment. Her mentor always joked that wizardry would be simple if they didn't have to deal with people. So much energy went into turning distrust and hostility into a working alliance. Up to that moment it was all just theory to the inexperienced Wizard.

"She's been a rogue Wizard for many years," Goodemer began carefully. Gain trust by giving information freely, her mentor's voice echoed in her head.

"Is she called Misner?" Tigh sat forward, pinning the young Wizard with her compelling eyes.

"Yes," Goodemer responded, tilting her head in curiosity. "How do you know that?"

Tigh crossed her arms, holding the Wizard's gaze. "I had some...dealings with her. Several years ago."

"Dealings?"

"I was sent to kill her." Tigh watched as Goodemer's pupils dilated. She was as nervous as a rabbit, yet the warrior couldn't detect any concealment of truth from her. "I thought I succeeded. Time has proven me wrong."

Goodemer tried to swallow, but her throat was too dry. "May I ask why you were sent to kill her?" Her voice was amazingly steady under the gaze of intense blue.

"The Northern powers wanted her to create an army that could defeat the Elite Guards," Tigh casually explained. "Five Guards before me were sent to kill her. She killed them. When I faced her, she taunted me with their names and played havoc with my mind. I somehow fought through that and sliced off her head. Something fed back from the blow and knocked me unconscious for over a day. When I came to, what was left of the Wizard was still there, so I had no reason to doubt that she was dead."

"It would have been an easy enough illusion," Goodemer mused, her nervousness slipping away unnoticed.

"Why would she pretend to let me kill her when she killed the other Guards?" Tigh looked around the discreet kitchen helpers who were quickly laying out platters of food on the table.

"Why is she playing games with your people?" Goodemer asked before her eyes gazed with delight on the feast before her.

"Tigh is not Emoran, and we were attacked before she ever visited Emoria." Argis scooped a thick meaty stew into a small bowl. "Eat up. Jyac presides over an informal table."

"Thank you." Watching how the others filled their plates and bowls, Goodemer took a little of everything within her reach. Traveling introduced her taste buds to some interesting treats. Glancing around the table, she noticed a different type of food sitting in front of Tigh and Jame. "Do you follow a special diet?"

Jame looked up from her plate. "Tigh is Ingoran. I cook according their customs because it's easier than preparing two different things for every meal." The arbiter gave Goodemer a charming smile, but refrained from looking at the Queen. No need to drag out the Ingoran joining at that moment.

"This is very good. Different from the food in Maymi." Goodemer smiled at Jyac.

"Thank you. We take pride in our cuisine," Jyac responded.

They ate, keeping the conversation to inconsequential matters and exchanging cultural differences. The spiced tea had turned into spiced wine at some point in the meal and Goodemer relaxed in the presence of these seemingly benign women. Thinking more and more on how strange that was, she realized that they should have been treating her with suspicion. She was a Wizard after all, capable of creating great mayhem even as she sat eating.

"I am curious about one thing," she found herself saying, the alcohol taking a stronger hold on her than she was aware. "I have to admit that I was expecting to be treated with a little more suspicion, being a Wizard and all."

Six sets of eyes were immediately on her, lifted forks and cups momentarily forgotten. She blinked at them, realizing that the wine might have loosened her tongue too much.

Tigh sucked in a breath and cleared her throat, bringing Goodemer's attention her way. "A part of our training in the Elite Guards was to learn how to detect deception in others. I have not felt any deception from you."

"How do you know that I'm not covering my deception with an illusion?" Goodemer returned with a friendly challenge.

"Illusion only works when the illusion is unexpected," Tigh replied steadily. "We have learned in the past few days not to trust anyone or anything, so naturally we were looking for deception from you. Your illusion would have been shattered immediately and I would have seen it."

"You understand the ways of the Wizard?" Goodemer's eyes had widened during Tigh's little speech.

"I understand what I have observed," Tigh simply stated. "What I don't understand is the total lack of deception coming from you. Each of us has something to hide and there is always a degree of evasion when we talk with others, especially strangers."

"Wizards can't lie." Goodemer, once again, found all eyes on her.

"What do you mean—can't?" Jame asked, slowly.

"We take an oath on the staff of Hatliz, swearing that only the truth can be spoken by a Wizard."

"What happens if you don't speak the truth?" Jame frowned.

"We die," Goodemer returned with a shrug.

A shocked silence dropped over the chamber. All eyes shifted to Tigh.

"She's telling the truth," the warrior confirmed.

Jyac sat back, allowing a catlike grin to stretch across her features. "Well then. That changes everything. Welcome to Emoria, Goodemer. I think we may be able to help each other."

****

They heard the gathering crowd before rounding the last switchback and walking the final long incline to the fields above the city's south cliff. Unlike the tree-covered northern rim, an extended meadow spread away from the southern rim before it rose into the distant pale snowy peak.

Centuries-hardened sparring fields and archery ranges splotched the meadow outside of a well-kept ceremonial circle that was large enough to hold much of the population of Emor around its perimeter. Most Emorans' strongest memories were of events as witnesses or participants within the ceremonial circle. Whether in celebration or in mourning, whether receiving a first braid or witnessing a severe reprimand, it all happened on that high meadow.

The event that day was an uncommon occurrence in Emor—the first step in accepting an outsider into their society. In light of all that had happened since the challenges were made, the sixteen Emoran warriors were actually less apprehensive of their opponent than before. They had witnessed Tigh's formidable skill and control and they knew that they were as safe as lambs in a stable in a fight with her. The warriors looked forward to watching a master, and maybe picking up a few tricks in return.

Jame almost collided with Tigh when the warrior abruptly stopped. "What...?" Jame looked around her partner, eyes widening larger than Tigh's. "You're going to have a bit of an audience." Tigh scowled at Jame. The arbiter hid a smile behind a hand.

"Is this a good thing or a bad thing?" Tigh took a few steps away from the edge of the bluff, allowing Jame onto the grass.

"They're smiling and laughing. Sounds like a celebration to me." Jame grinned, feeling a joyful jolt through her body.

"But what are they celebrating?" Tigh raised an eyebrow.

"The initiation of a new member into the tribe." Jame almost laughed at Tigh's stunned expression. "The challenges are for you to prove your worth. You've done that in battle, no less. Now the challenges are to prove your solidarity with the other warriors."

"So I can have fun?" Tigh's face lit up.

Jame wrapped an arm around the warrior. "Have fun. Give them a show." Tigh's delighted grin was a gift that Jame treasured.

The groups of women shifted as Tigh and Jame strolled to the center of the circle where Jyac was in an animated discussion with Argis.

"Probably trying to figure out the order of challengers," Jame commented.

"Unless they've decided I take them all on at once." Tigh flashed innocent eyes at her.

"And why would they think of doing that?" Jame gave her partner a knowing look. Sighing at the guilty child expression that she could never resist, Jame just shook her head. "Warriors." She quickened her pace, missing Tigh's broad grin.

Jyac and Argis, noticing that the crowd had grown more hushed and the air dense with anticipation, glanced up to see Jame and Tigh strolling towards them.

"Are you going to tell them?" Argis asked in a low voice.

"I'd better in case there's trouble," Jyac sighed, not able to keep her eyes off the approaching warrior. In her black leather and armor Tigh exuded a strength and confidence that she could only hope her warriors emulated. Not that the Emoran warriors weren't the best fighters in the known world. They had no counterpart until the formation of the Guard. If they could learn the combat secrets of the Guard, they would be great and unstoppable. Jyac feared that these special skills were necessary to defeat their latest adversary.

"Good morning," Jame greeted cheerfully.

"Good morning." Jyac smiled back. "A good morning for a challenge or two or sixteen."

Argis and Tigh rolled their eyes. Jyac, a fearsome warrior in her day, understood the excitement and anticipation of meeting a fighter with a different and interesting technique. But she never passed up a chance to tease the warriors a bit about their occasional over-enthusiasm.

"I'm glad we were able to find a way of keeping the city entertained." Jame's voice twisted with irony as she glanced around the outer perimeter of the circle.

"Looks like we're going to get more than our wool trade worth," Argis' worried voice cut in. The others followed her gaze back towards the city. The Council, in full ceremonial garb of supple intricately embossed leather, was trampling across the meadow, faces set and determined.

"I thought you were going to talk to Gindor." Jame turned to her aunt.

"She wouldn't see me." Jyac shook her head. Why couldn't the meddlesome old women just let this one little breach of tradition be?

Within a heartbeat the only sound in the meadow was the breeze playing with the grass and the soft crackle underneath the Council members' boots. From long years of practice, the Council formed a ring around the foursome standing in the middle of the larger circle.

"That woman is not allowed to carry a sword in Emoria," Gindor announced, pointing to Tigh. "We have not accepted her presence here."

"I've had enough of this bothersome, daughter-of-a-shaggy-goat talk about tradition!" Every head whipped around as an angry Tas strode out from the crowd, rotating her sword with negligent skill. Gindor was too shocked to come up with a reaction before the indignant Tas stood tensely before her.

"You know better than to challenge the Council," Gindor, finally recovering, growled before seeing threescore warriors, including the challengers, emerge from the stilled onlookers, with swords drawn and ready to stand for what they thought was right over the Council's old-fashioned traditions.

Jame turned to her aunt, wondering why she wasn't surprised to see that Jyac was smiling.

Chapter
14

Gindor shook an accusing finger at Jyac. "You put them up to this to make it look like what was written in the Mysteries," the older woman croaked at her Queen.

"I did no such thing," Jyac bristled back. "Our warriors have enough sense to see when you are using tradition as an excuse."

Gindor glared at Jyac, then broke away from her place in the Council ring and strode angrily to her Queen. So threatening was her demeanor, Argis instinctively pulled her sword. Gindor ignored what she considered foolhardy behavior from the young warrior and concentrated her rage on Jyac.

"You dare speak to me about tradition?" Gindor's voice dropped low and menacing, her natural strength of presence trying to penetrate the rebellious resolve around her.

Jyac straightened, presenting a calm, controlled demeanor, trying to cast aside the trembling terror that unsettled her stomach and made her light-headed. Gindor had been her weapons master and the Elder's anger brought back memories of a young warrior in training. Not speaking until she was sure her voice was strong and steady, the Queen replied, "Traditions are created to protect our society from threat and from losing its identity. A princess taking a consort from outside the community only departs from tradition, it does not break any of our written laws. The law states that a princess must be joined in an Emoran ceremony, it does not forbid her from being joined in a ceremony of another culture. The fact that you refuse to acknowledge her joining doesn't make it any less real according to our laws. And the fact that you refused to approve her joining to an outsider doesn't make your words law. And as for the matter of bearing arms, I think that Tigh has proven that she is an asset rather than a threat to our society."

"The Council has the last word on the interpretation of the law," Gindor reminded her Queen. "Jame has brought a potential threat to our society by entering into a union with an unstable and menacing woman whose deeds are worse than any stories from the Book of Horrors. It is our responsibility to protect Emoran society. Especially when our people are sometimes too blind to see the true threat."

Jame moved so fast, even Tigh was caught by surprise. The arbiter was nose to nose with the startled Elder in a heartbeat. "Show me the proof that she is a threat. Tell me what you have heard in the last few years or seen in the last few days to support this accusation. You have no argument. I am an arbiter for the Southern Districts and Emoria, by treaty, is under my jurisdiction. Let me advise you, as your counsel, you have no case."

It was all of two heartbeats before the meadow erupted in deafening support for the impassioned princess. Argis stepped forward behind Jame's right shoulder. At the same time Tas strode through the opening in the Council's circle and stood behind Jame's left shoulder, their swords resting on their shoulders in a show of casual menace.

Keeping a steady eye on Jame, Gindor took a step back and folded her strong arms over her chest. The spectators fell into silence. After long heartbeats of studying the indignant princess she raised her eyes to Jyac. "Spoken like a true princess of Emoria." The large blue-gray eyes then returned to Jame. "You are right. We have no evidence against Tigh. Everything points to the fact that she has been fully cleansed and that she lives a life dedicated to peace and justice. The Council met last night and decided to accept Tigh into our society and recognize your joining, if you agree to an official Emoran joining before you leave our territory again."

Anger rushing through her, Jyac was tensed to confront Gindor when a hand wrapped around her arm. Whipping her head to one side, her resolve was stopped by a pair of steady blue eyes. Tigh gave a slight nod in Jame's direction. Her eyes told her that this was Jame's fight. Relaxing a little, Jyac returned her attention to her niece.

Jame's own anger wasn't much less than her aunt's, but her training taught her to capture that energy into carefully formed words rather than action. "Excuse me for being a little confused, but didn't you just say that you haven't accepted her presence here?"

"It's not official until we make the announcement." Gindor straightened.

Jame, knowing that the Council loved keeping everyone off balance, decided that this was one time they needed to be confronted with it. "I thank the Council for accepting Tigh into our society." She paused to give her next words the appropriate weight. "But I have a problem with the tactics you used today. You made the decision to allow Tigh Emoran rights, yet the first thing you did was to fling threats at everyone when all you had to do was make the announcement."

"You must see it from our point of view. You did not know of our decision, yet you were going against our law by letting a stranger to bear arms in Emoria. It doesn't matter that she wore a sword to fight for Emoria. She made the honorable decision to give up the sword after the battle but no one would accept it," Gindor explained, evenly. "The question of the joining may be more a part of tradition than law. The ban on strangers bearing arms in Emoria is law and no matter how silly it seems to enforce it sometimes, we have to continue to take it seriously. We needed to remind you that a law has been broken."

"Perhaps a less dramatic reminder next time might be wise," Jame gently suggested.

Gindor studied her, realizing for the first time that Jame did not fear her. It was rather refreshing to see. "Perhaps. We'll take your words under consideration." Raising her eyes to her Queen, her grim features transformed into a grin. "Now, Jyac. I think you have a challenge to oversee."

****

Goodemer, still pondering the curious scene involving the Council, followed Eiget to the other two strangers in Emoria. She was thankful to be encased in warm Emoran leathers since the chill of the morning was as cold as it ever got in Maymi. Eiget quietly explained what the confrontation with the Council was about and that the ensuing challenge was not a serious fight. "Warriors' idea of fun," was the way the taciturn guard put it.

Seeran and Gelder stood on the edge of the crowd gawking around like children at a summer revel. Tas, feeling good about her part in the little drama with the Council, sauntered by, then noticing Seeran, stopped a few paces away, keeping the historian in sight. Just as Goodemer and Eiget joined Seeran and Gelder, wild drumming started up, signaling that the challenge was about to begin.

Jame, Jyac and Ronalyn lounged in low chairs, slung with shaggy mountain goat skins, on a platform built of meadow stone. Tigh was on one side of the circle and the sixteen challengers casually stood on the opposite side. The low morning sun shimmered as the dew vaporized, casting the scene into an ethereal tableau.

"What's she doing?" Gelder nudged Seeran. Curious eyes were turned to Tigh and low murmurs of speculation filled the air. The warrior was tugging off her boots and neatly putting them aside. Eyes that strayed to Jame caught the arbiter throwing up her hands and appearing to be uttering some colorful phrases.

"I don't know. Maybe it's some Elite Guard ritual." Seeran shrugged.

Jyac stood and raised a hand. The women, not wanting to wait another heartbeat for the challenge to begin, were silenced by this signal. "Sixteen of our warriors have challenged Tigh of Ingor, partner of Jame, princess of Emoria, to a battle of skill. The rules of engagement have been agreed upon between the challengers and the challenged. Tigh of Ingor will take on all the challengers at once, in any fight formation chosen by the challengers." A shocked murmur rose and fell as Jyac waited. "The only weapons will be swords. Because there are sixteen challengers and only one challenged and the intent is to show skill and not to do harm, three touches of aggression will constitute a defeat."

The spectators exchanged incredulous looks. Surely Tigh would receive three blows before being able to strike sixteen three times over. Only those who witnessed her display against the Lukrians maintained a knowing silence.

Jyac nodded to Tigh and settled into the low-slung chair. The tall warrior's eyes shifted to her partner's. Jame glanced down at the bare feet, then raised an eyebrow at Tigh. A quirky grin flicked across the war-

rior's face and she shrugged. Jame shook her head a
little before yielding to her warrior with a grin. Tigh's
dazzling smile in return was enough for Jame to completely give in and let Tigh engage in what she considered fun. Even if it were fighting sixteen warriors at
once.

Tigh, feeling the cool, dewy grass against her bare
feet, strode to the center of the circle. The damp air
tickled her skin, waking up her body, opening her mind
to the thrill of balancing on the sharp edge of her warrior skills. Experienced eyes took in her adversaries,
reading much of their present state of mind by the language their bodies spoke. Instructing her own body,
she had to take their nervousness and relative inexperience into consideration to ensure that no serious inju-
ries happened on the field that day. Jame needed every
warrior to be whole and ready when they faced their
adversary in the mountains.

Eight warriors stepped forward and separated into
two lines of four with the intent of surrounding Tigh
once they were close enough. Tigh deliberately lifted
each of her feet, checking the soles, creating a break in
the warriors' concentration long enough for her to
sprint towards them. Just shy of entering the space
between the two groups, still only about three paces
apart, Tigh dove into a somersault and kicked both feet
out, collapsing the legs of the two closest warriors.

Just as swiftly, she was on her feet behind the warriors. Feeling a tap on her shoulder, a tall blonde
whirled her sword around only to have a pair of hands
slap against the flat of the blade. Her body caught off
balance by the unexpected jolt, the blonde sailed over
the black-clad warrior when Tigh leapt straight up and
shot both legs out parallel to the ground. The flying,
startled blonde released the blade, which was still
secure between Tigh's palms. The two warriors unfortunate enough to be behind the blonde were doubled over
from blows to their midsections.

With an arch of her back, Tigh was on her feet in time to whack the blades of the three remaining warriors with the hilt of the sword before flipping the sword into her hand and ducking. Four swords crashed above her as she rolled free, leaving the sword in the grass for its owner to claim.

The remaining eight warriors, recovering from the startling quickness with which their comrades received their first touches of aggression, let forth whoops and yodels as they rushed forward. Tigh flipped to her feet and ran towards the oncoming flashing swords. Catching a nice soft patch of dirt with her toes she catapulted into a single casual flip over them. Before they had a chance to turn around, she scuttled down the line, slapping each one on the arm, then plunged sideways, causing two warriors to ungracefully crash into each other.

The crowd shifted and strained to decipher what looked like a mad free-for-all as sixteen warriors chased and slashed at the capering former Elite Guard, teasing and slipping away from them like a fabled mountain sprite. Blades flashed and crashed and bare feet caused creative havoc and aching bruises. Blood sprayed from an unlucky nose, a mumbled apology lost as the crowd roared. One by one the warriors stepped away from the fray, one holding a leather rag to her nose, another limping, another flexing her hand. All were stunned by Tigh's unnatural fighting ability, her body whirling like a snow devil and as quick and unerring as a slick-coated panther.

The last three challengers facing the barefooted, aggravating, daughter of a shaggy goat realized that the honor of Emoria pressed mightily on their shoulders. Tigh took the slight breather to plop down onto the grass and pluck a small stone from the tough sole of her foot. The warriors, seeing their chance to give the inattentive Tigh her three blows at once, rushed forward, preparing to whack the black-clad warrior with the flat of their blades.

They ended up whacking each other and never saw the flying body that introduced their backs to the hard ground. The roaring crowd hushed as the three slowly climbed to their feet. Facing Tigh, they whipped their swords into a salute before turning and joining their fallen comrades. Tigh, having lost count of the touches of aggression, frowned with disappointment that the fight was over.

The tall warrior faced the platform with a hopeful expression on her face. "I forgot to use my sword. Can we do it again?"

The hiss of a sword sliding along a leather sheath was her answer. Whirling around she faced the warrior who dared challenge her skill.

****

Expecting Argis or Tas, Tigh had to quickly hide her surprise. Gindor stood ten paces away, casually twirling her sword, a mocking smile creasing the aging face.

"Let's show these baby lambs how to fight," Gindor purred, straightening to her full height, head and shoulders shorter than Tigh.

Jame and Jyac were on their feet but knew better than to interfere with the Elder. There was some laughter from the crowd but many remembered Gindor in her prime. She more than made up for her height with a fluid quickness and incomparable skill. The stories told of her encounters with brigands and skirmishes with the Lukrians bordered on exaggeration, yet the fear and respect she commanded was a legacy from that time.

Tigh did not laugh. She turned to the platform to gauge Jame's reaction to this challenge. The arbiter was clenching her fists, tensely watching her partner. Their eyes met briefly, but long enough to tell Tigh that she had to be careful with Gindor.

The former Guard's weapons instructors had been hardened veterans of wars, past what many considered their prime but still possessing the ability to push the younger, stronger warriors to exhaustion. Although still young, Tigh, a veteran of the most deadly war in several generations, was hardly a novice. Resting pale eyes on the older woman, Tigh slowly drew her black-bladed sword.

"We're both honorable warriors. We don't need rules of combat to have a nice friendly fight." The bold words rolled from Gindor as her eyes flashed with anticipation.

"As you wish." Tigh nodded, resting her blade against her shoulder.

Gindor strolled around the warrior and Tigh turned to follow her path. "That was quite a spectacle you just put on. Don't they teach warriors to stand up and fight anymore?"

"They taught us how to survive a fight with as little injury as possible." Tigh absently kicked up a small stone and caught it on the flat of her blade, bouncing it into the air a few times before bunting it away.

Gindor rushed forward with her sword raised only to clash with the black blade. The startled Elder hopped backwards. She had known Tigh would counter the blow, but she expected the tall warrior to at least be caught off-balance. The former Guard was both quick and unhurried at the same time, with no excess of movement. Gindor, narrowing her eyes, realized that Tigh put her opponents off-guard by pretending to get distracted away from the fight. Clever.

To test Tigh's handling of her weapon, Gindor traded a series of strokes with the tall warrior. Nice. The Elder nodded with approval. "Now do you think we can do something a little more fun without any fancy playing?"

"Play? Me?" Tigh pointed to herself with one hand, while flipping her sword in the other.

"Yes, you." Gindor almost laughed at the warrior-child as the meadow rang with an impressive flourish of parries and thrusts. Both warriors displayed an easy control over their art, working together in a smooth, deadly dance. Delicately probing for weak spots in technique and pushing the level of skill, they played with the melodies and the rhythms of their strokes. Reveling in the sweet joy of putting body and mind on a deadly edge, they grinned as their swords created new variations to dance to.

Tigh kept her mischievous streak in check, concentrating on simple sword work. She was impressed by the older woman's skill. Every stroke made it obvious that Gindor practiced regularly. Muscles bulging from strained arms and legs held as solidly as those of a warrior in her prime. The joy of battle glinted in Gindor's eyes as a wild grin brightened the usually dour features. Tigh was face to face with her own future. Too old to be a warrior. Having to give up something that was as much a part of her as her own soul. Not having the sharp reflexes to protect Jame.

Blinking, Tigh caught the surprise in Gindor's eyes as the Elder backed off from a parry. Looking down at her shoulder, the former Guard saw a rip in the leather between her light armor plates and a thin line of blood on the exposed skin. From the crowd's point of view it looked as if Tigh had skillfully deflected the side blow. But Gindor's blade had slipped through a half heartbeat before Tigh got her sword in place.

Straightening, Tigh flipped her blade in a respectful salute to Gindor, conceding defeat. A puzzled murmur wafted across the meadow, but the two warriors remained focused on each other.

"You have a strange sense of honor," Gindor commented.

"You drew first blood. The victory is yours," Tigh simply stated.

Gindor kept hold of the pale blue eyes for a bit longer. She didn't think that Tigh allowed the blow so the Elder could win. But she was curious about what caused the lapse in concentration. Even the strongest warrior had a weak spot. "You just beat sixteen warriors at once without even getting hit. How does an old woman like myself get in a nick like that one?" she asked in a voice meant only for Tigh to hear.

"You reminded me of my greatest fear," came the quiet answer.

"Growing old." Gindor nodded, knowingly.

"Not being able to protect Jame someday."

The Elder wasn't expecting that. She thoughtfully studied the tall warrior, now relaxed. "If you ever feel that time has come, don't be foolish and refuse to recruit a younger warrior for the job. Our history is filled with too much unnecessary tragedy because of a warrior's pride."

Tigh, puzzling out the kind of lecture that her grandmother loved to give, slowly sheathed her sword. Shaking her arms out, she finally settled her thoughts. "I hope that I will have the wisdom to do that when the time comes."

Gindor slowly nodded her head, then straightened and whipped her sword into a salute. "I think we should have had more confidence in Jame's ability to choose the right companion. Perhaps we were wrong to reject her choice based only on rumor and campfire stories. We cannot wander through our past to try a different path. We can only find a new path to follow into the future. I believe Emoria needs you and Jame to join us on that journey."

"Whatever path Jame takes, I'll follow," came the only truth that Tigh lived by.

****

Sometimes Tigh acted like a bashful child, especially after engaging in something that she knew Jame didn't quite approve of.   Jame found it endearingly sweet and she greeted her partner with a twinkling grin.

This inner child peeking through had caused Jyac to be both amused and perplexed by Tigh's antics. During the bout with Gindor, the Queen finally questioned Jame about it. Jame wasn't sure if her explanation put Jyac's mind at ease, but it at least gave insight into the tangled complexity of the former Elite Guard.

When the Guards recruited her, Tigh had been a sheltered, emotionally immature fifteen-year-old. As the oldest daughter, she was the heir to the Tigis dynasty and had been spoiled and coddled by those wanting to be in her favor. Although Tigh possessed an aptitude for scholarship and was on the verge of rebelling against being a merchant, the social dynamics of her life were woven into her psyche from birth. Jame did not begrudge Tigh's belated discovery of the child she was never allowed to be as a youngster, but accepted it for the precious gift it was.

Around them, women gathered in chatty knots while others followed the persistent drumming and wound braids of rhythmic dances across the meadow. Once the challenge was officially over the atmosphere quickly dissolved into a festival in honor of the newest member of the tribe.

Wrapping her arms around her sweat-soaked warrior, Jame let the knowledge that she wouldn't ever have to choose between Tigh and Emoria spread a warm feeling through her soul. She felt the old injury that had ached through the years heal with barely a scar. Chuckling to herself, she realized that all the carefully worded arguments and pleas she had composed for her ultimate confrontation with the Council had been a waste of mental energy. Sometimes her partner's way was better. Sometimes.

Jame looked up into affectionate azure eyes. "Good work," she softly praised, coaxing a dazzling smile from the warrior. "I suppose they want you to play with them some more." Jame's eyes sparkled as Tigh sheepishly shrugged.

"You don't mind?" Tigh bent down and brushed her lips against Jame's irresistible cheek.

"I'm delighted that they've accepted you," Jame murmured back, soaking in the warrior's closeness.

"They want me to show them a few fancy moves, then they'll drag me off to the tavern," Tigh breathed into her ear.

"Emoran ale is stronger than most," Jame gently warned. "According to legend, it's distilled from the souls of ancient Emoran warriors."

"You have such quaint traditions," Tigh chuckled.

"I'm sure Ingor has its share of quirky customs." Jame casually inspected the sword cut on Tigh's arm. The shallowness of the wound was a tribute to Gindor's control and skill.

"It's just a nick."

"My idea of a nick has never quite agreed with yours." Jame grazed her warrior with an affectionate glance. "But I have to agree on this one. Your sleeve, however, is a different tale." The arbiter flicked the torn leather flap.

"One of the hazards of being a warrior," Tigh deadpanned. "Hard on the wardrobe."

Looking past Tigh, Jame saw the three guests of Emoria breaking from a knot of women and trudging across the grass towards them. A faintly puzzled expression creased her brow as she noticed Tas strolling next to Eiget. "That's strange." Tigh turned to see what had caught Jame's attention, then turned back to her partner for enlightenment. "What's Tas up to?"

Tigh returned her gaze to the bantam warrior, seeing something familiar in the furtive glances cast in Seeran's direction. "It's a warrior thing." She shrugged.

Jame whipped suspicious eyes around to her innocent-eyed partner. "Warrior thing?" the arbiter repeated.

"I'll explain later," Tigh muttered as Seeran, Gelder and Goodemer stepped within listening range.

"Tonight. If you're not too drunk." Jame's knowing look was met with mock indignation. "Yes, you," she laughed before turning to the others. "Did you enjoy the challenge?"

"I feel so honored. So honored," Seeran stammered out. Her training had prepared her to be an impartial observer and chronicler with emphasis on the word impartial, but she was so attracted to the Emoran society that the historian became lost in her purely personal reactions. "It's like being caught in the time of legends and myths."

Jame laughed. "Emoria is hardly mythical. We like to call it Paradise with Wasps."

"That's because of our tendency to greet newcomers with the sting of the sword," Tas, standing nearby, put in.

"I feel fortunate that I was spared such a greeting." Seeran grinned at the amiable warrior. Tas, feeling a jolt of confidence, stepped next to the historian.

"If you'd like, I'd be honored to explain some more of our traditions to you." Tas scuffed the toe of her boot into a soft patch of dirt, her eyes trained on the puffs of dust. This action alone caused Jame and Tigh to exchange a quick glance. The greatest foe of a warrior's boldness was the emotion of the heart.

"The honor would be mine." Seeran felt an uncharacteristic shyness as she puzzled at Tas' strange bashfulness. She was surprised at her pleased reaction to the quick grin and sparkling eyes of the compact warrior.

"If you don't mind, I'd like to visit the stables. Kas promised me she'd let me help with the horses," Gelder spoke up hesitantly.

"Take that as a compliment." Jame smiled at her. "Kas is very particular about who she lets near those beasts."

"Give Gessen a few extra strokes," Tigh quietly requested. "I'll try to visit her tomorrow."

"I'll make sure she's nice and shiny." Gelder grinned as she excitedly trotted away.

"I'd better get over there." Tigh nodded at the cluster of warriors watching her with expectant eyes. "See you later." She pulled Jame into a one-armed hug and strode towards the now-grinning group of warriors.

Tas and Seeran had already wandered off, leaving Jame and Goodemer watching with amusement as two lines of dancers nearly collided when their movements grew more enthusiastic.

"Would you like to join me for a bite to eat?" Jame asked the reserved Wizard.

"Only if I can try some of that interesting-looking Ingoran cuisine."

"I'll send someone to fetch the food," Jame agreed amiably. "I don't want to miss Tigh playing with the warriors."

Chapter 15

"This is it," Argis slurred. Tigh held the torch as Argis felt for the hidden door latch in the intricately carved wall blocking their way.

"I can't believe we're doing this," Mularke muttered before taking a nip from a half-full skin.

"Got it." Argis straightened and pulled on one of several carved handholds. As the stone slowly pivoted to reveal an opening, a puff of cool stale air touched their senses.

Tigh held the torch into the deep blackness of the opening. "You've been in here before?"

"When I was young," Argis clarified. "Tas and I stumbled on it when we were looking for somewhere to hide after we put indigo in the ceremonial waterfall."

"You two were in so much trouble for that," Mularke drunkenly giggled.

Tigh cast an amused eye back at the Emoran warrior. "What was Jame doing at the time?"

"She, uh, masterminded the plot." Argis grinned.

"And got you to actually do it." Tigh shook her head before stepping into the long-forgotten chamber. It was a good size with the walls extending far beyond the light from the torch. Sniffing the air, Tigh detected an unexpected freshness and water. "What do you remember of this cave?"

"Not much, except that it was large and dark." Argis shrugged, wandering around within the range of the torchlight. "It's a nice cave. I wonder why we've never used it?"

Tigh dug the toe of her boot into the sandy ground, noticing a darker color just beneath the surface. "Water. Probably floods."

Mularke nodded as she took fire from Tigh's torch with a taper that all Emorans carried and lit a small oil lamp she had picked up in the outer corridor. "The water that feeds Laur's waterfalls is on the other side of that wall."

Tigh illuminated the craggy wall. Her quick eyes picked up a set of markings that did not look natural.

"What's that?" Argis stumbled over to the markings and peered at the circular design. Tigh ran a finger over the brown substance. It didn't smudge or rub off.

"Wizard marks," Tigh muttered. Mularke joined them, putting a chin on Argis' shoulder as she stared at the design. "This is where the illusion in the Temple was created."

The three warriors allowed the words to penetrate their ale-soaked brains. "That means the enemy..." Mularke's unfinished statement hung in the cavern as the trio lost consciousness.

****

Jame stepped into her chamber and immediately sensed that Tigh wasn't there. The low fire crackling in the fireplace was the only noise that reached her ears. It was late—closer to dawn than dusk. She had spent the evening learning about Goodemer and their enemy, gathering together as much knowledge as possible for her to present her case. That was how she approached the daunting responsibility of leading the Emorans to a victory against the Wizard in the mountains. She decided to prepare the facts and evidence as if she were putting together a defense. After all, she had never lost a case.

Sighing, she ran a hand through her hair, frowning at the empty bed. She knew she wouldn't be able to sleep knowing that Tigh was probably passed out somewhere. Tavern first. If Tigh wasn't there, she could follow the trail. Emor had a discreet, well-organized security, so much so that it was difficult to move around the city without being observed.

Walking into the tavern and an odorous cloud of stale ale and leather, Jame stepped around passed-out warriors and avoided the wild uncontrolled movements of the few who hung onto consciousness. The long tables were tightly packed together and Jame took her time peeking under the furniture and into the darkened corners of the domed cavern.

Not seeing her warrior, she approached the bar where a battle-hardened white-haired woman was cleaning up for the night. "Have you seen Tigh?"

Teniar, the tavern keeper, glanced up from her task, then recognizing Jame, straightened. "My princess," she murmured in a voice made rough from years of barking orders to novice warriors. "She was here all night. These young pups couldn't get enough of her. Bragging about how she busted their shaggy-goated noses or flipped them onto their worthless behinds."

"The ale flowed pretty freely?" Jame arched an eyebrow.

"They were pressing drink on her all night." Teniar waved a scarred hand. "But between us, I noticed that she'd slide every other full mug in the direction of one of her table mates."

Jame frowned at this. "So she wasn't falling down drunk when she left?"

The tavern keeper scratched her nose in thought. "She left with Argis and Mularke, if I recall. They'd been having some kind of discussion about hidden caves around the city. Argis was drunk but no worse than usual. Mularke was stumbling around a bit, but that's Mularke. Tigh seemed to be in a relaxed state, the most sober of the three, I think."

"How long ago did they leave?" Jame felt a chill that had nothing to do with the cool night air wafting through the open tavern doors.

"Let me think." Teniar frowned. "It was probably about one mark on the sand glass."

Jame squinted at the tall sand clock behind the bar. "That was about two marks ago. Do you have any idea where they could have gone?"

"Not really. But, by the sound of their discussion, it seemed as if they were going somewhere specific," the tavern keeper mused. "You know how focused warriors can get. Just add a bit of ale and you have them making bets on who can hit Laur's eye at two hundred paces in the dark. And they can't live another heartbeat unless they meet the challenge."

"If they went off on some crazy warrior bet two sand marks ago, they'd be finished by now." Jame shook her head and smiled at the tavern keeper. "Thank you, Teniar."

"They probably couldn't stop betting." Teniar cast a sympathetic eye at the princess.

"It's hard to get them to stop once they get started." Jame nodded before stepping into the quiet square. She concentrated on the silence, opening up her senses like Tigh taught her to. A movement near the Temple caught her attention. Staring into the deep shadows she saw two struggling women holding each other up.

Without thinking, her feet started moving and when she was close enough, she recognized Argis and Mularke. Their sober, pain-filled expressions told Jame that their condition wasn't from drunkenness.

Breaking into a trot, the arbiter got to them in time to stop Argis from pitching forward.

"Jame," the miserable warrior rasped. "It's our fault. We're so sorry. So sorry." Argis sank to her knees, sobbing, breaking the old code that warriors never cried.

"What happened?" Jame managed to push sound through her suddenly arid throat.

Trembling, Mularke put a hand on Argis' shoulder to steady her own weak body. "We were showing Tigh a cave. A close one just beneath the Temple. We found some strange markings—Wizard markings, according to Tigh. The next thing we knew we were waking up and Tigh was gone."

Panic and fear crashed through Jame's mind, making her lightheaded. But she couldn't give in to it. Tigh was in trouble. "Guards!" she shouted, knowing she had to do something, even if it was too late to stop whoever had taken her warrior.

Several footfalls came from different directions. "What happened?" Jame looked up, surprised to hear Tas' voice.

"We think Tigh's been captured," Jame said steadily, focusing on what needed to be done at that moment. She could give in to despair later. "Mularke will tell you where they were when this happened. Get two squads of scouts and try to find out how whoever took her got into the cave and follow where they went."

One of the guards ran to a heavy bell outside the barracks and pulled back a metal shaft suspended on rope. Letting the shaft go, it shot into the bell and bounced several times, sending a deep rumble through the city. Several other guards ran into the barracks shouting, "Rouse the scouts, no time to lose!"

Tas helped Jame get Argis back onto her feet. "She and Mularke need to see a healer," Jame said softly. Tas nodded at a young eager-looking guard to take charge of Mularke.

In a matter of heartbeats, the square was filled with torches and scouts, pulling on leathers and weapons. Shouted commands quickly brought order to the chaos as the leaders of two squads of scouts approached Jame for instructions.

Jame explained to them what had happened and the location of the cave. "Be careful. Approach everything as if it were a deception, from the solid rock wall to the ground you step on. If anything is covered by only illusion, that will break it." Pausing in thought, she turned to a wiry curly-haired guard with alert eyes. "Go wake Goodemer. We need her here." The guard, grinning at being given a special task, sprinted to the palace. "If the passage out of the cavern is hidden by a spell, Goodemer will find it. Stay alert, they can take you down in a heartbeat with darts covered with a potion." The scouts nodded their understanding, having heard about the effects of the potion from their three comrades who found Jame.

As the scouts stormed through the Temple door, Jame was momentarily alone. It took every bit of strength she had to keep the tears, pooling in her eyes, and a dark despair wrapping a thick fog around her mind, from taking over. Tigh was in trouble and Jame wouldn't rest until her warrior was safely back with her.

****

The first things Tigh noticed were that her hands were bound in front of her instead of in back and that the pallet she was lying on was filled with down rather than straw. A slight movement of her legs told her that her feet were loosely tied together. Absent was the dank chill of a cavern or the stale, unwashed odors of a prison cell. Muffled voices touched her ears. Concentrating on the sound, she realized that one of the voices was Meah. Tigh could tell by her tone that the rogue Guard was irritated.

Meah, Tigh sighed. She was in trouble. Her foggy mind drifted to how she was captured. Jame was going to kill her for being so careless. At least Argis and Mularke wouldn't be mistreated because the Lukrians wanted their people released.

Through a slightly opened eye, Tigh quickly assessed that she was in a tidy chamber. The furnishings suggested that it was a private sitting room. Determining that she was alone, she allowed both eyes to open. A fire wanly burned in a stone fireplace, giving off enough light to illuminate a puzzle that kept getting more and more confusing. She tensed at the sound of footfalls.

"Misner is tired of hearing about your people." Meah's voice was suddenly distinct and close. Tigh squinted at the door, realizing that the wood was too thin to stop sound from coming through. Meah and whomever she was talking to must have just entered the neighboring chamber.

"What kind of honor does this Wizard have that she won't let us get our warriors out of the hands of the enemy?" a weary yet strong voice responded to Meah's words. It was the voice of a leader, steady and confident.

"She doesn't care about your quaint sense of honor." Tigh could hear the scowl in Meah's voice. "There is only one thing she wants right now."

"The great warrior, Tigh." It sounded like an old argument. "We deliver Tigh, Misner delivers Emoria to us."

"Your honor will be more than restored when you have the Emorans bowing at your feet," Meah purred.

"Misner must be patient. Now that the Emorans know that we can enter their city unseen, they're on extra alert. Tigh is rarely where we can easily capture her." The warrior in question was impressed by how

the Lukrian carefully worded her statement so it wasn't
a lie. "I still don't understand how Misner can deliver
Emoria to us and not be able to capture Tigh herself."

The soft pacing of boots replaced words for several
heartbeats. "Misner has a tendency to treat people like
sheep." Was there a trace of bitterness in Meah's
voice? "I guess she didn't think you'd figure out that
little inconsistency."

"Go on," the other woman prompted.

The sigh from Meah sounded genuine enough, but
Tigh would have given anything to see the rogue
Guard's face. "What I'm about to tell you must not be
told to any one. I'm risking my place in Misner's circle
by saying this to you. But you need to know it to follow her orders without question." Meah hesitated for a
heartbeat. "Misner's magic doesn't work on Tigh."

The shock of the words to Tigh was like being hit in
the head with her own sword. Several blank pieces of
the puzzle suddenly gained meaning and slipped into
place.

"What do you mean—'doesn't work'?" The
Lukrian was naturally incredulous of this idea.

"Many years ago, Tigh was sent to kill Misner,"
Meah's resigned voice began. "She somehow was able
to fight through the Wizard's magic. Misner became so
weak that she barely escaped with her life. To get
away, she created one final illusion of her death at
Tigh's hands. It took her many long years to recover
from what Tigh did to her."

Tigh didn't notice the long silence as the Lukrian
weighed the veracity of the seemingly outrageous tale.
She pulled out the memories of that horrific encounter
on the Umvian plains. Slipping the explanation into the
holes left by the ensuing questions of how she defeated
the Wizard, she realized that her mentors had tried to
pull something out of her that she didn't know she possessed. She had no doubt that she had defeated Mis-

ner's magic, but it was through a warrior's belief that anything could be defeated with enough savage force.

"Tigh was a Guard then. Surely that power has been cleansed from her," the Lukrian reasoned.

"Five Guards possessing power and skill equal to Tigh's were easily defeated by Misner." Meah's voice was a little distant. One of the five had been the rogue Guard's lover. Tigh wondered if Misner was aware of this. "Misner believes that whatever defeated her had nothing to do with the Guard enhancements."

"Why hasn't Tigh just confronted her and stopped her?" the Lukrian countered.

"Tigh doesn't know how she defeated Misner." Meah's voice betrayed her amusement. "She thinks she killed her by whacking her head off."

"All right. Your explanation is outrageous enough to probably be true," the Lukrian slowly accepted. "I can see why Misner wants Tigh out of the way."

"Her patience has been stretched much farther than she likes." The cold warning was back in Meah's voice. "She wants Tigh. Do everything you can to deliver her. Soon."

Soft footfalls faded away, leaving Tigh focused intently on the silence. Long moments passed and then the door slowly opened.

****

As Jame watched Goodemer wander around the cavern muttering words that didn't sound encouraging, she felt an inexplicable pang of disappointment. Shaking her head, she realized that she had hoped that Goodemer would enter the cavern and in an impressive, colorful display, tear down Misner's illusions so the scouts had a chance to rescue Tigh. The methodical study of the markings and the casual poking of odd places in the rocky wall grated on Jame's heightened anxiety. Too many sand marks had passed for hope of catching Tigh's abductors.

Tas strode into the cavern, taking in the scene with a faint air of puzzlement. "Argis and Mularke are all right," she reported to Jame. "Aggie said that the combination of the alcohol and whatever knocked them out might take a while to wear off."

Jame mutely nodded her head, eyes returning to Goodemer. Tas gave her old friend a worried look. When they were children they could always tell how upset Jame was by how quiet she got. Her observation that Jame was Tigh's whole life seemed to go both ways. Sighing, the warrior thought back on her own evening. Never in her life had she just sat and listened to someone for endless sand marks without getting bored or falling asleep. What was more surprising, she had been so captivated by her talkative companion that she felt a strange loneliness just a few heartbeats after leaving Seeran's company.

"Clever, clever." Jame and Tas focused on the placid Wizard.

"What?" Jame could no longer hold in her frustration.

Goodemer blinked at her audience. "Several spells have been woven together in such a way that an attempt to unravel one weaves the other spells tighter." Pursing her lips she ran a strong hand over a rough patch of rock. "It's a rather clumsy weave, but works well enough." Goodemer's eyes had a wicked glint in them as she wrapped a hand around her wolf's head amulet. Soundless words formed on her lips as the head of the wolf incandesced for a scarce heartbeat. "If this is any indication of Misner's abilities, I don't think we have much to worry about."

A yawning darkness replaced the rugged wall in front of them. The astonished scouts had their hands on their belt knives before observing the grinning Wizard.

"You did it." Jame felt the weight of uncertainty about the young Wizard's ability tumble away. She and Tas rushed to the newly revealed tunnel.

Goodemer, peering into the darkness, soaked up the essence of the oddly flat air. Frowning, she held her amulet out in front of her, concentrating on the sensations that tingled through her fingers. "She makes up for clumsy weaving with excessive redundancy."

"Huh?" Tas blinked at the Wizard as Jame rolled her eyes.

"She means that Misner has compensated for her less than perfect spell weaving skills by repeating the weave within the tunnel," Jame explained patiently.

"Oh." Tas knitted her brow. "You mean she leaves a little trap like this every so often in the tunnel?"

"Excessively so," Goodemer sighed.

"Then how do the Lukrians get through?" Jame peered into the dim opening in the wall.

"All they need is a token that acts as a key so they can pass through without breaking the spells." Goodemer rubbed her chin, her mind analyzing the technique behind the weave of the magic.

"Exactly how excessive are these spells?" Jame cocked her head at the Wizard, realizing there was a reason for Goodemer's pensive behavior.

"Hundreds I would say," the Wizard mused. "And they have to be unraveled one at a time. Sometimes superior skill isn't all it takes to beat another Wizard, especially if that Wizard is clever like Misner."

"So Misner is not a proficient Wizard?" It was Jame's turn to ponder the possibilities.

"If this spell is any indication, I would guess her skills to be mediocre at best." Goodemer rubbed a fingertip on the wolf's head, reconfirming her original opinion of the spell.

"Then why would the Northern Territories ask her to create a rival warrior to the Guards?"

"She was probably the only Wizard who agreed to do such a thing." Goodemer shrugged. "It's against our covenant to engage in actions that do physical or mental harm. If we allowed that kind of behavior, no one would trust us to do our traditional work. To ensure that we cannot deceive those we are helping, we take the vow of truth. We would die on the spot if we attempted a deception. Wizards like Misner are cast-offs from our society. They deal in deception so they never have to worry about not telling the truth."

Anxious footfalls pounded in the outer corridor and they turned in time to see Poylin skid on the fine, powdery sand. Stepping forward, the scout handed Jame a long, heavy object loosely wrapped in soft leather. "This was delivered to the Northern outpost by a shepherd on horseback."

Pulling away the leather, Jame gasped. It was Tigh's sword. A piece of parchment, held in place by a thin strip of leather, was wrapped around the hilt. Taking a deep breath to steady her trembling hands Jame pulled the tie loose and removed the parchment. Handing the sword to Tas, she deliberately unrolled the stiff scrap.

The others watched intently as Jame's nervousness turned to puzzlement. A single word was elegantly traced, signed by an equally graceful solitary letter. Unexpected yet intriguing pieces hovered over significant parts of the puzzle that was their enemy.

****

The woman thoughtfully studying the prone warrior was tall and possessed a battle-hardened body. Like the Emorans, she was encased in a patchwork of red leather and armor that covered as much of her body as not. Absently running a powerful hand through white-streaked auburn hair, she eased onto a low-slung chair several paces from Tigh.

"If I'd known Meah was going to toss that little shock bomb at me, I would have chosen a different place for our conversation." The Lukrian's voice hinted at a gnawing frustration. "Perhaps it's for the best. I'm Kylara, by the way. Regent-General of Lukria."

"Why didn't you turn me over to Meah?" Tigh's voice was raw from the potion that was still playing havoc with her alertness.

"Because you're the only one who can convince the others that I'm telling the truth." Kylara rested inscrutable hazel eyes on the former Guard.

"Others...?" Tigh prompted.

"Emorans." The Lukrian was a study in weary resignation.

"What truth?"

Kylara contemplated the former Guard for long heartbeats. "The truth about how I made a decision that led my people to be used by an insane Wizard. I was in the Regulars." Tigh's eyebrow shot up in surprise. "We interact with the outside world a little more than the Emorans and we've never been above fighting in the major wars. Anyway, I was the leader of the Gold Corps under Meah's command."

"You were in the battle of Halt," Tigh whispered as shadowy memories of that horrific night battle assaulted her tired mind.

"Yes." Kylara nodded wearily. "Several moons ago, Meah showed up here in Lukria. She told us that a Wizard in the mountains had heard that the Emorans were planning to invade our territory and that she would help us fight them off for a few favors in return. Originally, these favors were to help train the small army the Wizard was building. A defense force, she called it, nothing more. To keep people from wandering too near to the Wizard's stronghold."

"The rumors were already abroad by then that she was building an army to re-take the Southern Territories," Tigh mused.

"We are sometimes cursed by our isolation. We rarely hear rumors until long after they have run their course," Kylara sighed. "Shortly after we agreed to help, Meah came to us with another offer. She said if we did everything that the Wizard asked, she would deliver Emoria to us. We told her that we would never accept a territory that we hadn't fought for. We were assured that the Wizard would do enough to enable us to capture Emoria on our own. We agreed." The Lukrian flicked an apologetic eye at Tigh. "Many traditions are too strong to give up, even long after their foundations have crumbled and washed away. We have been at odds with Emoria since before our written history. The idea of finally defeating them in battle is as much a part of our life as the blood in our bodies."

"She wanted you to raise money for her army," Tigh guessed. Kylara flashed a startled look at the former Guard. "You were selling everything you could get your hands on. When Misner showed you how to enter Emor undetected, you stole things that wouldn't be immediately missed but would bring in a great deal of money. Like Emoran ceremonial swords."

The Lukrian nodded. "You did more in Balderon than just rescue your scouts. It was frustrating, but we were sworn to our bargain with Misner. We first sent our scholars into Emor to read their Mysteries. I had gotten used to Guard mind games during the war and convinced our Council that mentally breaking down the Emorans would ensure victory against them. Your Council destroyed that deception when they escaped."

"The deception was broken before that," Tigh clarified. "We saw through the army in the meadow."

The Regent-General slowly nodded. "We were wondering what went wrong."

"So why am I here?" Tigh shifted a little.

"We're being used by a Wizard who has no honor," Kylara stated softly. "She wanted to continue the silly mind game instead of exchanging your Council for the prisoners. We began to question our alliance with this person."

"She didn't allow you to free the prisoners through the tunnels." Tigh nodded.

"You have no idea how frustrating it's been not to be able to reach them." Kylara shook her head. "Now we've learned that Misner is moving her army to Balderon valley. She has this insane plan to take over the Southern Territories—starting with Balderon. As far as she's concerned, only one obstacle stands in her way. You."

Tigh pondered this for several heartbeats. "So she used your traditional animosity towards the Emorans and my relationship to Jame to draw me here."

"Yes." Kylara nodded. "It took me a long time to figure out what she was really after." The Regent-General straightened and rose to her feet. "We have been dishonored by our dealings with this insane Wizard. Our only honorable path is to destroy Misner." Whipping out her knife, she cut the rope between Tigh's hands. "Our paths lie together."

Chapter 16

Dark, restless flashes of deep fears and horrors relentlessly subverted a tranquil sleep. The subconscious mind gave way to desperate images as Jame fought the growing anxiety... Something was tickling her cheek.

Her arm flew up in reflex only to be caught in a gentle but firm grip. Eyes popping open, it took just a half-heartbeat for her restive dream to vanish. She had her arms wrapped around her warrior, squeezing so tight that Tigh grunted. The low chuckling in her ear revealed a good mood, meaning hope.

Pulling back, Jame looked into gentle, affectionate eyes. "How...?"

Tigh glanced in the direction of the door and nodded. A stranger, in Emoran leathers, stood watching them. "That's Kylara, Regent-General of Lukria."

"What?" Jame pulled away from Tigh and gave the stranger her full attention. Slipping off the bed, the arbiter approached the leader of the traditional enemy of Emoria. She absently smoothed down her leathers, having simply collapsed onto the bed fully-clothed

early that morning. The Lukrian stood tall but her eyes
sparked like a skittish horse.

"Well met, Kylara." Jame bowed her head. "Thank
you for returning Tigh's sword and for your note."

"Well met, Jame." Kylara, relaxing a little, gave
the arbiter a deep bow. "I was hoping you'd be able to
understand the note. I couldn't risk writing down too
much. At least not until I talked with Tigh."

"Note?" Tigh strolled up next to her partner.

"Kylara sent a note with your sword." Jame turned
to her. "It had the word 'truce' and the letter 'K' on it."

"Did you show it to anyone else?" Tigh asked.

"I showed it to Jyac. She was wary but struggled to
keep an open mind." Jame faced the Lukrian. "Come,
let's sit down. I think we have some things to discuss."
Jame pointed to the pair of chairs in front of the fireplace.

Tigh went to rummage through their saddlebags for
some herbs to brew a much-needed mug of tea. Bringing the fire back to life, she set a heavy kettle full of
water on a shelf in the fireplace.

The Lukrian warrior cleared her throat and settled
into the chair. Her weariness was now from simple
exhaustion rather than bearing the weight of leading her
people to dishonor. She quickly realized that it was her
good fortune that the Emorans choose a worldly arbiter
to lead the campaign against Misner. "Thank you for
allowing me to present my case."

"That's my job." Jame smiled, flashing an amused
glance at Tigh, who was sitting cross-legged on the
hearth waiting for the water to boil.

"And that's the only reason that I feel that this may
work," Kylara stated as she held Jame's eyes.

"Just remember. By speaking to me, you have put
yourself in my care. It is my sworn duty as a peace
arbiter to defend your case and it is Tigh's sworn duty
as a peace warrior to protect you," Jame explained, settling into her accustomed job with surprising relief.

The Lukrian chuckled. "I had forgotten about that. It's hard to see beyond the Emoran princess."

"I understand. And thank you, by the way, for releasing Argis and Mularke and returning Tigh unharmed." Jame reached for the steaming mug that Tigh was offering and handed it to Kylara. Taking her own mug, she settled back into the chair. "Now why don't you tell me why you're here."

Kylara was surprised by how many details Jame had gently prodded from her during the course of her narrative. It was as difficult to hold the truth from Jame as it was from Tigh. Many of her fears and concerns that she had kept to herself tumbled from her tongue before she could catch them. In the end, she realized that she had entrusted this daughter of her ancestral enemy with her honor and her life.

An expectant silence settled over them as the last of Kylara's words seeped into the thick rock walls. Jame's brain raced as she chased after the best way of presenting Kylara to Jyac and the Council. Then she mentally banged her head on the wall. Like the Regent-General of Lukria, she was having problems getting past the Emoran princess. This wasn't any different than any other arbitration case. "I will write up your statement and present it to Jyac. We don't have much time to waste so it might be best if I can convince her to at least be reasonable before arranging a meeting between you. You and Tigh..."

Three sets of eyes were riveted on the door. A gentle rap was quickly followed by the scraping of wood against stone, rapidly displaced by the hiss of steel against leather. Jame rolled her eyes upward to whatever divine imp oversaw her destiny and shook her head.

****

Argis sensed the stranger before she actually saw her and the sword was in her hand, ready to defend her princess to the death if need be. Poised to strike, her eyes darted from Jame to Tigh, then to the stranger, all of whom were frozen and staring at her.

"Put the sword down, Argis." Jame's tolerant voice penetrated her confusion.

"Who is she and how did Tigh escape?" Argis remained tense.

Jame glanced at Tigh. The black-clad warrior rose from her place on the hearth and strode to Argis. A quick jab to the Emoran's wrist and the sword hit the woven mud catcher in front of the door with a thud.

"Why don't you come and keep our visitor company while I write up her statement?" Jame evenly requested as she rose from her chair.

"What's going on?" Argis demanded, exasperated. "Who is this...?" Suddenly getting a good look at the other woman, Argis made a dive for her sword, but Tigh beat her to it. The former Guard backed away, casually flipping the sword and wagging a finger at the Emoran.

"This is Kylara, Regent-General of Lukria. She is also in my protective custody." Jame remained calm and steady, knowing that Tigh could keep Argis under control if necessary.

Anger and confusion chased each other across Argis' face. "What's she doing here?" she finally sputtered.

"She's here to call a truce between Lukria and Emoria and to help us defeat Misner," Jame explained steadily.

"Truce? And you believe her?" Argis was beyond exasperated.

"Yes," came a calm voice next to her. Argis whipped around to face the warrior she had learned to call friend. "Jame could win any case she argued using her compelling personality alone, but she refuses to take a case unless whoever she defends is truly innocent of what they've been accused of. Fortunately, I can help her with that. Kylara is sincere in wanting a truce."

"Kylara let you and Mularke go when, by right, she should have taken you prisoner," Jame reasoned. "She returned Tigh's sword instead of keeping it as a badge of honor. And she wrote a note accompanying the sword that conveyed her wish to call a truce. She had the opportunity to turn Tigh over to Meah and did not take it. Do you know what she would have gotten in return for that simple act?" Argis, staring dumbfounded at her, shook her head. "Misner promised to deliver Emoria to the Lukrians."

"What?" Argis rasped.

"And we know Misner could have done it, given her ability to penetrate Emor with ease," Jame reminded her. "So why don't you sit here and let Kylara talk to you?"

"She's the enemy, Jame." If it had been difficult for Argis to accept Tigh as a decent human being, it was impossible to think of Lukrians as anything other than spawn of the underworld.

"Why?" Jame ambled over to Argis and crossed her arms.

"What do you mean, 'why'?" The warrior ran a frustrated hand through her hair. When did the certainties in her life suddenly become so complicated?

"Why are the Lukrians the enemy?" Jame repeated calmly, then put up a hand before Argis could say anything. "Think about it. We've been skirmishing for years, but can anyone remember why?" Jame paused, letting her irresistible voice mesmerize the warrior. "Isn't it time to leave behind that which has been long forgotten? We have a chance to defeat Misner and gain a valuable ally. Should we turn our backs on this opportunity because of something that happened countless generations ago? Or should we show that we have grown as a society, and put aside petty disputes for the

greater good of the world at large? Because that's what
this is all about. Once again, Emoria has a chance to
save the world from a powerful, ruthless force. It'll be
the Kuntic wars all over again, with a new Hekolatis
rising up to stand beside the old. But we can't hope to
succeed without the help of the Lukrians." Jame turned
to Kylara, who was just as entranced by Jame's words
as Argis was. "Our animosity towards the Lukrians is
traditional."   The arbiter turned back and captured
Argis' eyes. "We've spent the last few days liberating
some of our traditions from Emoria's dusty foundation.
This can be the dawn of a new age for Emoria. But we
must have the strength and courage to make it happen."

Having had her say, Jame looked around at her
audience. Argis and Kylara appeared to be stunned.
Tigh was grinning broadly. Jame couldn't help but
return the grin.

"I've got to think about this," Argis muttered to the
floor.

Jame took the stupefied warrior by the arm and led
her to the chair. Kylara followed both with her eyes,
not relaxing until Argis settled back. "Kylara, this is
Argis, Master Warrior. Chat a bit while I prepare the
statement."

As Jame backed away, Tigh took her place on the
fire hearth, pouring another cup of tea. The Emoran
warrior and the Lukrian leader eyed each other for long
heartbeats.

"So," Argis finally breathed, "tell me why you're
going against Misner."

****

Pride. It was a strong, satisfying feeling. Especially in a situation so volatile that a single, minor
action could undermine the spell that Jame had cast
upon the hushed crowd gathered around the ceremonial
circle as the day faded into night. Standing straight and

unmoving, Jyac swept her eyes around the transfixed women as the last of Jame's ardent plea floated away on the gusts of the evening breeze.

After long heartbeats, Jyac stepped forward next to her niece. Jame's eyes blinked with astonishment at the reception of her words. "You of all people shouldn't be surprised that they accept your judgment in this matter," Jyac murmured in her ear. "You are the wind of change for Emoria and they all want to be caught up in your wake."

Jame whipped her head around and stared at her aunt. "I can't believe that this is all that is needed for them to lay down generations of hostility towards the Lukrians."

"The Lukrians are not much different from us," Jyac responded. "We share the same sense of honor and tradition. I think our people were feeling a reluctant sympathy for the way the Wizard used the Lukrians. We could have very easily been in their place."

"We'll know in a few heartbeats, won't we?" Jame sighed.

A disturbance near the city bluff caused a wave of tension to flow over the silent gathering of women. The crowd opposite Jame and Jyac backed away from three figures walking deliberately towards the center of the circle. Flanked by Argis and Tigh, Kylara allowed a meditative calm to lift her awareness above the tense, well-armed women around her. She had fought under the Elite Guard. She understood, very well, the use of the mind over body. It also didn't hurt that the truest master of mind and body control was strolling casually next to her.

Studying the Emorans' reactions to this older, war-hardened woman walking bravely amongst them, Jame noted that they were more curious than vengeful. Tigh and Argis had carefully spread the word that Kylara had fought in the Grappian Wars in one of the Guard's own regiments. This was enough to pique the curiosity of these warriors to want to witness Kylara's fighting skills.

Jyac, followed by Jame, stepped from the stone platform and strode to meet their guest in the center of the circle. It was traditional for peaceful confrontations with the enemy to be witnessed by the people of Emoria. Kylara stopped several paces in front of the Queen of Emoria, noting that they were close in age. Jyac was a little shorter, but her body was still conditioned for battle.

"Well met, Kylara, Regent-General of Lukria." Jyac bowed her head.

"Well met, Jyac, Queen of Emoria," Kylara returned with a bow.

Jyac closed the space between them and held out her arm. Kylara met Jyac's steady gaze and clasped her hand around the Queen's forearm. They let the solid contact penetrate their senses for a long breath before releasing their grips.

"Kylara, Regent-General of Lukria, you have offered a truce between our two tribes to fight an enemy who could destroy both our territories." Jyac raised her voice so the surrounding women could hear her words. "The Council has allowed this truce to take place under the following condition: we must engage in a symbolic battle to bring our traditional hostilities to a satisfying conclusion. In this way, we can maintain our honor while resolving our differences. Do you accept this condition, Kylara, Regent-General of Lukria?"

"I accept the conditions of this truce, Queen Jyac." Kylara's voice rose on the breeze.

Jyac turned to Jame, who stepped between the two women. "The rules of combat have been agreed upon by the combatants. First blood ends the competition and the hostilities between Emoria and Lukria will be resolved in favor of the country that draws first blood. It has been agreed that this will end all hostility and aggression between Lukria and Emoria." Jame's steady voice rang out, casting a blanket of realization over those gathered in the meadow that their world was about to be changed forever. "It has also been agreed that Tigh of Ingor will judge the combat and her word will be the final decision."

For the first time since Kylara entered the circle, an excited rumble threatened to shake the ground as the anticipation of a fight that promised to become legend penetrated the crowd. It was nearly full dark, and an amber glow of thousands of torches added to the magic that crackled in the thin mountain air.

Tigh slid next to Jame. "You were wonderful," the warrior breathed into the arbiter's ear. "I think this will work."

Jame, still fighting a natural feeling of ambivalence, captured Tigh's eyes and saw a confidence that she wished she could share. "I hope you're right."

"Reach out with your senses," Tigh gently said. "Your people are ready for this change." The warrior then straightened and nodded to Argis, who stepped forward to escort Jame back to the royal platform.

"I'll try to believe." Jame looked back at her warrior and was rewarded by a warm, affectionate smile.

Turning to the leaders of Lukria and Emoria, Tigh pulled out a sword tucked into her belt. Kylara's sword. She had carried it for the Regent-General since they had entered Emoria. The warrior impaled a soft patch of dirt, allowing the sword to stand freely, and backed away. A tense silence ensued while Kylara strode over to her weapon.

The Lukrian circled her blade, putting it between herself and Jyac, who stood calmly with arms crossed. Tigh moved far enough away to be out of the intense focus of the two older warriors.

The veteran of the Grappian Wars pulled her sword from the ground and casually rested the blade on her shoulder, pretending to scrutinize the other woman. They were both canny warriors, well versed in the patient probing of an opponent's skills. Although they were both more inclined to wait for the other to make the first move, Kylara knew that in this particular situation, it was her place to give in to the honor of a Queen on her home ground and make the first motion of aggression.

With a relaxed flip of her sword, Kylara stalked around the equally loose Jyac, both looking as though they were ready to start a friendly conversation rather than a potentially deadly battle. Knowing that they could circle each other like cagey mountain cats all night, Jyac slipped her sword from its sheath on her back. The blade flashed in the light that flamed from tall stone lanterns within the circle.

The first clash of blades all but echoed off the distant mountain peaks as the crowd held a collective breath. Several more clashes sounded as the opponents tested each other's strength and movement. Both were pleased to find a well-conditioned foe. The more uneven the match, the more dangerous it could be. It was a relief to know that they could go at each other with greater freedom and less risk of serious injury.

"It's good to see that the Queen of Emoria stays battle ready." Kylara gracefully slid past a sideswipe, then whipped her blade around, only to have it neatly parried by Jyac's quick anticipation.

"With Lukrians lurking about my borders, it seemed a prudent thing to do." Jyac grinned. Her surprising admission allowed her to slip into Kylara's defenses enough to almost nick the Regent-General's ribs, but the veteran's sword moved as if it had a say in where it should be going.

Pushing Jyac's blade away from her vulnerable side, Kylara spun around, catching the Queen's rebound with the momentum of her blade. "I can see where your niece gets her ability to sweet talk a wolf into becoming a lap dog."

Jyac was airborne, deftly avoiding a swipe to the legs, plunging in the opposite direction of the movement of the sword and rolling to her feet to the side and a bit behind Kylara. The Regent-General whirled around in time to feel the sting of a ready sword against her own.

Rapid parries of jarring steel against steel set off a fireworks display of flame-touched reflections off polished metal. Caught hilt-to-hilt, faces close enough to smell remnants of the evening meal, steady eyes met, and each warrior was surprised to find a cautious respect in her opponent.

They pushed apart and broke into a brilliant dance of flying blades and nimble steps. Both women now realized that the enemy had only been a faceless name and that this opponent, whose attitudes and skills mirrored her own, did not fit the hateful words that always accompanied that name. Each woman saw herself in the other as she sought an advantage.

"I have a niece," Kylara commented as she feinted to one side before making a swift reverse, but was not quick enough to catch Jyac off-guard. "She has also turned her back on the ways of the warrior."

Jyac glided past Kylara's arcing sword and danced out of range. "Where do you suppose we went wrong?" the Emoran asked ruefully.

Kylara faced the Emoran with poised sword. "Perhaps they are reflections of a new world...a new society."

The pair lazily circled each other, flipping and casually waving their swords. "Perhaps," Jyac agreed. "Should we, as elders show the way?"

The roaring crowd dropped to silence as the opponents stopped circling and stood facing each other. "It is our duty." Kylara nodded. Never breaking eye contact, they slowly lowered their swords until the tips nuzzled the slick grass. The rustle of leaves and the crackle of the torches rose up to meet the silence as the two leaders simultaneously whipped their swords into a salute.

Long heartbeats passed before the Emorans realized that the battle was over. That, by some miracle, these two proud leaders chose to give up victory for a peace without conditions. The wall of cheering happened at once, causing more than one ear to pop. Grinning, Tigh stepped between the two combatants and motioned them to her. Sheathing their swords, Kylara and Jyac clasped forearms as the burden of generations tumbled off their shoulders.

Rapid footfalls brought Argis and Jame into the center circle of light. Jame wrapped her arms around her aunt, shock and relief making her speechless for once.

"It's your fault, you know." Jyac affectionately patted Jame's back.

"What do you mean?" Jame pulled back confused.

"We decided we had to set an example for the next generation." Jyac smiled at her startled niece.

"They chose peace." Tigh grinned.

"You're not hearing any arguments from me," Jame laughed. She was beyond stunned that this truce could have happened so easily and without any bloodshed at all. Looking back at Tigh, she caught the warrior gazing into the crowd. Releasing Jyac with a grin, Jame snaked an arm around Tigh's waist. "What is it?"

"Sometimes miracles need a little help," the warrior commented in a low voice. Frowning in confusion, Jame looked to where Tigh was staring. Goodemer stood with a grin that was ready to engulf her entire face.

"You think she had something to do with this?" It suddenly made a lot of sense of Jame.

"I could feel it. Like I was able to feel Misner when I fought her," Tigh sighed. "I didn't know that it was unusual to be able feel the spells. It took being captured and an admission from Meah to tell me more about myself than I ever knew."

"I'm glad you have that gift." Jame gave her warrior a loving squeeze. "If only to prove that these people I thought I knew couldn't change so suddenly overnight."

"I think it would have happened, even without a Wizard's help," Tigh mused.

"I guess we'll never know." Noticing that Kylara and Jyac were already halfway across the circle back to the city, the warrior and arbiter joined the trailing Emorans, off for yet another night of celebration.

Chapter 17

Two days later, Tas was picking at the shoulders of the red leathers that had been scavenged for the handful of Emorans who had volunteered to go to the Lukrian camp that was huddled around the entrance to the caves inhabited by Misner. After quietly freeing the Lukrian prisoners, it was agreed that representatives from each tribe should be exchanged, an action that could be interpreted as a show of good will and erase the last remnants of distrust between the two countries.

"Do you find these shoulder pads uncomfortable?" the compact warrior asked Olet, who didn't seem to have the same problems with the clothing as Tas.

"Actually, they're rather comfortable." Olet shrugged, focusing her attention on Tas' shoulders. "The problem is, they're made for someone with broader shoulders." She tugged and shifted the leather. "How's that?"

Tas flexed her upper body. "Better."

Hard, hurried footfalls sounded outside the entrance of the large tent they were in. A serious, sturdy woman rushed in. "Everyone up, Misner wants to review the troops," she barked sharply.

Two score warriors who were sleeping off night duty did not hesitate to voice their objections, even as they groggily pulled on their leather and weapons.

Spotting the pair of Emorans in the back of the tent, the fair-haired woman strode up to them. "I'm Tindal, Master Warrior."

"Tas, and this is Olet," Tas responded.

"Misner likes to play Supreme Commander," the Master Warrior continued in her no-nonsense way. Like Kylara, she was a veteran of the Grappian Wars and had no problem with Emorans or anyone else swelling the ranks of her army. If they proved to be good fighters, they were welcome. "Just follow what the others do and you'll be fine."

"Yes, Master Warrior," Tas and Olet said at once, straightening and saluting with their belt knives. Tindal gave them a long, appraising look before nodding and striding back out of the tent.

"I think she has Argis beat." Olet suppressed a grin.

"Can't wait to see them try to out-warrior each other." Tas' eyes twinkled mischievously.

"Fourth Regiment," a stocky Lukrian with a powerful voice barked into the tent opening. "Out to the review grounds."

The Emorans were impressed by the quickness with which the Lukrian warriors were out of the tent and trotting to the expanse of open fields surrounding the camp. In step with their Regiment, Tas and Olet had to concentrate on keeping their feet moving as their stunned senses took in the dusty mass of humanity streaming from the half-dozen camps around the edge of the well-trodden fields. Falling into place in the back line of their Regiment, the Emorans fought to shake off the shock of the enormity of the Wizard's army.

The Lukrians, being a ready-made defense force, held the place of honor as the personal guard to the

Wizard. The other Regiments lining the field were recruits and mercenaries, including a few men who proved they could fight and stand up to the strain of military life. The numbers had to be in the thousands. Tas and Olet exchanged wide-eyed glances. Never had they seen so many people in one place, much less a well-armed and disciplined army.

"We're supposed to defeat this?" Olet whispered as the five hundred horse cavalry, kicking up tufts of dust, cantered proudly to their place across the grounds.

"Tigh knows what we're up against and she thinks we can do it," Tas muttered back.

"You think she knows the army is this large?" Olet darted uncertain eyes at her companion.

"She once lead an army this size," Tas breathed, allowing the awe she felt color her words.

"Fourth Regiment! Stand at attention!" the rough-voiced group leader barked as Tindal trotted her proud horse past them.

Within heartbeats the entire field was silent and still except for the fluttering of the narrow banners proudly displaying the colors of each regiment. Enough time passed to allow the dust to subside and the breeze to chill the sweat-soaked skin of the fully armored troops.

A noise from the Lukrian camp tickled the edge of Tas' hearing. It took intense concentration to keep her eyes staring at the back of the head in front of her. No order had been given to pull on their masks. In Emoria and, she was sure, Lukria, masks were required for all formal military ceremonies and reviews. Shifting her eyes to the rows of troops across the field and facing her, she couldn't help but think how Seeran would love to witness this. The warrior pledged to try to remember as much as possible of this experience in the midst of the enemy. She just barely stopped the smile that always seemed to happen when she thought of the gentle historian.

Barked orders and names of Regiments from the direction of the caves told Tas that Misner was on the field and that she was not rushing her inspection. It felt like a whole sand mark had passed before a cluster of horses and riders played on the edge of Tas' vision. A shout and the Regiment next to the 4th pulled out their swords and whipped them into a sharp salute.

Before she even had time to think, "We're next," their group leader was shouting the Regiment name and giving the orders to salute. Fortunately, Tas was concentrating on performing the salute in rhythm with the Lukrian in front of her. If she had raised her eyes before she safely executed the move, she would have surely faced a Lukrian dressing down.

Five black-clad figures sat atop strong, tall warhorses. A cold deadness wafted off these creatures of death. Blinking, Tas realized that they were not monsters but women, arrogant and confident, sweeping their stone-hard eyes across the Regiment and dismissing it with a sneer. Tas remembered Tigh saying something about how certain enhancements for the Guards were rejected because they made the Guard detectable. That coldness would certainly not go unnoticed. *By the Children of Bal,* the warrior's mind clenched in horror, *Tigh used to be one of them.*

Calming down her suddenly pounding heart, the compact warrior's eyes shifted to a round, diminutive figure on a pony. Because the woman's head was bent in a discussion with Tindal, Tas couldn't see her features, but she knew that this was the mad Wizard.

Just then, Misner raised her head and turned to the indolent brown-eyed Guard on the other side of her. Tas had to blink. Then she closed her eyes and opened them again. Expecting an insane, cold monster, she couldn't accept that this sweet-faced, motherly woman with gentle light eyes was the mad Wizard, Misner.

"Very nice, Tindal." A soothing, light voice, raised high enough for the Regiment to hear, sweetly touched her ears. Then the small group trotted down the line to the next regiment.

"Welcome to Misner's army." The young warrior on the other side of Olet winked at them.

* * * * * * * * * * * * * * * *

Goodemer fidgeted with the leather bracer on her forearm, wondering how anyone could get used to wearing something so tight and unforgiving. Looking down at herself, she didn't think there was enough leather and armor in the known world to make her look like a warrior.

"That looks great on you," Jame commented as she wandered into the armory. Goodemer snorted at the idea. Jame raised an eyebrow at Argis, who was hefting swords in search for one light enough for Goodemer to carry. "You don't think you look good in that?"

"I look ridiculous," Goodemer muttered, looking down at herself.

"You may feel ridiculous but you look fine." Jame grinned.

"I'm not a warrior." Goodemer stared at the weapons of war hanging from the walls and piled under leather covers on the floor.

"But that doesn't mean you can't look like one, and you have to blend in with the rest of us." Jame's attention was diverted to a low opening in the back of the cavern. Tigh emerged, cradling a rough wooden ball. A thick layer of dust and cobwebs fell away from the object, telling a tale of long neglect.

"Do you still have the catapults for these?" Tigh asked Argis.

The warrior rubbed the back of her neck trying to mentally put the balls together with the heap of junk gathered in one of the storage chambers. "Maybe. We've got odds and ends of things from when we battled the invaders from the east. The stuff in those balls has probably rotted by now."

"We can make more." Tigh shrugged. "What is important is whether you still have the mechanism to propel them."

"I'll get someone on that." Argis nodded and strode out of the chamber.

"I just got a report from Tas," Jame said as Tigh carefully put the filthy ball on the floor and dipped her hands into the water the smithy used for cooling metals. "She says that Misner's army is roughly four thousand foot soldiers and five hundred on horseback." The arbiter carefully watched Tigh's reaction to this, relieved to see no surprise in the warrior's grim eyes. "So you think we can handle them?"

Goodemer, on the other hand, was wide-eyed with alarm at the size of the army they were going to try to stop. "By the Children of Bal," she whispered.

"Has Tas seen any of the leaders?" Tigh asked, absently testing several of the swords lying about.

"While Misner was reviewing the troops, Tas saw five Elite Guards," Jame elaborated.

"Five," Tigh mused.

"She also mentioned that she could feel the cold coming off them, like what we felt from Meah in Balderon." Jame's optimism rose as a wicked gleam danced in Tigh's eyes. "You've got a plan?" she asked, cocking her head at the warrior.

"I think so," Tigh mused, resting her eyes on Goodemer. "That was a neat spell you used on Kylara and Jyac."

The startled Wizard almost tripped on a bundle of spears as she unconsciously stepped back at the shock of Tigh's words. "What do you mean?" she stammered out, regaining her composure.

"I said that was a neat spell you used on Kylara and Jyac," Tigh repeated steadily. "Very subtle."

Goodemer stared at the warrior, cursing her inexperience at getting around the truth. "How do you know I had anything to do with that?"

"I've recently learned that I can detect when a Wizard is casting a spell." Tigh casually spun a staff, nodding in appreciation of its balance. "But I don't seem to be able to detect spells that have already been cast."

"I've heard of that gift," Goodemer slowly said. "It's extremely rare. So you could sense even the minor spell I used on Kylara and Jyac?"

"Yes. It felt quite tangible to me." Tigh frowned a little. This was something that she would have to explore in depth.

"That's how you defeated Misner." Thick, wavy hair bobbed as the Wizard vigorously nodded her head. "Whatever allows you to sense the spells also makes you immune to them."

"Her spells felt pretty real to me." Tigh rested the staff on her shoulder.

"Of course, you were able to feel them and understand what they were trying to do to you, but you also resisted them," Goodemer explained, astonishment now replaced by excitement. "Since magic doesn't affect you, I can channel it through you."

"Why would you want to do that?" Jame asked curiously.

"So far I've been able to mask my presence from Misner," Goodemer explained. "The bit of magic the other night was not enough to break through my mask and capture her attention. There will be some point when she'll become aware of me and that could ruin our attempts to take her down. My magic would have to be carefully coordinated with your actions or I'd give everything away too soon. But if I could channel the magic through Tigh, I'd be able to maintain the mask and Misner would never be able to detect it."

Tigh and Jame stared at the Wizard for long heartbeats. It seemed too good to be true. "Is this something that's been tried before or just theory?" Jame finally asked.

"The great Wizard, Gryplor, is said to have defeated a rogue Wizard by channeling through a small girl who was immune to magic." Goodemer looked from one face to the other. "It can work."

Tigh knew that Wizards were cautious of using their skills, so Goodemer's confidence was based on her understanding of magic rather than wishful thinking. "Sounds good." She nodded, gazing at Jame and arching a brow.

"Is this going to harm Tigh in any way?" Jame asked, pushing down the natural apprehension she felt any time Tigh was in danger.

"Only resistance to channeling may cause harm." Goodemer studied the black-clad warrior.

"I have no reason to resist." Tigh grinned, snuggling up to the idea and liking it more and more.

****

Seeran sat at the little table tucked in the corner of the airy gallery turned war room. Her intent scribbling in her journal was the only sound echoing through that part of the palace. She had to call upon all her powers of memorization to capture the intricate detail of the plan Tigh had calmly laid out for the battle leaders. The casual mixing of magic with troop placement sounded like an impossible plot from a novel. But this was real. The scraping of quill against parchment stopped in mid-word. Tas was in enemy territory. She knew that the small warrior had the tendency to put herself into dangerous situations, but it had been a shock when Tas volunteered to go behind enemy lines. Shaking the thoughts from her head, Seeran forced herself to concentrate on the amazing tale she had the good fortune to be a witness to.

Jame stood watching Tigh, still bent over the scattering of maps on the large stone table in the middle of the gallery. The battle leaders had long gone to bed, not knowing when their next opportunity for rest would be. The arbiter felt a rare uncertainty radiating from the warrior. The intent frown and the resigned sag of the shoulders told Jame that her warrior had more than a few worries about her plan.

Nodding to Seeran, as the historian blinked up from her work, Jame softly padded around the table. She looked down at the maps, quietly studying them until Tigh came back from wherever she was and turned to her. "Looks...interesting," Jame ventured, glad to see the furrow between Tigh's brows relax.

Being the Supreme Commander of the campaign to stop Misner and her army, Jame knew the general outline of the plan, but she left the detailed placement of individuals at any given time to the person who commanded the decisive battle of the Grappian Wars. Jame had tried, one more time, to get Jyac to lead the campaign, but the Queen of Emoria, still clinging to her faith in the Emor Mysteries, refused.

"It'll be interesting all right." Tigh nodded.

"Where will Argis be?" Jame asked, peering at the different colored lines and matching small blocks of wood.

"Here." Tigh laid a finger on an artistic rendering of a hill. "And Mularke will be here and Kas with her horse troops will be next to Argis, here." She indicated a line of trees.

"Where will we be?"

"In these caves." Tigh tapped the place. "Kylara convinced Misner to allow the Lukrian regiments to be the rear guard for the main army. Her excuse was that they could scour the area for Emorans who might be trying to get to Misner. In reality, they will keep close behind the main army and make up the third side of our little box."

"And the fourth side is Balderon, hopefully armed and ready, thanks to our swift-footed scouts." Jame nodded.

"All we have to do is disable the Guards and Misner right before the signal to attack is made." Tigh grinned.

"And we know how to find the Guards and we have the potion to disable them, thanks to Tas." It really did seem possible. Jame cocked her head at her partner. "Maybe the army will surrender without any bloodshed."

"Then Argis won't have any fun." Tigh affectionately messed up Jame's bangs.

"So, everything seems to be falling into place. What's bothering you then?"

"We're dealing with a set of events that have to happen between two places that are a good four days' march from each other. Too many things can go wrong," Tigh sighed. "I had a long talk with Goodemer about this. We have to get into Misner's stronghold and wait for her to cast the spells that will make her army invincible. If we stop her too soon, the Guards, who will be in some kind of contact with her, will be suspicious. So we have to stop her as she is preparing that spell."

"Why doesn't she just cast the spell over them now?" Jame asked, noting out of the corner of her eye that Seeran was jotting down their conversation.

"She'd alert every Wizard in the area of what she was up to," Tigh returned. "I don't think she's willing to take that chance."

"It'll work," Jame confidently stated. "Misner doesn't know that we know what she's up to."

"That's the only thing we have in our favor." Tigh's eyes drifted to the map once again.

"So." Jame wrapped an arm around Tigh. "Are you going to stand here and stare at these maps all night?" she gently teased.

Tigh cast an amused glance at her partner. "Depends."

"I happen to know a nice warm bed that's big enough for two," Jame purred as she nuzzled the warrior's shoulder.

Tigh's arm snaked around Jame. "If you can't think of anything better, I guess that'll have to do."

Jame playfully punched the warrior's shoulder. She suddenly found herself in the air, cradled in Tigh's strong arms. The grinning warrior bounced a few times on her toes and launched them into a quick flip over the table.

"Show off. Good night, Seeran." Jame waved at the wide-eyed, slack-jawed historian, as Tigh strode into the corridor with her beloved burden.

****

Carved out of the natural landscape, Emor tenuously clings to life, but the absence of most of its inhabitants is a disturbing reminder of how civilizations can slip to dust in just a short span of time...

Seeran, seated cross-legged on the wide stone ledge of the fountain in the center of Emor, looked up from her writing at the first noise she heard that morning that wasn't one of the nesting cliff birds. Emerging from the Palace was the small band of reluctant heroes embarking on the kind of adventure that the historian had only dreamed of witnessing first hand. She had quickly found that reality had a way of mixing living dreams with nightmares. It was her own fault for forgetting the first rule of being a historian—never get emotionally involved. But she couldn't help it. The Emorans had captured her heart and soul, and for the first time in her life she found something that was greater than her love of history.

Seeran jumped to her feet as the group approached.
"Good luck." She mustered a smile as she observed the
casualness they strained to project.

"Thank you, Seeran." Jame smiled graciously,
stepping forward and taking the historian's hand in
hers. "I'll try to bring back a story that will make you
the envy of Artocia."

"Just bring yourselves back," Seeran whispered,
lowering her eyes, not wanting to give in to the sudden
pressure of tears.

"No fear." Jame gave her hand a gentle squeeze.
"Tigh and I have made a promise to each other." Seeran
raised sad but curious eyes. "We promised that
we'd have a long life together after we've given up
being on the road. And we always keep our promises to
each other." The arbiter turned to catch Tigh's tender,
affectionate look.

"I wouldn't want to have Jame angry with me,
would you?" Tigh's eyes twinkled.

"I guess not." Seeran smiled, fighting harder to
keep the tears back.

"See you soon, Seeran." Tigh nodded as they continued across the square, followed by a pensive Jyac.

Goodemer, looking oddly at home in her warrior
gear, paused in front of Seeran. The Wizard fished
from her belt pouch a small amulet with the image of a
wolf pup engraved into it. "In case some magic strays
this way, just wrap your hand around this and think
about those things you love the most. This will protect
you." Glancing around, Goodemer leaned closer to the
historian. "It will also protect a loved one, if you speak
protective words to it."

Seeran blinked up at the Wizard with a profound
sense of thankfulness and relief. "Thank you," she
stammered, clutching the small amulet.

Goodemer simply smiled and hurried to catch up
with the others who were waiting for her at the door to
the Temple of Laur. Sometimes being a Wizard wasn't

such a bad job as long as she never lost sight of the individuals around her. Small magic was as powerful as attention-getting, flashy displays and more often than not, much more satisfying. Goodemer ruefully shook her head. Her mentor would call her a mushball and she would most amiably agree.

The Wizard had yet to set foot in the Temple and so was surprised at the feat of engineering that allowed the continuous flow of water. A little mental probing told her that no mortal magic was involved in this impressive aquatic display. Any deity who could provide warm water for indoor bathing was well worth cultivating.

Jyac took Jame by the arm and led her away from the others to the altar at the other end of the main worship hall. "My faith in the Emor Mysteries gives me the confidence that we will be victorious," Jyac began, studying the floor, polished by generations of worshipers. "But the side of me that is your aunt can't help but feel apprehensive about all this." She lifted proud eyes to her niece. "You left Emoria an idealistic girl. The road you chose to follow returned to us a strong, likable young woman as prepared for leadership as any Emoran princess. Be careful and come back to us safe and victorious. Let no harm come to your partner. She has won the hearts of our people and will be a worthy Consort for their future Queen."

"Thank you, Jyac." Jame wrapped her arms around her aunt, refusing to give in to the intense emotions that swarmed at her like relentless bees. "Tigh has led campaigns many times greater than this one and has never lost. We will succeed because she has the ability to focus on not being defeated. She can pluck more tricks from her bracers than a street magician. I have placed my life in her hands more times than I can count and she has always kept both of us from harm. This time will be no different."

Jyac nodded, knowing that their only hope was in the fact that Tigh had once defeated Misner. She prayed that Misner's power hadn't grown strong enough to overpower the former Elite Guard, even with Goodemer's help. Sighing, she wished a more experienced Wizard had been sent to deal with the rogue Misner, but she wasn't in any position to question the decisions of that secretive society.

The small group entered the neglected chamber where Tigh had been kidnapped. During the four days since word had come to them that Misner's army was on the move, Goodemer and the warrior had practiced channeling magic through Tigh by breaking the spells in the tunnel. Even though the Lukrians could pass through the spells without a problem, the Emorans still couldn't penetrate them without being in some kind of physical contact with a Lukrian.

"Good luck and may all of Bal's Children be with you." Jyac clasped each of them on the shoulder. "May the waters of Laur flow through you and safely bring you back to the mother head waters."

"We follow the waters' journey to victory and back," Jame intoned.

As the unlikely trio of Wizard, arbiter, and warrior disappeared around the first bend in the cavern Jyac fought back the urge to follow. One of the hardest parts about being the Queen was being left behind to wait while others set off to fight for the fate of the country. Sighing, Jyac turned and trudged back to Laur's Worship Hall. She hated waiting more than almost anything.

Chapter
18

"Have you ever seen anything like it?" Kas whispered in awe. The three Emoran battle leaders were sprawled on their stomachs on the top of a small windy hill with only knee-high grass as cover. Spread before them was the night-darkened Balderon valley. Far to their left, they could see the torches sparkling along the thick impenetrable walls of Balderon. In front of them, close enough to hear voices and to detect the main ingredients of the stews bubbling in the numerous cauldrons, was Misner's army.

The troops had spent most of the day setting up camp within sight of Balderon. Confident in their belief that no one would dare go against them, they didn't even send out patrols to scout the area. Tigh had predicted this behavior. This arrogance was a part of the Elite Guards' psyche. The Guards were invincible and they made sure everyone knew it.

Argis sucked in the cold night air. To her shock, she'd found herself hoping to disable the leaders so they wouldn't have to engage that terrifying force in battle. Never in her life had she turned away from the opportunity to fight. Her soul longed for the edgy rush she felt when her sword became an extension of her body as she danced with the enemy. She had waited all her life to be in this place, leading her army to victory. Now, gazing at the neatly spaced watch fires surrounded by shadowy soldiers, the whole camp confounding her imagination by its immense size, she realized that she would be satisfied if the victory came without bloodshed.

"To think Tigh used to lead an army four times this size." Mularke drew in an awed breath. Shouts from the camp signaled a changing of the watch.

The grass crunched behind them and three hands were on dagger hilts before they recognized the red leathers and white-streaked hair of the Regent-General as she dropped to the ground and slithered up next to them.

"I've got some news," Kylara said softly, settling quietly in the grass. "Have you noticed that there are only four command tents down there?" Argis remembered Tigh telling her that each Guard leader always had her own command tent, no matter the number of troops she commanded. "There are five Guards. One is missing."

"Which one?" Argis finally found her voice.

"I've seen all but two out there," Kylara mused. "They don't like to show themselves if they can help it. I haven't seen Patch or Meah."

"Meah," Argis sighed, dropping her chin onto clenched fists. "I hope she's still not playing with Tigh."

Kylara rubbed a brittle, brown weed between her fingers. "They do have a bit of a history together."

"They were friends." Argis nodded.

"More than friends," Kylara clarified. "Meah was obsessed with Tigh back then. That's one of the reasons why Misner recruited her. It seems that Meah has been holding some kind of grudge against Tigh for a long time."

Argis frowned as the conversation in the Balderon safe house tickled her memory. "Meah had been cleansed, which means she was at Ynit the same time as Tigh. Was this relationship still going on at the end of the War?"

"Close to the end, at least." Kylara thought back to the exhilarating and confusing last days of the War. "Meah was one of several commanders under Tigh by that time. You have to remember that the Meah you've met was not the one I served under. She was like most of the Guards, arrogant and ruthless to be sure, but also a good commander. Tigh was the monster." The Regent-General shook away terrifying memories that still twisted her deepest dreams into nightmares. "She was many times worse than this Wizard-enhanced Meah, if you can imagine such a thing."

The Emorans exchanged wary glances. Argis certainly could imagine it after witnessing Tigh's brief relapse. "I was just thinking that things must have cooled down between them by the time they were returned to Ynit for cleansing because Jame was close to Tigh from almost the beginning." Argis was sure Jame would have mentioned Meah if she had been more of a presence in Tigh's life while in Ynit.

"Sounds like a reason for a grudge to me," Kylara returned.

Argis thoughtfully nodded her head. "We don't have time to send back a warning that one of the Guards is at large."

"I know," the Regent-General sighed, staring at the endless army camp in front of them. "It's never easy, is it?"

* * * * * * * * * * * * * * *

The spidery network of caverns beneath the Phytian Mountains was illuminated with permanent fire spells, and carefully etched maps, showing the intricate routes,

were at each intersection of chambers and tunnels.
Jame ran a hand over the neatly inscribed writing, wondering how many years Misner ruled these caverns
without anyone knowing she was right below their feet.

"This way." Tigh peered down a wide tunnel. As
always, Goodemer went first. Cunning spells hid traps
and treacherous openings so the travel was slow as
Goodemer found and unraveled the spells one at a time.

They had gone just a few paces into this new tunnel
before Goodemer shook her head and waved her amulet
over the ground. A circle of sharp, pointed finger-
length spikes protruded from the floor before them.

"That would have been painful," Jame commented
as they eased around the spikes.

"Are you sure Misner won't be able to detect your
magic?" Tigh asked Goodemer as they continued down
the tunnel.

"As long as my mask is in place, she can't detect
me," Goodemer reassured her. "The little magic it
takes to break these spells can't be distinguished from
the stray magic that is always charging the air around
us."

"Stray magic?" Jame repeated.

Goodemer shook her amulet at a rock wall, revealing a shadow trigger—a mechanism that clicked into
action when a shadow passed over it. Snapping her fingers at it, a half dozen darts flew out and landed harmlessly on the ground. "Wizards do not make magic, we
simply learn to harness the magic that exists around us,
all the time. If you can detect magic it cannot harm
you. Tigh can detect magic."

"But I can't detect a spell that's already been cast."
Tigh frowned as they paused for Goodemer to set off
another shadow trigger that catapulted several stones
into their path.

"That's because the magic in a cast spell is dormant
until the circumstances are in place to awaken the
magic and set off the spell. These caverns would be

extremely noisy with magic if the spells weren't protected in this way. So noisy that it could confuse the spells, and unpleasant and unwanted things could happen," Goodemer explained as she revealed a gaping hole in the middle of the path.

Jame stared down into the dark hole as they carefully skirted it. "Isn't this protection a little extreme? It seems to me setting off just one of these spells would stop someone."

"Several backup spells aren't unusual, but this obsessive repetition betrays an unstable mind," Goodemer sadly reflected. "They are also attempts to make up for being a mediocre Wizard at best. A mad and mediocre Wizard is a dangerous foe to go up against."

"Now is not the time to have second thoughts," Tigh growled.

"Not second thoughts," Goodemer assured her. "We just have to be alert to her weaknesses and use them against her. Just as you do when you fight."

Tigh nodded in understanding as something brushed the edges of her memory. She had defeated Misner once. Unconsciously she had found Misner's weakness. "If I recount what I can remember of my last meeting with her, do you think we can figure out how I was able to get the upper hand and beat her?"

Goodemer grinned as she looked back at the warrior. "We can certainly try."

＊＊＊＊＊＊＊＊＊＊＊＊＊＊＊

"Kylara just told me there are only four Guards out there." Tas entered the ring of light at one of the watch fires that illuminated the Lukrian camp sprawled in the barren, narrow strip of land between the foothills and the mountains. Holding a plate filled with stew and a hunk of bread, she plopped down on the cold ground next to Olet and the other four Emorans masquerading as Lukrians.

"We saw all five of them leave." Olet frowned before scooping some stew into her mouth. "It wasn't hard to miss them at the head of each of their regiments. They could make the snow shiver."

"All the regiments are out there," Tas nodded in the direction of Balderon, "but only four command tents are set up."

"So what does that do to our plans?" Wolfie asked, her wild hair catching the firelight and shadows, reminding the others where her nickname came from.

"We stick to the original plans. If we can't stop all five, at least we can get four of them," Tas responded.

"I wonder which one is missing," Olet mused.

Tas shrugged. "We'll find out tomorrow."

They were quickly on their feet as Tindal approached. Lukrian or not, they had grown to respect this no-nonsense Master Warrior. She was tough but fair and never mentioned their Emoran origins. More importantly, she made certain that the other warriors in the Lukrian regiments treated them civilly. Under other circumstances it may have been different, but everyone knew that there just wasn't time to gnaw at old hostilities when they had a greater foe to face.

"They plan to attack Balderon at first light," Tindal reported, pleased with the six serious sets of eyes watching her. Rumors that the Emorans had grown wild and undisciplined were obviously unfounded. "Kylara will enter the main camp with an escort of twelve, including you six. You must do what needs to be done, and all but one of you will rejoin the escort when Kylara is ready to return."

"What about the missing Guard?" Tas asked in a low voice.

Tindal pondered the question. "There's a possibility she may be in camp by the time we get there. We are scouring the area for her, in case she's thinking of making trouble. The Guards play mind games and Misner may have some tricks for tomorrow. We can't be certain of anything we think is going to happen. We have to stay alert and be ready to adapt. I'm hoping we won't have to implement the backup plan, but we must be prepared for it."

"We will do whatever it takes to stop them." Tas straightened.

"Good luck on your mission." Tindal nodded. "Show us Lukrians that legendary Emoran ability to sneak up on the enemy in a field of snow and have to tap them on the shoulder to let them know you're behind them."

The Emorans grinned. A challenge from the enemy was enough of a blow to their honor to succeed or die trying.

****

As soon as Tigh's eyes adjusted to the clear, half-moon lit sky, she determined that it was closer to dawn than dusk. The Lukrian camp, fifty paces in front of them, was quiet except for a handful of guards posted around the outer perimeter.

She turned to Jame, a dozen emotions scuttling across her night-darkened features. Not able to find words to match the feelings roiling within her, Tigh simply reached out and pulled Jame to her.

Jame wrapped her arms tightly around her warrior. This little adventure was going to greatly test the promise they had made to each other. "You're going to have to wear Emoran leathers for the joining," she murmured as she lifted her head and looked up at her partner.

Tigh blinked down at her. "Hope they're more comfortable than they look." She brushed her lips against Jame's cheek.

"I'll make sure they are cut to fit you perfectly." Jame nuzzled Tigh's neck.

"Is that a promise?" Tigh purred in Jame's ears.

"It's a promise." Jame nodded as she captured her partner's eyes. "And I always keep my promises to you."

A faint smile danced across Tigh's features as she lowered her head and reaffirmed their bond with a gentle kiss. "Time to go play with Misner."

Goodemer stood a few paces apart from them and studied the opening in the craggy bluff beyond the Lukrian camp tents. Raising her eyes, she wished her mentor were there to whisper words of guidance. *Take one step at a time and work with whatever is at hand.* Blinking out of her reverie, she turned to her companions, who were watching her expectantly.

"The magic in this place is disturbed and unstable," Goodemer softly stated. "It's as if she can't quite control what she's trying to do. That, in itself, can be extremely dangerous."

"Let's go and stop her then." Tigh let a wolfish grin overtake her features.

Goodemer followed Tigh and Jame to the edge of camp, wishing it was as simple as strolling into the cavern and beating up Misner. She paused and gave that thought another look. An idea wove an intriguing pattern in her mind.

Approaching a Lukrian guard, Tigh's fingers flashed the code that had been agreed upon to allow them safe entry into enemy territory. The tall, slender guard straightened and simply nodded as they walked past her. Tigh opened her senses, taking in all the sounds and movements around them. The air was tense but that was to be expected. The Lukrians left behind to guard the Wizard would be in a deadly position if this unlikely looking trio of heroes failed to stop her.

Pausing at the mouth of the cave, Goodemer held her amulet and gently probed the wards and spells spilling out to them like a pile of string after a kitten was tired of playing with it. It was confusing magic and not particularly effective. If too much magic is pulled into too many spells at once, the result is more messy than useful. Yet, Goodemer didn't have the time to gently push the magic aside. "There are too many spells. We'll need a Lukrian to get through them."

"Wonder if we can convince someone to volunteer." Tigh ran her eyes over the all but deserted tents. Her head snapped back, as a chill that had nothing to do with the cold mountain air flowed out of the cave.

The trio, eyes alert to any movement, backed slowly away from the dark opening, knowing they were in grave trouble when the blackness materialized into Meah.

****

The outer guards signaled the small band on horseback through the lines. Even though it was still two sand marks before dawn, the camp was awakening and the aroma of oat gruel permeated the air. The thirteen riders trotted through the camp to a ragged hide tent where they dismounted and tied their horses to a nearby picket line.

Kylara poked her head through the tent's opening, relieved that there was only one occupant sitting at a small table, illuminated by a single lamp.

"Come in, old friend." A silver-haired, war-hardened woman looked up from the book she was reading.

Nodding to six of her escort to remain outside, Kylara entered the low-pitched tent accompanied by the Emorans. "Good evening, Yanajin." Kylara walked over to the older woman and they clasped arms.

"Please sit." Yanajin nodded to the chair opposite her. "Relax while your friends relieve us of a handful of trouble."

"Are there still only four?" Kylara asked as she settled into the goat hide chair.

"As of a half sand mark ago, yes," Yanajin answered, her dark brown eyes resigned to whatever fate Bal had arranged for her. "One can't do the damage of five, so the odds are still with us."

"It would still be better to know where the fifth one is and what she's up to." Kylara shrugged.

"Ah, but that would make this game of war too easy and predictable." The older woman grinned.

Shaking her head, Kylara turned to the waiting Emorans. "Good luck to you, and get back here as swiftly as you can."

"We'll be back before you know it," Tas announced as she flashed a feral grin.

Slipping through the back slit of the tent, the four Emorans paused to make sure that no one was looking in their direction. Tas met each set of serious, intent eyes before they disappeared in four separate directions.

Tas strode past the kitchen fires where soldiers were lining up for what passed for the morning meal in Misner's army. The small warrior would be happy if she never again saw another bowl of the pasty stuff they had the audacity to call porridge. Across the camp before her, the dark shadows draping the ground came alive as regiment after regiment responded to the insistent shouts of their group leaders to wake up and get their bellies filled.

The Emoran pushed down thoughts that if they didn't succeed, they would have to actually fight this formidable army. They had to win. For Emoria and for the odd reason that Tas wanted to present Seeran the story of a lifetime.

Her target was in sight. Tigh was right. The imposing tent made from white goat hides was not guarded. A part of the Elite Guard mystique was that they feared no one, and all but dared any one to try to sneak up on them with the intent to do harm.

Striding purposely by the tent, Tas could feel the cold radiating from it as if it were made of ice. A meal line snaked relatively close to the front of the tent and the light from the kitchen fires sank the darkened sides and back of the tent into deeper shadow. Circling away from the tent and approaching it from behind, Tas disappeared into a shadow and immediately dropped to her stomach. She scanned the area outside the shadow for long heartbeats until she was certain no one had seen her.

Slowly, making no more noise than the wind, she pulled herself to the tent's edge. Using her knife, she carefully worked a hole around the seams that held the hides together, listening intently for sounds inside.

A cold arm shot through the hole so swiftly that Tas froze for half a heartbeat before fumbling open her belt pouch and pulling out a sharpened dart. The steely fingers wrapped around her throat, freezing her skin, but her hand shot up in reflex and the dart pricked the arm.

Gasping to bring both air and warmth back into her throat, Tas concentrated on completing her task. After carefully pushing the arm back through the slit in the tent, she grasped the wolf pup amulet around her neck and held it until it tingled her fingers.

One down. She prayed to Laur that the other three were successful.

* * * * * * * * * * * * * * *

"We do seem to meet in the oddest places." Meah grinned wickedly. The frozen tension snapped in the thin mountain air.

"Is she real?" Tigh turned to Goodemer.

"She's real." Goodemer nodded, not taking her eyes off the cold menace before her.

"Have you finally figured out whose side you're on?" Tigh crossed her arms, ignoring Jame's startled glance.

"I've always known whose side I'm on." Meah casually strolled out of the cave. "My side." Her night-deepened eyes swept over Jame. The arbiter tightened her grip on her staff.

"Misner never found out about Ocarla?" Tigh raised an eyebrow.

Haunted eyes flew up to capture Tigh's. "No," Meah whispered. Jame was taken aback by the raw emotion in the Guard's voice. It touched old memories from her time during the cleansings in Ynit when she witnessed the Guards teetering between being ruthless warriors and the gentle souls that were their true selves.

"I have only one question." Tigh took a step closer to Meah. Jame and Goodemer were shocked to see the Guard struggling to stand her position. Whatever had been between them went beyond the knowledge that Tigh had the means to disable the Guard. Meah betrayed a frightened awe of her former commander. "Why have you waited until now to take your revenge?"

"The other Guards." Meah's eyes were like granite. "I had to wait until they were far away from Misner."

"What would you have done if Kylara had turned me over to you?" Tigh suddenly asked. Meah's confused stare solidified their trust in the Lukrians. "I was bound and helpless within a few paces of you in Kylara's quarters in Lukria." Meah was so shocked, she couldn't find any words to respond, even if she somehow found her voice. "You didn't need the Lukrians to capture me. Misner must not be very clever to have believed the stories you fed her about how I kept slipping through your fingers."

Meah stared into the dark camp for long heartbeats. "I would have let you escape. That would have been enough to break the Lukrians' trust in Misner when she didn't deliver Emoria to them for your capture. Misner doesn't understand warrior honor. She wouldn't have understood that the Lukrians expected payment for your capture whether you were delivered to her or not."

"Did you have something to do with the wording of that agreement?" Tigh raised an eyebrow.

A sly grin touched Meah's eyes. "She doesn't know much about how Guards operate, either."

"Not if she thought you were jealous of Jame." Tigh returned the grin.

"Hey, what's that supposed to ⸳ mean?" Jame, momentarily forgetting the seriousness of their situation, shot her partner an indignant look.

"It means, little princess, that Misner learned from the Lukrians of our relationship during the last campaigns of the War and mistook my devotion to my commander as something more than an admiration for her skills as a master warrior. As I said, Misner has no understanding of the Guards." In a blinding motion, Meah's sword hissed from its sheath. "I told you back in Balderon that we would lead the dance together." The rogue Guard whipped the blade into a salute. "It's an honor to be a part of another one of your brilliant campaigns, my commander."

Jame and Goodemer stared in shock at the former Guard.

"We need to get into that cave," Tigh stated.

Meah held out an arm, eyes level with Tigh's. Tigh slowly reached out and grasped it. Not letting go of Meah's eyes, she stretched her other hand out to Jame. Keeping a wary eye on the Guard, Jame took the hand. Goodemer quickly grabbed Jame's free hand. Unable to keep back a pleased grin, Meah pulled them into the Wizard's stronghold.

✳✳✳✳✳✳✳✳✳✳✳✳✳✳✳

"That's three." Tas breathed as another warrior slipped through the back slit of Yanajin's tent "Any problems?"

The young woman shook her head. "It was just as Tigh said. The Guard heard me cut the slit and I was able to dose her as her hand reached out."

Kylara peeked out the front opening of the tent. "We don't have much time."

"Come on, Wolfie," Tas muttered tensely as she stared at the amulet in her hand.

"We need to go." They had to get out of the camp before the unconscious Guards were discovered. No alarm had been sounded yet but their discovery was just a matter of time. Kylara beckoned to one of her escorts outside the tent. "Get the horses and bring them here."

"Come on, Wolfie," Tas growled in frustration.

The soft footfalls of the horses sounded outside the tent. Kylara turned to her old friend. "Keep safe, Yanajin."

"I will be satisfied with ending this day as your prisoner." Yanajin bowed. "It is not the fate of this old warrior to die in a dishonorable battle."

"It's done," Tas gasped as the amulet in her hand briefly flared yellow. "Olet. Go."

Tas grasped her friend's shoulder. Olet nodded and slipped through the slit in the tent and was off and sprinting through the dusty chaos of the awakening camp.

By the time the others were mounted, Wolfie, wild hair flying, barreled towards the horse that Tas held for her. Deftly vaulting onto the animal's back she caught the reins Tas tossed to her.

"You decide to do a little sightseeing?" the smaller warrior casually asked.

Wolfie let out a wild laugh in reply as the twelve riders galloped through the camp to the foothills.

Chapter 19

Cluttered was the best word to describe Misner's world. Parts of just about everything imaginable filled corners of chambers and barely negotiable corridors. Machines, weapons, kitchenware, furniture, toys...all broken and haphazardly thrown together.

A questioning look on her face, Jame picked up a piece of a crystal tribute to Laur.

"According to Misner, everything has magic in it." Meah shrugged. "She consumes it from this stuff like a drunk drinks ale. I think the Lukrians' rebellion really started when they were sent out to collect these things. Demeaning work for anyone, much less a people born to be warriors."

Goodemer absently rubbed her chin at this unexpected information. "This could be useful," she mumbled to herself.

"This way." Meah paused at the opening of a narrow, twisting tunnel. If coldness wafted off the Guard, an uneasy evil radiated from the tunnel.

"I was afraid you were going to say that," Jame weakly joked. Tigh put a hand on her shoulder and gave it a reassuring squeeze. Jame smiled at her part-

ner. They had done their share of crazy things for the
greater good. It sometimes seemed that each adventure
was just a little crazier than the last.

Goodemer pulled a wolf pup amulet sculpted from
purple quartz out of her belt pouch and spoke a few soft
words to it. "Put this around your neck."

Jame took the amulet and did as Goodemer
instructed. "That's much better." The arbiter grinned.
"That's amazing. I can't feel anything but the good
coming off all of you." She walked up to Meah, who
was watching them with an amused smirk. "Even you."
The former Guard mustered her most uncaring sneer for
the arbiter.

"Save it for Misner, Meah," Tigh laughed. "You
were always more show than action."

"We had *you* around for any action that needed
doing." Meah flashed an evil grin at the black-clad
warrior.

"Some things never change," Tigh responded as she
brushed past Meah and Jame and strode into the tunnel.

They had gone maybe fifty paces when a howl of
frustration and an echoing crash sounded from further
down the tunnel. The four exchanged glances and continued at a more deliberate pace until they rounded a
tight bend. Six paces away, the tunnel spilled into a
large, brightly lit cavern. Low muttering followed by a
splintering commotion sounded frighteningly close.

Tigh put a hand on Jame's tense shoulder. The arbiter captured her partner's eyes, reading a confidence in
her abilities and an overwhelming concern for her.
Jame reached out and squeezed Tigh's arm, telling her
through their contact that she was ready. The warrior
raised her eyes to the waiting Meah and nodded. The
rogue Guard and the arbiter, blinking a little in the
bright illumination, strode into the cavern.

In the middle of the rough cave, a short, round
woman rummaged through haphazard piles of unbroken
objects, mumbling incoherent words. Tas had warned

them that the evil Misner had the sweet face of a grand-mother so Jame wasn't shocked when the Wizard looked up and latched onto Meah with startled eyes.

"Meah." a sugary voice filled the cavern. "What are you doing here? Why aren't you with your regiment?"

"My second in command is with them." Meah shrugged.

"And who is this?" Misner squinted at Jame. "An Emoran spy? You left your regiment to bring me an Emoran spy?" The Wizard straightened and faced the rogue Guard, her features hardening into anger. "I'm preparing to give the order to attack. You're supposed to be with your regiment to receive that order."

Leveling a cold gaze on Misner, Meah folded her arms and sauntered closer to the Wizard. "My second can lead the troops," she scoffed. "This is no ordinary Emoran spy. She is the Emoran princess and companion to Tigh the Terrible." Misner's eyes widened at the name of the one person she feared above all others.

"Tigh the Terrible," Misner muttered. "It's too late to draw her to me, even with such a perfect hostage. I'm ready to attack. Tigh can't stop me now."

"You see, that's my point." Meah casually picked up a ceramic mug from a pile of objects and pretended to study it. "She's not *my* hostage. I'm *her* hostage." She innocently shrugged at the incredulous expression on Misner's face.

"What game are you playing here, Meah?" Misner's sweet voice took on the quality of hard candy.

The rogue Guard appeared amused by this. "Game? Why, a Guard's game. It's the only kind I know how to play. But Tigh has always played it better than any of us."

Misner, sensing that she didn't have much time to cast her spell, wrapped a hand around her vulture's head amulet. After several heartbeats, she struggled to keep panic from her expression. She concentrated a little harder, flashing suspicious glances at Meah and Jame.

"Looking for your Guards?" Jame's casual voice captured Misner's attention.

"How do you know what I'm doing?" The hard sugar of Misner's voice crystallized and the spell wrapped around it was enough to leave Jame shaking with fear, but Jame didn't know that. Her wolf pup amulet made her blissfully unaware of the magic being cast her way.

"I know a lot of things, Misner," Jame responded. "Like, for instance, how my people disabled your Guards."

"Disabled my Guards?" Misner chuckled through her puzzlement at Jame's lack of reaction to her spell. "You do not possess the means to do that, even if your people could sneak through my army undetected."

"Why do you think we can't disable Guards?" Jame lifted up a stone vial tied to her belt. "I have the means right here to disable Meah. I don't think she'd be so amiable a hostage if it were otherwise."

Misner stared at the vial and at the confident fair-haired young woman. "Unfortunately for you, young princess, that won't stop me." The Wizard dramatically lifted her amulet in Jame's direction.

"Are you trying to do something?" Jame inquired, taking in the startled reaction from Misner. Frowning, the Wizard thrust the amulet at Jame. "Maybe that thing is wearing out," the arbiter calmly suggested.

Misner threw her senses out to encompass the stronghold and the camp outside. Certainly, another Wizard had to be behind this impertinent young woman's immunity to magic. Her probing picked up nothing out of the ordinary. Only the usual flow of stray magic touched her mind. Squeezing her amulet once again, she knew that she was conjuring magic, but it dispersed before completing its purpose. Staring at

Jame, she realized that this calm young woman was truly stopping her magic.

"Why are you here?" the Wizard rasped from the failed effort of casting a spell.

"To stop you, of course." Jame shrugged, putting on her best impression of Tigh's casual disinterest.

Picking up an octagonal object crafted from clear crystal, Misner's fearful expression was quickly replaced by a confident smirk. "You may have been able to stop my Guards. But you won't be able to stop my army. The spell has already been cast into this crystal. All I have to do is smash it against the ground and my army will be imbued with the belief that they are invincible. The seconds-in-command know to lead the army with or without the Guards."

Jame's training as an arbiter allowed her to keep her expression impassive as her mind prayed that Goodemer was able to work around this unexpected twist in this deadly game. "We know," she said softly, thinking fast to give Goodemer some time. "That's why we have your army surrounded."

"And you think your puny forces can beat my mighty, well-trained army?" The grandmotherly face lit with pride.

"We have the element of surprise and have had the time to prepare for the most efficient attack on your troops," Jame answered, steadily. "We can defeat you."

"Not if my army is invincible." A warm laughter filled the cavern as Misner raised her plump arms and flung the crystal as hard as she could against the ground. Where it bounced upon impact.

Staring startled at the crystal, Misner did not see Tigh's dagger until it was protruding from her chest. Looking up into Jame's eyes, her face creased into an insane grin before she sank lifeless to the ground next to the crystal.

A startled yelp from behind caused Jame and Meah to whip around in time to see Goodemer bolt into the cavern, face scrunched in concentration and arms waving in strange rapid movements. The others stood frozen watching this bizarre demonstration. Goodemer finally slowed her arms and appeared to be tying off invisible strands in the air, before stepping back and taking a deep breath.

"Is there a problem?" Tigh asked pointedly.

"When Misner died, she released the spell of invincibility," Goodemer gasped, her voice raw from the effort of stopping a sudden surge of intense magic.

"But you stopped it. Right?" Jame pressed, hopefully.

"For a while, I think." Goodemer shook her head. "It's struggling against my hold even now. I don't know how long I'll be able to restrain it."

Meah, always one to enjoy a good twist in the game, grinned, as her former commander rolled her eyes up to whatever demented deity oversaw her destiny.

****

Before Olet scrambled over the hill rising up from the valley, she glanced back to see if the others escaped the camp unharmed. The shadowy band was flying across the open flats to the foothills adjacent to the small mound Olet was on. Relieved, she sprinted down the other side of the hill into the Emoran camp and was pleased to see the warriors positioned at the old fashion catapults that Tigh had shown them how to use. Goodemer had spent a good amount of time handling the rough balls for the catapults. Olet hoped her efforts would give them the power needed to clear the small mound between them and the enemy.

"Success?" Argis, running to greet her, asked.

"Yes," Olet gasped. "And the others are almost to the Lukrian camp."

Argis nodded, staring down the line of catapults. Tigh had told her to make their presence known as soon as the Guards were out of the way. Without their leaders, Misner's army was just a group of volunteers and mercenaries whose loyalties didn't go beyond the next payday, and this could be used in their favor.

Strolling up the small mound, Argis stood—not even attempting to conceal herself—and stared at the sprawling camp as it churned to life in the weak dawn light. Reaching into her belt pouch, she pulled out a stone amulet in the shape of a wolf pup's head. Wrapping her hand around it, she concentrated on the words that Goodemer had instructed her to repeat over and over again. Warmth suddenly emanated from the amulet and it first turned blue from Kylara and then green from Mularke. "That really works," the warrior muttered as she returned the amulet to her pouch.

As she turned, every warrior's eyes were on her. It was time to meet her destiny. Shocked by this unbidden thought, she blinked at her waiting force as if seeing them anew. If this was her destiny, then she was not going to settle for anything less than complete victory. Strolling back down the hill, she unsheathed her sword with a sibilant hiss that hung in the still pre-dawn air. Positioning herself at the end of the catapult line, Argis held her sword up high, every eye focused on her blade.

"For Emoria!" Argis cried out as she slashed the sword towards the ground. Yodels and battle cries rose up first from the warriors, then echoed by the horse troops, picked up by the Lukrians in the adjacent hills, and then spread to the archers on the opposite side of the enemy camp. At the same time, the first volleys sprang from the catapults, sailing easily over the hill. The catapults from the Lukrians and the archers mirrored this display with their own. "Fire at will!" Argis cried as she and Olet scrambled back up the hill, flattening themselves when they topped the crest.

The catapulted balls spewed thick, misty clouds upon impact, surrounding three sides of the Wizard's camp and slowly spreading to the Balderon side. Shouts of commands and chaotic efforts to get into defensive positioning were undermined by a growing sense of confusion within the camp. Seconds-in-command, upon discovering that their Commanders had been taken down, struggled with their own commitments to this mercenary army. The only thing clear to them was that they were under attack and it was no longer a matter of fighting Misner's war but one of simple survival.

The first finger of light from the sun, as it popped up between distant mountain peaks, illuminated a strange tableau in the valley overlooking the city of Balderon. Four thousand foot soldiers and five hundred mounted troops were lined up in tense formation in defense of their lives. Before them was a creeping, impenetrable mist, no closer than a hundred paces from the edge of the Wizard's camp.

Misner had promised them the gift of invincibility when the battle began, yet they felt only fear and uncertainty. Rumors, as thick as the mysterious fog, about the Guards being poisoned, dead or missing turned their uncertainty into the knowledge that they were on their own.

"What's that?" Olet stammered as the sun penetrated the mist. "By the Children of Bal..."

Both Emorans rose to their feet, staring dumbfounded at the impossible vision before them. The warriors at the bottom of the hill, taking in the stunned expression of their leader, cautiously trod up the mound until they also stood staring, unbelieving.

Argis finally barked out a laugh and shook her head. "That daughter of a Yitsian snow monster of a Wizard told me to expect some small illusions."

"I'd hate to see what she calls a large illusion," Olet snorted.

Before them, where the thick mist had been, stood ten thousand Emoran warriors, swords drawn, facing Misner's slack-jawed, wide-eyed army.

****

"Is there any way you can break the spell?" Jame sank down on a rather opulent chair, staring at Goodemer, who was tensely concentrating on holding Misner's spell within a sphere of magic.

"I can't break it." Goodemer's voice was strained. "There's only one thing I can do."

"And that is?" Tigh paused from prowling around the chamber and looked up at the Wizard.

"Redirect it," Goodemer replied through clenched teeth. "At least most of it."

"Redirect. Most." Tigh latched on to the important words hanging in the air.

"It's a complicated spell," the Wizard muttered as she struggled with her hold.

"The only thing you can do is come up with the best way of dealing with it and tell us what to expect." Jame's steady, reassuring voice helped Goodemer push through her inexperience, which was draining her confidence in her own skills.

The Wizard nodded with jaw tensed in concentration. "I'm going to have to redirect the spell into something."

"Something." Tigh, once again, focused on the troublesome aspects of this little drama.

"I don't know what will happen exactly, but I can redirect it into something large enough to absorb it," Goodemer explained as she subtly shifted her arms to strengthen her magic.

"All of it?" Tigh asked.

"Most," Goodemer sighed. "I've frozen it like an arrow in mid-flight. The moment it's released, it will be moving at the same speed as when it was captured. Some of the magic will slip through."

"What will happen?" Jame thought about Argis trying to deal with the formidable army in the Balderon valley.

"It will have some effect on Misner's army, but not as strongly as if they were hit with the full spell."

"Something large," Tigh mused. "Can you hold it long enough to get out of these caverns?"

"I can try." Goodemer nodded.

"Let's get out of here." Tigh held a hand out to Jame and pulled her from the chair.

"With pleasure." Meah, who had been lounging on a pile of broken rubble, stretched and hopped to her feet. "This place has lost its charm."

"If you feel you can't hold it any longer, cast it into the walls." Tigh turned to Goodemer. "Everyone else be ready to run."

Fortunately for them it took less time to navigate the tunnels and caverns without having to worry about traps and spells. Goodemer looked as if she was ready to explode, but her face showed a determined strength. She wasn't going to fail. She had to prove her mentor's faith in her. Stumbling, she suddenly felt strong hands grasping her arms as Jame and Tigh pulled her along through the rubble-strewn tunnels.

It was full light by the time they emerged from the cavern, but they staggered ahead, not stopping to adjust their eyes to the sudden bright early morning sun. Tigh pulled Goodemer through the Lukrian camp into the surrounding meadow where towering boulders sat like solitary brooding giants casting long shadows on the foursome.

"Pick a boulder." Tigh waved a hand.

"I don't know what will happen." Goodemer eyed the looming granite rocks. "Misner could have anticipated something like this happening."

"We have no choice. Pick a rock." Tigh leveled clear blue eyes on her.

"Go on," Jame softly encouraged. "We'll get through this."

Goodemer nodded at the gentle arbiter and focused on the farthest boulder within their view. Taking in several calming breaths, she pulled in all the stray magic she could. She sliced her hands through the air, and the spell exploded from her hold. Flying several paces backwards from the force, Goodemer landed hard on the rocky ground. The funnel of stray magic held, guiding the spell to the boulder with only bits of magic sparking off and darting down the mountain slopes to the valley of Balderon. The ground shook and rumbled for long heartbeats as the boulder took the impact of the spell.

Silence hung in the air as they stared unmoving at the boulder. When it appeared that nothing was going to happen, Tigh and Jame trotted over to the stunned Wizard and helped her to her feet. The Lukrians from the camp had gathered on the edge of the meadow, mystified by what looked like a strange pantomime followed by an earth-shake.

As Jame opened her mouth to speak, another small tremor captured their attention. Four sets of eyes were riveted on the boulder. The tremors increased as the rock moved.

"Misner certainly knows how to keep things interesting," Meah commented as she sauntered up next to the other three.

Blinking several times, they realized that the rock was doing more than just moving. It was reshaping.

"This doesn't look good," Tigh muttered, as the shape became more defined.

"Uh, Tigh." Jame grabbed her partner's sleeve. "You're not planning on fighting that, are you?"

"Well, I don't think it's capable of reasonable discussion." Tigh arched an eyebrow at Jame.

"I'd fight it, but Tigh was always so much better at this kind of thing," Meah put in with a shrug.

The rock had grown from being round and squat to tall with limbs as a human shape quickly emerged as if manipulated by an inspired sculptor.

"It's invincible." Jame wrapped her hands around Tigh's arm, fully capturing the warrior's attention.

"It only thinks it's invincible. Right?" Tigh turned to Goodemer.

The Wizard, staring at Misner's handiwork, mutely nodded.

"It's a rock, not a person. It's not in the habit of thinking," Jame pressed.

"It's a spell." Tigh met Jame's eyes. "How long is the spell of invincibility supposed to last?" Tigh looked over Jame's head at Meah.

"Until the battle is over," Meah responded.

"I'm just going to whack at it and keep it out of trouble and hope that Argis has a good day fighting." Tigh returned her attention to Jame.

Jame slowly nodded as their eyes met with the understanding that working together always kept their focus on their promise to each other. "We'll help as best we can."

An earth-rattling pair of thuds caused all eyes to look up. Tigh sighed as she unsheathed her sword. She swore she would never again complain about not having enough challenge in her life.

****

Kylara shut her eyes and gave her head a shake. The incredible vision was still there when she slowly opened them again—thousands of Emoran warriors. The Regent-General applauded Goodemer's attention to detail, right down to the casual arrogance that was trained into the Emorans as intensely as any weapons skill. It was an unbelievably disquieting scene, even for those who knew it to be only an illusion.

Shading her eyes, she viewed the adjacent hills where Argis was quickly recovering from her shock and shouting commands to her equally stunned warriors as they scrambled into formation. It wouldn't do to let Misner's troops know that this sudden army of Emorans was not expected and not real.

Kylara signaled her warriors to the top of the hill, proud that they held their composure at their first glimpse of the unimaginable spectacle dominating the Balderon valley. Turning to the hills opposite Argis, she nodded with approval as Mularke was efficiently commandeering her archers into neat double lines following the contour of the hills.

Tindal, following her warriors up the hill, joined Kylara. "Wizards can be handy to have around," she commented.

"I think I'm glad we didn't have them during the Wars," Kylara responded, dryly. "The Guards were unpredictable enough."

"So what now?" Tindal shaded her eyes as she scanned the rows of tense soldiers in Misner's camp.

"That depends on if Tigh and Jame can stop Misner," Kylara sighed. A sudden unpleasant chill shot through them, causing a visible shrug of the shoulders. "What was that?"

The answer came quickly as the defeated posture of the Wizard's army suddenly snapped into alertness. The seconds-in-command, who were conferring on the least ruinous battle plans, were all at once convinced that they could defeat this unimpressive army surrounding them with barely drawing a sword.

"Looks like Tigh and Jame have run into some problems," Tindal murmured, gesturing to her group leaders, who in turn shouted directives to the lines of warriors who were trying to shut out of their thoughts the significance behind the sudden change in the enemy.

Barked commands echoed through the camp and a thousand arrows arced over the outer circle of foot soldiers into the illusionary army. Kylara locked her eyes onto Argis as the Emoran prepared to give the signal to attack. Too many heartbeats passed by as Argis intently studied the scene before her. Puzzled, Kylara returned her gaze to the valley and was surprised to see that the illusion not only held, but was slowly moving forward.

The shouts from Misner's camp were precise and confident as the foot soldiers drew their swords and advanced on the menace before them. Not waiting for the illusion to be broken, Argis' sword flashed. Mularke's distinctive yodel penetrated the air and hundreds of arrows sparked off the intense morning sun.

Kylara waved her sword and shouted, "For Lukria!" before charging down the hill followed by four hundred bellowing warriors with swords flaring and the sharp glint of joy in their eyes.

Olet and Argis watched as the Lukrians raced through the outer edge of the counterfeit warriors. At first, Argis couldn't distinguish between the Lukrians and the illusions because of the sunlight on the mist surrounding them. Then her eyes lit up and she gave off a surprised whoop. Instead of dissipating the illusion, a whirling mixture of mist and Emoran warriors covered the Lukrians' wake.

"Remind me to kiss Goodemer." Argis grinned wildly, now seeing the difference between the puny magic of Misner and the illusions of a skilled and imaginative Wizard like Goodemer. "The confusion just may be enough to put this in our favor."

Kas, galloping down the line of her horse warriors, let the suddenly charged air fill her lungs, and she couldn't keep a maniacal grin from her face. Yodels and shouts rose up as she passed, then the ground rumbled as two hundred horses draped in leather and armor rounded the smaller mounds closer to Balderon and flew across the plain, swords waving in unrestrained ecstasy.

"For Emoria!" Argis' voice rang out and the Emoran warriors bolted down the hill, filling the air with high-pitched cries of "Emoria!" Argis' entire body was galvanized as she crashed through the misty illusion, the magic-soaked vapors penetrating her skin and heightening her sense of awareness.

Argis' army pressed through the illusions as Misner's troops charged into the vaporous warriors, discovering that they had been cleverly deceived. But they didn't have time to ponder the duplicity because they were immediately battling real warriors mixed with the counterfeits with no way of telling which was which.

Argis almost stumbled in amazement when her sword finally rang against another. Her defensive blow had the inexplicable power to repel her opponent. With swift, agile movements that she knew were beyond what she truly possessed, she downed her stunned opponent. A crazy laugh erupted from deep within her soul as she slashed through the line of Misner's so-called invincible warriors.

"We've been given the skill of the Guards." Argis' hoarse voice reached those closest to her. "Pass the word." Kiss Goodemer? By all the Children of Bal, she'd take the Wizard as her life partner and beg for the honor on her knees.

Chapter 20

"Oh look, it has a sword." Meah clasped her hands in mock delight. "A very sharp looking sword."

"Glad you didn't pick one of the largest boulders," Tigh commented as the stone giant staggered to a halt, as if trying to remember what it was just doing. In a short time, the granite face had transformed into disquieting human-like features. "Are you going to help with this or are you concentrating on what's happening in the valley?" Tigh flashed Goodemer a quick look before fixing her attention on the stone menace.

"I think they're going to be just fine," Goodemer replied as an intriguing half smile touched her lips.

"But they're fighting soldiers who think they're invincible." Jame frowned.

"But the Lukrians and the Emorans think they have the skills of the Elite Guards." Goodemer sheepishly dropped her eyes.

Tigh half-turned to the Wizard, impressed by her strategic use of magic. "That beats invincible any time." The former Guard grinned.

"Wonder if that works for invincible rocks?" Meah mused, staring at the struggling stone creature.

Jame shot dagger looks at the rogue Guard as she struggled to bring her own fears for Tigh's safety under control. Tigh's stance was casually indifferent as she absently flipped her sword and strolled to meet the animated stone warrior. The arbiter knew that Tigh was fighting a battle against her own fear and apprehension towards this unknown foe. But she also knew that the warrior had the incredible ability to harness the energy of fear and transmute it into another weapon to use to her advantage.

"She'll be fine," a quiet, confident voice said softly in Jame's ear. "She's beaten Misner's magic before. It may look nasty, but it's still made from the same kind of magic."

Jame turned astute eyes to the Wizard. "You know something that we don't know," she stated.

"All I know is what I've seen and heard." Goodemer spread her hands and shrugged.

"You're going to help her, aren't you?" Jame pressed.

"If I can," Goodemer sighed. "I have to keep watch over the spells in the valley. One slip and it would be disastrous for your warriors. Tigh has the skill to beat Misner's magic without me. You must believe this."

Before Jame had a chance to probe further, the ground shook again. This time the rhythm of the tremors reflected a more confident movement from the stone creature. Staring at the threat, terrifyingly close to Tigh, another transformation had changed the stone giant's limbs from blocky and cumbersome to sleek and muscular.

"Be careful," Jame whispered, as Tigh whipped her sword above her head to stop a brutal blow from the stone warrior's blade. The arbiter winced as the clash echoed in the still morning air.

Tigh held onto her sword with little more than stubborn determination. Fortunately, her blade didn't shatter and basic sword-handling skills did not appear to be a part of the magic that filled the stone warrior. Instead of holding the blade against Tigh's, the rocky giant let it bounce off, giving Tigh the chance to hop out of striking distance.

This lack of skill could be good or bad, Tigh wryly mused as she nimbly flipped away from another clumsy swipe of the large blade. The stone face worked into a dozen planed expressions of frustration. Shaking her head, Tigh whacked a solid rocky knee with the flat of her blade, just to test the reaction.

The stony features labored to express annoyance at the clout, while Tigh cursed in three languages as the painful jolt from the blow reverberated through her body. "Great," she sighed as she backed away. Why didn't she think to have Goodemer channel the spell into a tree? At least a sword had a chance against living wood.

The stone warrior straightened to twice Tigh's height as the spell rippled across the rocky surface, smoothing it, as if finely chiseled by a master sculptor. With this change came a more fluid movement as the giant whipped the sword over its head and with a graceful downward swipe tried to split Tigh in two. The black-clad warrior sideswiped the blade, then jumped on its upper edge. Balancing on the sword, Tigh grinned mockingly as the frustrated stone warrior reacted with an upward swing, effectively flicking Tigh over its head and delivering a staggering blow to its own forehead.

As the rocky tormentor clumsily careened around in the grass, Tigh sheathed her sword and vaulted onto the giant's back, climbing until she had one arm wrapped around the huge neck. She carved into the top of the stone head with her sharp hunting knife, narrowly avoiding a cleft in her own head from the monster's enormous blade, before shimmying down the stone body.

The ground trembled as the stone warrior crashed to the ground in a rocky daze.

"Amazing," Goodemer murmured.

"What?" Jame blinked at her.

"Every time the stone giant injures itself, Misner's army falters." The Wizard grinned. "I wasn't sure if the redirected spell would work under the same rules as the original spell. It does. This means that it doesn't matter if Argis or Tigh wins, either one can break the spell."

❉❉❉❉❉❉❉❉❉❉❉❉❉❉❉

Tas felt as if her body was under the control of a manic warrior. Being agile and quick was already a given for someone of her size, but this was beyond anything she had ever dreamed. It took her senses to an exhilarating battle high as she slashed and spun and flipped past her victims. *Daughter of a shaggy mountain goat. This is what it's like to be Tigh.*

A wild, demented sound erupted from her throat as she faced a wide-eyed soldier, her sword finding its mark before the soldier had time to react. Suddenly there was no one in front of her to fight. She had battled all the way through the enemy line. The sight of the abandoned camp reminded her that the rogue Guards could give them trouble if they regained consciousness.

"Wolfie!" The bantam warrior squinted in the misty swirl of the battle before catching the unruly hair of the Council's guard. Her voice was barely audible above the chaotic din.

Wolfie caught her eyes, then grinned as she enthusiastically removed the three soldiers in her path. The Council's guard greeted Tas with a joyous laugh. "Can you believe this?" She flipped and swung her sword with graceful abandonment.

"I'd give anything to feel this every day." Tas grinned wildly. "But I'll be happy if it lasts as long as this battle. It's been several sand marks since we knocked out the Guards. Goodemer said she wasn't sure how long that potion would keep them under. Interested in checking them out with me?"

"Let's go." Wolfie bounced on the balls of her feet, unable to control the manic energy flowing through her.

The two Emoran warriors jogged through the camp. Taking in the litter of abandoned plates and cups and blankets, they couldn't help but feel pleased that the enemy had been caught off-guard.

"Do you think that this is Goodemer's doing?" Wolfie asked as they padded past a picket of nervously nickering horses.

"Who else do we know with the skill to turn us into Guards?" Tas grinned.

"And she created that magical army..." Wolfie sighed with a faraway look in her eyes. "I swear, I'm ready to join with her forever. I'll even plead for the honor on my knees."

Tas laughed. And everyone called her the impulsive one.

Cautiously approaching the front opening of a large, light colored tent, they paused as the small warrior took a deep breath and looked inside. Slowly pulling her head back from the tent opening, she blinked at Wolfie with an expression of surprise and fear. Wolfie stuck her head through the opening and took a long look around.

"She's not here," Tas gasped. "Argis needs to know."

Wolfie nodded. "There's only four of them and we already have the upper hand in this battle. How much trouble can they make?"

A blood-freezing chuckle floated to them. Their words had been picked up with the enhanced hearing of four black-clad warriors casually standing barely fifty

paces away. Quickly, harsh cries of a blue jay emerged
from the Emorans' throats as they prayed that Argis
would hear the incongruous sounds above the battle
noise.

"Look, Patch," mocked a black-haired Guard with
dead gray eyes. "It's a half warrior." The four chuckled with an evil glee that touched every nerve in the
Emorans' bodies. "Emoria must be desperate to allow
such tiny women to become warriors."

Tas labored to fight the paralyzing chill that wafted
off the arrogant foursome. She desperately wished she
had more of the potion-covered darts. Wait. Her mind
froze for a heartbeat on the most astonishing revelation.
She possessed the same fighting skills as these menacing Guards. Raising confident eyes, she looked upon
the Guards as equals. "This from a former peace-lov-
ing book pusher?"

The Guards' grating laugh almost undermined the
Emoran's confidence. "There's a fine line between
being courageous and being stupid. Although in this
case, it comes to much the same thing," the one called
Patch purred.

The crunch of grass caught their sensitive ears and
the four Guards twisted around. Tas and Wolfie held
their breaths as they watched Argis and Kylara rush
through the camp towards them. The newcomers prudently stopped a good distance from the Guards, eyeing
them warily.

"Kylara." A tall light-haired Guard sounded the
name with malicious delight. "What an interesting surprise."

"Let's just say I came to my senses about Misner,"
the Lukrian Regent-General said steadily.

"You think joining the losing side means coming to
your senses?" The blonde Guard's laugh was like sleet
against their ears.

"No. I joined the winning side." Kylara grinned. "Look around. Our army has all but cut through your lines."

"You think a little illusion can stop us?" Patch scoffed. "Have you forgotten about the spell of invincibility?"

"I haven't forgotten. But it doesn't seem to be very effective against the spell our Wizard has cast over us." Kylara casually flipped her sword before allowing the blade to rest on her shoulder. "After all, the four of us fought through your invincible army without a scratch."

"Your Wizard?" the blonde repeated, as the four Guards exchanged enigmatic looks.

"A Wizard much more skilled and powerful than Misner," growled Argis, impatient with all the talk. She straightened to her full height and casually sauntered up to the Guards, ignoring the shivers caused from the icy air surrounding them. "As I see it, as long as you four are around, your army will continue to labor under the illusion that they can win this battle. I know only one solution to that problem."

The Master Warrior, sending a quick prayer to Laur, swung her sword, only to have its progress stopped by four black blades. Her arms felt as though they had been plunged into an ice packed river, but by some miracle, she was able to push all four Guards back, giving the other three time to join in the battle.

Feeling the snow-cold sting of the sword of a worthy opponent, Argis thanked Goodemer a thousand times over for the ecstasy of negligent skill that wiped the arrogant smirks off these offspring of Yitsian snow creatures.

****

"You sure you don't want to join in the fun?" Tigh shot a look at Meah, who was lounging on a nearby boulder.

"Don't tell me that a rock-brained invincible, stone giant is too much for you?" Meah blinked innocently at her former supreme commander.

Tigh gracefully flipped away from another clumsy swipe of the stone warrior's sword. "Nah. Just making sure you don't mind me having all the fun."

"Tigh." Jame's strained voice reached her. The warrior turned sheepish eyes to her intently watching partner.

"I'm being careful." Hearing the movement of air behind her, she sideswiped what would have been a rather messy encounter with the insistent blade of her rocky opponent. The sword penetrated the ground with the ease of a hand through water. Face contorted with anger and frustration, the stone warrior focused on pulling the stubborn blade from the hard-packed soil.

Tigh picked up a fist-sized stone and pitched it at the rocky body. The stone warrior flinched at the impact but continued to tug at the sword hilt. "Start throwing stones at it," Tigh shouted to the others. "Try to get it away from the sword."

Goodemer and Jame quickly picked up stones and lobbed them at the rocky creature. The impacts sounded like loose stones scuttling down steep cliffs. Tigh scanned the boulder-strewn meadow for anything that could be used to their advantage. The hole to the underground tunnels was too small. Then her mind snagged on a fleeting memory from when they emerged from the hole.

The arbiter and the Wizard were performing their task with enthusiasm and the stone warrior's attention was now on avoiding the strength reducing chipping of stone against stone. Noticing the monster's instinct to lunge in the direction of its attackers, Tigh ran behind the rocky being and whacked its leg with the flat of her blade. Snarling at this stinging sensation, the stone giant twisted around and glared at the black-clad warrior.

"Stop throwing the stones," Tigh called out to Jame and Goodemer. She hopped out of the way of the blocky hand grabbing for her. "You want me, you have to catch me." Tigh scooped up a rock with her boot and kicked it into the stone giant's forehead. The sculpted features grimaced in anger as the warrior gave chase with earth-shaking steps.

"What's she doing?" Jame's voice was raspy with fear for her warrior. "Why is she leading that thing away from us?"

Goodemer laid a hand on Jame's tense arm. "Have faith."

Raptly staring at Tigh, who was playing a deadly teasing game with the angry stone warrior, Meah slid off her boulder.

"Come on, you pebble," Tigh taunted the stone warrior, kicking up the occasional rock for emphasis. "You think you're invincible?" The stone warrior flung deadly legs out and propelled the heavy body faster, arms wildly swiping the air, just missing the aggravating black-clad pest. Each unsuccessful attempt to knock the life out of the warrior added a new layer of frustration for the stone giant. It was invincible. It could not be beaten. It will destroy all these puny creatures...

Tigh flipped ten paces away, landing on her feet but immediately grimacing and falling to the ground.

"Tigh!" Jame's shout echoed through the thin mountain air, followed by the crunch of grass as her feet quickly moved.

Seeing the agonized pain in the former Guard's eyes as she sprawled helplessly on the ground, the stone giant's planed features shifted into a hardened smile. Wanting to squash the soft flesh and hear the grinding together of crushed bones, the stone warrior took a lunging step forward.

A thunderous avalanche of noise echoed through the meadow as an unexpected cloud of stone dust puffed into the air, obscuring the giant and Tigh. Jame skidded to a stop, just paces from the dust cloud, frantically trying to see through it.

"Tigh!" she cried in a raw voice that only fear could produce.

A black figure flew through the stone dust. Tigh stood a pace away, unharmed, only to be toppled onto her back by the hurtling body of her partner. Jame choked back a sob as she wrapped her arms around her warrior's neck, letting the tension flow out of her. A grinning Tigh was content to hold the arbiter as her own nerves settled down.

Staring down into the pit that was used for transporting oversized equipment and supplies into the tunnels, Meah could barely make out the shattered remains of the stone warrior. Cleansing certainly didn't harm her former commander's ability to find on-the-spot solutions to impossible situations.

Goodemer stood next to the rogue Guard, probing the stone remnants for any trace of the spell. "The spell is broken," she whispered, feeling an incredible joy that almost made her lightheaded.

Laughing, Tigh rolled to her feet, bringing Jame with her. Hand-in-hand they walked to the edge of the pit. "Clever." Jame nudged Tigh. "But if you scare me like that again, I'll stop speaking to you."

"Seeran wouldn't have been very happy if there wasn't some suspense and excitement." Tigh lifted an innocent eyebrow at Jame.

Jame gave her partner a mocking glare before shaking her head and grinning. "Something for the Chronicles, indeed. I wonder how Argis is doing."

Casting her mind to the valley of Balderon, Goodemer simply smiled.

****

It was one thing to fight an ordinary soldier while possessing the skills of a Guard. Fighting someone who possessed the same skills was an entirely different matter. The arrogant Guards had the advantage in that they were comfortable with their enhancements. Fortunately for their foes, their reaction time was ragged from the potion that had knocked them out, making the encounter deadly and exhilarating at the same time.

Kylara nimbly sidestepped a sword thrust from the blonde Guard. "You'll have to do better than that, Nark," she taunted.

"Meah should have killed Tigh when she had the chance," Nark growled as she swung her sword in angry swipes at the Regent-General. "Only Tigh could have worked out a plan to beat us."

"So you think you've been beaten?" The Regent-General took the Guard through a series of wildly executed thrusts and parries.

"This puny army, perhaps. Misner, perhaps. But never the Guards." Nark's guttural response was like ice against Kylara's spine. But she concentrated on warming her reaction with a skillful thrust that ended with the two blades scraping together down to the hilts.

"That reminds me." Kylara knocked Nark's sword away. "Where is Meah?"

"She disappeared before we got here." Nark shrugged before her sword crashed against Kylara's. The Lukrian's arms ached from the bone deep frost flowing off the Guard's body. "We thought maybe Tigh got her."

Kylara remained silent at this, hoping it was true.

Argis stared into the cold gray eyes of Patch Lachlan. Patch was almost as legendary as Tigh for her skill and cruelty. She had been well on her way to equaling Tigh when the Grappian Wars ended. Which meant...Argis almost missed a parry in her realization

that this sneering warrior had been a gentle soul before
the Guard enhancements. Reeking with cruelty, Patch
lunged at the Emoran with a dizzying quickness. Argis
flipped, catching her boot on the Guard's chin and
snapping her head back.

Patch tumbled backwards hitting the ground hard,
shock overwriting her smirk. Fighting the agonizing
frostbite that tightened around her foot, Argis stomped
the same boot onto the Guard's wrist, forcing the hand
to open and the sword to clatter to the stony ground.

In a blur of movement, the Emoran warrior kicked
away the blade and whipped her own around until the
point was pressed against Patch's throat. Staring down
at the cold anger, Argis struggled not to kill her. She
growled in her frustration but wouldn't give in to her
desire for blood. She couldn't shake the knowledge
that deep within this person, who would kill her without a thought, was a peaceful, gentle soul. Someone
who had been used, first by the Southern Territories and
then by an insane Wizard. Replacing her blade with her
boot, she bent down and slammed the hilt of her sword
against Patch's head.

Argis took the opportunity to check the progress of
the battle. She was surprised to see that the fighting
was now scattered throughout the camp and the Emorans looked as though they were whittling down the
enemy with little problem. "Good spell, Goodemer.
Good spell," Argis breathed.

Kylara was holding her own with the blonde Guard,
but Argis was ready to put an end to this battle. Taking
a step, the Emoran collapsed to the ground. Face
creased in agony, she pounded her cold, numb foot trying to work some warmth back into it. Growling, she
spewed enough curses to curl every hair on the heads of
Laur's acolytes until the feeling returned to her foot
that she could hobble on it.

Stepping behind the blonde Guard, Argis feinted a
movement that she expected Nark to detect through her

enhanced senses.   The Guard parried a thrust from Kylara, then spun to stop what she thought was a blow from Argis, but the Emoran moved around to her blind side and slapped the side of her head with the flat of her blade.   Nark, with a stunned expression on her face, slumped to the ground.   Kylara blinked at Argis in confusion.

"Don't kill them," Argis rasped.   "I think Tigh should be the one to deal with them."

Kylara allowed the idea to sink in for a few heartbeats before slowly nodding.   "Let's help the others."

The other two Guards were quickly knocked out and Tas and Wolfie took a few heartbeats to rub the feeling back into their frozen hands.   "Now I know what it's like to fight a Yitsian snow creature," Tas grumbled as she held her sword hand beneath her other arm.

"Now what?"   Kylara stared down at the Guards. "They're not going to stay out for long."

"Let's tie them up.   Not that it will do much good when they come to," Argis muttered, looking around for rope.   Pulling out her knife, she sliced one of the ropes holding up a nearby tent. "This'll do."

Tas and Wolfie efficiently divided the rope and tied the Guards' ankles and wrists.   With the help of Argis and Kylara, they dragged the Guards near one of the tents, out of the way of the fighting.

The air crackled.   The hairs on their arms lifted and a whirlwind almost swept them off their feet.   Just as quickly, the flapping tents and the dust settled down. Shouts of dismay rose up from around them.   Emorans and Lukrians stopped blows in mid-strike, staring as the enemy dropped their weapons and fell, sobbing, to their knees.   Terror-stricken cries for mercy replaced the grunts of battle.

Argis dashed to the picket of horses and untied a noble warhorse.   Throwing herself onto the beast, she galloped through the camp, waving her sword.   "Vic-

tory is ours! Secure the prisoners. Victory is ours!"
she exulted as jubilant cheers rose up in her wake.

In the distance, shouts and drums erupted from the
walls of Balderon. The city gates opened and people
bolted onto the meadow as if it were the first day of
spring. Argis pulled up on the horse and stared at the
thousands of ordinary people rushing out to welcome
them as their saviors. She had just led the army that
saved Balderon from an invading army. The realization
made her lightheaded. The prediction on the statue of
Hekolatis came true.

"You did it." Olet was jumping up and down,
unable to contain the incredible elation from a good day
of fighting.

Argis rested weary eyes on her. "*We* did it. *All* of
us."

"But *you* led us." Olet stopped her movement and
grabbed the horse's reins. "Let them honor you for
that." She glanced at the Balderons who filtered
through the camp, helping with the prisoners and the
wounded.

"They will remember us all," Argis said decisively.

Chapter
21

Jame toppled over from laughing so hard. Fortunately, she was sitting on the large cushions in Jyac's private eating chamber. A long, strong hand gently wrapped around her arm and pulled her back upright. Capturing the affectionate blue eyes of her relaxed warrior, she forgot about her fit of laughter and allowed herself to be pulled into the wonderful depths of Tigh's beautiful soul.

"Poor Argis." Jyac wiped a tear from her eye, her face flushed from laughing. Sharing the midday meal with Poylin was quite entertaining but made eating and drinking difficult.

"If you think the expression on her face when that artist asked Argis to pose for him was funny, you should have seen her actually trying to pose." Poylin could barely squeeze the words out, she was laughing so hard. "He kept insisting that she hold her sword in a heroic way and she kept insisting that you couldn't hit a full grown cow holding a sword like that. It went on and on until, in sheer frustration, she showed him the proper way to hold a sword by slicing his pile of wet clay into a thousand flying bits." The small group around the table was holding their sides from their aching mirth. The tension had been so strong for the last several weeks that this release was as much from relief as from the amusing tales of the battle of Balderon.

"Here's to Argis. Hero of Balderon." Jyac raised her mug of spiced wine.

"Here's to Argis," the others intoned with raised mugs.

"Here's to Jame, Tigh and Goodemer. Heroes of Emoria." Jyac looked over at the trio with a sly grin. Jame shook her head, Tigh rolled her eyes and Goodemer reddened as she suddenly found the pattern of the ceramic plate in front of her fascinating.

They were saved from further embarrassment by the sound of quick footfalls in the outside corridor. A few heartbeats later a beaming Eiget stepped into the chamber.

"They're on their way?" Jyac knew she didn't even have to ask.

"They've cleared the outer border." Eiget nodded, unable to keep the silly grin from her face. Her partner was among the returning heroes and she had a special celebration planned.

"Let's go welcome our victorious army." The Queen of Emoria rose and put a hand out to Ronalyn, who took it and was gracefully pulled to her feet.

They strolled out the doorway, followed by Sark and Goodemer. Tigh stepped back to let Jame go ahead of her, but the arbiter put a halting hand on her arm. The warrior blinked at Jame's enigmatic expression.

"What's wrong?" Tigh asked.

"I just wanted a quiet moment before all the excitement," Jame returned a little sheepishly. "I'm missing just the two of us. Being on the road. Not having to share you with anyone else."

Tigh captured Jame's lips in a long, reaffirming kiss. She had been half prepared to settle in Emoria if Jame wanted to stay. Deep down she didn't think either of them was ready for such a stable existence, but Tigh wanted to make sure that it was Jame's decision. "Anytime you want to leave, just say the word," she breathed in the arbiter's ear.

Jame sighed as her mind did some rapid calculations. "We can't leave until we are joined in an Emoran ceremony, but everyone's going to want to celebrate this victory first. Being a princess sure can be a pain sometimes."

A pondering hum rumbled in Tigh's throat. "Maybe it can have its advantages, too. You can request to make our joining ceremony a part of the victory celebration. Two rabbits with one arrow."

The answering grin from Jame was enough to weaken the mighty warrior's knees. "I like the way you think," Jame purred as she nuzzled against Tigh's strong neck. "In fact I like everything about you."

"That's good to know, because we're about to be joined." Tigh cast an indulgent eye downward, feeling Jame smile contentedly against her skin.

****

The stillness of the valley was the only indication that something out there was threatening enough to silence the birds and put the habitually grazing deer on alert. The women lined the top of the gate wall, focused on the single entrance into the valley. Long heartbeats passed during which they all realized that they were putting themselves at risk from passing out because they were holding their breath.

The silence was broken by the endless echoing of hooves that were clattering against the rocky floor of the tunnel that led into the valley. Kas, atop her elegant white mare, both decked out in full battle gear, shot out into the valley floor and galloped towards the opposite bluff before pulling up and turning to face the tunnel.

A sharp whistle cut through the fading echoes of the horse's hooves. A heartbeat later horses and riders in full, shiny battle gear galloped single file from the tunnel, trampling out intricately coordinated designs in a proud display of horsewomanship. Each design, building on the one before it, elicited louder and louder shouts and cheering from the several hundred intently watching Emoran citizens who had been left behind in the city.

Much too soon the patterns wound down as the horses, one by one, pulled into a line next to Kas, stretching from bluff to bluff beyond the furthest side of the tunnel.

"Do you think they spent the whole journey back planning this?" Jame bent her head to Jyac.

"Of course." Jyac grinned. "How many chances does one have to lead a victorious army home from battle?"

Kas sounded three shrill whistles and a line of archers marched from the tunnel, their gear so polished that the afternoon sun glinted off the tips of the arrows bobbing in the quivers on their backs.

When a double line of archers stood at attention in front of the horses, Mularke ran from the entrance. The archers, in formal age-old embellishment and enviable precision, strung their body-length bows and nocked an arrow as the Master Archer rushed by them. The effect was a smooth ripple of movement from one end of the double lines to the other.

After the last two archers snapped into readiness with bows tightly drawn, a cutting whistle sounded and the cavalry tossed banners from Emoria, Lukria and Balderon, anchored with stones, upward and over the archers. A sharp shout from Mularke and the front line of archers raised their bows and let the shafts hurtle through the air, impaling and carrying each banner further into the air before they fluttered gracefully to the ground. As soon as the first wave of arrows hissed through the air, the front line of archers dropped to one knee and the second line let their own shafts capture the colorful cloth filling the sky.

The gate wall came alive with movement and deafening noise. This legendary salute had not been attempted since Hekolatis' victorious homecoming.

"I think the Balderons got to Argis," Tigh murmured in Jame's ear.

"I bet Kas and Mularke pestered her to do it until she had to give in or explain why she had caused her friends bodily harm," Jame said, knowingly.

Tigh straightened, chuckling. "That I can believe."

When the crowd on the walls noticed the rigid stillness of the horse warriors and archers, their shouting faded into a tense silence of anticipation. The late afternoon wind brushed against the dry grasses, reminding them that the cold season was upon them.

A pair of warriors on horseback, holding large standards that displayed carefully embroidered images of Laur's waterfalls, emerged from the tunnel and took positions on either side of the opening.

Yodels and battle cries suddenly crashed around the cavern as if fighting to burst into the valley. Hundreds of warriors, waving flashing swords and making enough noise to reach Hekolatis' sleeping ears, sprinted from the cave, tearing through the space in front of the archers and horse warriors. Swords crashed in mock battles as the warriors flipped and capered in abandoned ecstasy.

The Emorans gathered on the wall gasped and twittered in wonderment, staring so hard that it was a wonder that their eyes stayed in their heads.

Sucking in a sharp breath, Tigh's head whipped around to Goodemer, who was watching the spectacle with childlike delight. Sensing the warrior's eyes burning into her, the Wizard calmly met the wide-eyed startled look staring back at her.

"It's only their fighting skills." Goodemer shrugged. "They haven't changed in any other way."

A haunting uncertainty flickered across her face before Tigh slowly nodded.

"I think it's a wonderful gift." Jame, observing the exchange, wrapped reassuring hands around Tigh's arm and grinned at Goodemer.

"It's an incredible gift," Jyac breathed, feeling a swell of pride for her warriors. Truly the greatest fighters in the world once again. "Thank you." She rested grateful eyes on the smiling Wizard.

"A Wizard always leaves a little something behind for people to remember her by," Goodemer modestly explained.

Piercing whistles bounced off the bluff walls. The crashing of swords halted as the warriors sprinted into rows of eight down the middle of the valley.

The next sound from the tunnel was the rhythmic stomping of soft boots. A puzzled murmur rose from the women on the wall.

In rows of four, a column of Lukrians marched into the sunlight. The stunned silence gave way to a thunderous cheer of greeting. Jyac nodded and straightened, her pride for her people so strong that it was a wonder that it didn't explode from her.

The column of Lukrians marched to the front of the Emoran warriors. In a smooth movement the Emoran column transformed into a crosshatch of Lukrians and Emorans as the Lukrians wove into the Emoran rows.

Something profound caught in Jyac's throat and she was shocked to find her eyes brimming with tears. Glancing around, she was relieved to see that the others were struggling with their own intense emotions. The sudden vision of a united Emoria and Lukria was so appealing that she sent a prayer to Laur in hopes that it was truly their destiny.

"Argis knows what she's doing." Tigh nodded thoughtfully.

As if hearing her name, a clatter of hooves was followed by Argis and Kylara entering the valley at a dig-
nified pace atop horses trimmed in full commander
dress. Tas and Tindal trotted behind them on equally
resplendent horses, gifts from the grateful people of
Balderon.

Pausing at the cave entrance, the foursome let the
standard bearers guide their mounts to positions before
them and lead them at a rousing gallop to the front of
the column.

If the noise from the City had been great up to that
point, it did not compare to what was rising up just
then. Every bit of portable metal had been dragged
from cupboards and chamber corners in anticipation of
this moment. The clanging rang out in such a deafening clatter that none doubted that it could be heard all
the way to Balderon.

Halting at the head of the column, Argis kicked her
horse and sprinted away from the others, then spun
around, taking in the hundreds of solemn eyes riveted
on her with an unshakable respect. This was an army
that could hold its own against any army in the world
and at that moment, it was her army. Fighting a wave
of lightheadedness as she allowed the reality of the last
few days to flood through her, she took a steadying
breath and raised her sword. The clean sound of an
army moving in precise unison as she aimed the point
of her sword to the ground was the sweetest noise she
had ever heard.

****

Argis let out a healthy selection of curses as she
paused at the threshold of one of the tiny meditation
chambers in Laur's temple. Sprawled on one of the
stone benches was Tigh, clothed in formal Emoran
leathers, dead asleep. A chuckle behind Argis told her

that there was another witness to this disgusting spectacle.

"You lost that bet, Argis," Tas purred in her ear.

Argis shook her head. "I've never seen a warrior who wasn't as nervous as a mouse around a cat on her joining day."

"She's been through this before, you know," Tas reminded her.

Argis fiddled with the unfamiliar addition to her dress uniform—a single purple sleeve draping down her right arm to the elbow. She balked at it but Jyac insisted that she wear the sleeve of Hekolatis on formal occasions at least. "Why does it have to be so uncomfortable," Argis muttered.

"I don't think it's the sleeve that's uncomfortable." Tas eyed her friend knowingly. "I think you're just uncomfortable wearing it."

"I don't think I'm the one who should be wearing it," Argis sighed, gazing at the peacefully slumbering warrior.

"She may have drawn up the battle strategy, but you made the decisions on the field that led our army to victory." Tas struggled to keep down her exasperation at the reluctant hero.

"It was Jame's plan, Tigh's strategy and Goodemer's magic..."

"And your quick thinking," a groggy voice mumbled. Tigh carefully stretched before pulling her body around to sit on the bench. "Don't fight it, Argis. The opportunities to be a hero are too few. Treasure them when you can."

"It's time." Tas raised her chin at Tigh.

In a disgusting display of casual ease, the warrior got to her feet, taking the time to make sure all the intricate parts of the unfamiliar Emoran uniform were in place. Both Argis and Tas were struck with how much she embodied the ideal Emoran warrior, wearing the crosspatch of armor and leather as if it were a part of her skin.

"Ready?" Tigh quirked an eyebrow at the staring warriors, who immediately blinked in embarrassment at being caught in their open admiration of Jame's partner.

"That's what we should be asking you." Argis cocked her head at the tall warrior.

"There are worse things than being joined to Jame." Tigh grinned as she and Argis followed Tas into the main chamber of the Temple.

"You're very lucky," Argis said softly, looking across the chamber at a vision as shimmering as the waterfalls around them. Tigh's attention was already fixed on the center of her world. Surrounded by a lavender cloud of flitting acolytes, Jame stood in her warrior uniform looking as natural as Tigh in the intricate armor and leather. Her calling may be peaceful arbitration, but there was no doubt that she had the heart of a warrior. The easy way she carried herself under the weight of the armor and the ceremonial sword on her back showed that she had the physical soundness to back up her mental strength.

Looking up, green eyes met blue as Tigh strode quickly to her.

"I could only dream of this day," Jame said softly, as Tigh took her hand.

"I'm open to any opportunity to reaffirm my love for you," Tigh murmured in her ear. Jame's answering expression made the warrior's knees as liquid as the gurgling pools around them.

"All right. Save it for after the ceremony." Argis scowled good-naturedly.

"Come on, your highness." Tas grinned as she took Jame's arm. "We go first."

Jame squeezed Tigh's hand as they shared a private smile before Tas tugged the arbiter towards the Temple door. Thunderous cheering exploded, affirming that every Emoran was in the City that night.

Argis took a deep breath and shook out her arms. "Remember what you have to say?"

"Say?" Tigh raised an eyebrow at the Emoran.

"The words for the ceremony," Argis said, nervously.

"Not offhand." Tigh shrugged. "But I'm sure they'll come to me when needed."

Argis' startled stare at Tigh was almost comical. "Aren't you afraid of messing up?" she managed to rasp.

Tigh turned puzzled eyes to the tense Emoran. "It won't be the end of the world. It's not a life or death situation if I don't get the words exactly right."

"I'll never understand you," the hero of Balderon muttered, catching a signal from the door. "It's time. Try not to improvise too much."

Grinning, Tigh stepped into place next to Argis.

Torchlight burnished the square as it seemed to pulse in rhythm to the drums thundering from different parts of the City. A straight path was cleared from the Temple door to the fountain in the middle of the square, and smartly uniformed warriors lined the way to maintain the distance of the excited throng. The Council formed an arc in front of the fountain creating a space for Jyac to stand. The Queen beamed at her niece as Jame walked towards her on Tas' arm.

The radiance that drenched the princess was enough of a gift to last Jyac the rest of her life. This kind of happiness was so rare that everyone wanted to be around it and share in it. Although she would protest the thought, Jame looked the perfect Emoran princess in the ceremonial uniform with the supreme commander braid dangling from her belt.

Jame stood before Jyac as Tas took a step to the side, behind her princess. Aunt and niece exchanged wry grins as a new wave of shouts and cheers caused the bells in the temple tower to juggle against each other from the vibrations. It was a struggle to not turn around and stare at her approaching warrior. Jame's mind's eye captured the vivid spectacle as it was reflected in the faces of the Council. The approving expression in Jyac's eyes as she watched Tigh told Jame that the warrior's eyes were on only her.

After what felt like an eternity, Jame finally soaked up Tigh's warm presence next to her. Argis stepped back and winked at Tas, who couldn't keep from beaming.

Jyac reached over her shoulder and pulled her delicately etched ceremonial double-edged sword from its soft leather scabbard. Holding the sword in both hands, she slowly lowered it, flat side up between Jame and Tigh until it was pointed straight out.

"Jamelin Ketlas, princess of Emoria, and Paldar Tigis, adopted warrior of Emoria, have come before the citizens of Emoria to be joined," Jyac intoned. "They are here to declare their lifelong pledge to each other. If anyone feels that they are not meant to speak these words make your protest now."

The silence was so profound that the only sound was the fluttering of the banners and the hiss of the torches. Nodding, Jyac raised her eyes to Tigh.

The tall warrior and the arbiter turned to face one another. The sword blade hovering between them kept back the yearning to reach for the other's hand. Tigh couldn't help thinking how torturous Emoran ceremonies were. Capturing the brimming green eyes with her own blue ones, Tigh pulled a wrist bracer of woven leather from her belt pouch and held it up. "I give my life to be with Jamelin Ketlas, princess of Emoria, for as long as I walk this earth and until Laur's waters stop flowing."

Jame, with trembling hands, pulled a matching wrist bracer from her belt pouch. Holding it up, she gently tried to clear the roiling emotion from her throat by narrowing her world around those wonderful familiar eyes gazing at her with raw adoration. With a clear voice, she repeated the words that Tigh had intoned.

Tigh reached over the sword and took Jame's free hand, slipping the bracer onto the only part of Jame's body not covered. The contact after even such a brief time of denial sent a warm jolt through both of them. Jame, in turn, took Tigh's hand and carefully pulled the bracer onto her sword-strengthened wrist.

Tigh ran a finger over the sharp edge of the sword, then held up her hand. Jame, trying not to wince at the cold blade followed by the sting of her skin slicing open, slid her finger across the blade and held her hand in front of Tigh's. Slowly the two hands touched, then pressed together as the warm blood mingled.

"Let it be written that the citizens of Emoria have witnessed the joining of Jame and Tigh." Jyac dropped the sword out of the way and Tigh gathered Jame in her arms for a gentle kiss. The magic that crackled in the air needed no help from Goodemer. Noisemakers baffled their hearing with wild metallic sounds and the tops of the bluffs erupted in an astonishing fireworks display that could only be the work of the good Wizard.

Tigh reached up and gently wiped away an errant tear from Jame's cheek. A gaping hole in Jame's psyche was finally healed and she felt fully home, at last.

* * * * * * * * * * * * * * *

The bemused Wizard strode into the Great Hall trailed by a half dozen warriors. Warriors had been following her, doing little chores for her, helping her get around the City...basically making nuisances of themselves since they returned from Balderon. She understood that they were grateful for the warrior skills she had given them, but this was going on much too long.

"I would be honored if you joined me at the table."

Goodemer spun around to find Argis standing next to her. The Emoran flicked her eyes at the Wizard's entourage and lifted an eyebrow.

"The honor would be mine." Goodemer smiled, grateful for one levelheaded warrior in the bunch. Knowing that it would be extremely bad form to protest their commander, the cluster of warriors looked on, disgruntled, as Argis led Goodemer away.

"Thank you for rescuing me." Goodemer grinned.

"I'm the one who should be thanking you for rescuing all of us," Argis said, sincerely. A crash from the middle of the room followed by a stream of creative curses told them that Mularke and Tas were giving an impromptu floorshow. "Perhaps I can talk you into teaching a few of my warriors some social skills."

"You crazy archer," Tas snorted as Mularke stared at what was left of her meal on the floor. "You either have to try that completely sober or drunk out of your mind before it can work." With that, Tas tossed her a half-full skin. "Since you're halfway there, you can try it later when you're stinking drunk."

Mularke, grabbing the skin out the air, nodded. "Good idea."

"If you don't rescue Tas soon, she'll be passed out in a doorway somewhere," Jame observed from the long table on a rise at the end of the hall.

"Let her have her fun tonight." Seeran watched the small warrior with great affection. "I won't have any chance to speak to you or Tigh for a while, now that you're leaving."

"I'm glad you decided to stay here." Jame smiled at the historian. "Emoria needs a chronicler."

"Thank you for bringing me here. It's strange, but it feels like I've come home," Seeran responded shyly. "Tas and I are going to visit Artocia in the spring to get my things. I'll be able to show her a bit of my world."

"And you'll also have quite a story to add to the Archives there," Jame teased.

"Now that's an understatement," Seeran laughed. "There's still one thing I don't understand. Why did Meah go against Misner?"

Jame darted a glance at Tigh, who was engaged in a discussion on battle strategy with Jyac. "Meah was never on Misner's side to begin with. You see, one of the Guards that Misner killed before Tigh disabled her was Misner's lover, Ocarla. She pretended to join Misner's army to get close enough to get her revenge. It turns out that she never stopped being loyal to her old supreme commander, Tigh."

"Now she's on her way back to Ynit with the others to be cleansed." Seeran nodded.

"Hopefully she'll finally be able to find some peace in her life," Jame softly mused.

"So where are you going next?" Seeran broke off a piece of thick bread and sopped up the remains of her meal with it.

"We're continuing over the mountains. We haven't been that way yet." Jame wrapped an arm around Tigh, capturing the warrior's attention.

Jyac gave them an indulgent look before lifting her mug. "Thank you, Jame, for restoring my faith in the Mysteries and leading Emoria into a new age."

The arbiter shook her head, hiding the blush that crept onto her cheeks. "Emoria has entered a new age because it was ready and willing to do so," she responded, looking up into the indulgent blue eyes that gazed down at her. "Now I know how you feel about being called a hero."

Laughing at this, the small party gathered around the table raised their mugs to Emoria.

Here ends the first Tale from the ancient scrolls entitled The Tales of Emoria by the Artocian bard, Mindancer, as translated by modern Emoran scholar C. A. Casey.

Coming next from
Silver Dragon Books

Thy Brothers' Reaper

By Devin Centis

Gillian Montague, an apprentice P.I., is tracking down the cause of a series of brutal and vicious deaths where victims' skulls are punctured. The assailants appear to be large and abnormally powerful men.

Through research and her own close encounters, Gillian discovers that these men are clones bred by the government to form an omnipotent military. In addition to this, the local water becomes contaminated and food shortages become the norm. She comes to believe that secret government organizations and conspiracies are behind it.

Her investigation puts her in grave personal danger which increases with each new fact she finds.

Will Gillian survive to discover and expose the truth?

Available July 2000.

Available soon from
Silver Dragon Books

The Chosen
By V. H. Foster

The setting is Ryshta, a mythical, medieval world where a sadistic Sovereign rules the land, a world of extremes where you are either slave or master. When Lord Athol sends his only daughter to meet the man he has chosen as her husband, she is caught in the middle of a slave rebellion, and falls in love with a rebel slave, who is keeping a dark secret.

Tales of Emoria: Future Dreams
By Mindancer

In this *prequel* to <u>Tales of Emoria: Past Echoes</u>, Jame, an Emoran princess and assistant arbiter, takes on the most difficult case at the military compound at Ynit: arguing for the rehabilitation of former Elite Guard, Tigh the Terrible. Tigh and Jame discover that they are kindred spirits in their personal struggles against the expectations of their families in order the pursue the path they want their lives to take. The friendship that develops from this common bond transforms into a dream of breaking away from their pasts and facing the future together.

The Eighth Day
By Greg Gosdin

Taking place over the final week of a year in the very near future, from December 24th through January 1st, the Earth passes through the tail of a comet, causing a spectacular Christmas Eve meteor storm. But, the meteors bring something else to Earth as well. In the small West Texas town of Monahans, something is happening to people, causing them to behave like wild, murderous animals, killing with a relentless blood lust. They are aware of what they are doing, and are helpless to stop it. And it's spreading! On Christmas morning, Monahans is suddenly swarming with helicopters and soldiers in environmental suits. Martial law is declared and two young physicians, both virologists, are caught up in a maze of secrecy, desperation, and fear in their efforts to find out what is happening. Each situation pushes the characters to their absolute limits, and beyond, forcing them to decide what is truly worth living for, fighting for, sacrificing and possibly dying for.

Other titles to look for in the
coming months from
Silver Dragon Books

Forest of Eyulf: Instincts of Blue By Tammy Pell

The Claiming of Ford By T. Novan

The Athronian Chronicles Series By C. A. Casey

Well of Souls By Sheri Young

Mindancer was a scholar at the University of Artocia sometime at the end of the 4th century of the Modern Era. Her claim to fame are the Tales of Emoria, which, she has always maintained were based on first hand accounts by the legendary Emoran Queen, Jamelin Ketlas.

Originally from the midwest, noted Emoran scholar, C. A. Casey is currently a librarian at a university in the northwestern United States. Along with her forays into writing fantasy and translating ancient documents about Emoria, she has written several sleep-inducing articles published in library and education journals. These articles have earned her a biographical entry in the 2001 edition of Who's Who in the World. Her interests range from outdoor activities such as hiking and bird-watching to collecting Celtic music, and, of course, reading fantasy literature. Her two cats and self-proclaimed literary critics, Mac and Domino, fuss at her about the lack of felines in her stories but never right before dinnertime.